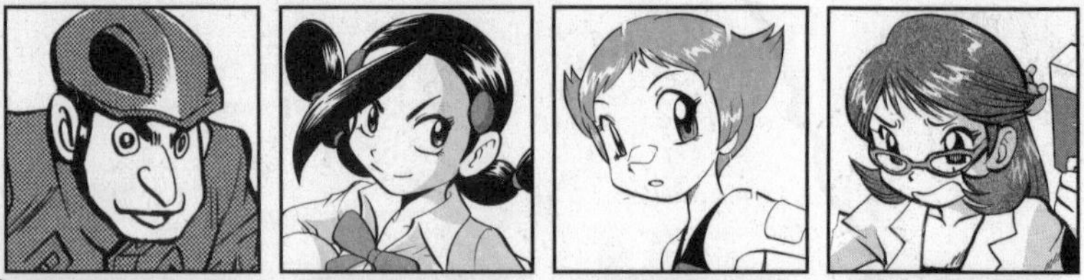

Rad Rickshaw

THE OWNER OF A BICYCLE SHOP IN ETERNA CITY.

Candice

THE SNOWPOINT CITY GYM LEADER. A POWERFUL GYM LEADER WHO USES ICE-TYPE POKÉMON.

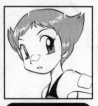

Maylene

THE VEILSTONE CITY GYM LEADER. HER EXPERTISE IS FIGHTING-TYPE POKÉMON.

Roseanne

PROFESSOR ROWAN'S ASSISTANT. SHE IS ACCOMPANYING DIA TO LAKE VERITY.

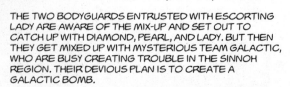

THE TWO BODYGUARDS ENTRUSTED WITH ESCORTING LADY ARE AWARE OF THE MIX-UP AND SET OUT TO CATCH UP WITH DIAMOND, PEARL, AND LADY. BUT THEN THEY GET MIXED UP WITH MYSTERIOUS TEAM GALACTIC, WHO ARE BUSY CREATING TROUBLE IN THE SINNOH REGION. THEIR DEVIOUS PLAN IS TO CREATE A GALACTIC BOMB.

DIAMOND AND PEARL FINALLY REVEAL THAT THEY ARE NOT LADY'S REAL BODYGUARDS, AND THOUGH IT SHAKES HER UP FOR A MOMENT, LADY (WHOSE REAL NAME "PLATINUM" HAS NOW BEEN REVEALED) RESOLVES TO STICK BY HER FRIENDS AND TRUST IN THEM AGAIN. BUT THEN THE TRIO SEPARATE AND EACH SETS OUT ALONE FOR ONE OF THE THREE SINNOH LAKES WHERE THREE POKÉMON OF LEGEND—UXIE, MESPRIT, AND AZELF-SLUMBER.

WITH ALL CLUES POINTING TO "OUTER SPACE," OUR FRIENDS GRADUALLY BEGIN TO FIGURE OUT THEIR ENEMY'S NEFARIOUS PLAN. BUT BEFORE THEY CAN ACT, THE DAY THE "GALACTIC BOMB" IS TO BE DROPPED ARRIVES AND THREE EERIE-LOOKING AIRSHIPS SLOWLY MAKE THEIR WAY TOWARD THE LEGENDARY LAKES...!

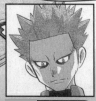

Cyrus

TEAM GALACTIC'S BOSS. AN OVERBEARING, INTENSE MAN.

Galactic Grunts

THE TEAM GALACTIC TROOPS, WHO CARRY OUT THEIR LEADER'S BIDDING WITHOUT QUESTION. CREEPY!

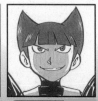

Saturn

HE IS IN CHARGE OF THE BOMB AND RARELY STEPS ONTO THE BATTLEFIELD HIMSELF.

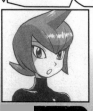

Mars

A TEAM GALACTIC LEADER. HER PERSONALITY IS HARD TO PIN DOWN.

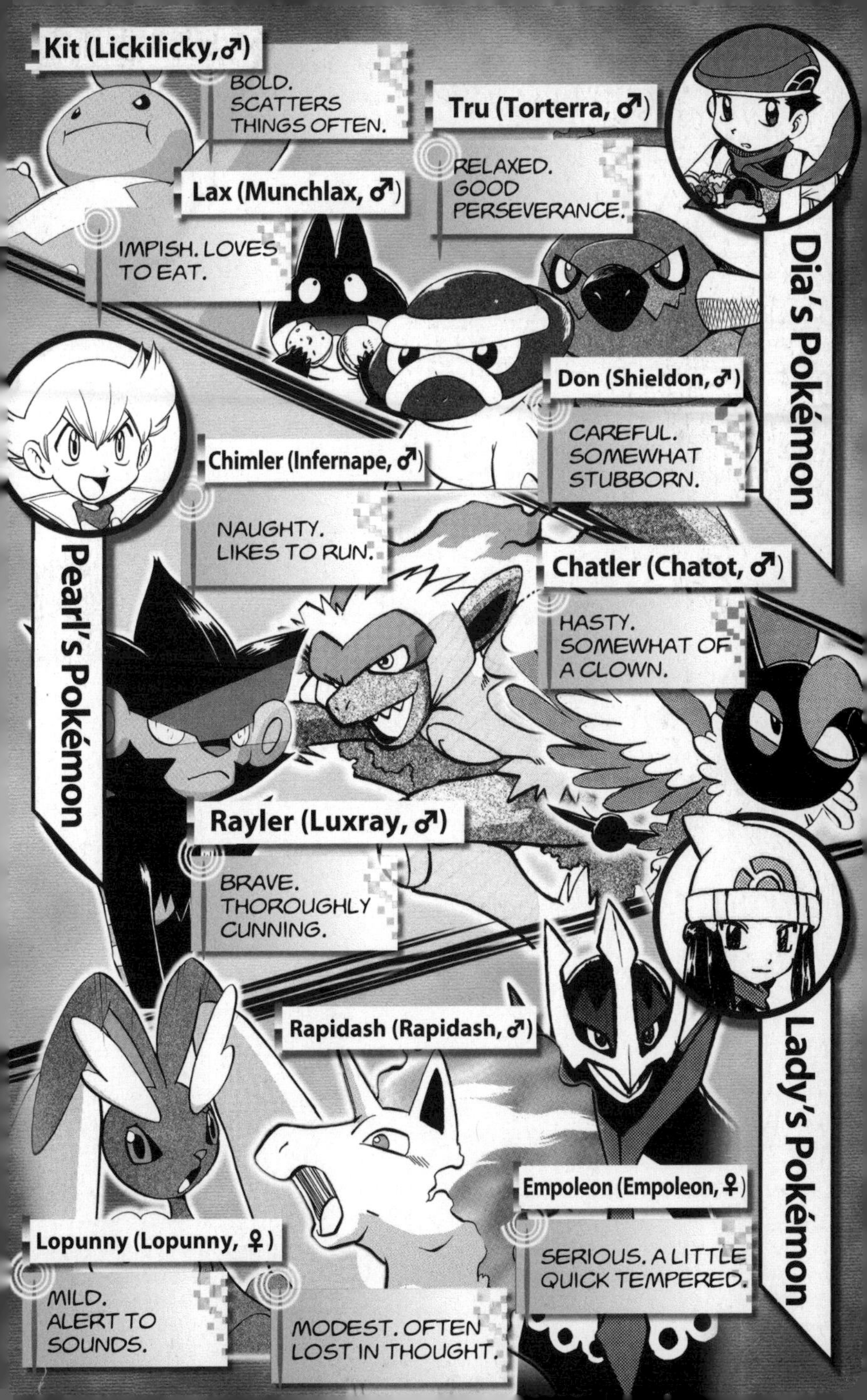

Dia's Pokémon
Kit (Lickilicky, ♂)
BOLD. SCATTERS THINGS OFTEN.
Tru (Torterra, ♂)
RELAXED. GOOD PERSEVERANCE.
Lax (Munchlax, ♂)
IMPISH. LOVES TO EAT.
Don (Shieldon, ♂)
CAREFUL. SOMEWHAT STUBBORN.
Pearl's Pokémon
Chimler (Infernape, ♂)
NAUGHTY. LIKES TO RUN.
Chatler (Chatot, ♂)
HASTY. SOMEWHAT OF A CLOWN.
Rayler (Luxray, ♂)
BRAVE. THOROUGHLY CUNNING.
Lady's Pokémon
Rapidash (Rapidash, ♂)
MODEST. OFTEN LOST IN THOUGHT.
Empoleon (Empoleon, ♀)
SERIOUS. A LITTLE QUICK TEMPERED.
Lopunny (Lopunny, ♀)
MILD. ALERT TO SOUNDS.

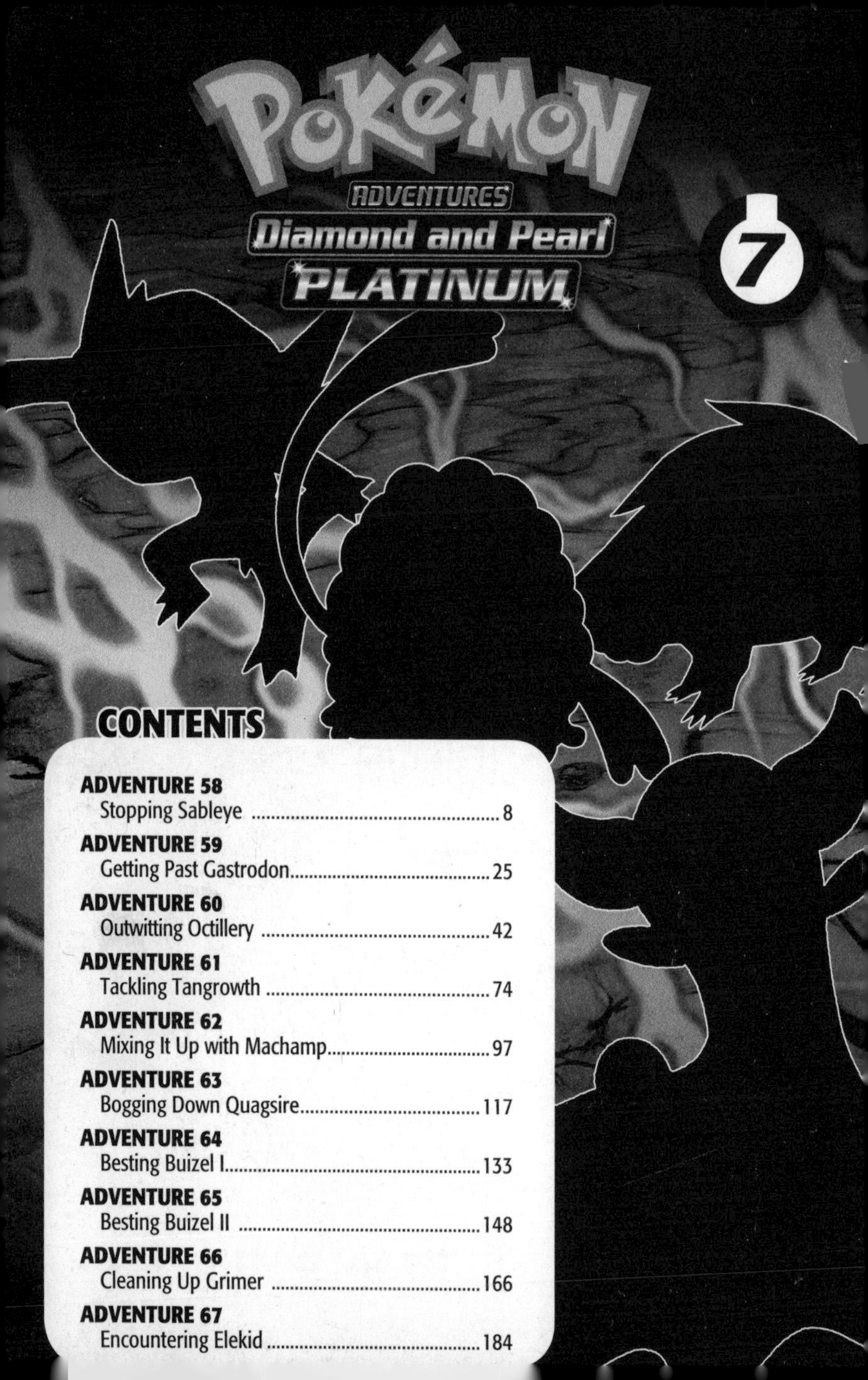
POKÉMON
ADVENTURES
Diamond and Pearl
PLATINUM
7

CONTENTS

58

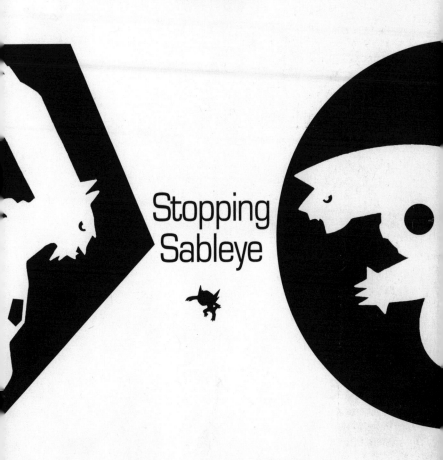

Stopping
Sableye

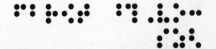

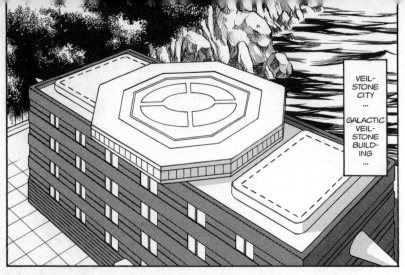

VEIL-
STONE
CITY
...
GALACTIC
VEIL-
STONE
BUILD-
ING
...

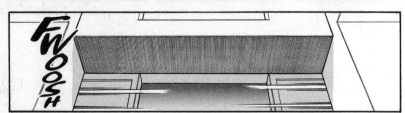

FWOOSH

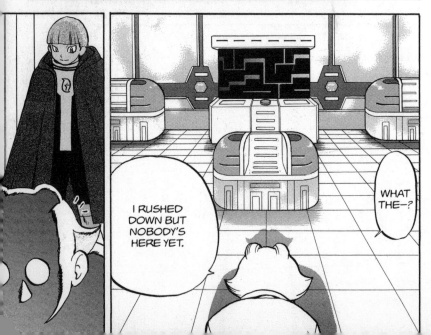

I RUSHED DOWN BUT NOBODY'S HERE YET.

WHAT THE—?

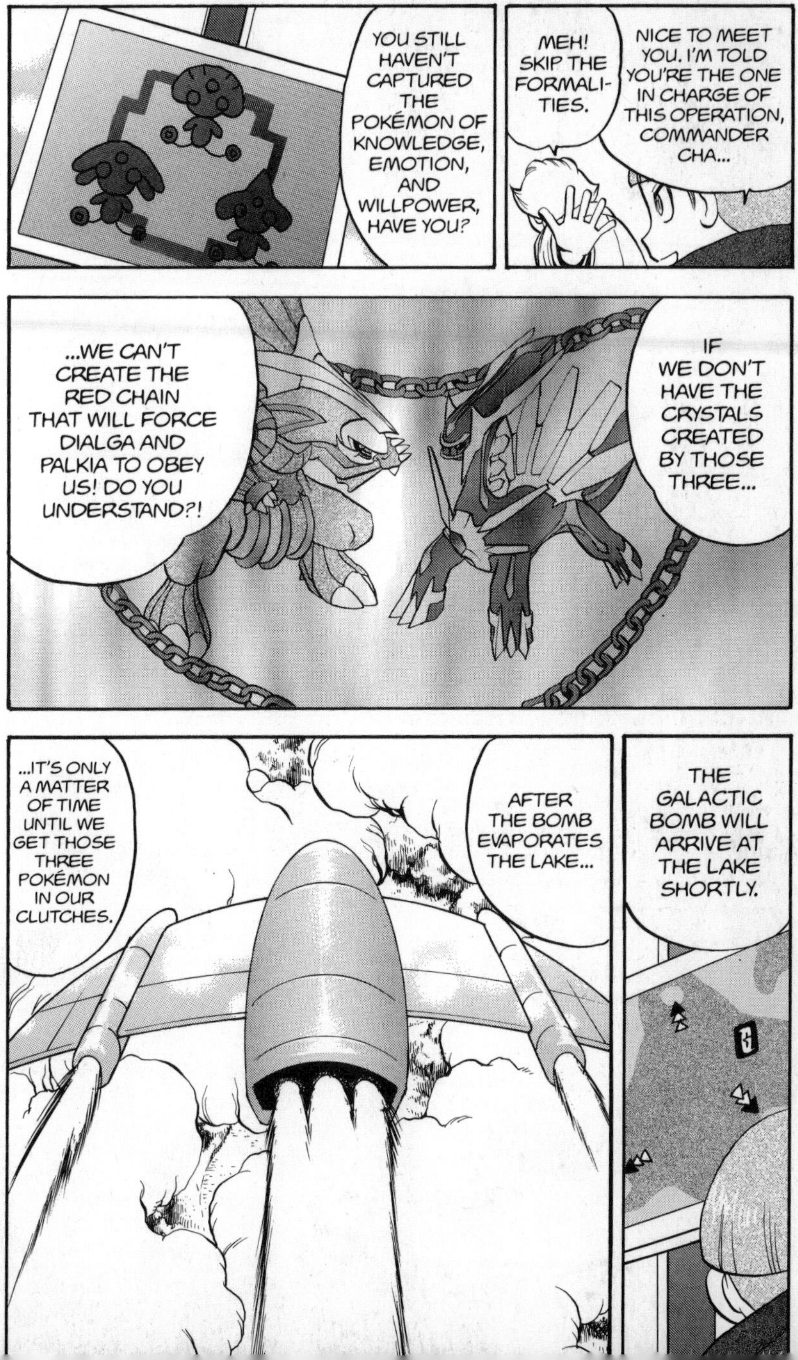
NICE TO MEET YOU. I'M TOLD YOU'RE THE ONE IN CHARGE OF THIS OPERATION, COMMANDER CHA...
MEH! SKIP THE FORMALI-TIES.
YOU STILL HAVEN'T CAPTURED THE POKÉMON OF KNOWLEDGE, EMOTION, AND WILLPOWER, HAVE YOU?
IF WE DON'T HAVE THE CRYSTALS CREATED BY THOSE THREE...
...WE CAN'T CREATE THE RED CHAIN THAT WILL FORCE DIALGA AND PALKIA TO OBEY US! DO YOU UNDERSTAND?!
THE GALACTIC BOMB WILL ARRIVE AT THE LAKE SHORTLY.
AFTER THE BOMB EVAPORATES THE LAKE...
...IT'S ONLY A MATTER OF TIME UNTIL WE GET THOSE THREE POKÉMON IN OUR CLUTCHES.

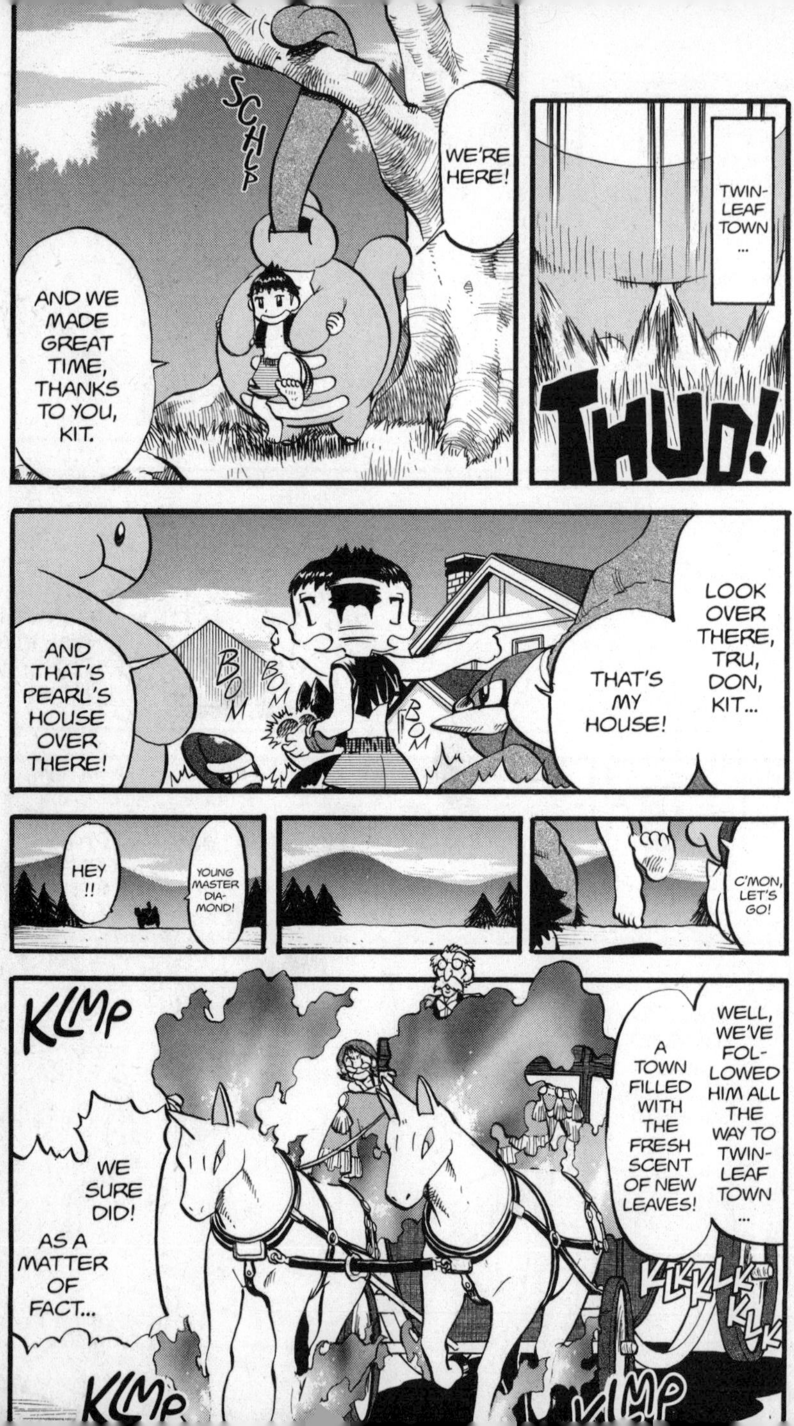
TWIN-LEAF TOWN ...
THUD!
WE'RE HERE!
SCHLP
AND WE MADE GREAT TIME, THANKS TO YOU, KIT.
LOOK OVER THERE, TRU, DON, KIT...
THAT'S MY HOUSE!
BOM
BOM
BOM
AND THAT'S PEARL'S HOUSE OVER THERE!
C'MON, LET'S GO!
YOUNG MASTER DIA-MOND!
HEY !!
WELL, WE'VE FOL-LOWED HIM ALL THE WAY TO TWIN-LEAF TOWN ...
A TOWN FILLED WITH THE FRESH SCENT OF NEW LEAVES!
KLMP
KLKKLK KLK
WE SURE DID!
AS A MATTER OF FACT...
KLMP
KLMP

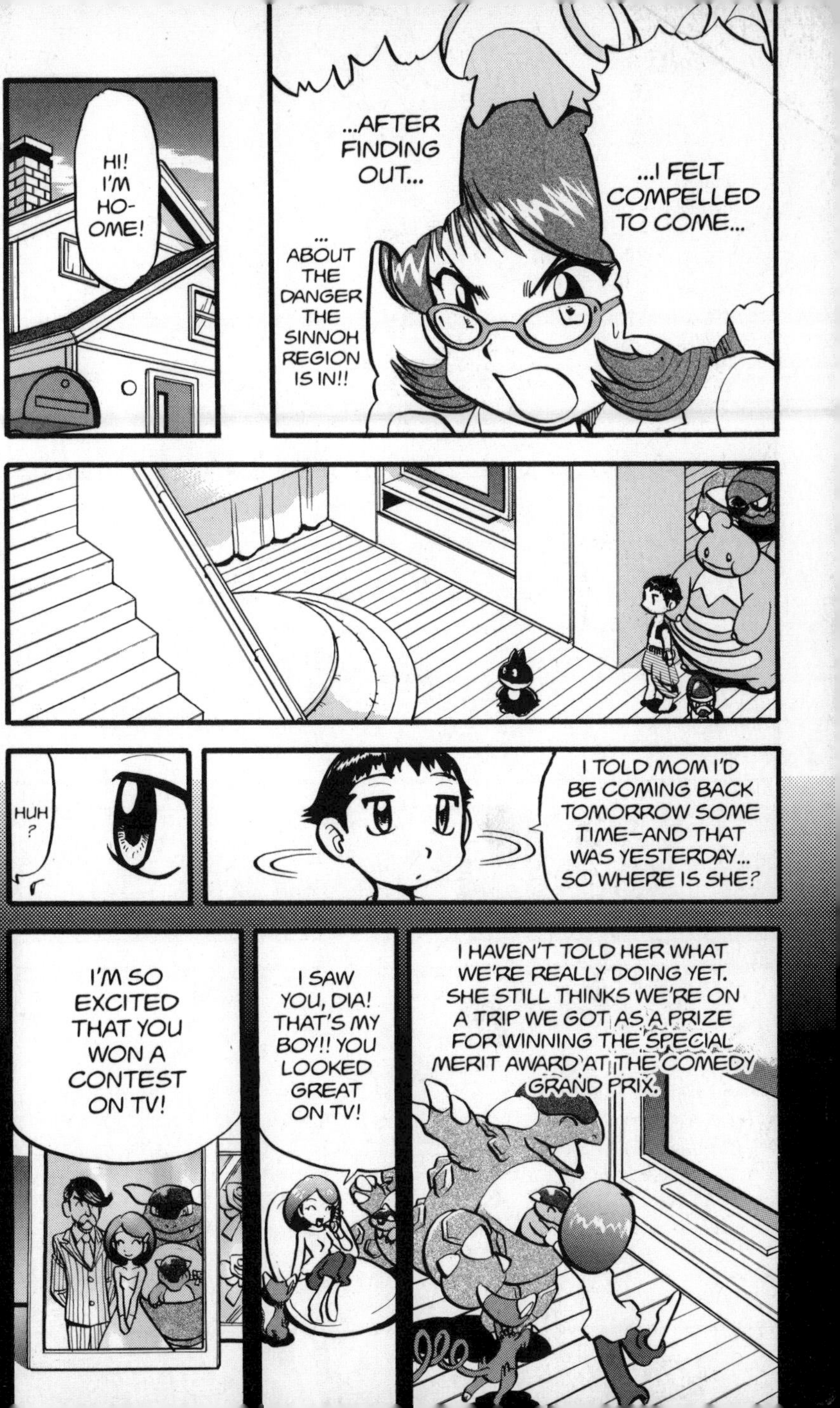
...AFTER FINDING OUT...
...ABOUT THE DANGER THE SINNOH REGION IS IN!!
...I FELT COMPELLED TO COME...
HI! I'M HO-OME!
I TOLD MOM I'D BE COMING BACK TOMORROW SOME TIME—AND THAT WAS YESTERDAY... SO WHERE IS SHE?
HUH?
I HAVEN'T TOLD HER WHAT WE'RE REALLY DOING YET. SHE STILL THINKS WE'RE ON A TRIP WE GOT AS A PRIZE FOR WINNING THE SPECIAL MERIT AWARD AT THE COMEDY GRAND PRIX.
I SAW YOU, DIA! THAT'S MY BOY!! YOU LOOKED GREAT ON TV!
I'M SO EXCITED THAT YOU WON A CONTEST ON TV!

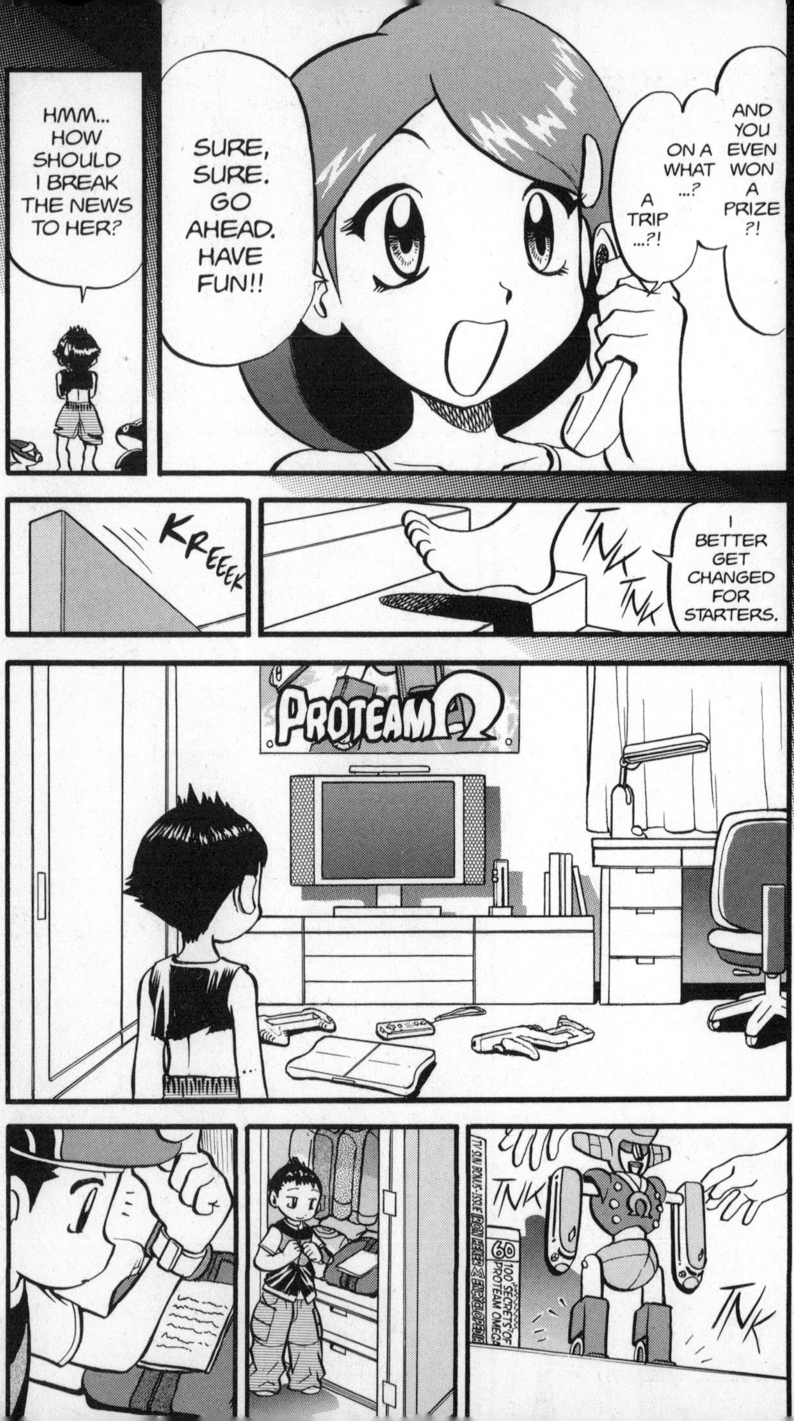
A TRIP ...?! ON A WHAT ...? AND YOU EVEN WON A PRIZE ?!
SURE, SURE. GO AHEAD. HAVE FUN!!
HMM... HOW SHOULD I BREAK THE NEWS TO HER?
I BETTER GET CHANGED FOR STARTERS.
TNK TNK
KREEEEK
PROTEAM Ω
TNK
TNK
TV SUN BONUS-ISSUE IRON HEXER Σ ENCYCLOPEDIA
60
100 SECRETS OF PROTEAM OMEGA

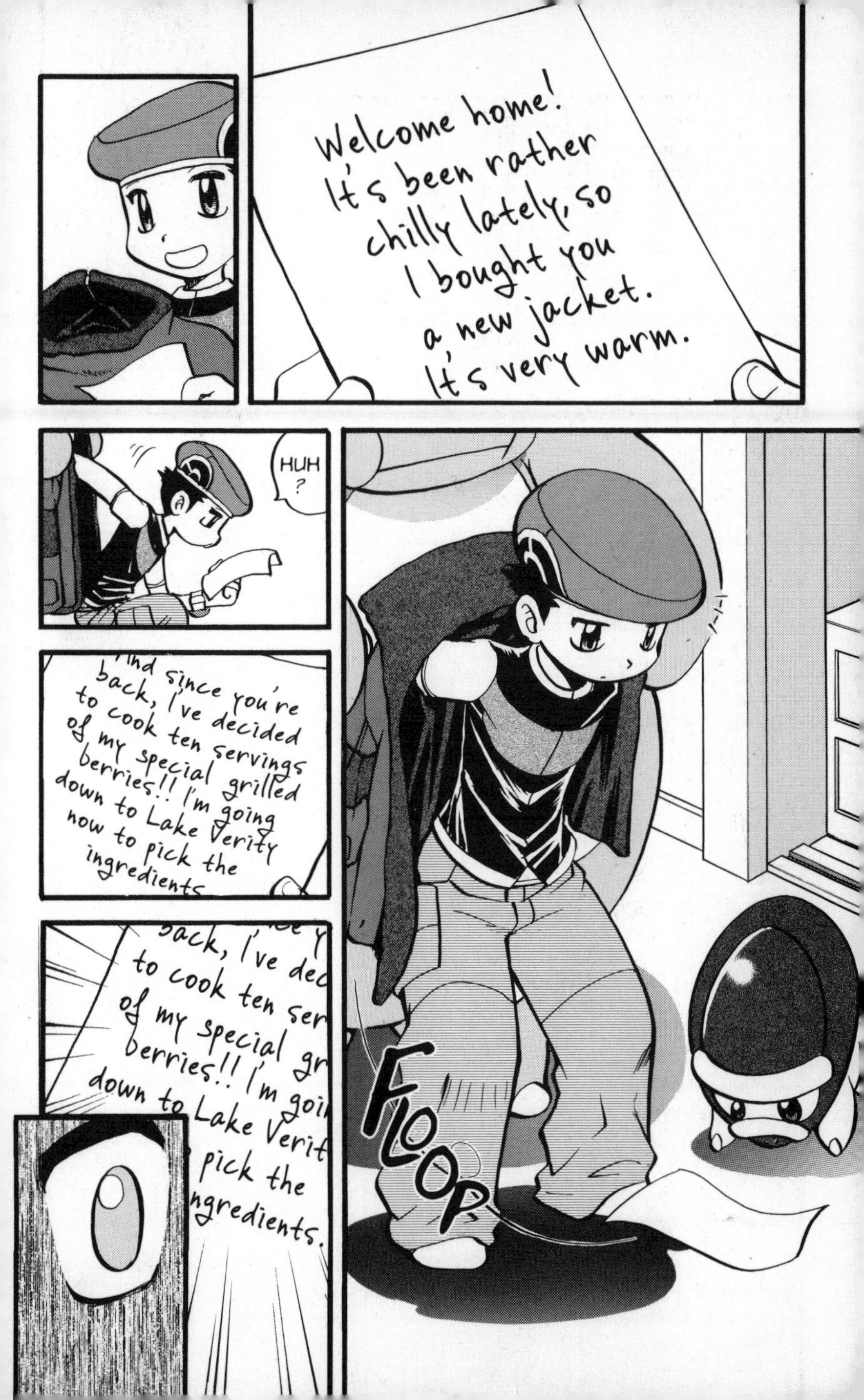
Welcome home! It's been rather chilly lately, so I bought you a new jacket. It's very warm.
FLOOP
HUH?
And since you're back, I've decided to cook ten servings of my special grilled berries!! I'm going down to Lake Verity now to pick the ingredients
back, I've dec to cook ten ser of my special gr berries!! I'm goi down to Lake Verit pick the ngredients.

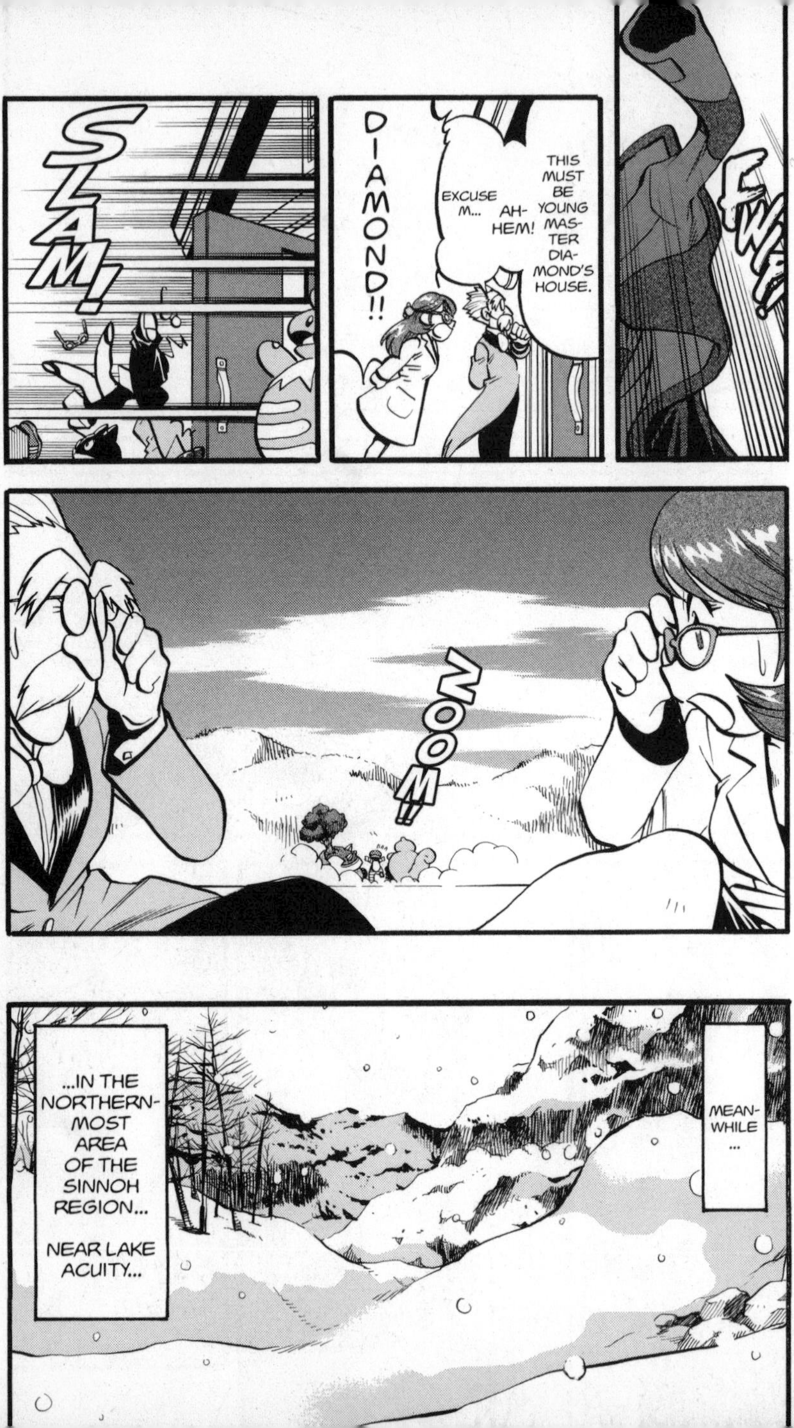
FWIP!
THIS MUST BE YOUNG MASTER DIAMOND'S HOUSE.
AH-HEM!
EXCUSE M...
DIAMOND!!
SLAM!
ZOOM!
MEANWHILE...
...IN THE NORTHERNMOST AREA OF THE SINNOH REGION...
NEAR LAKE ACUITY...

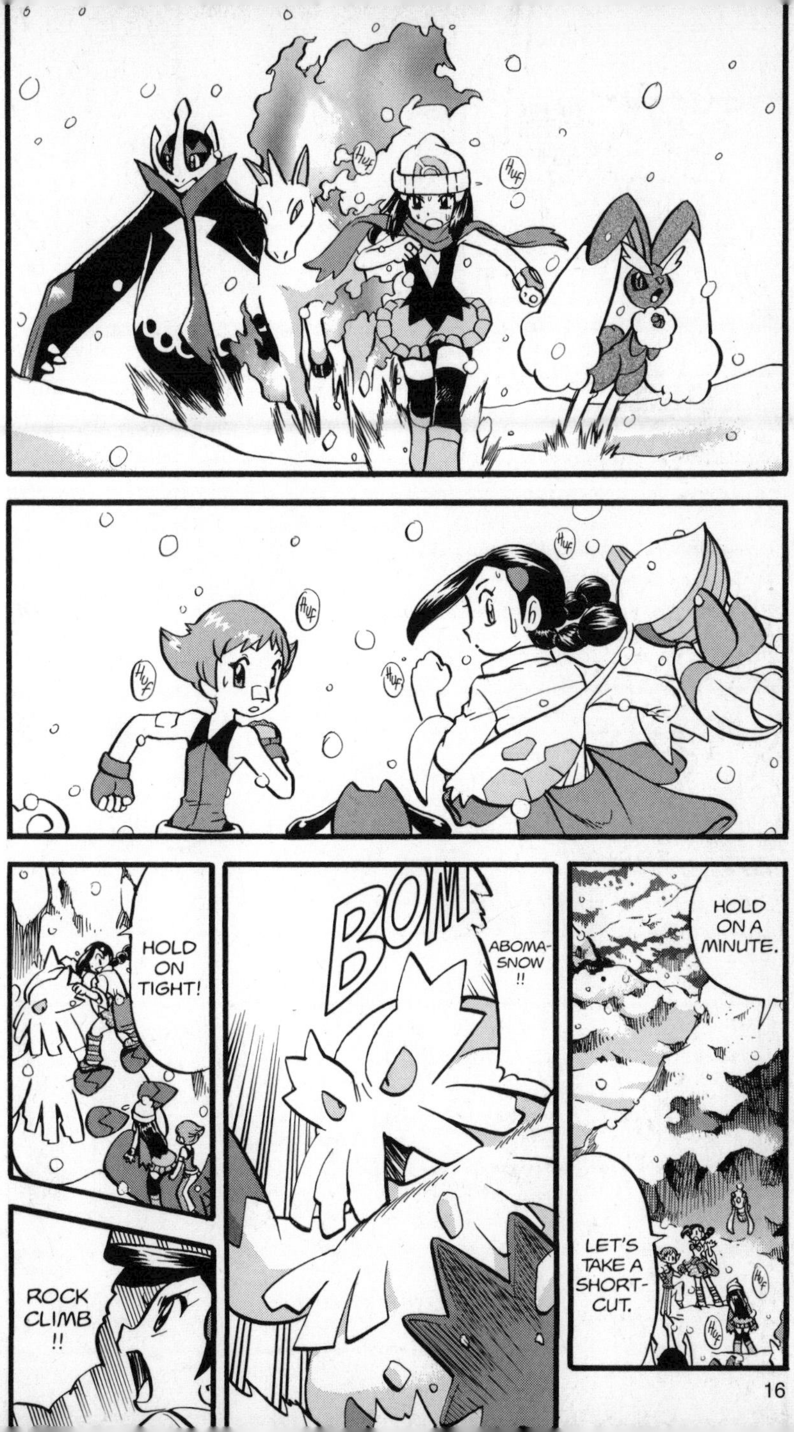
Huf
Huf
Huf
Huf
Huf
Huf
HOLD ON A MINUTE.
LET'S TAKE A SHORT-CUT.
Huf
Huf
BOM
ABOMA-SNOW !!
HOLD ON TIGHT!
ROCK CLIMB !!

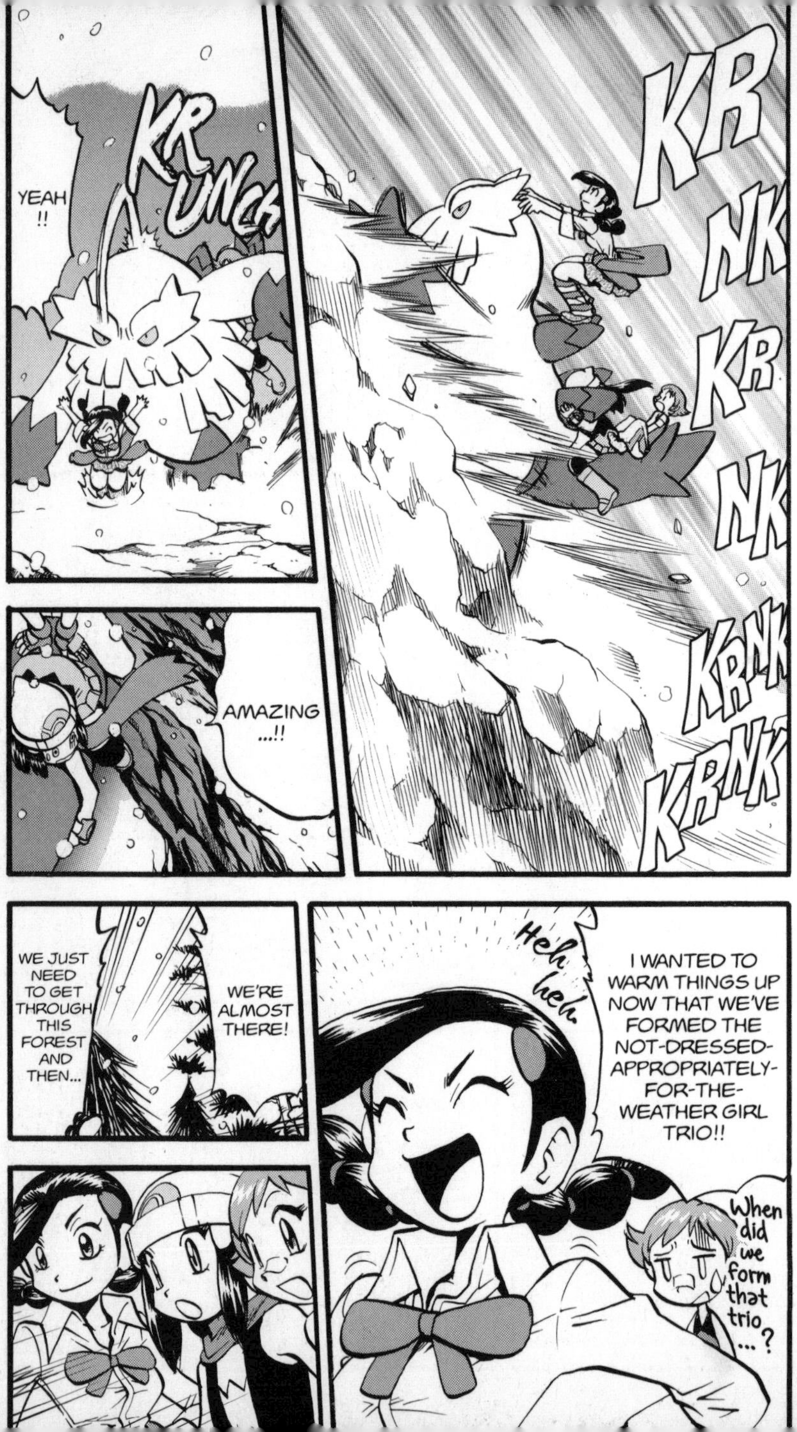
KRNK KRNK KRNK KRNK
KRUNCH
YEAH !!
AMAZING ...!!
I WANTED TO WARM THINGS UP NOW THAT WE'VE FORMED THE NOT-DRESSED-APPROPRIATELY-FOR-THE-WEATHER GIRL TRIO!!
Heh heh
When did we form that trio...?
WE'RE ALMOST THERE!
WE JUST NEED TO GET THROUGH THIS FOREST AND THEN...

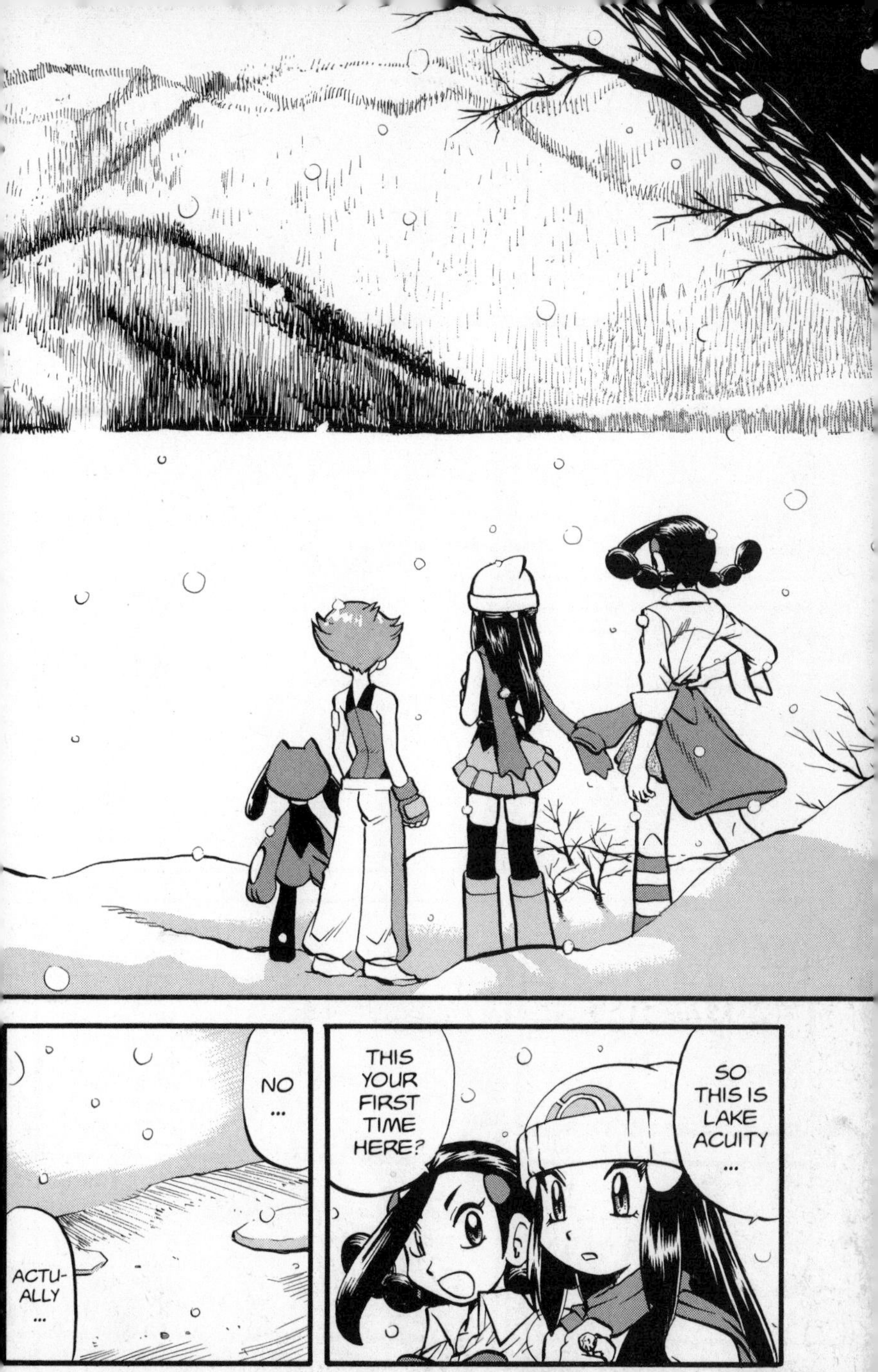
SO THIS IS LAKE ACUITY ...
THIS YOUR FIRST TIME HERE?
NO ...
ACTU-ALLY ...

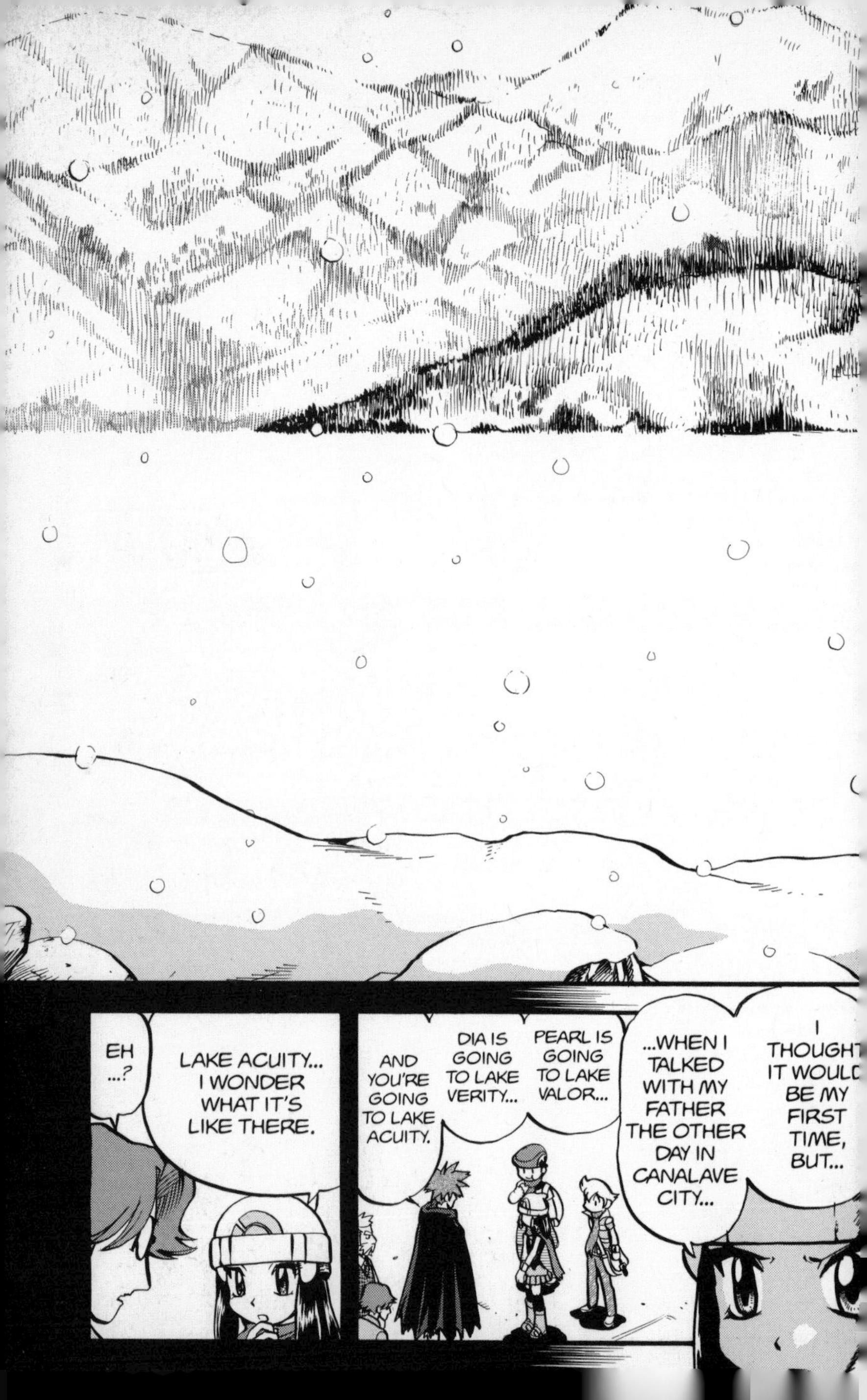
I THOUGHT IT WOULD BE MY FIRST TIME, BUT...
...WHEN I TALKED WITH MY FATHER THE OTHER DAY IN CANALAVE CITY...
PEARL IS GOING TO LAKE VALOR...
DIA IS GOING TO LAKE VERITY...
AND YOU'RE GOING TO LAKE ACUITY.
LAKE ACUITY... I WONDER WHAT IT'S LIKE THERE.
EH ...?

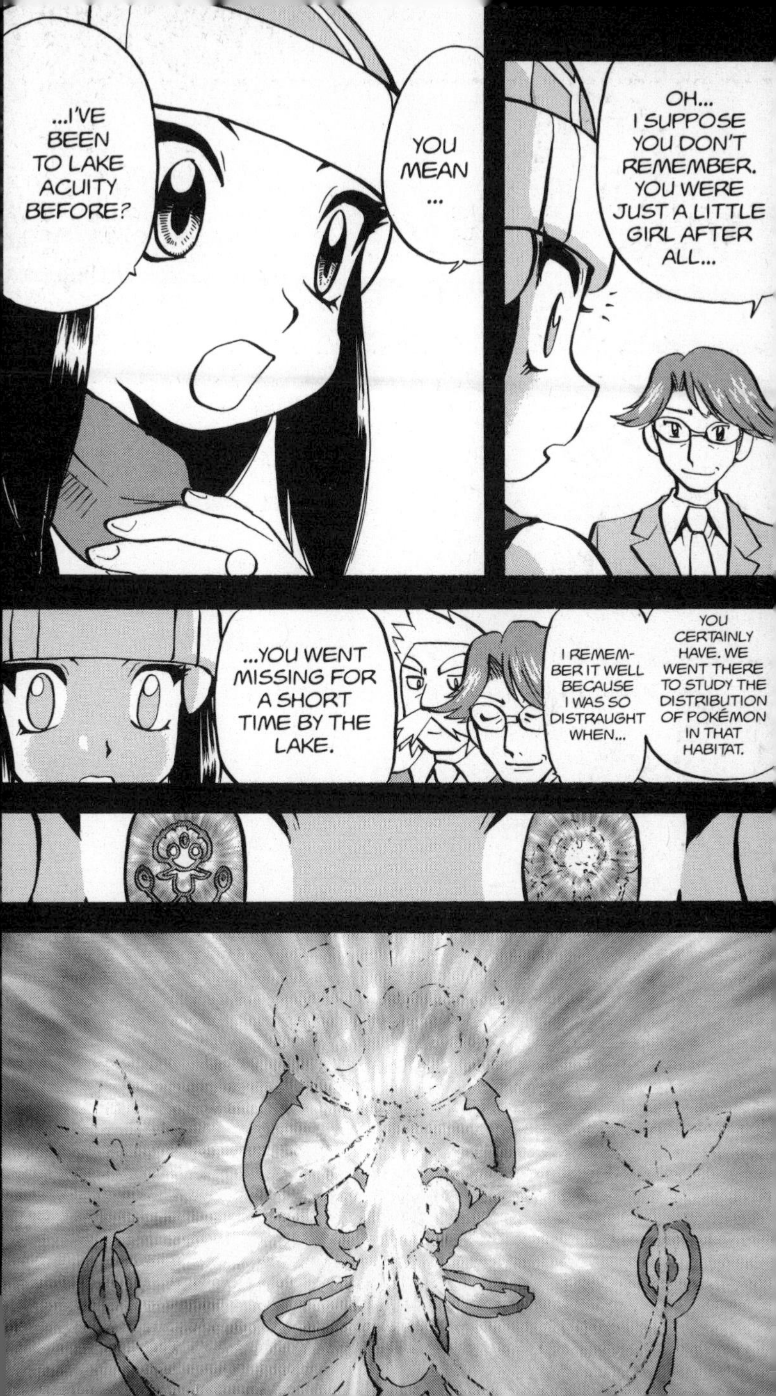
OH... I SUPPOSE YOU DON'T REMEMBER. YOU WERE JUST A LITTLE GIRL AFTER ALL...
YOU MEAN...
...I'VE BEEN TO LAKE ACUITY BEFORE?
YOU CERTAINLY HAVE. WE WENT THERE TO STUDY THE DISTRIBUTION OF POKÉMON IN THAT HABITAT.
I REMEMBER IT WELL BECAUSE I WAS SO DISTRAUGHT WHEN...
...YOU WENT MISSING FOR A SHORT TIME BY THE LAKE.

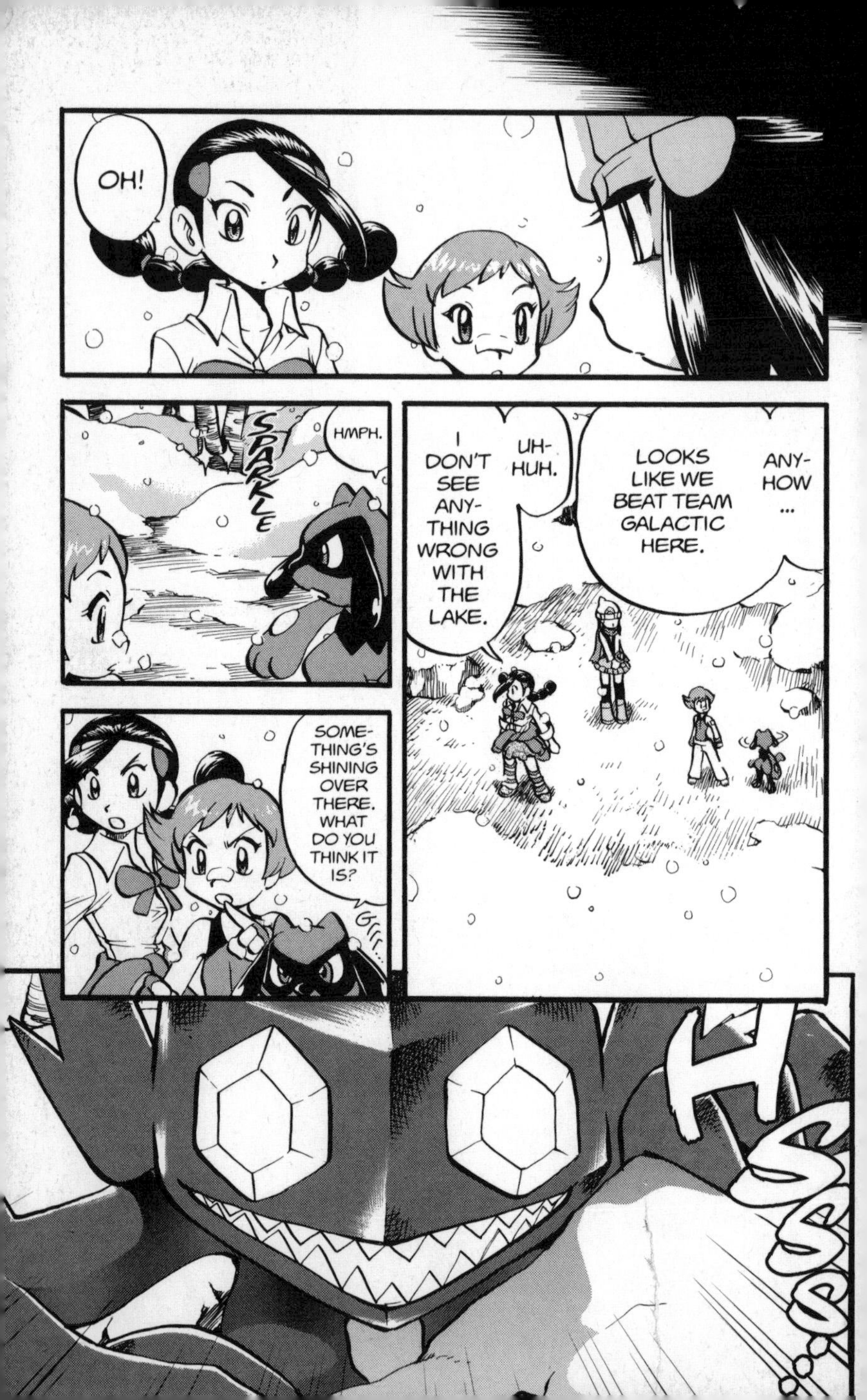
OH!
ANY-HOW ...
LOOKS LIKE WE BEAT TEAM GALACTIC HERE.
UH-HUH.
I DON'T SEE ANY-THING WRONG WITH THE LAKE.
HMPH.
SPARKLE
SOME-THING'S SHINING OVER THERE. WHAT DO YOU THINK IT IS?
HSSS...

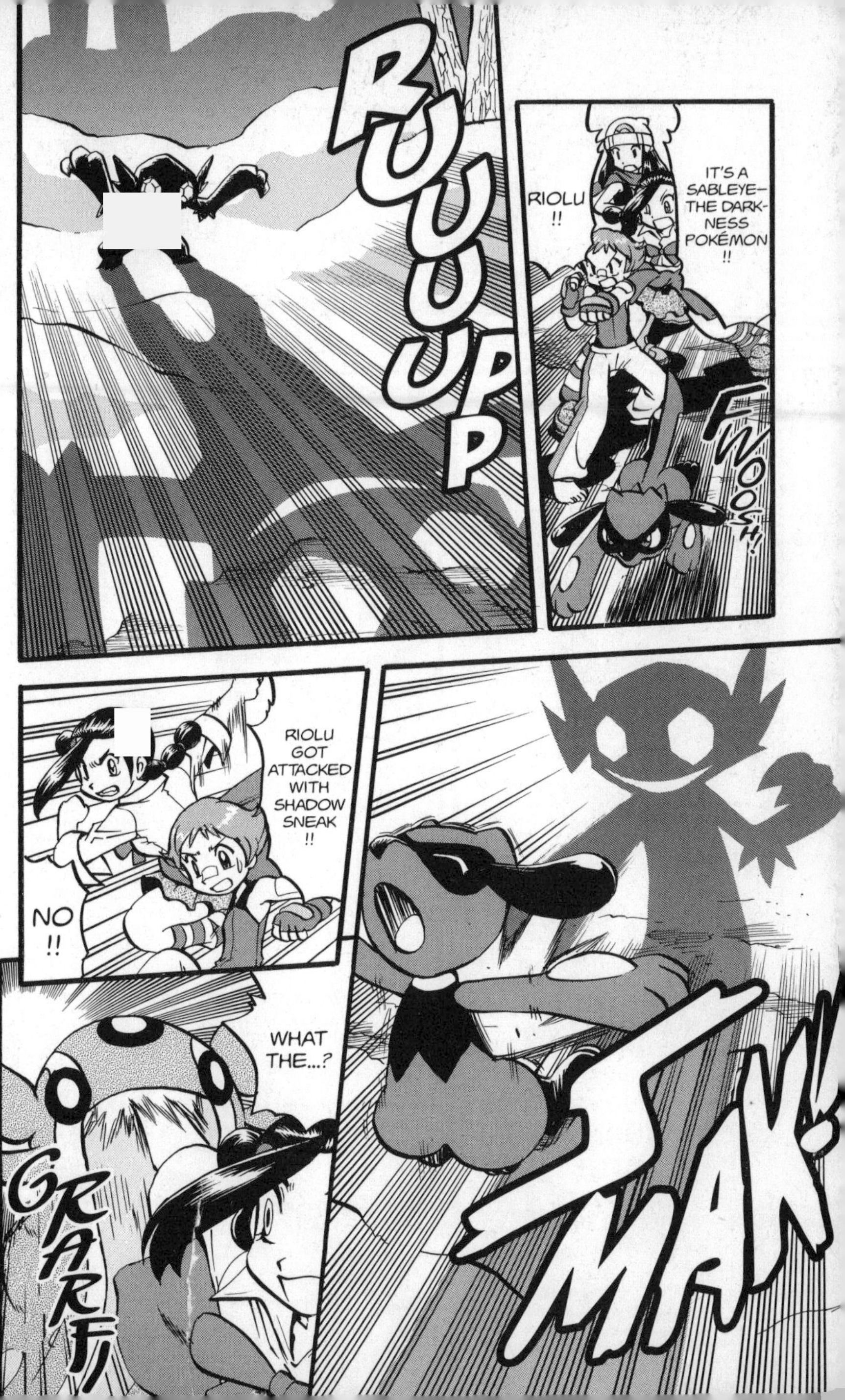

IT'S A SABLEYE—THE DARKNESS POKÉMON!!
RIOLU!!
FWOOSH!
RUUUUPP
SMAK!
RIOLU GOT ATTACKED WITH SHADOW SNEAK!!
NO!!
WHAT THE...?
GRARF!

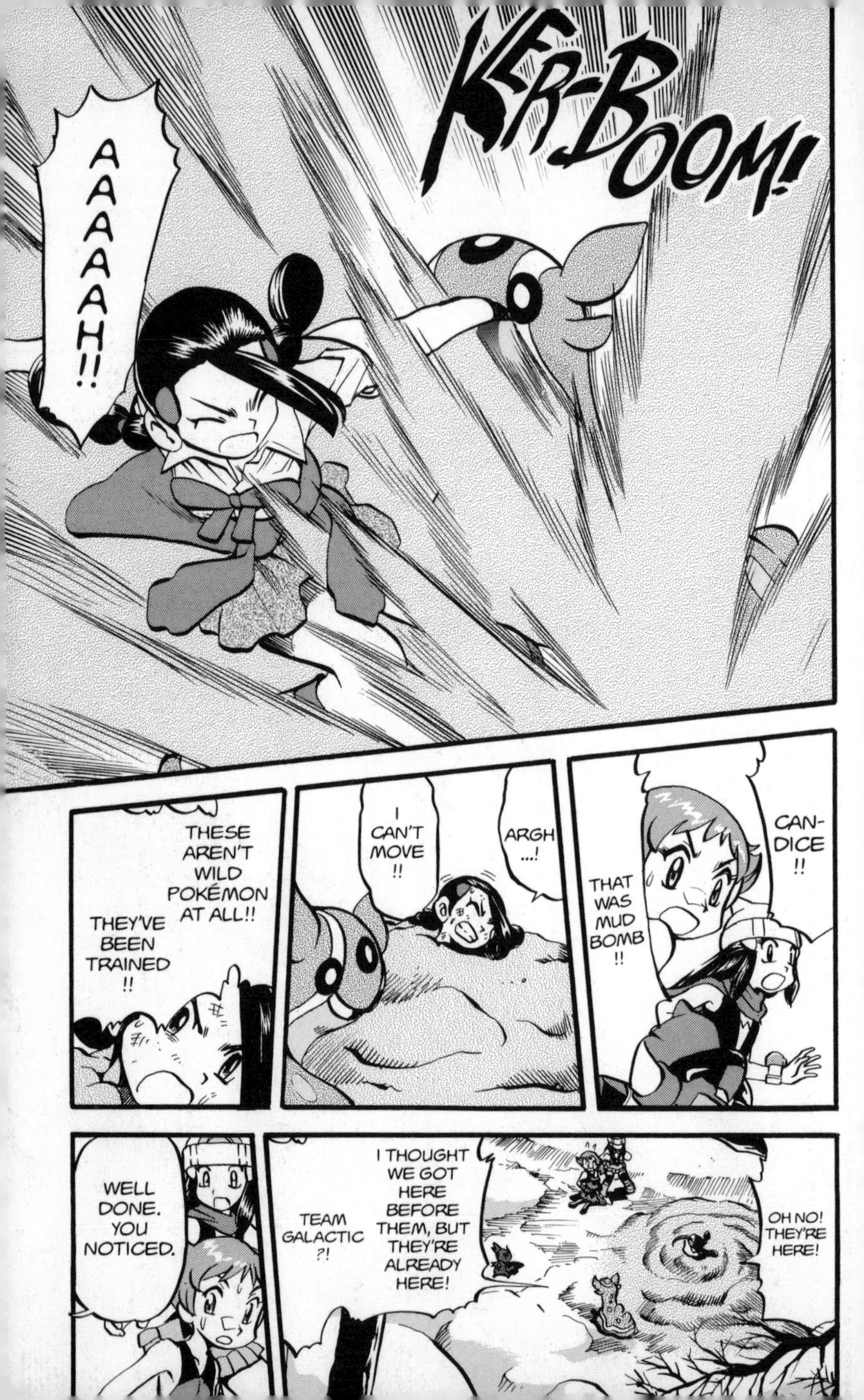
KER-BOOM!
AAAAAH!!
CAN-DICE!!
THAT WAS MUD BOMB!!
ARGH...!
I CAN'T MOVE!!
THESE AREN'T WILD POKÉMON AT ALL!!
THEY'VE BEEN TRAINED!!
OH NO! THEY'RE HERE!
I THOUGHT WE GOT HERE BEFORE THEM, BUT THEY'RE ALREADY HERE!
TEAM GALACTIC?!
WELL DONE. YOU NOTICED.

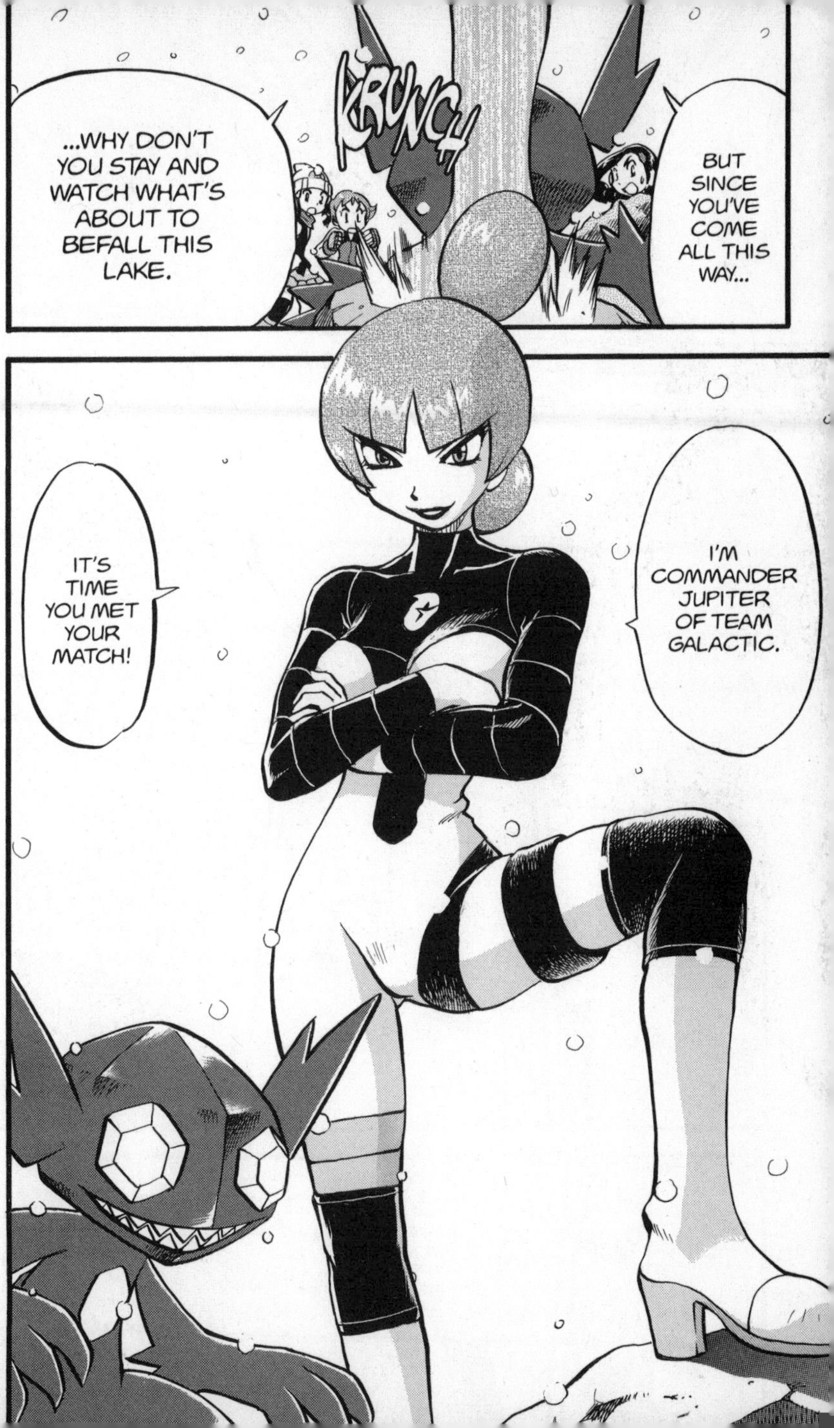
BUT SINCE YOU'VE COME ALL THIS WAY...
KRUNCH
...WHY DON'T YOU STAY AND WATCH WHAT'S ABOUT TO BEFALL THIS LAKE.
I'M COMMANDER JUPITER OF TEAM GALACTIC.
IT'S TIME YOU MET YOUR MATCH!

59

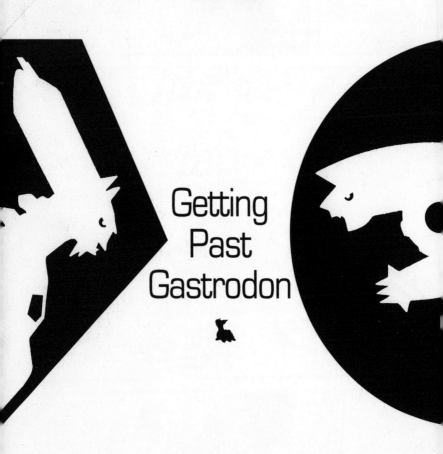

Getting
Past
Gastrodon

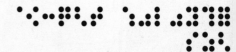

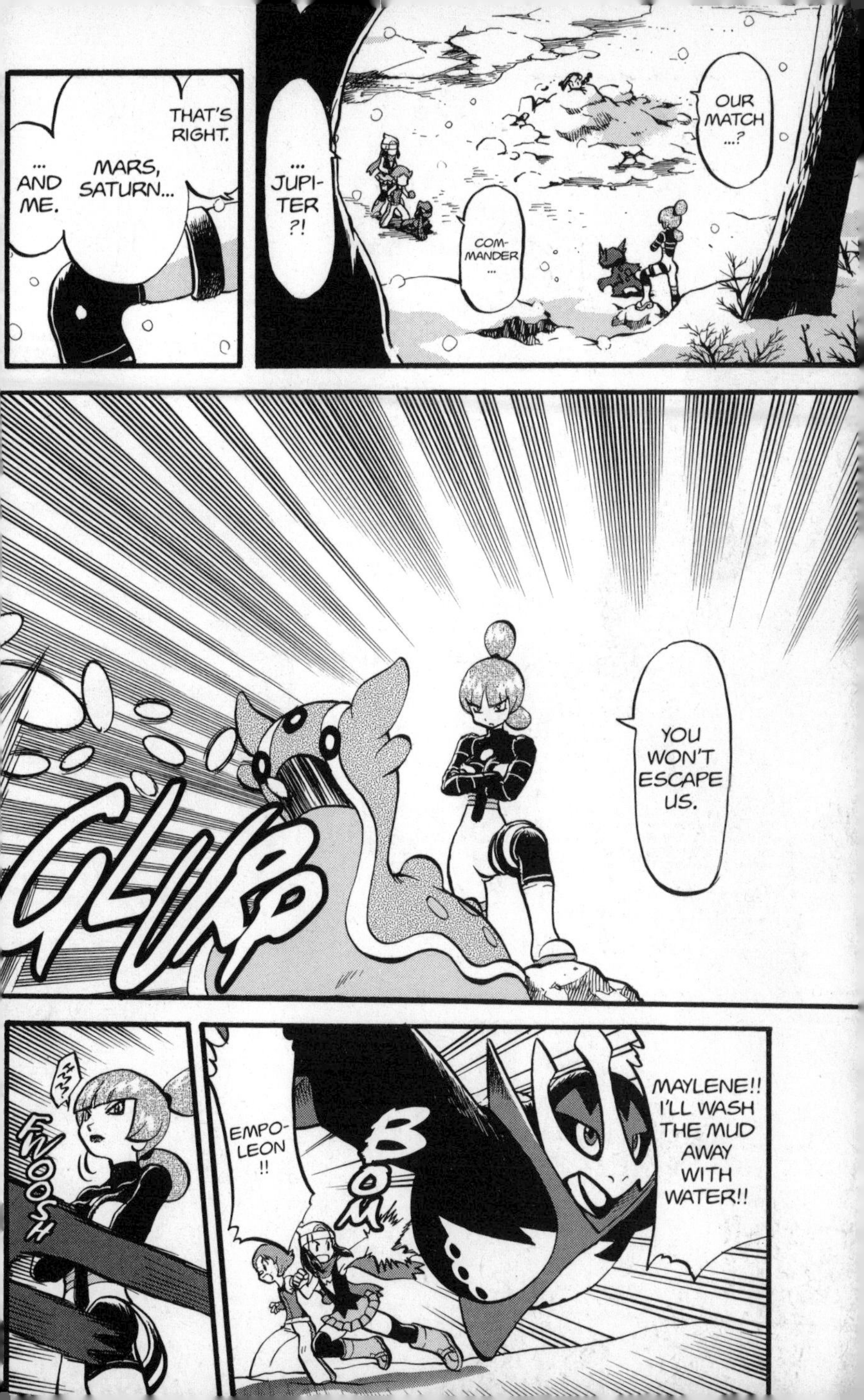
OUR MATCH ...?
COMMANDER ...
... JUPITER ?!
THAT'S RIGHT.
MARS, SATURN...
... AND ME.
YOU WON'T ESCAPE US.
GLUB
MAYLENE!! I'LL WASH THE MUD AWAY WITH WATER!!
BOM
EMPOLEON !!
HMM.
FWOOSH

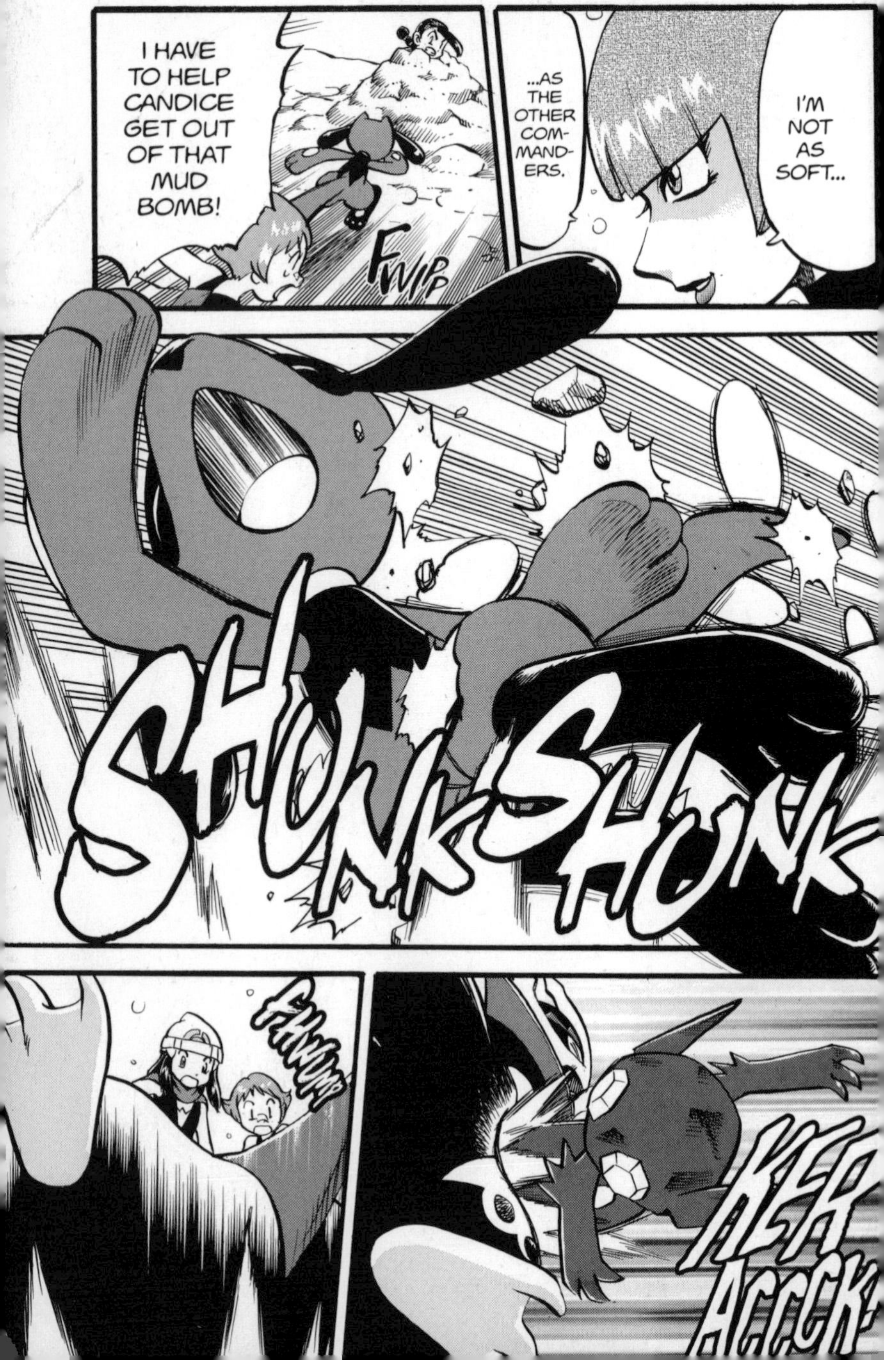
I'M NOT AS SOFT...
...AS THE OTHER COM-MAND-ERS.
I HAVE TO HELP CANDICE GET OUT OF THAT MUD BOMB!
FVVIPP
SHONK
SHONK
ACCCK

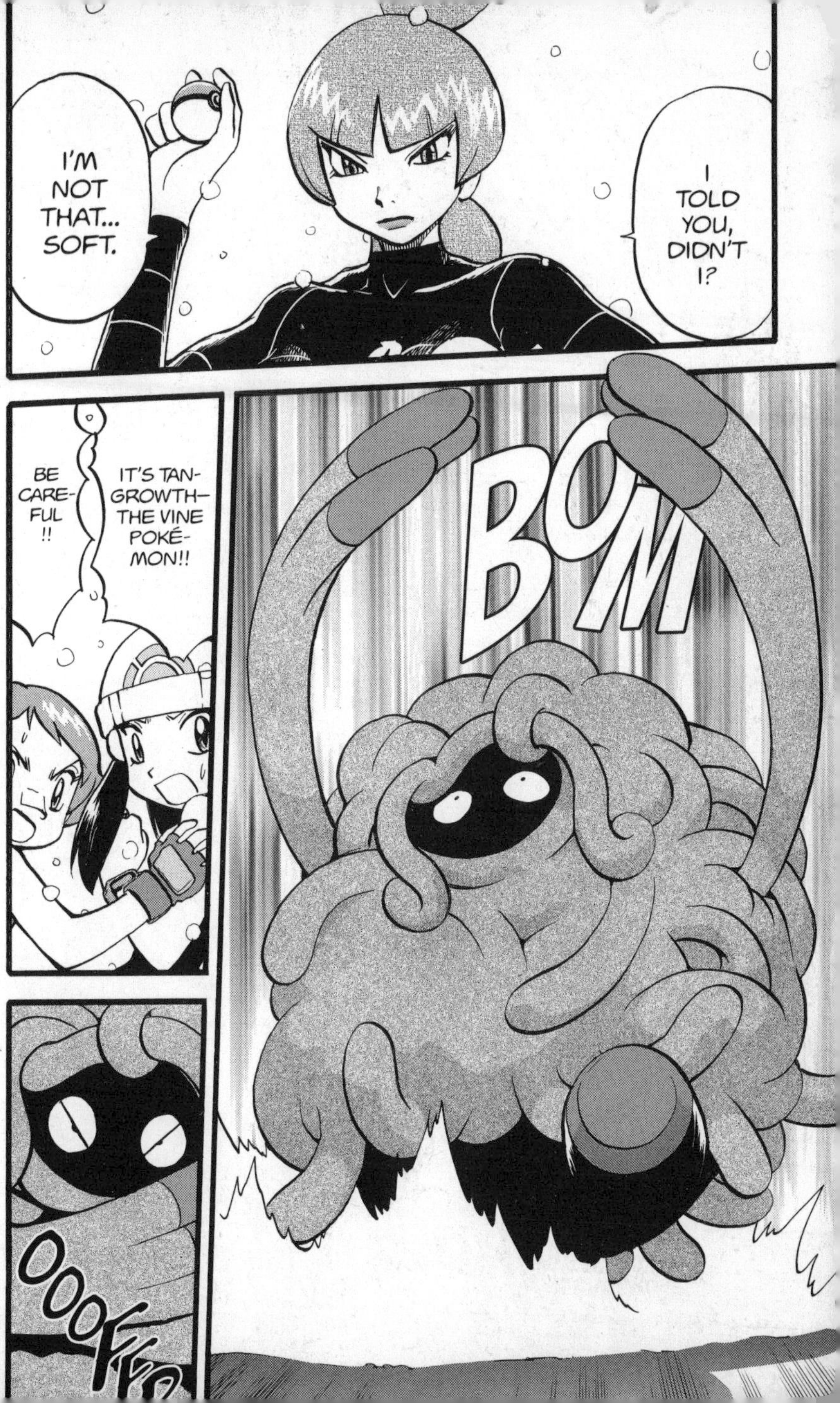
I TOLD YOU, DIDN'T I?
I'M NOT THAT... SOFT.
BOM
IT'S TAN-GROWTH—THE VINE POKÉ-MON!!
BE CARE-FUL!!
OOOFF

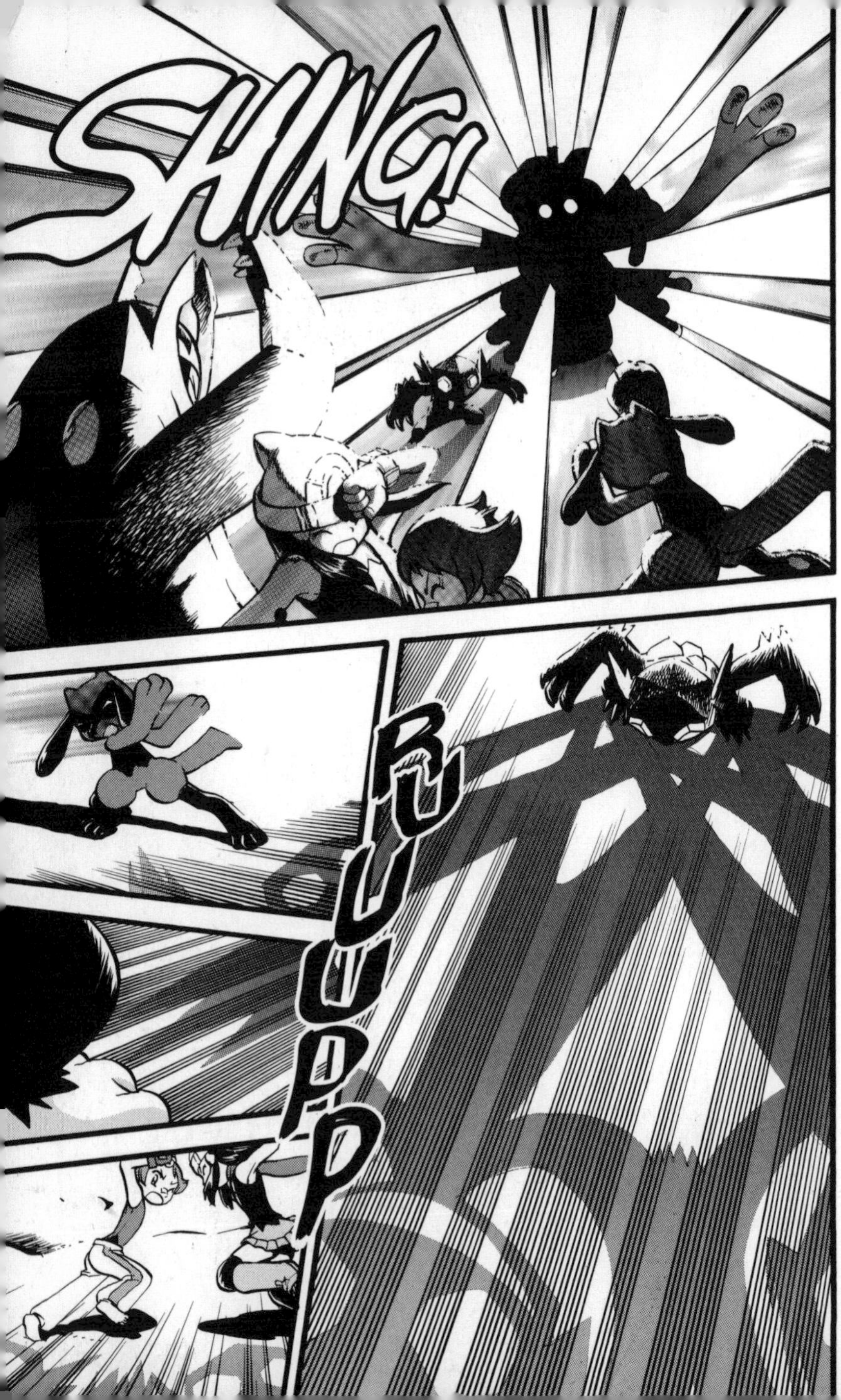
SHING!
RUUUPP

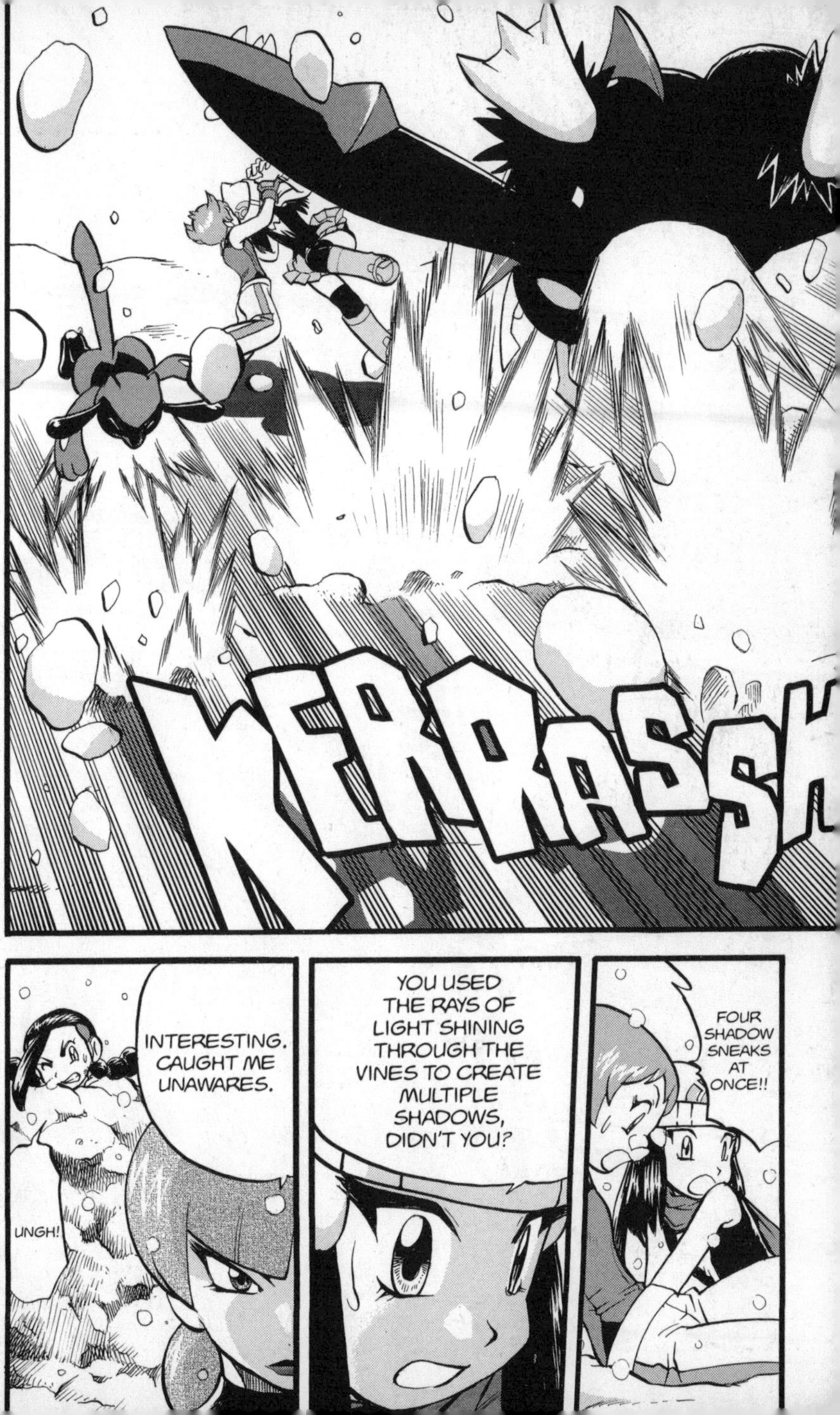
KERRASSH
FOUR SHADOW SNEAKS AT ONCE!!
YOU USED THE RAYS OF LIGHT SHINING THROUGH THE VINES TO CREATE MULTIPLE SHADOWS, DIDN'T YOU?
INTERESTING. CAUGHT ME UNAWARES.
UNGH!

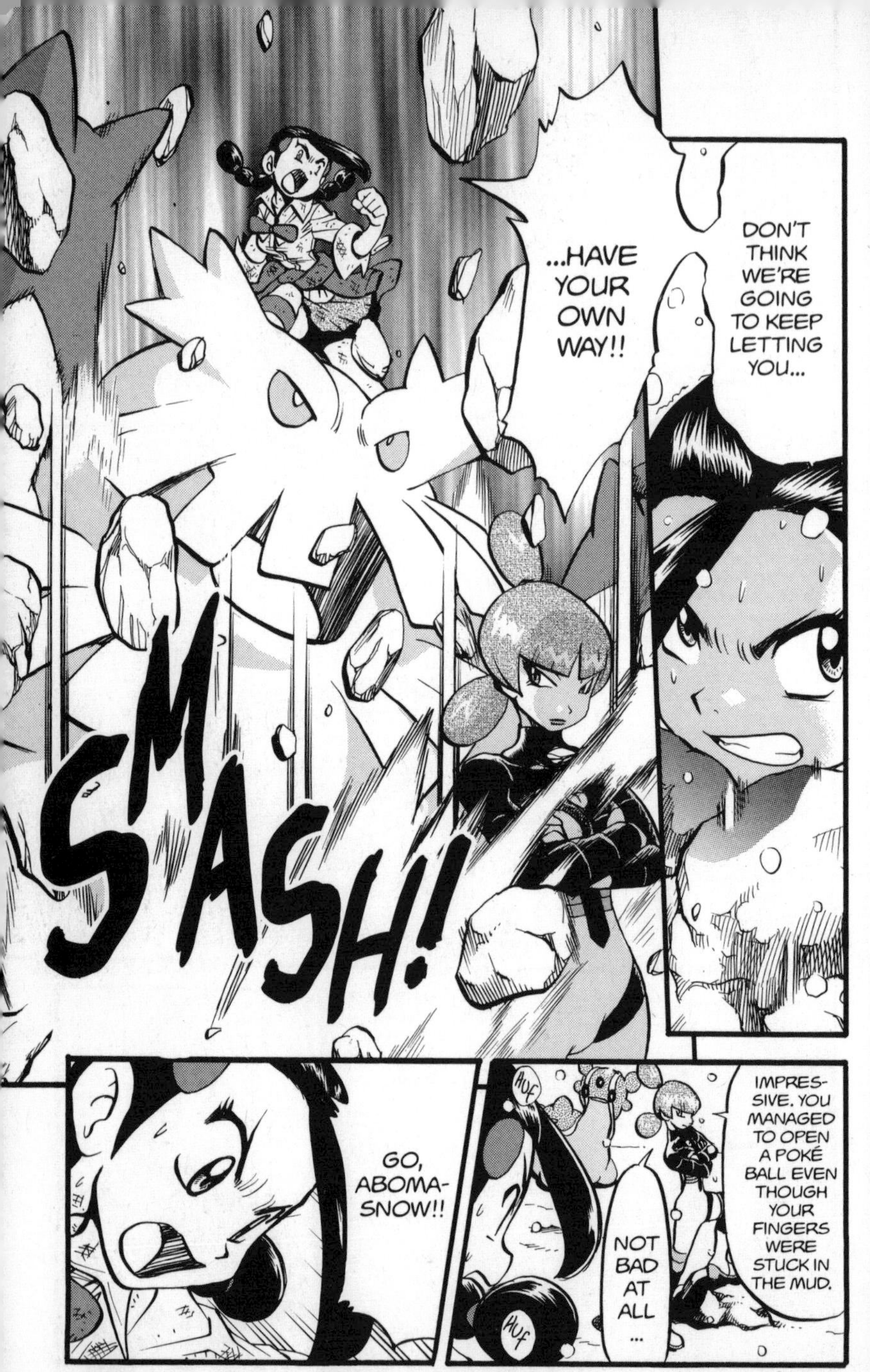
DON'T THINK WE'RE GOING TO KEEP LETTING YOU...
...HAVE YOUR OWN WAY!!
SMASH!
IMPRES-SIVE. YOU MANAGED TO OPEN A POKé BALL EVEN THOUGH YOUR FINGERS WERE STUCK IN THE MUD.
HUF
NOT BAD AT ALL...
HUF
GO, ABOMA-SNOW!!

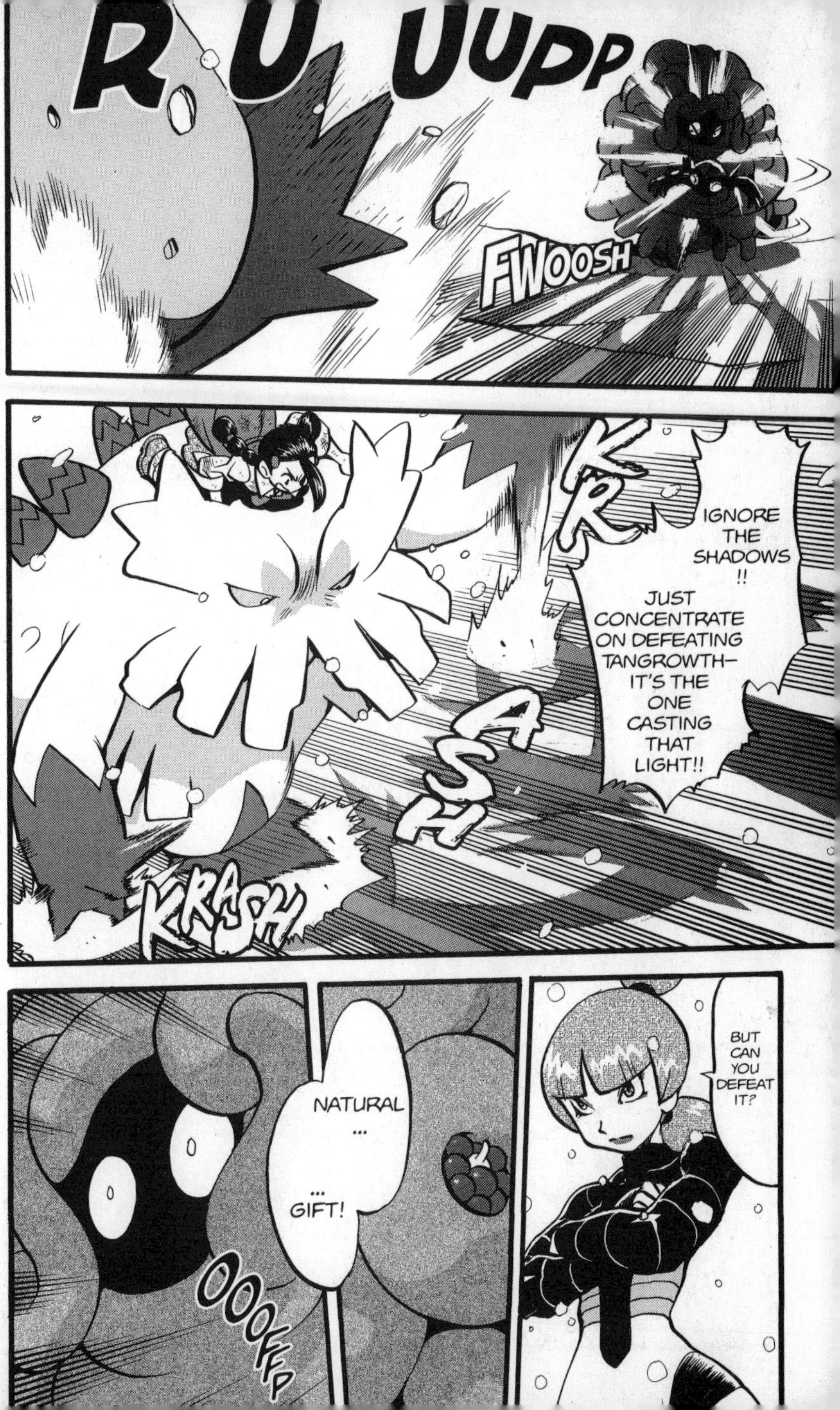
R U UUPP
FWOOSH
KRASH
IGNORE THE SHADOWS!! JUST CONCENTRATE ON DEFEATING TANGROWTH—IT'S THE ONE CASTING THAT LIGHT!!
KRASH
BUT CAN YOU DEFEAT IT?
NATURAL...
...GIFT!
OOOFFP

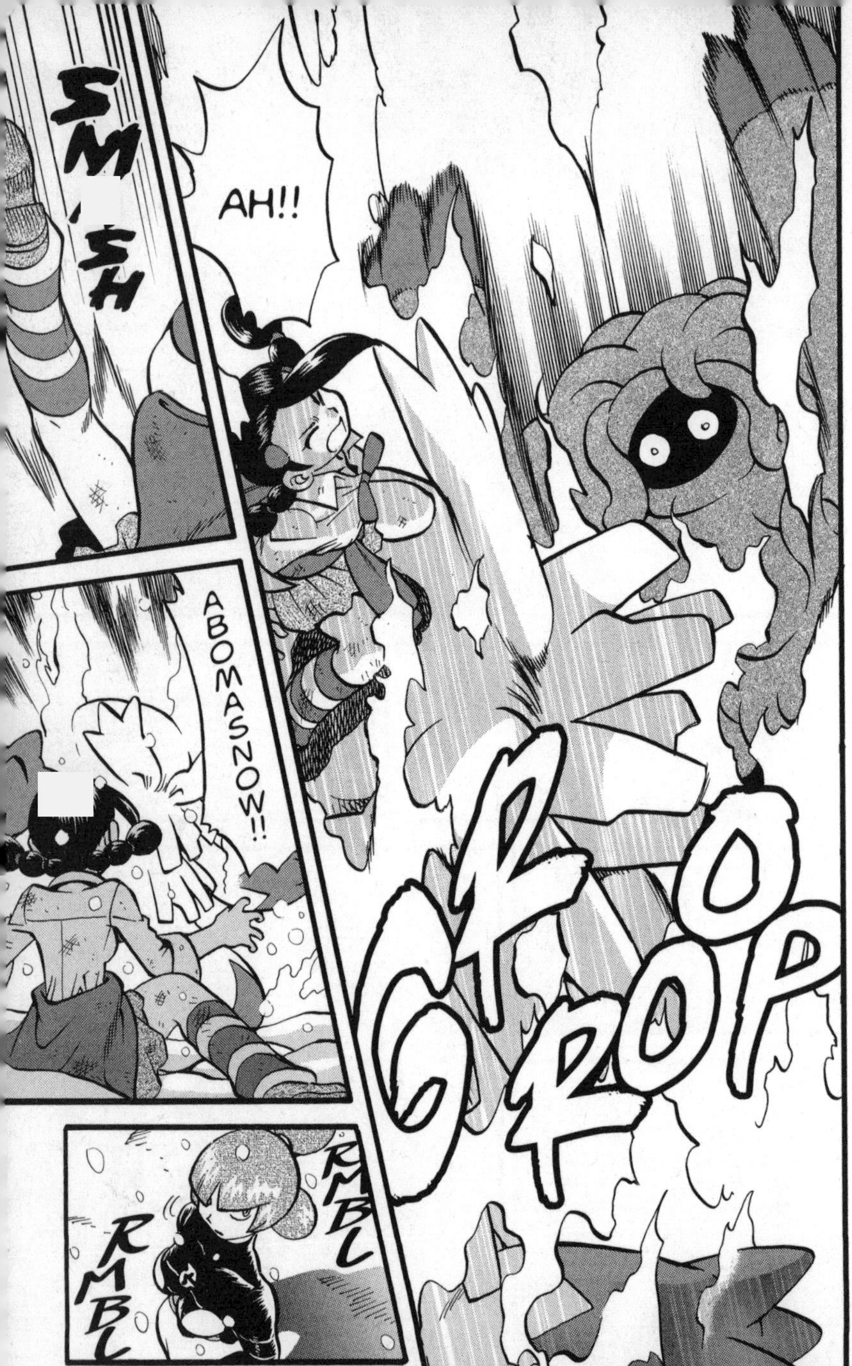
AH!!
GROP GROP
SMASH
ABOMASNOW!!
RMBL RMBL

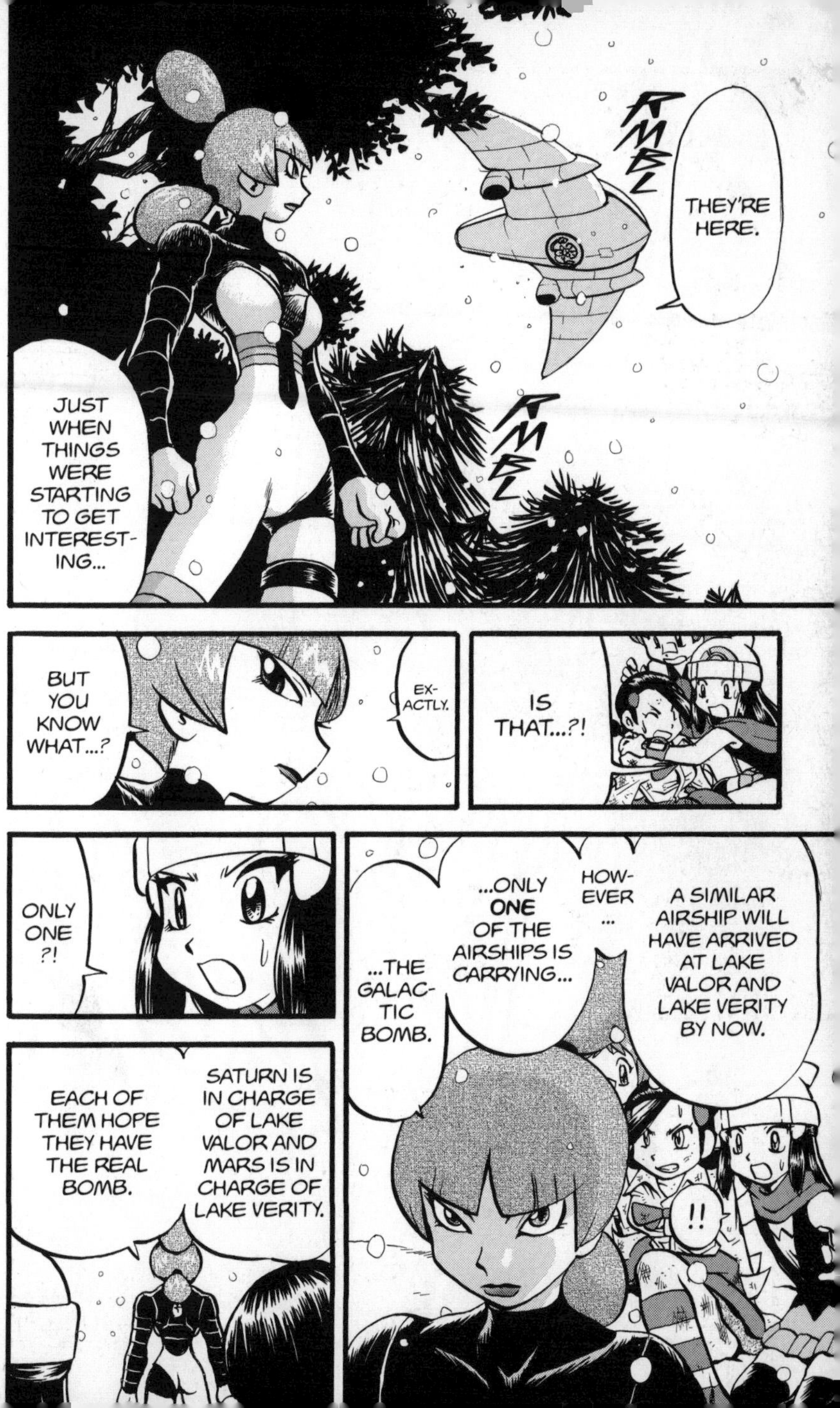
THEY'RE HERE.
RMBL
RMBL
JUST WHEN THINGS WERE STARTING TO GET INTEREST-ING...
IS THAT...?!
EX-ACTLY.
BUT YOU KNOW WHAT...?
A SIMILAR AIRSHIP WILL HAVE ARRIVED AT LAKE VALOR AND LAKE VERITY BY NOW.
HOW-EVER...
...ONLY **ONE** OF THE AIRSHIPS IS CARRYING...
...THE GALAC-TIC BOMB.
!!
ONLY ONE ?!
SATURN IS IN CHARGE OF LAKE VALOR AND MARS IS IN CHARGE OF LAKE VERITY.
EACH OF THEM HOPE THEY HAVE THE REAL BOMB.

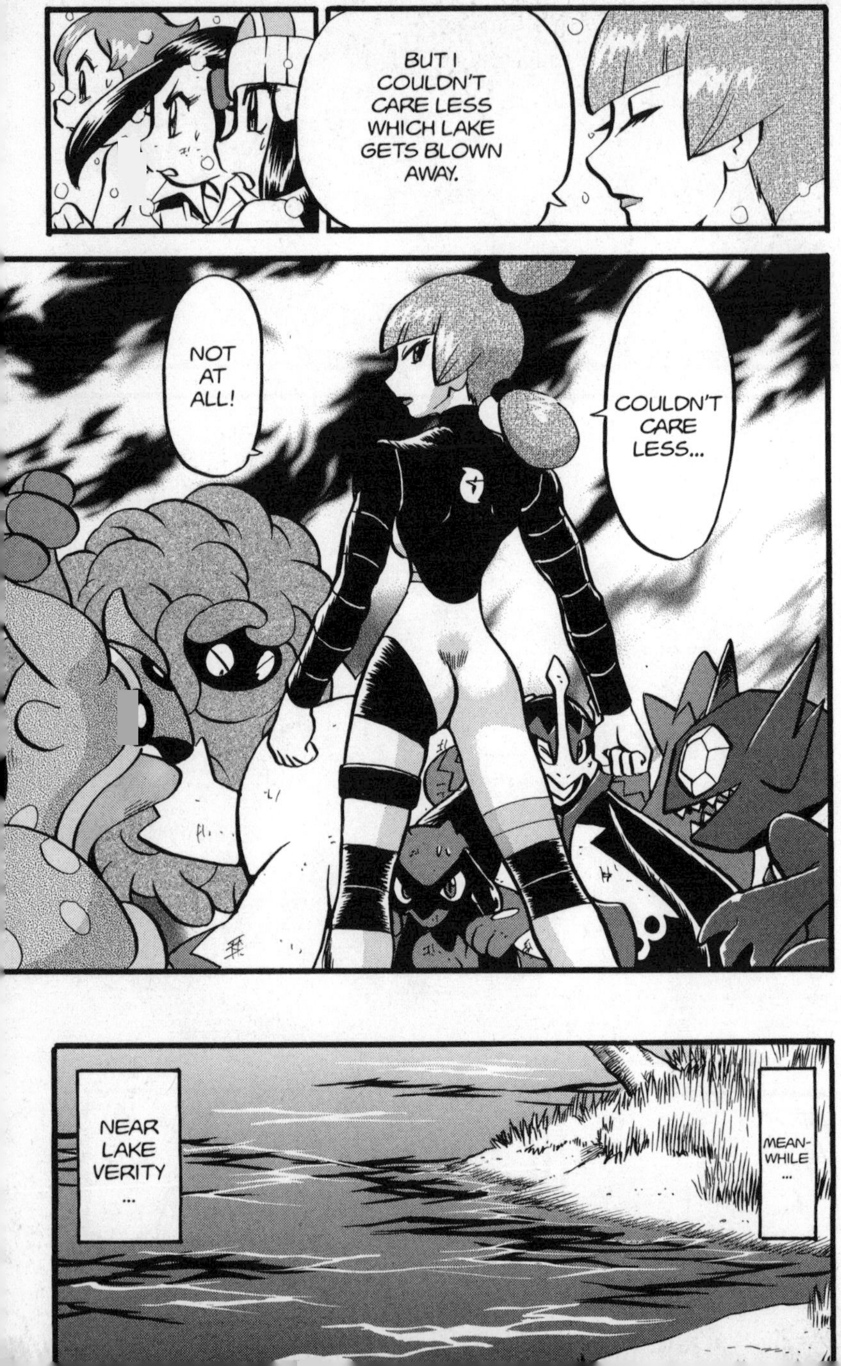
BUT I COULDN'T CARE LESS WHICH LAKE GETS BLOWN AWAY.
COULDN'T CARE LESS...
NOT AT ALL!
MEAN-WHILE...
NEAR LAKE VERITY...

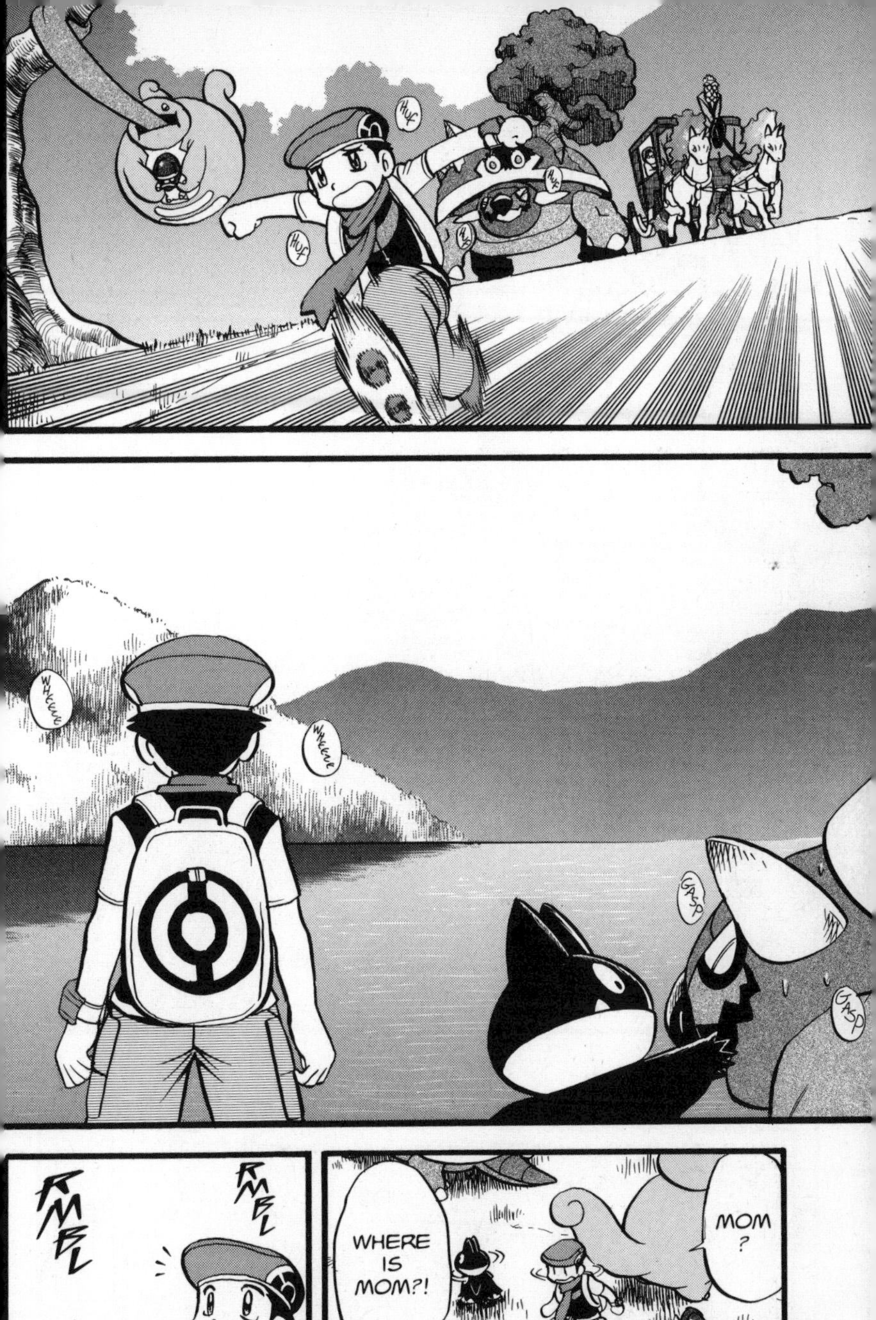
HUF
HUF
HUF
HUF
WHEEEE
WHEEEE
GASP
GASP
MOM ?
WHERE IS MOM?!
RMBL
RMBL

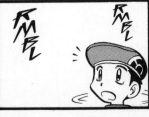

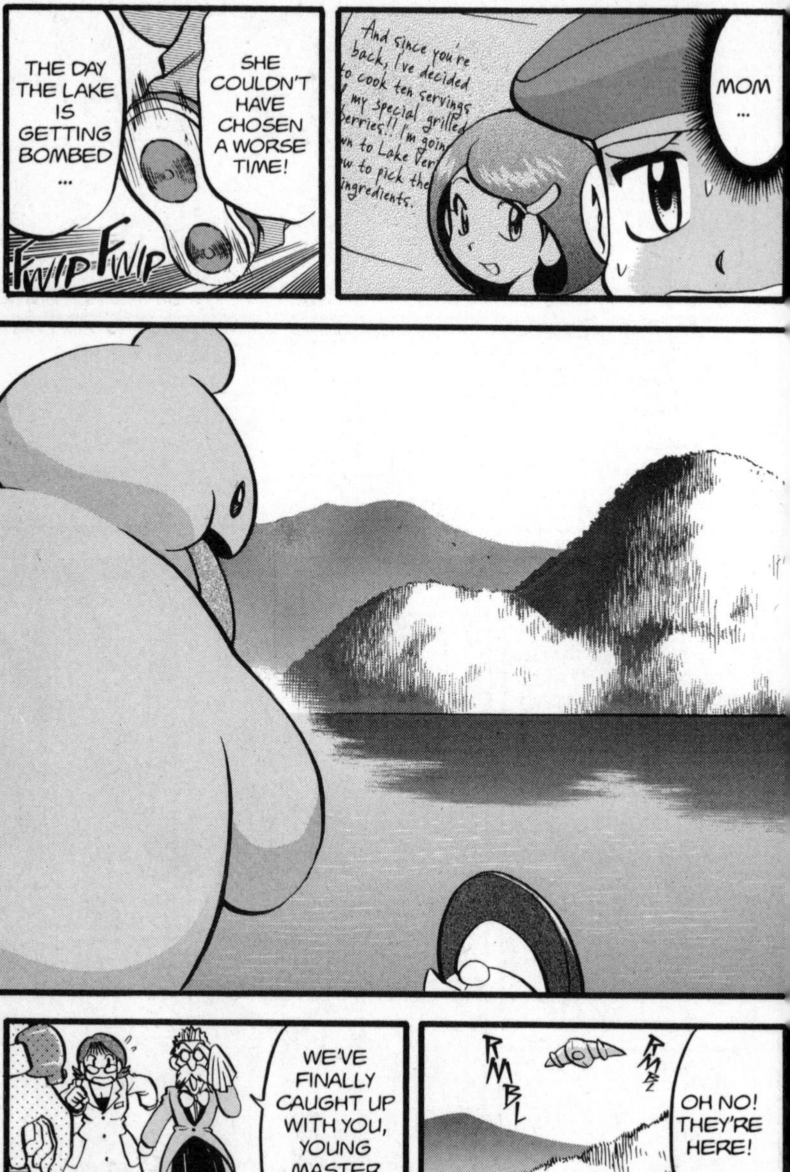
MOM ...
And since you're back, I've decided to cook ten servings my special grilled berries!! I'm goin to Lake Ver w to pick the ingredients.
SHE COULDN'T HAVE CHOSEN A WORSE TIME!
THE DAY THE LAKE IS GETTING BOMBED ...
FWIP FWIP
RMBL
RMBL
OH NO! THEY'RE HERE!
WE'VE FINALLY CAUGHT UP WITH YOU, YOUNG MASTER DIAMOND.

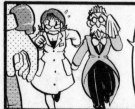

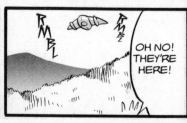

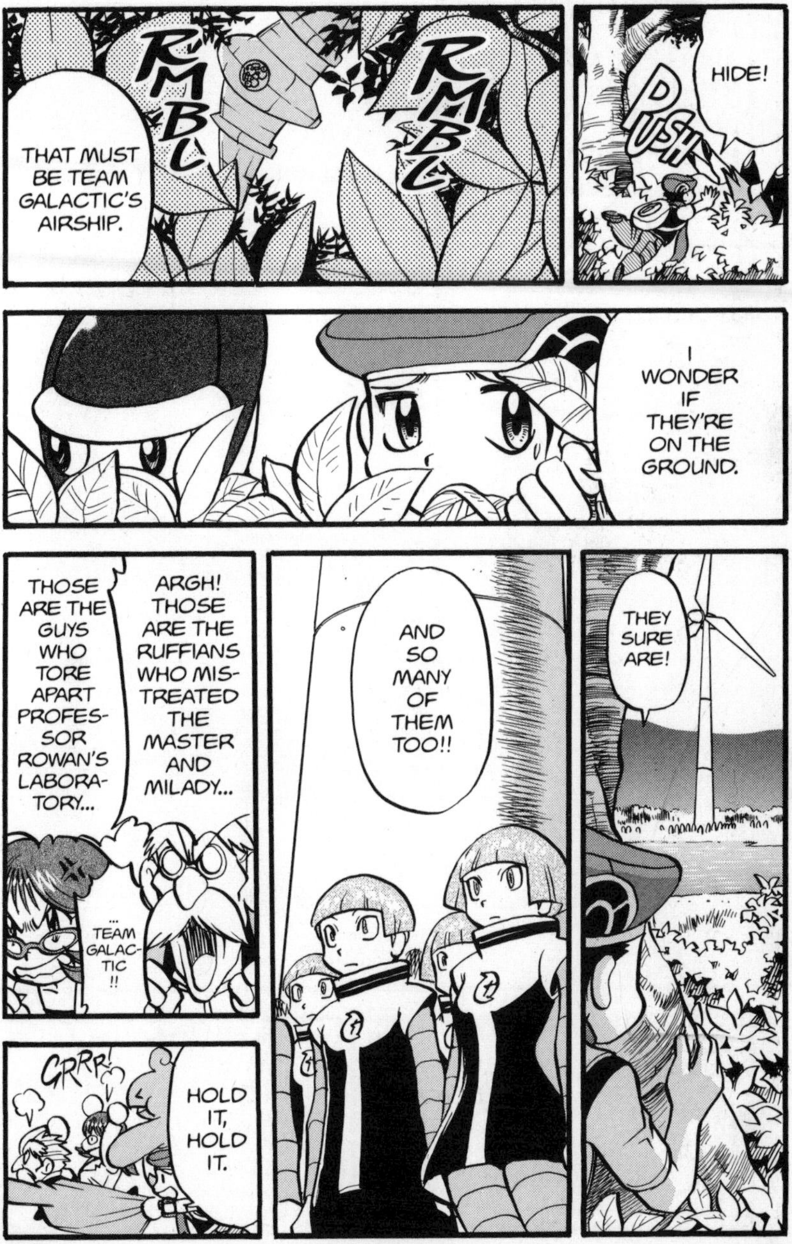
PUSH
HIDE!
RMBL
RMBL
THAT MUST BE TEAM GALACTIC'S AIRSHIP.
I WONDER IF THEY'RE ON THE GROUND.
THEY SURE ARE!
AND SO MANY OF THEM TOO!!
ARGH! THOSE ARE THE RUFFIANS WHO MISTREATED THE MASTER AND MILADY...
THOSE ARE THE GUYS WHO TORE APART PROFESSOR ROWAN'S LABORATORY...
...TEAM GALACTIC!!
HOLD IT, HOLD IT.
GRRR!

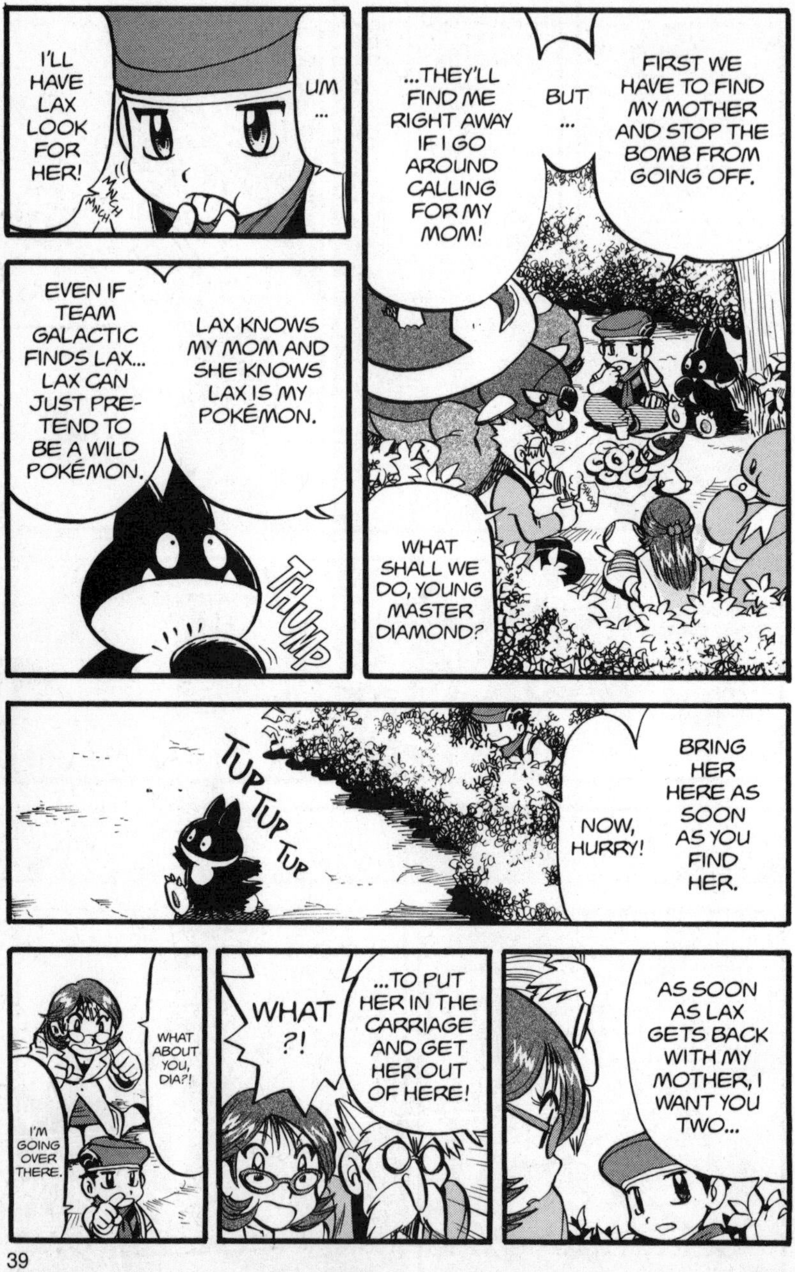
FIRST WE HAVE TO FIND MY MOTHER AND STOP THE BOMB FROM GOING OFF.
BUT ...
...THEY'LL FIND ME RIGHT AWAY IF I GO AROUND CALLING FOR MY MOM!
WHAT SHALL WE DO, YOUNG MASTER DIAMOND?
UM ...
I'LL HAVE LAX LOOK FOR HER!
MNCH MNCH
LAX KNOWS MY MOM AND SHE KNOWS LAX IS MY POKÉMON.
EVEN IF TEAM GALACTIC FINDS LAX... LAX CAN JUST PRE-TEND TO BE A WILD POKÉMON.
THUMP
BRING HER HERE AS SOON AS YOU FIND HER.
NOW, HURRY!
TUP TUP TUP
AS SOON AS LAX GETS BACK WITH MY MOTHER, I WANT YOU TWO...
...TO PUT HER IN THE CARRIAGE AND GET HER OUT OF HERE!
WHAT ?!
WHAT ABOUT YOU, DIA?!
I'M GOING OVER THERE.

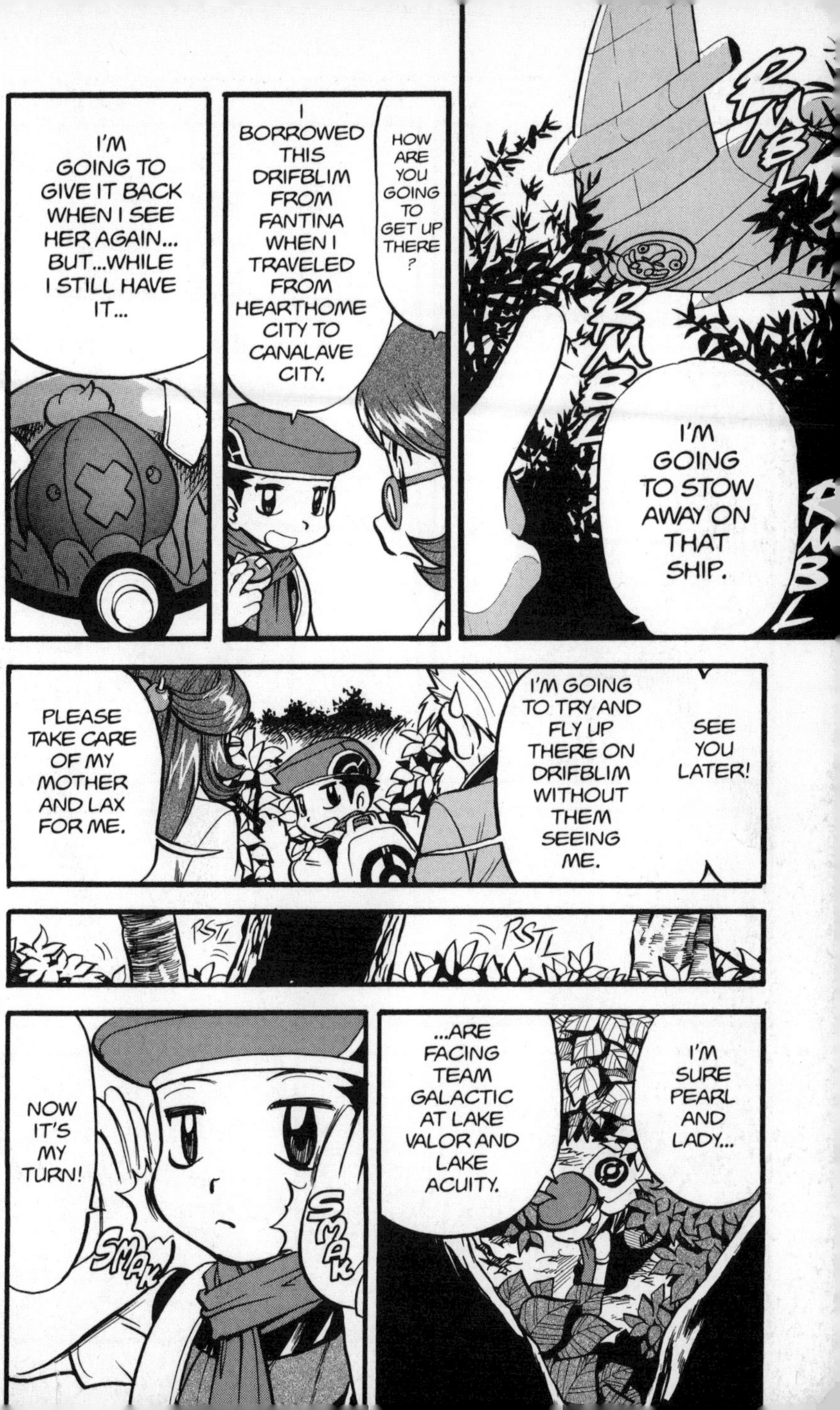
RMBL
RMBL
RMBL
I'M GOING TO STOW AWAY ON THAT SHIP.
HOW ARE YOU GOING TO GET UP THERE?
I BORROWED THIS DRIFBLIM FROM FANTINA WHEN I TRAVELED FROM HEARTHOME CITY TO CANALAVE CITY.
I'M GOING TO GIVE IT BACK WHEN I SEE HER AGAIN... BUT...WHILE I STILL HAVE IT...
SEE YOU LATER!
I'M GOING TO TRY AND FLY UP THERE ON DRIFBLIM WITHOUT THEM SEEING ME.
PLEASE TAKE CARE OF MY MOTHER AND LAX FOR ME.
RSTL
RSTL
I'M SURE PEARL AND LADY...
...ARE FACING TEAM GALACTIC AT LAKE VALOR AND LAKE ACUITY.
SMAK
SMAK
NOW IT'S MY TURN!

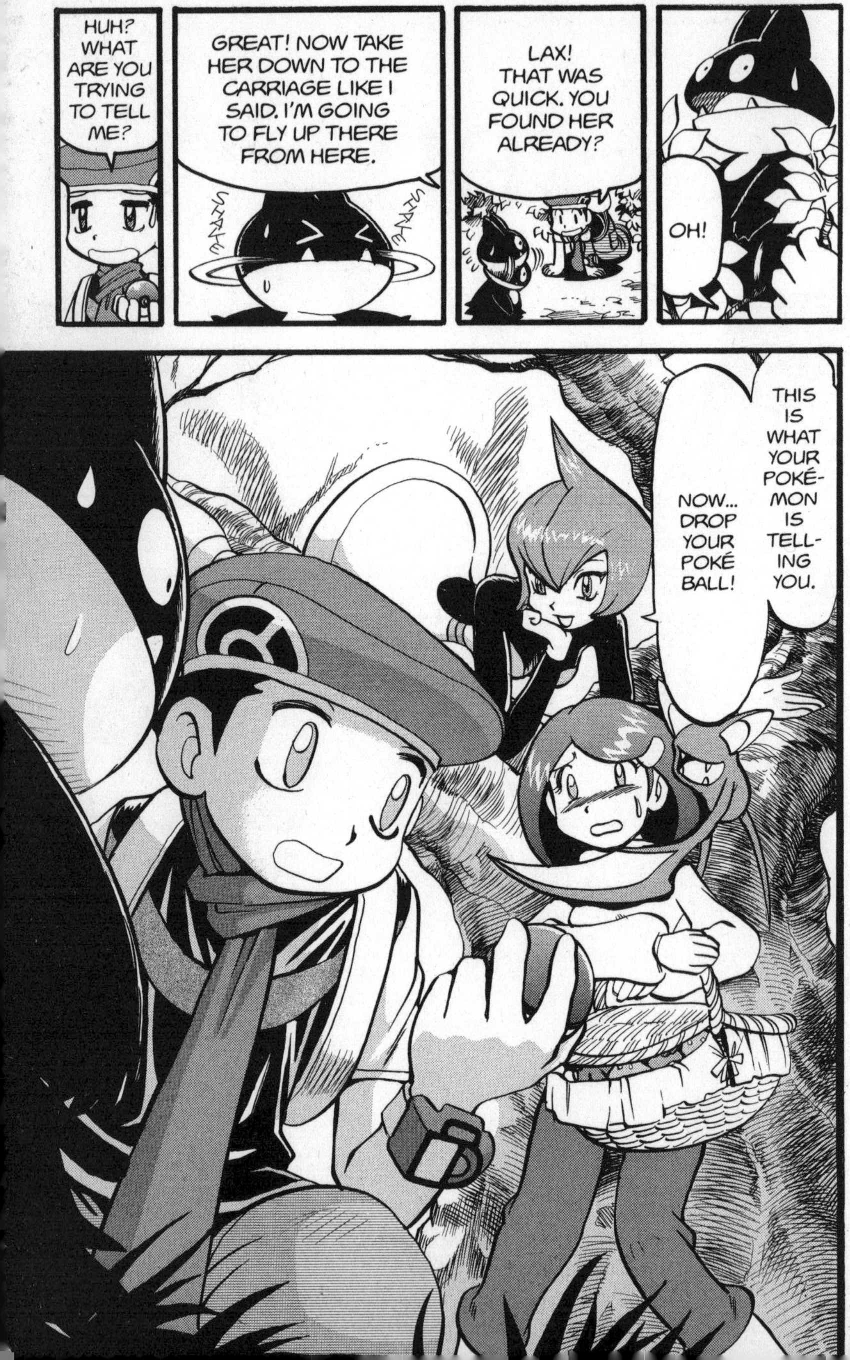
OH!
LAX! THAT WAS QUICK. YOU FOUND HER ALREADY?
GREAT! NOW TAKE HER DOWN TO THE CARRIAGE LIKE I SAID. I'M GOING TO FLY UP THERE FROM HERE.
SHAKE
SHAKE
HUH? WHAT ARE YOU TRYING TO TELL ME?
THIS IS WHAT YOUR POKÉMON IS TELLING YOU.
NOW... DROP YOUR POKÉ BALL!

60

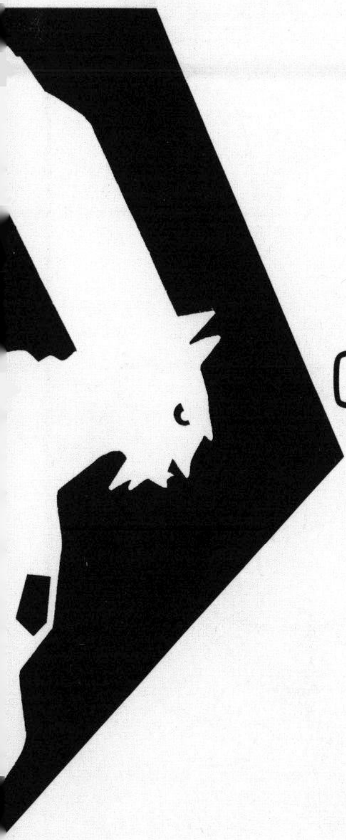

Outwitting Octillery

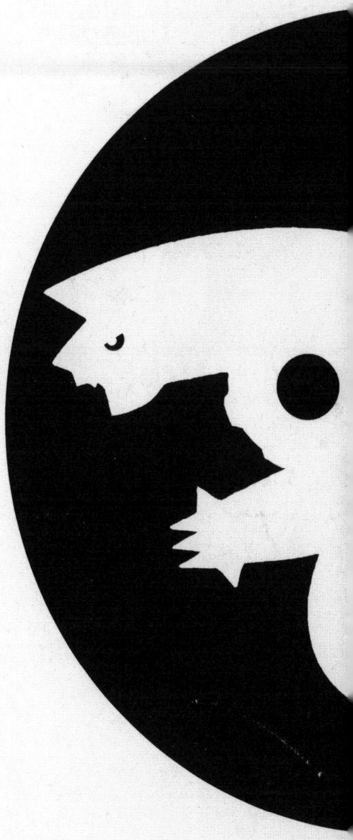

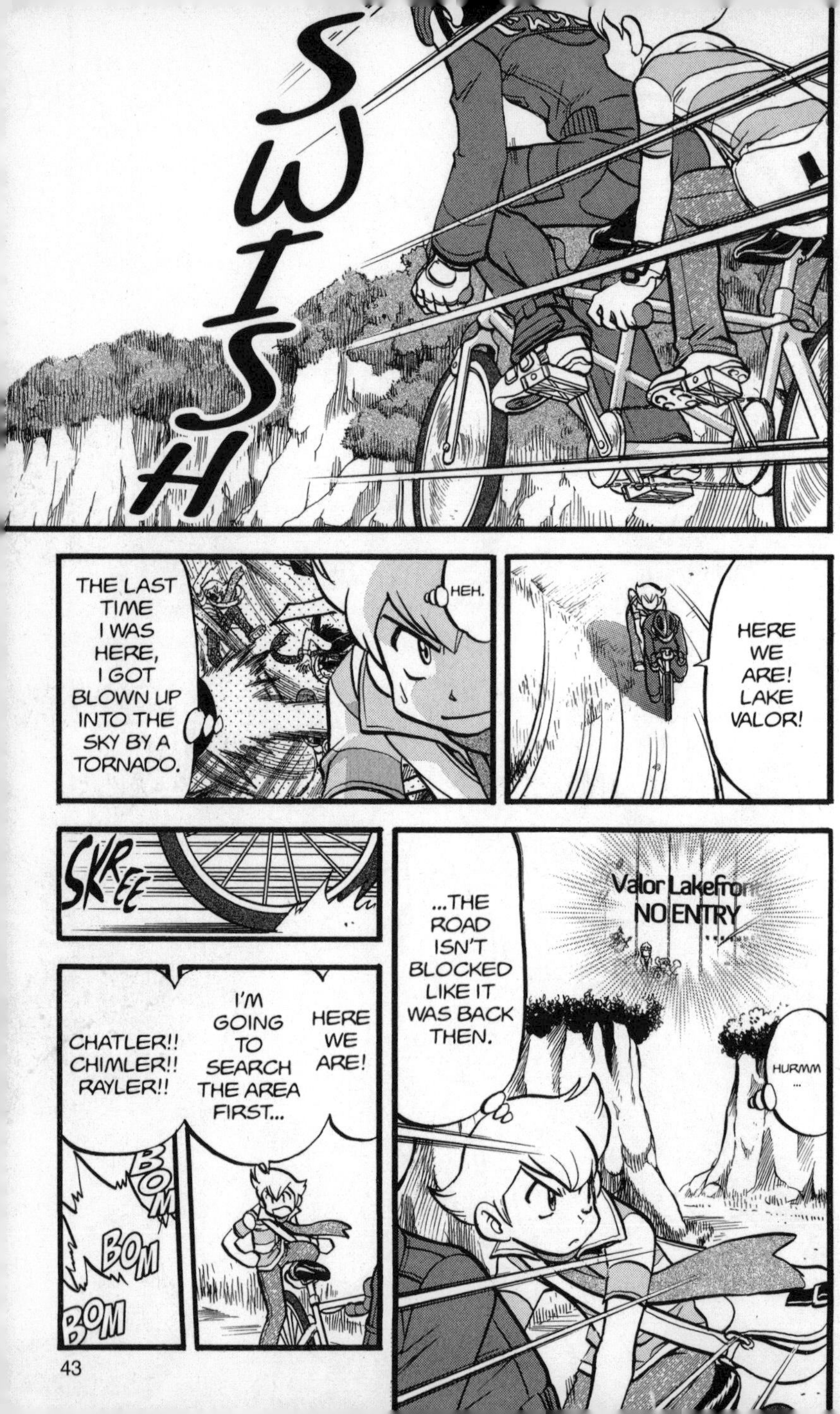
SWISH
HERE WE ARE! LAKE VALOR!
HEH.
THE LAST TIME I WAS HERE, I GOT BLOWN UP INTO THE SKY BY A TORNADO.
Valor Lakefro
NO ENTRY
...THE ROAD ISN'T BLOCKED LIKE IT WAS BACK THEN.
HURMM ...
SKREE
HERE WE ARE!
I'M GOING TO SEARCH THE AREA FIRST...
CHATLER!! CHIMLER!! RAYLER!!
BOM
BOM
BOM

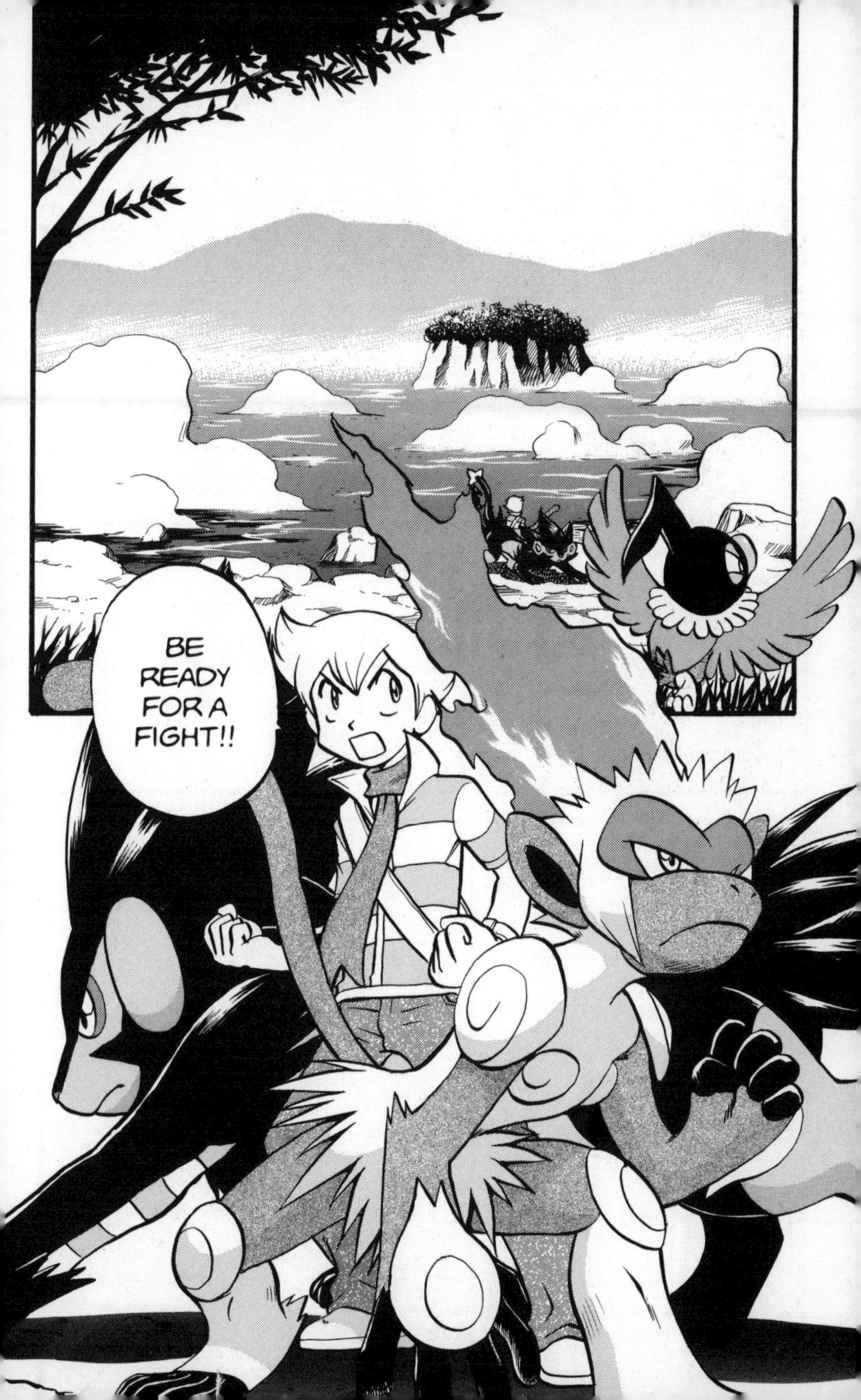
BE READY FOR A FIGHT!!

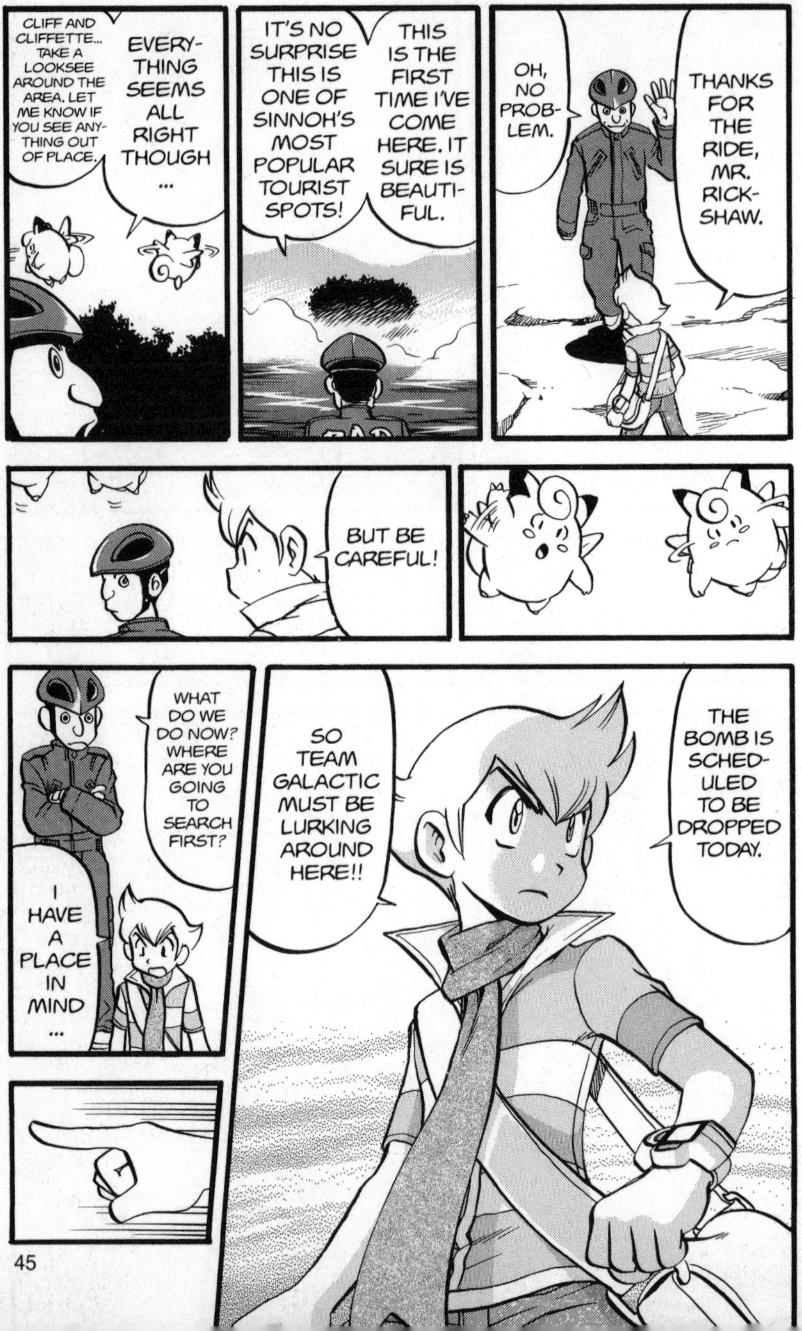
THANKS FOR THE RIDE, MR. RICKSHAW.
OH, NO PROBLEM.
THIS IS THE FIRST TIME I'VE COME HERE. IT SURE IS BEAUTIFUL.
IT'S NO SURPRISE THIS IS ONE OF SINNOH'S MOST POPULAR TOURIST SPOTS!
EVERYTHING SEEMS ALL RIGHT THOUGH...
CLIFF AND CLIFFETTE... TAKE A LOOKSEE AROUND THE AREA. LET ME KNOW IF YOU SEE ANYTHING OUT OF PLACE.
BUT BE CAREFUL!
THE BOMB IS SCHEDULED TO BE DROPPED TODAY.
SO TEAM GALACTIC MUST BE LURKING AROUND HERE!!
WHAT DO WE DO NOW? WHERE ARE YOU GOING TO SEARCH FIRST?
I HAVE A PLACE IN MIND...

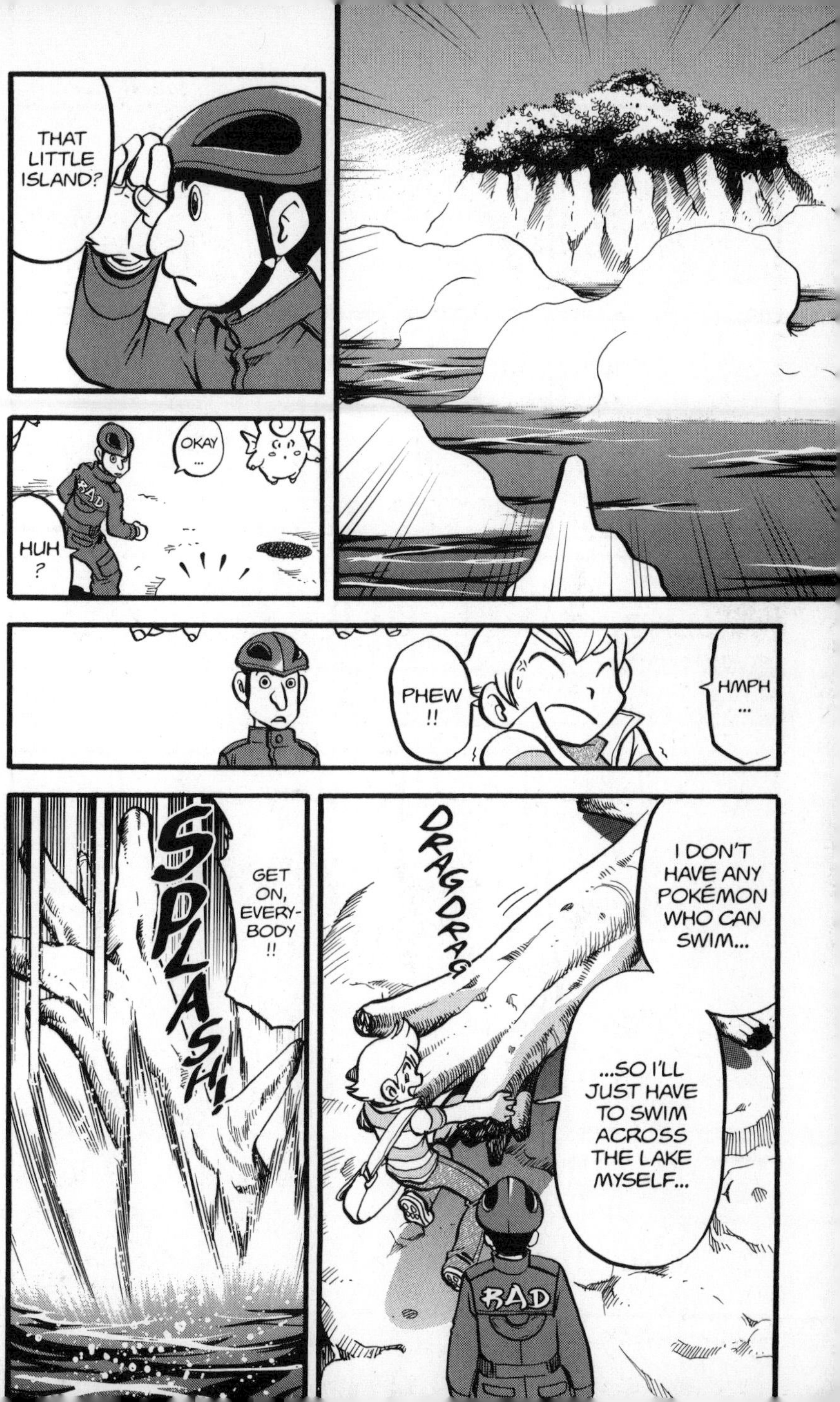
THAT LITTLE ISLAND?
OKAY ...
HUH ?
HMPH ...
PHEW !!
I DON'T HAVE ANY POKÉMON WHO CAN SWIM...
DRAGDRAG
...SO I'LL JUST HAVE TO SWIM ACROSS THE LAKE MYSELF...
GET ON, EVERY-BODY !!
SPLASH!

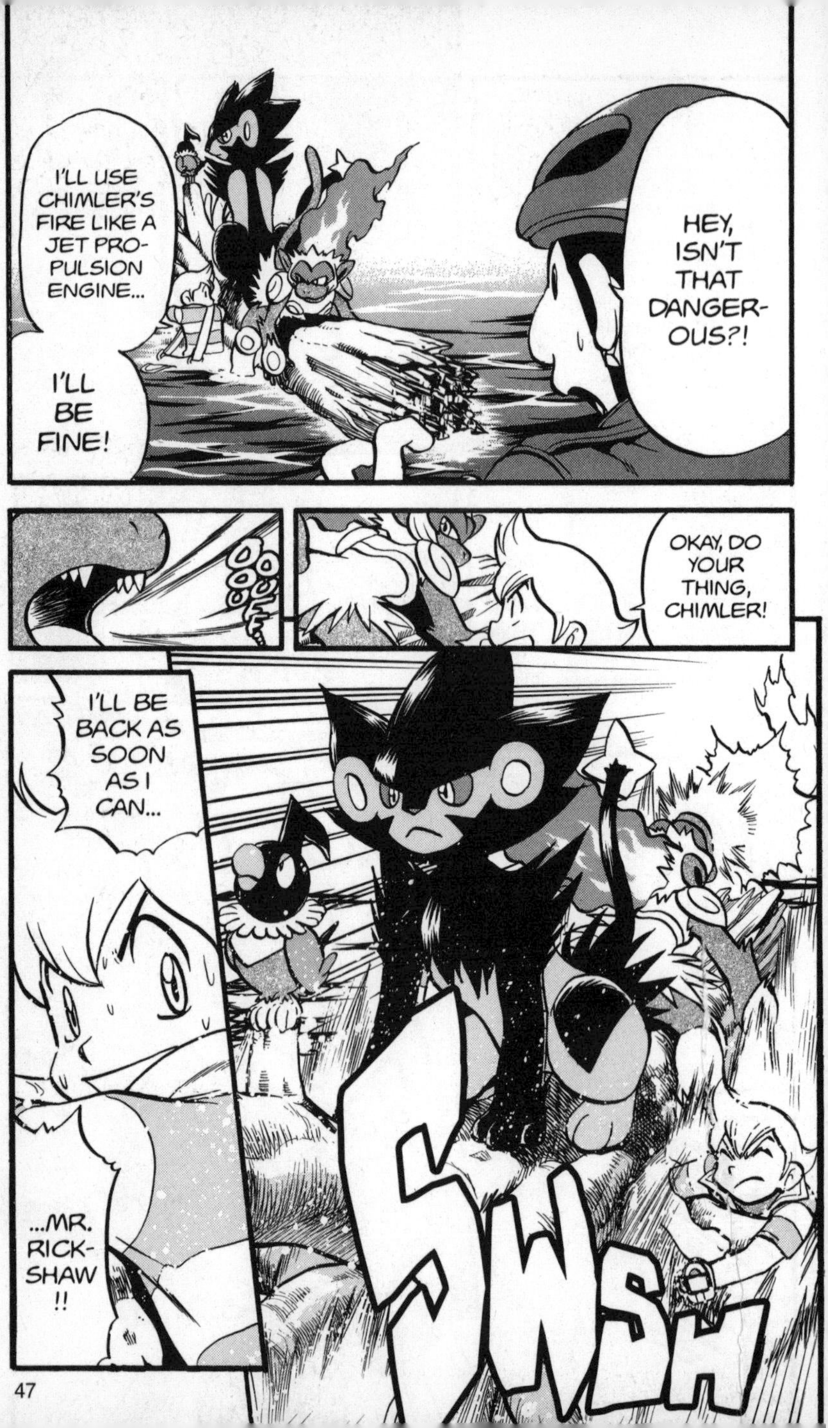
HEY, ISN'T THAT DANGER-OUS?!
I'LL USE CHIMLER'S FIRE LIKE A JET PRO-PULSION ENGINE...
I'LL BE FINE!
OKAY, DO YOUR THING, CHIMLER!
SWSH
I'LL BE BACK AS SOON AS I CAN...
...MR. RICK-SHAW!!

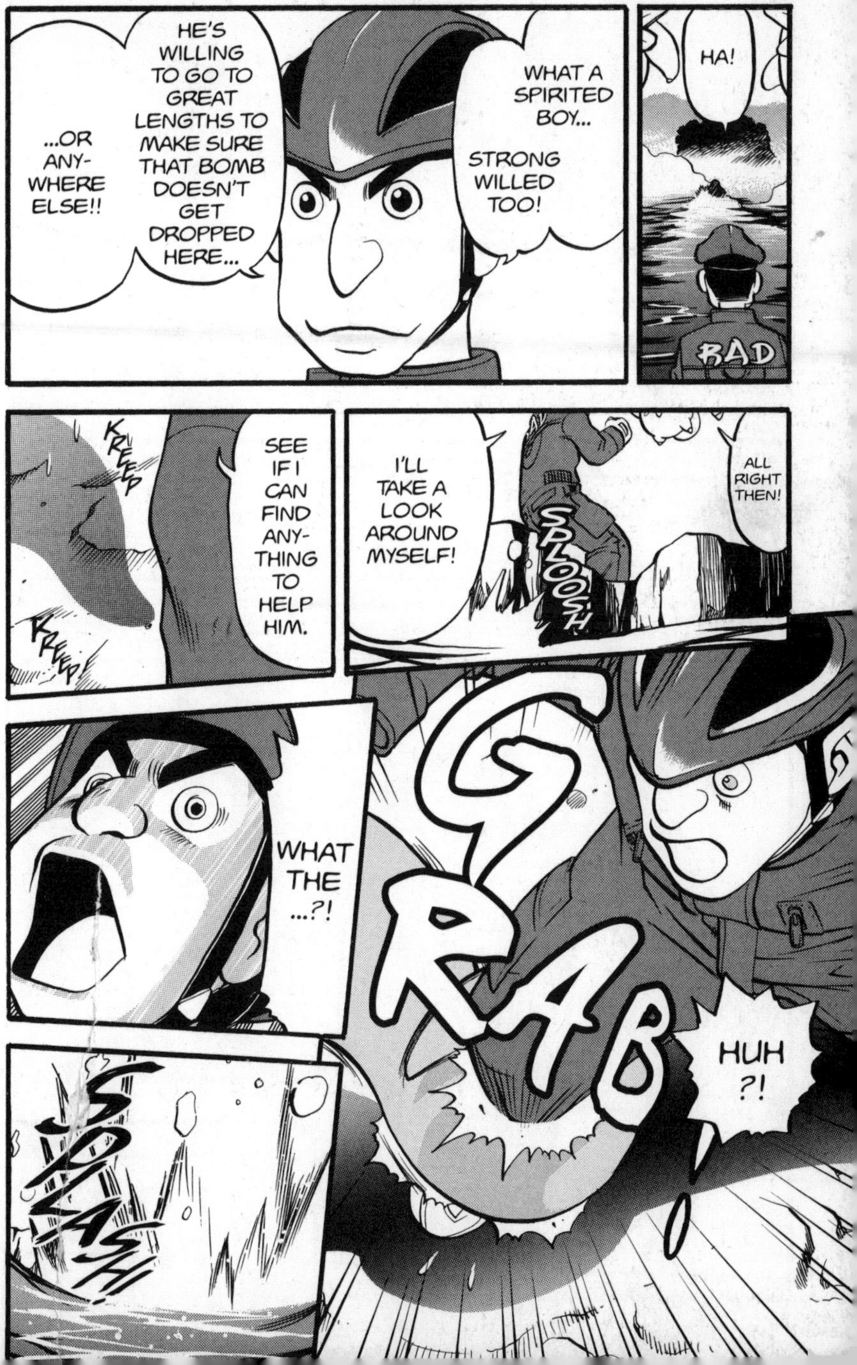
HA!
BAD
WHAT A SPIRITED BOY...
STRONG WILLED TOO!
HE'S WILLING TO GO TO GREAT LENGTHS TO MAKE SURE THAT BOMB DOESN'T GET DROPPED HERE...
...OR ANY-WHERE ELSE!!
ALL RIGHT THEN!
I'LL TAKE A LOOK AROUND MYSELF!
SPLOOSH
SEE IF I CAN FIND ANY-THING TO HELP HIM.
KREEP
KREEP
GRAB
HUH?!
WHAT THE...?!
SPLASH!

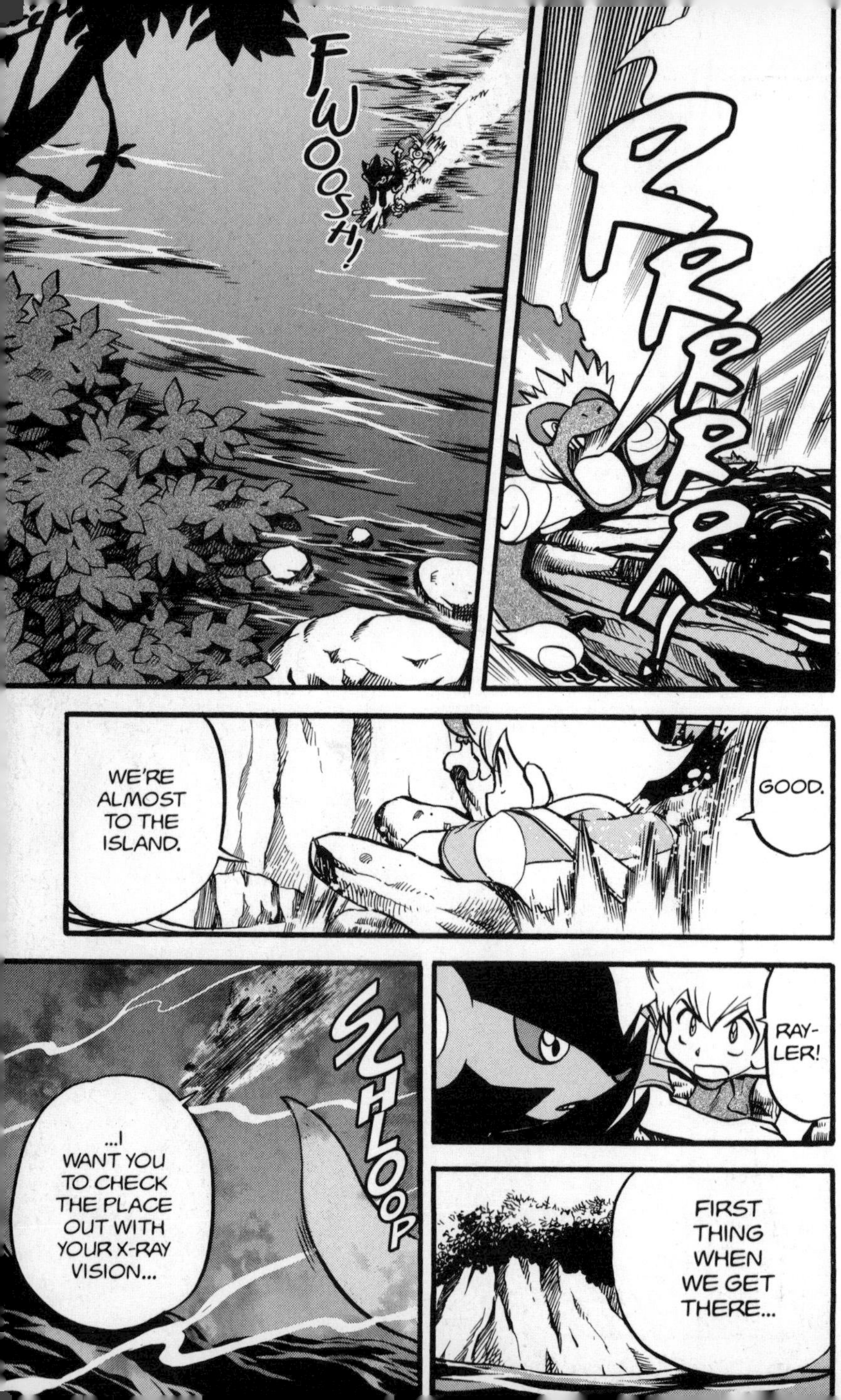
PRRRR!
FWOOSH!
GOOD.
WE'RE ALMOST TO THE ISLAND.
RAYLER!
FIRST THING WHEN WE GET THERE...
SHLOOP
...I WANT YOU TO CHECK THE PLACE OUT WITH YOUR X-RAY VISION...

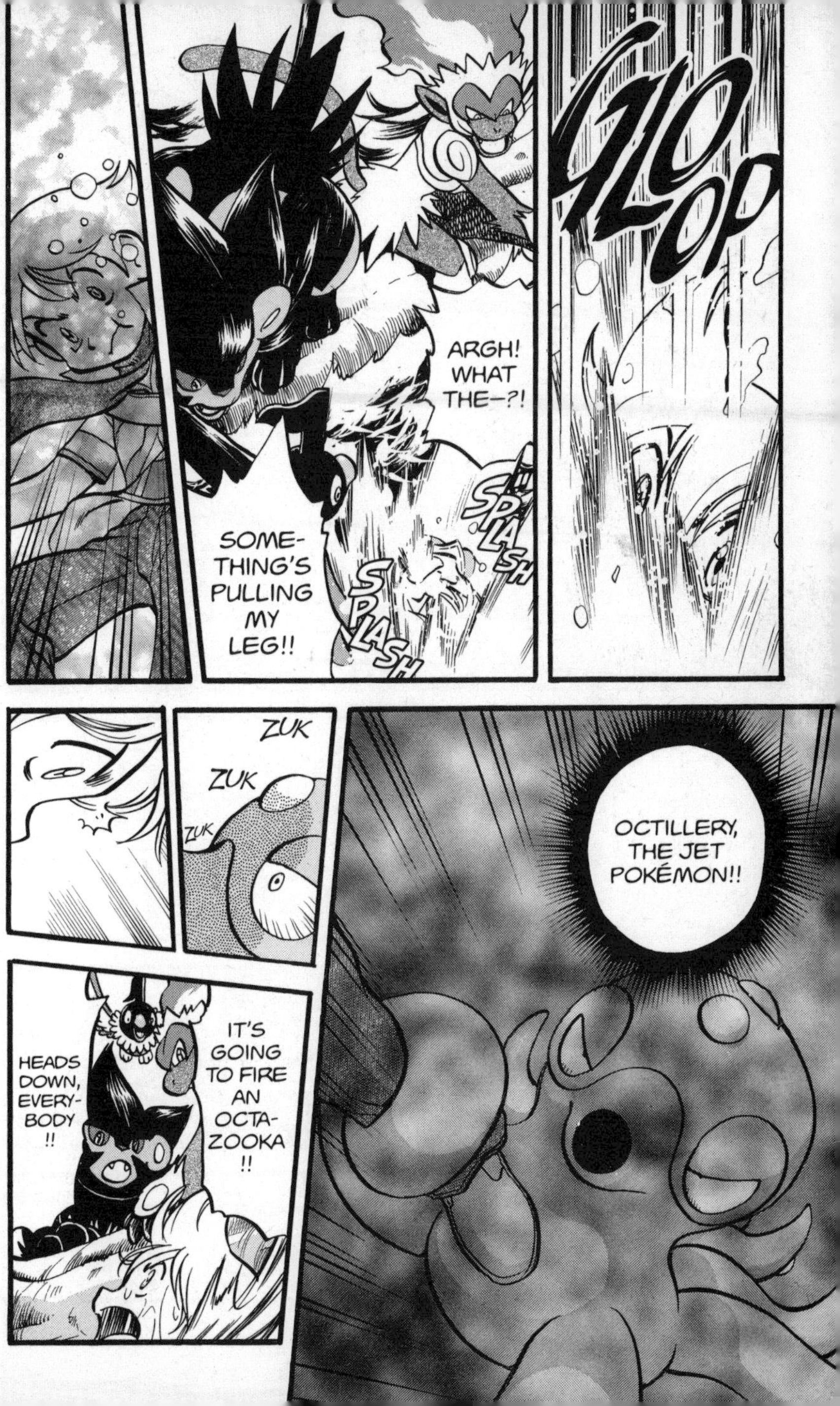
ZOOP
ARGH! WHAT THE–?!
SOME-THING'S PULLING MY LEG!!
SPLASH
SPLASH
OCTILLERY, THE JET POKÉMON!!
ZUK
ZUK
ZUK
IT'S GOING TO FIRE AN OCTA-ZOOKA!!
HEADS DOWN, EVERY-BODY!!

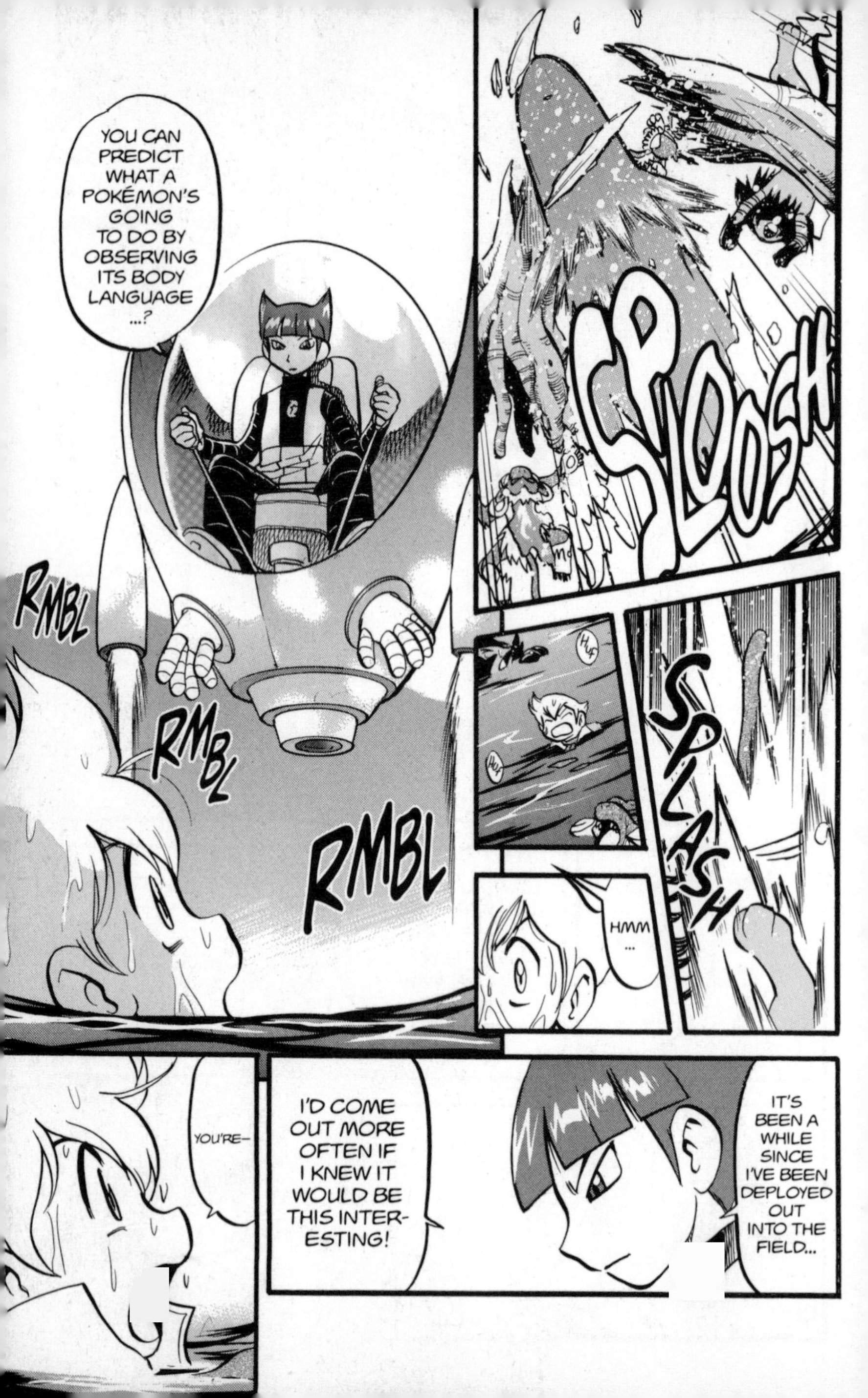
SPLOOSH
SPLASH
HUF
HUF
HMM ...
YOU CAN PREDICT WHAT A POKÉMON'S GOING TO DO BY OBSERVING ITS BODY LANGUAGE ...?
RMBL
RMBL
RMBL
IT'S BEEN A WHILE SINCE I'VE BEEN DEPLOYED OUT INTO THE FIELD...
I'D COME OUT MORE OFTEN IF I KNEW IT WOULD BE THIS INTER-ESTING!
YOU'RE—

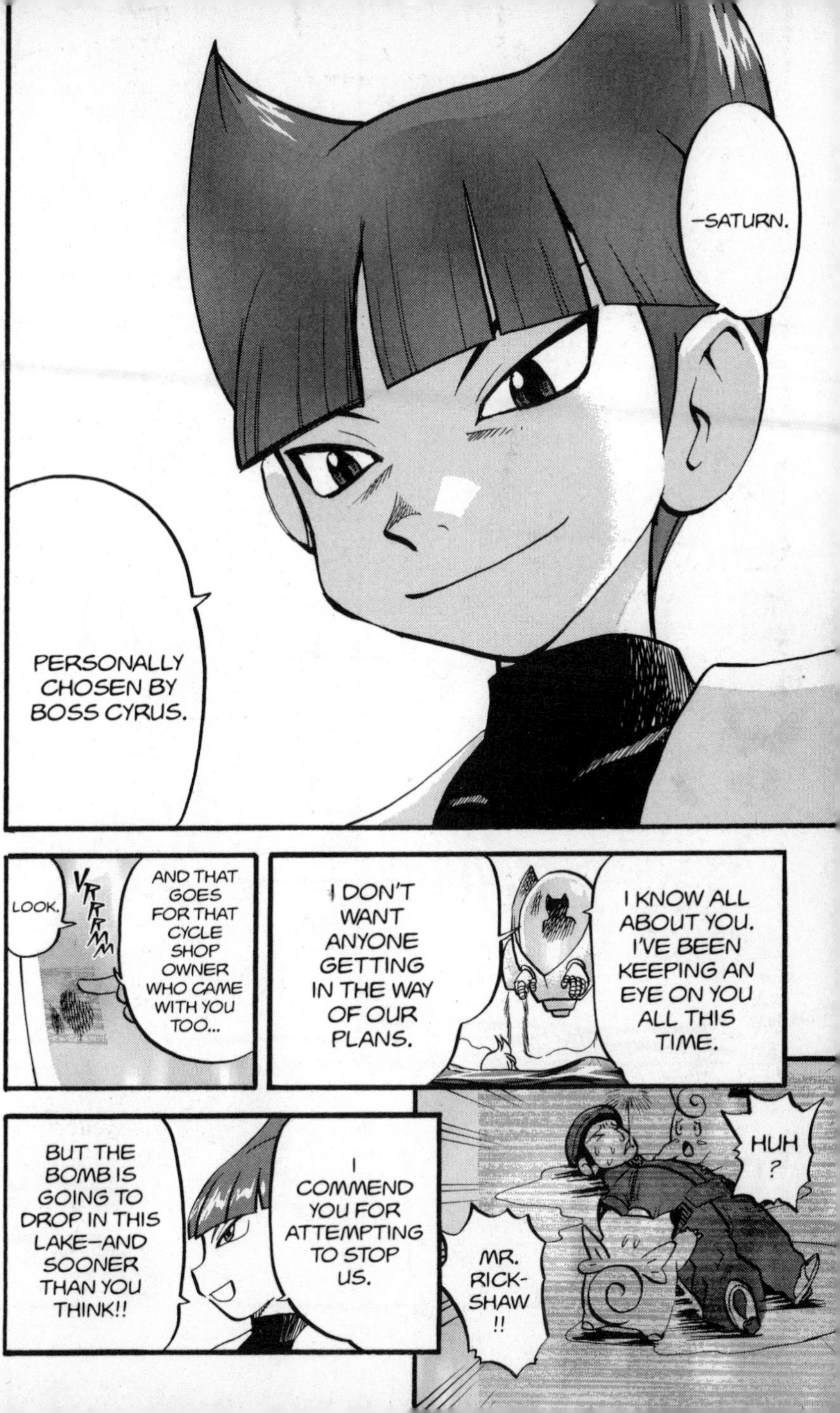
—SATURN.
PERSONALLY CHOSEN BY BOSS CYRUS.
I KNOW ALL ABOUT YOU. I'VE BEEN KEEPING AN EYE ON YOU ALL THIS TIME.
I DON'T WANT ANYONE GETTING IN THE WAY OF OUR PLANS.
AND THAT GOES FOR THAT CYCLE SHOP OWNER WHO CAME WITH YOU TOO...
VRRRMM
LOOK.
HUH?
MR. RICK-SHAW!!
I COMMEND YOU FOR ATTEMPTING TO STOP US.
BUT THE BOMB IS GOING TO DROP IN THIS LAKE—AND SOONER THAN YOU THINK!!

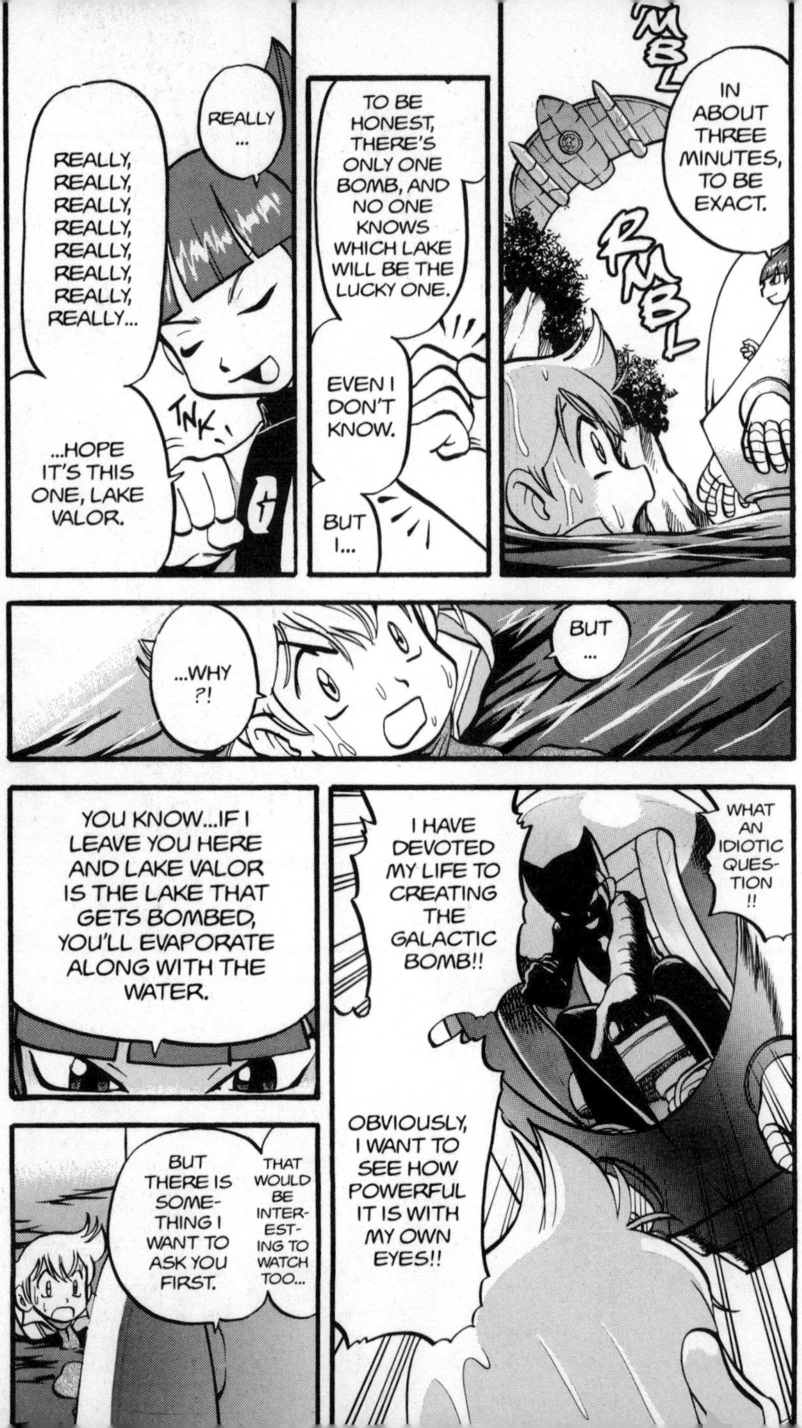
IN ABOUT THREE MINUTES, TO BE EXACT.
RMBL
TO BE HONEST, THERE'S ONLY ONE BOMB, AND NO ONE KNOWS WHICH LAKE WILL BE THE LUCKY ONE.
EVEN I DON'T KNOW.
BUT I...
REALLY ...
REALLY, REALLY, REALLY, REALLY, REALLY, REALLY, REALLY, REALLY...
TNK
...HOPE IT'S THIS ONE, LAKE VALOR.
BUT ...
...WHY ?!
WHAT AN IDIOTIC QUESTION !!
I HAVE DEVOTED MY LIFE TO CREATING THE GALACTIC BOMB!!
OBVIOUSLY, I WANT TO SEE HOW POWERFUL IT IS WITH MY OWN EYES!!
YOU KNOW...IF I LEAVE YOU HERE AND LAKE VALOR IS THE LAKE THAT GETS BOMBED, YOU'LL EVAPORATE ALONG WITH THE WATER.
THAT WOULD BE INTERESTING TO WATCH TOO...
BUT THERE IS SOMETHING I WANT TO ASK YOU FIRST.

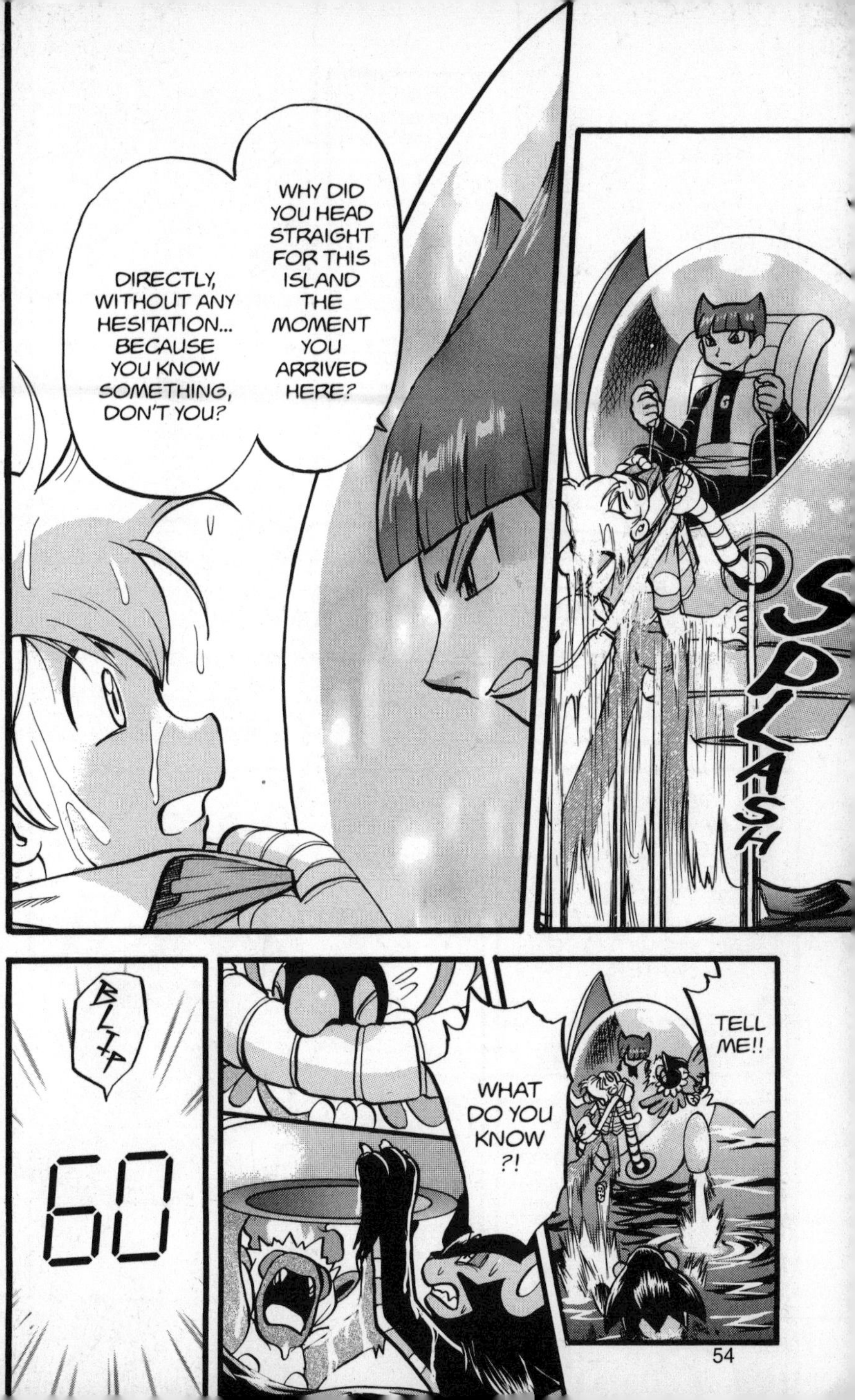
SPLASH
WHY DID YOU HEAD STRAIGHT FOR THIS ISLAND THE MOMENT YOU ARRIVED HERE?
DIRECTLY, WITHOUT ANY HESITATION... BECAUSE YOU KNOW SOMETHING, DON'T YOU?
TELL ME!!
WHAT DO YOU KNOW ?!
BLIP
60

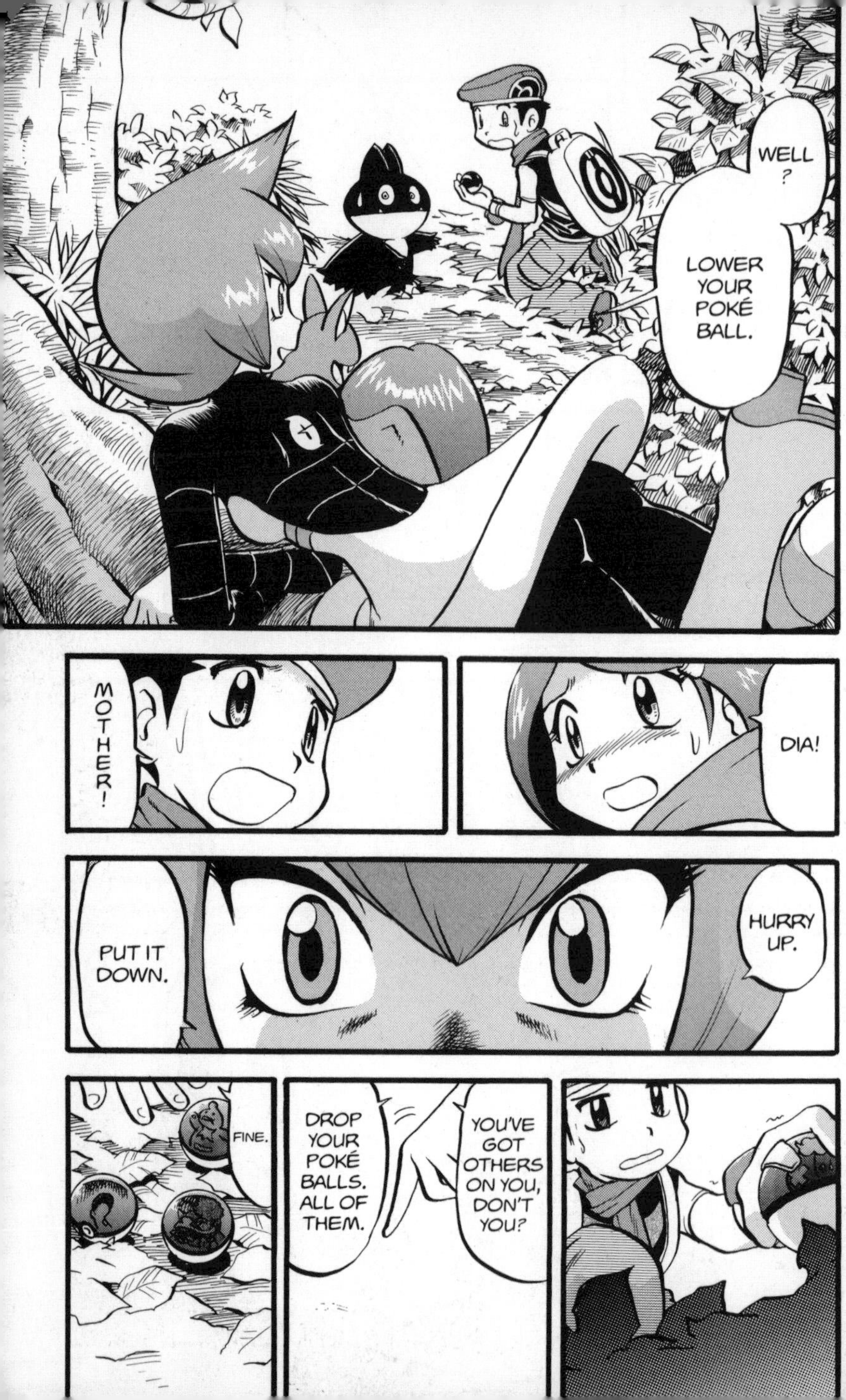
WELL?
LOWER YOUR POKÉ BALL.
DIA!
MOTHER!
HURRY UP.
PUT IT DOWN.
YOU'VE GOT OTHERS ON YOU, DON'T YOU?
DROP YOUR POKÉ BALLS. ALL OF THEM.
FINE.

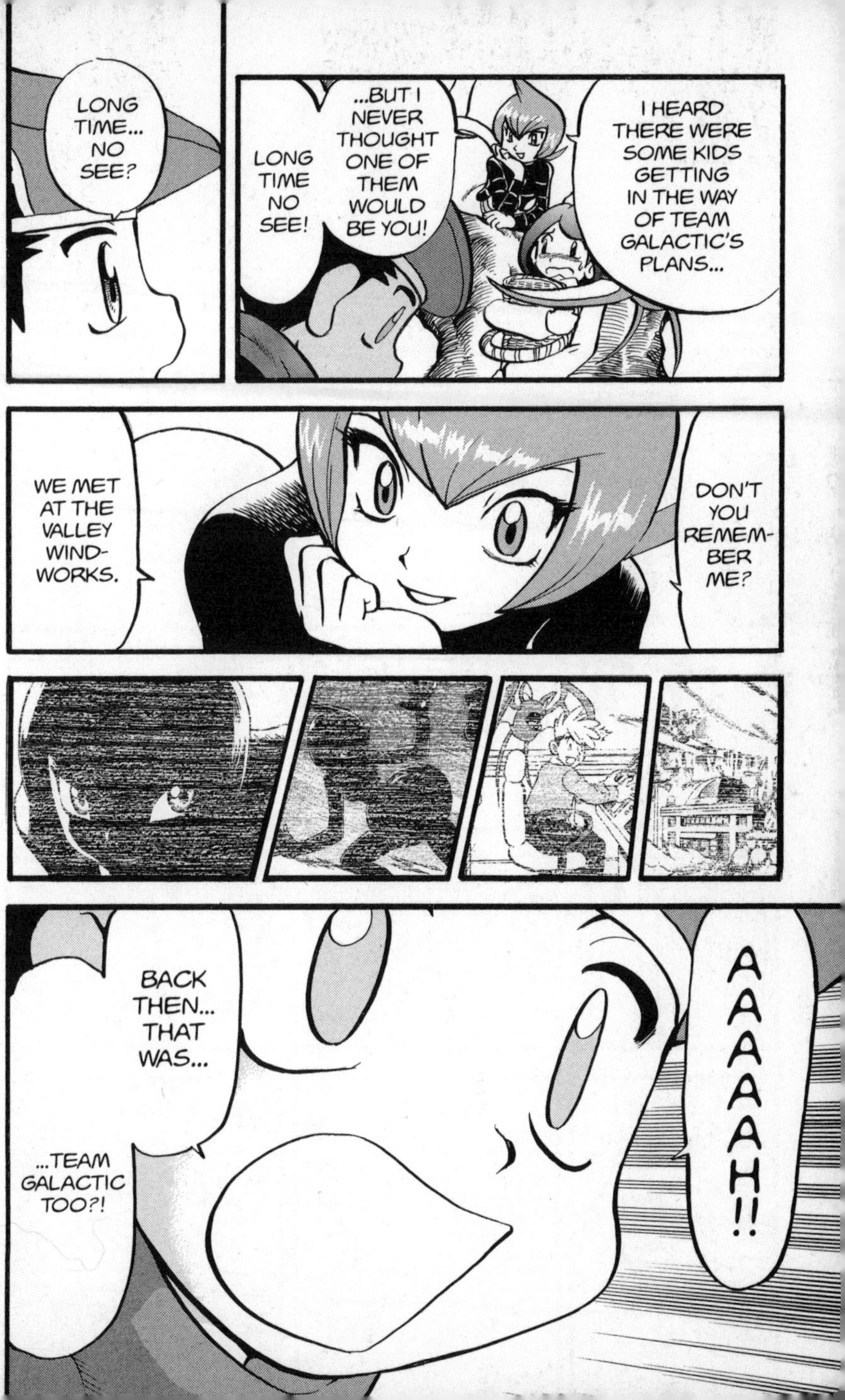

I HEARD THERE WERE SOME KIDS GETTING IN THE WAY OF TEAM GALACTIC'S PLANS...
...BUT I NEVER THOUGHT ONE OF THEM WOULD BE YOU!
LONG TIME NO SEE!
LONG TIME... NO SEE?
DON'T YOU REMEM-BER ME?
WE MET AT THE VALLEY WIND-WORKS.
AAAAAH!!
BACK THEN... THAT WAS...
...TEAM GALACTIC TOO?!

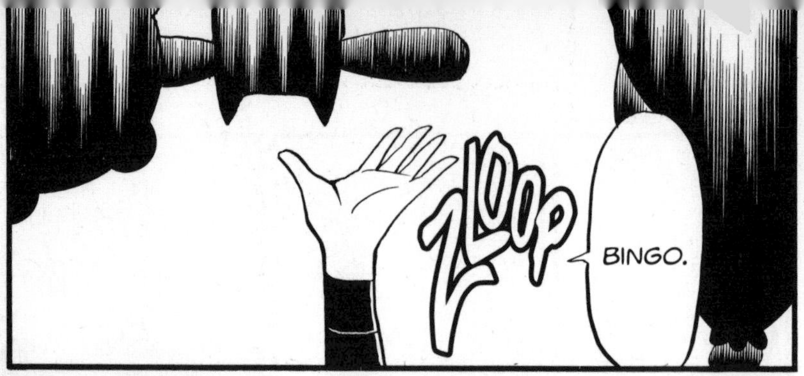
ZLOOP
BINGO.
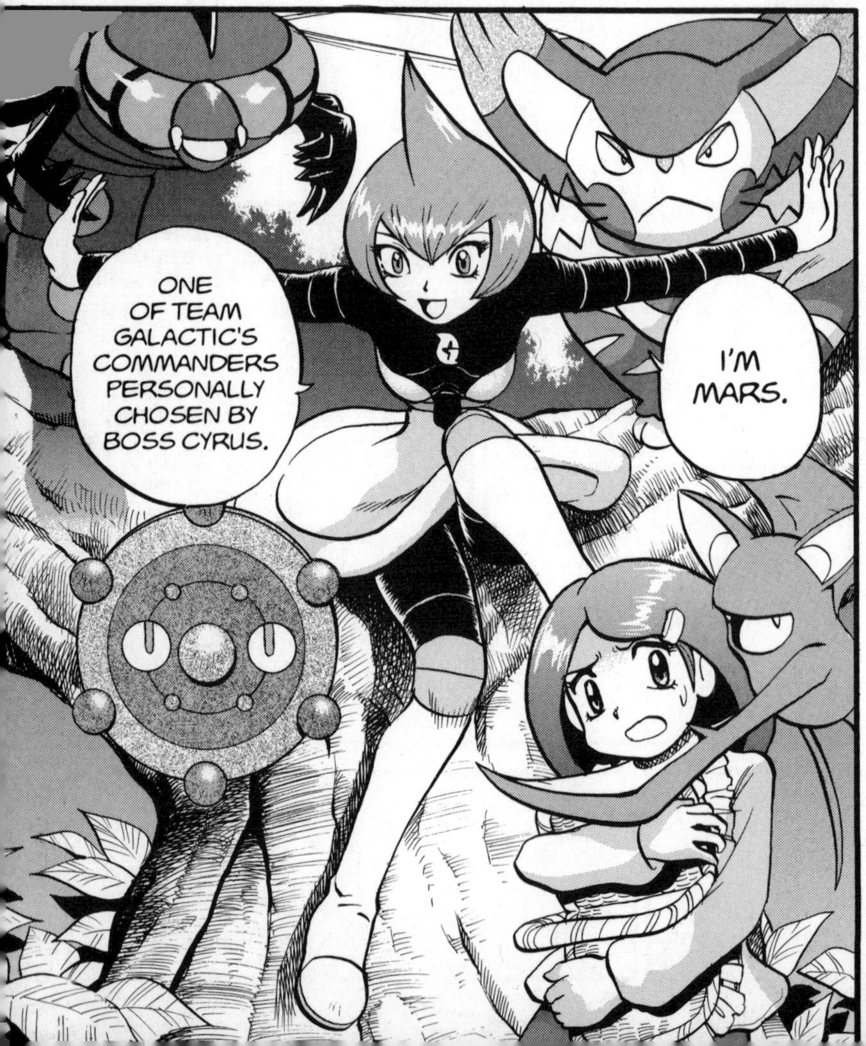
I'M MARS.
ONE OF TEAM GALACTIC'S COMMANDERS PERSONALLY CHOSEN BY BOSS CYRUS.

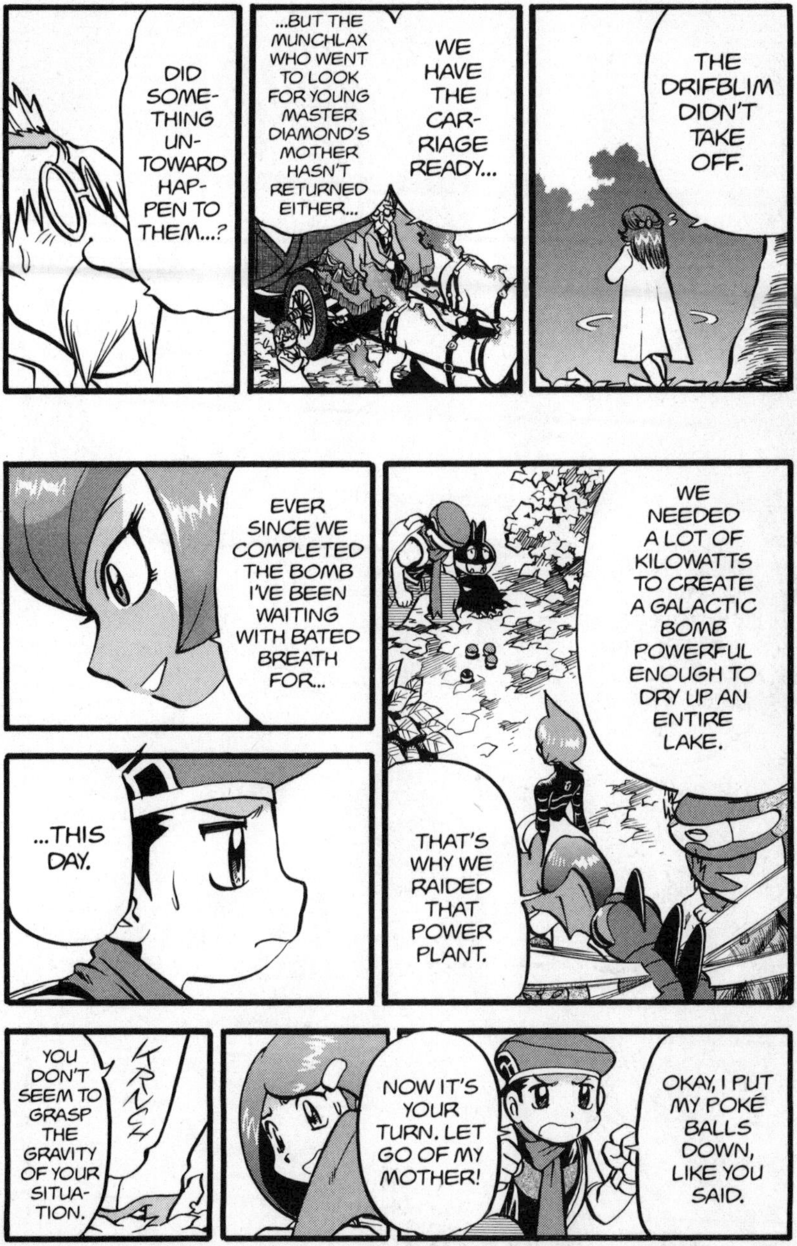
THE DRIFBLIM DIDN'T TAKE OFF.
WE HAVE THE CARRIAGE READY...
...BUT THE MUNCHLAX WHO WENT TO LOOK FOR YOUNG MASTER DIAMOND'S MOTHER HASN'T RETURNED EITHER...
DID SOMETHING UNTOWARD HAPPEN TO THEM...?
WE NEEDED A LOT OF KILOWATTS TO CREATE A GALACTIC BOMB POWERFUL ENOUGH TO DRY UP AN ENTIRE LAKE.
THAT'S WHY WE RAIDED THAT POWER PLANT.
EVER SINCE WE COMPLETED THE BOMB I'VE BEEN WAITING WITH BATED BREATH FOR...
...THIS DAY.
OKAY, I PUT MY POKÉ BALLS DOWN, LIKE YOU SAID.
NOW IT'S YOUR TURN. LET GO OF MY MOTHER!
KRNCH
YOU DON'T SEEM TO GRASP THE GRAVITY OF YOUR SITUATION.

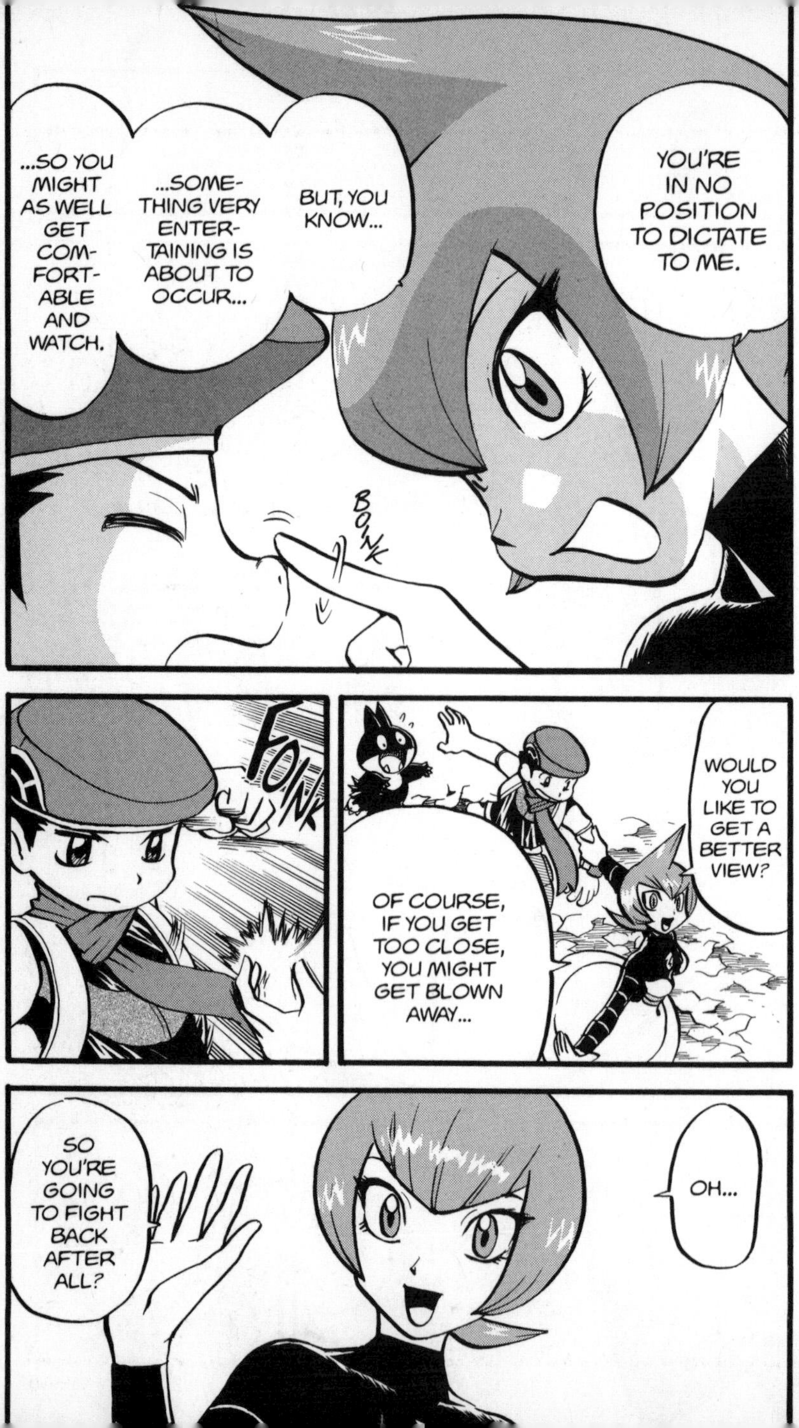
YOU'RE IN NO POSITION TO DICTATE TO ME.
BUT, YOU KNOW...
...SOMETHING VERY ENTERTAINING IS ABOUT TO OCCUR...
...SO YOU MIGHT AS WELL GET COMFORTABLE AND WATCH.
BOINK
WOULD YOU LIKE TO GET A BETTER VIEW?
OF COURSE, IF YOU GET TOO CLOSE, YOU MIGHT GET BLOWN AWAY...
FOINK
OH...
SO YOU'RE GOING TO FIGHT BACK AFTER ALL?

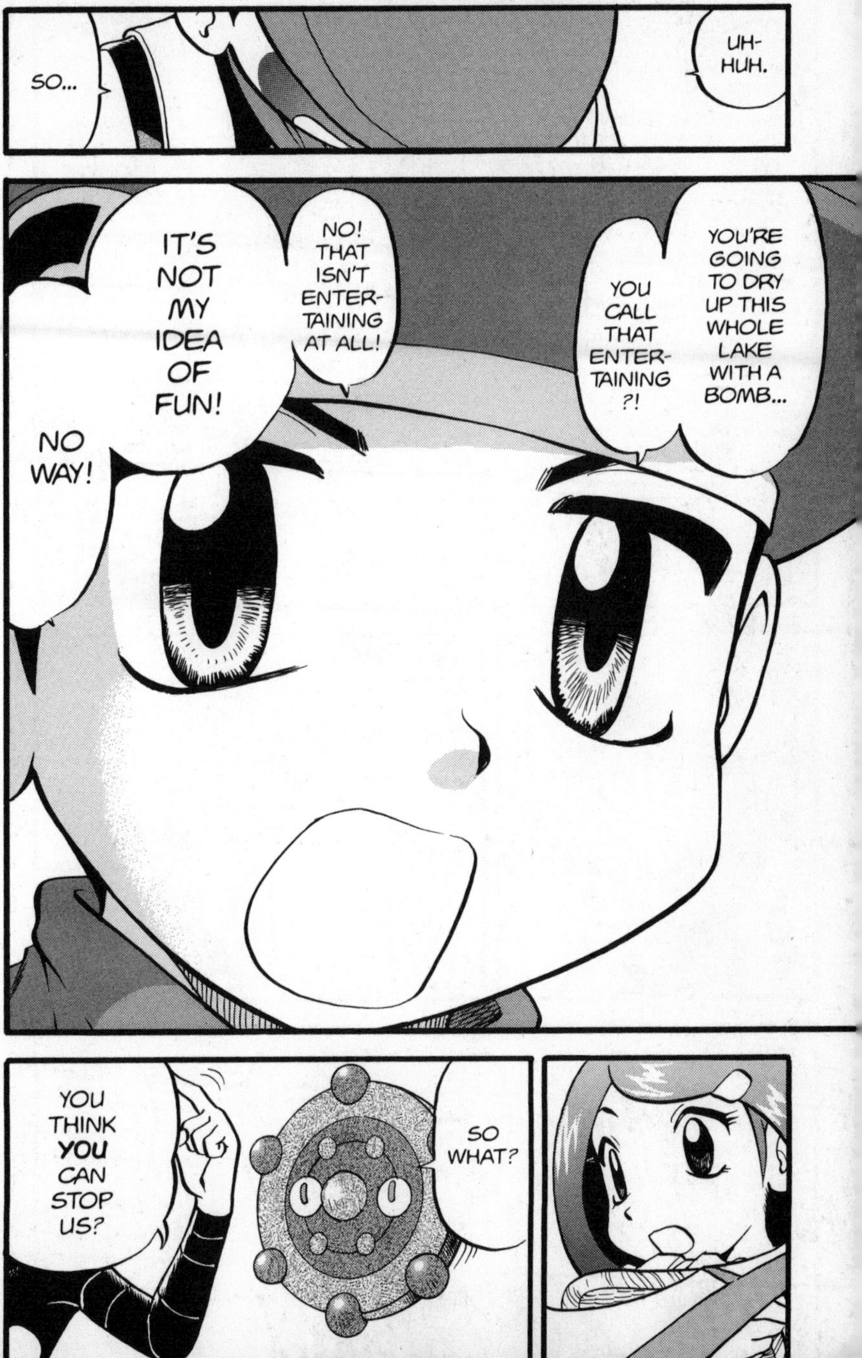
UH-HUH.
SO...
YOU'RE GOING TO DRY UP THIS WHOLE LAKE WITH A BOMB...
YOU CALL THAT ENTER-TAINING?!
NO! THAT ISN'T ENTER-TAINING AT ALL!
IT'S NOT MY IDEA OF FUN!
NO WAY!
SO WHAT?
YOU THINK **YOU** CAN STOP US?

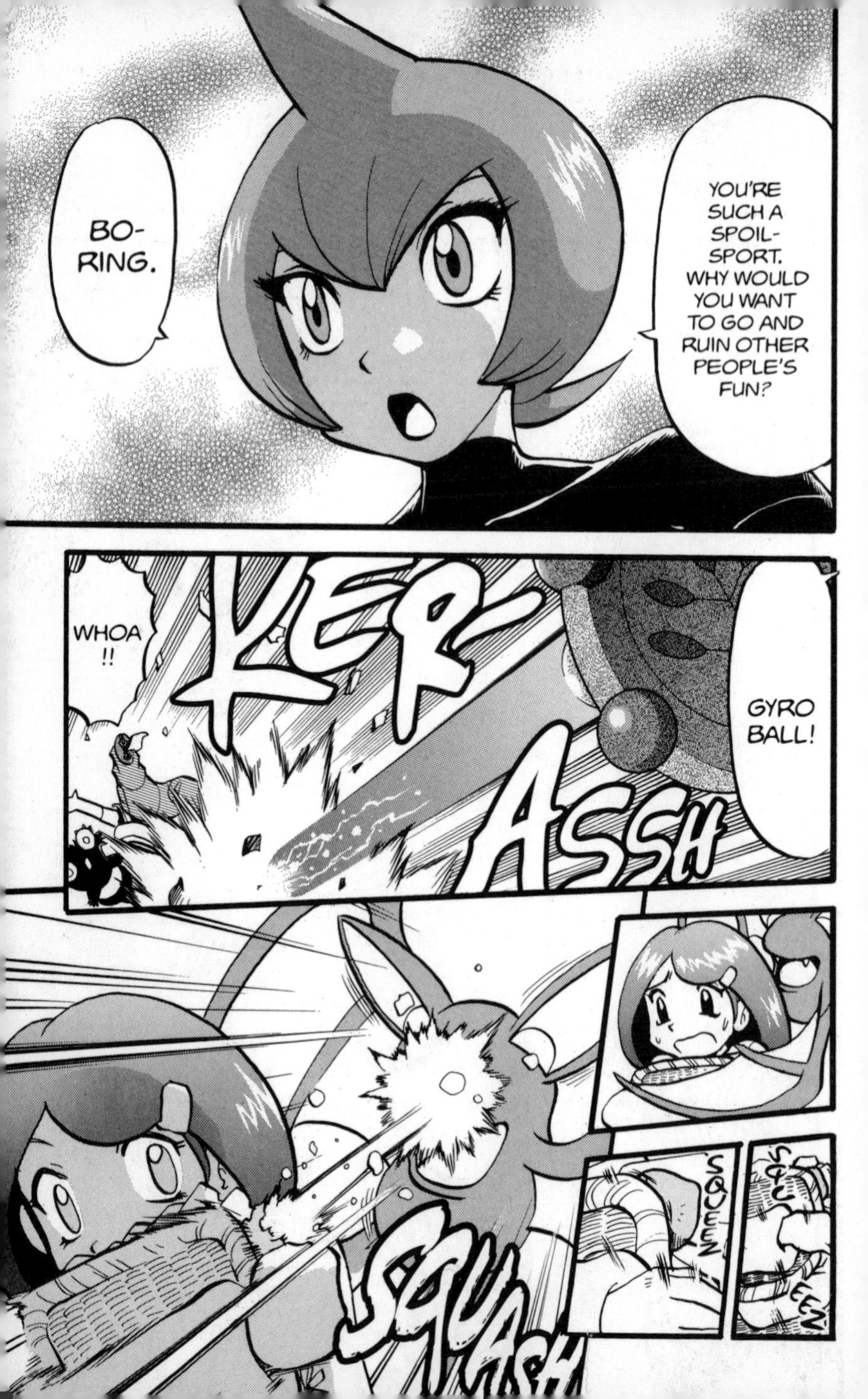

YOU'RE SUCH A SPOIL-SPORT. WHY WOULD YOU WANT TO GO AND RUIN OTHER PEOPLE'S FUN?
BO-RING.
GYRO BALL!
VER-
ASSH
WHOA !!
SQUEEZ

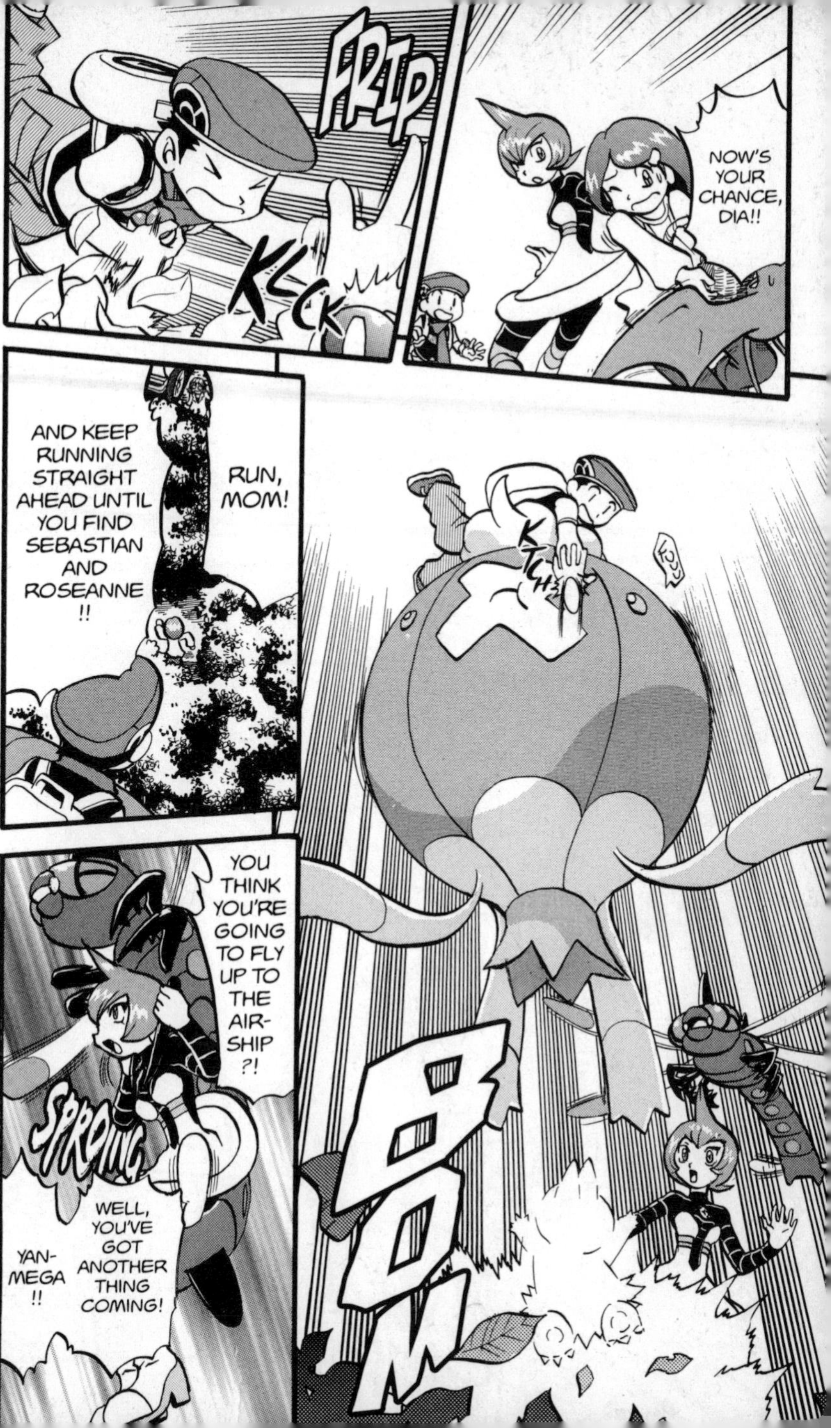
NOW'S YOUR CHANCE, DIA!!
FRIP
KLICK
KTCH
FUU
BOM
RUN, MOM!
AND KEEP RUNNING STRAIGHT AHEAD UNTIL YOU FIND SEBASTIAN AND ROSEANNE!!
YOU THINK YOU'RE GOING TO FLY UP TO THE AIR-SHIP?!
SPROING
WELL, YOU'VE GOT ANOTHER THING COMING!
YAN-MEGA!!

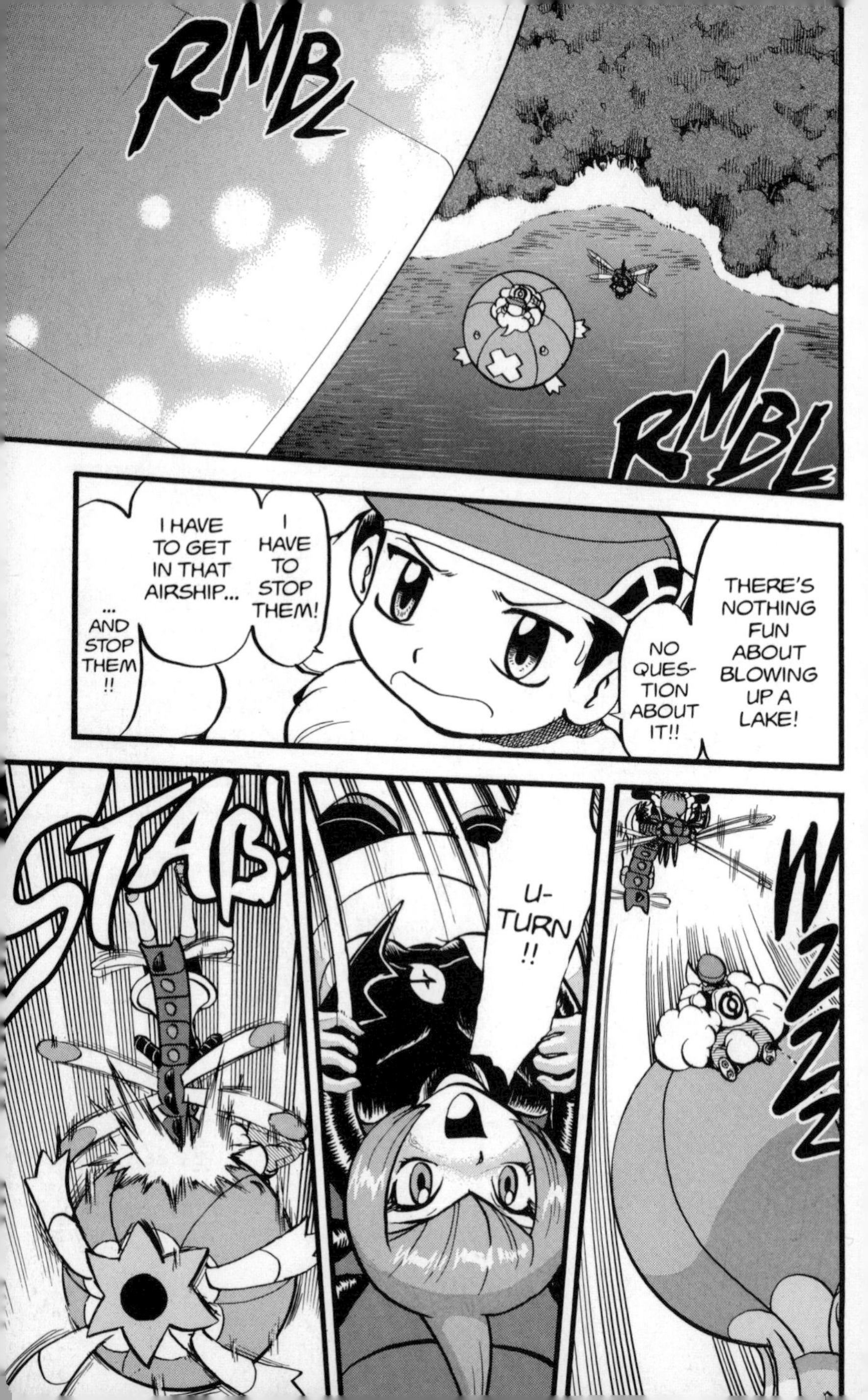
RMBL
RMBL
THERE'S NOTHING FUN ABOUT BLOWING UP A LAKE!
NO QUES-TION ABOUT IT!!
I HAVE TO STOP THEM!
I HAVE TO GET IN THAT AIRSHIP...
...AND STOP THEM!!
WZZZ
U-TURN!!
STAB!

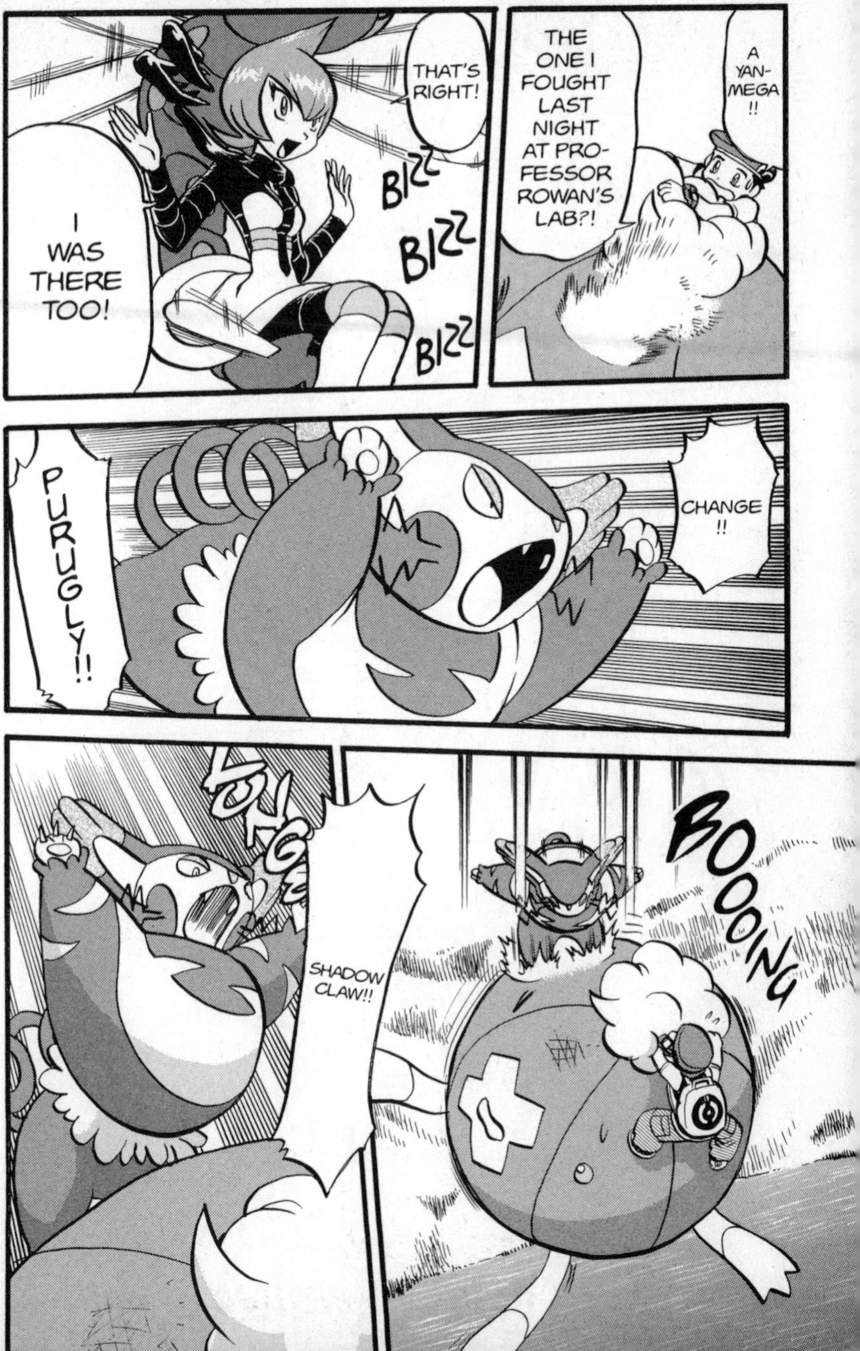
A YAN-MEGA!!
THE ONE I FOUGHT LAST NIGHT AT PRO-FESSOR ROWAN'S LAB?!
THAT'S RIGHT!
BIZZ
BIZZ
BIZZ
I WAS THERE TOO!
CHANGE!!
PURUGLY!!
BOOOING
SHADOW CLAW!!

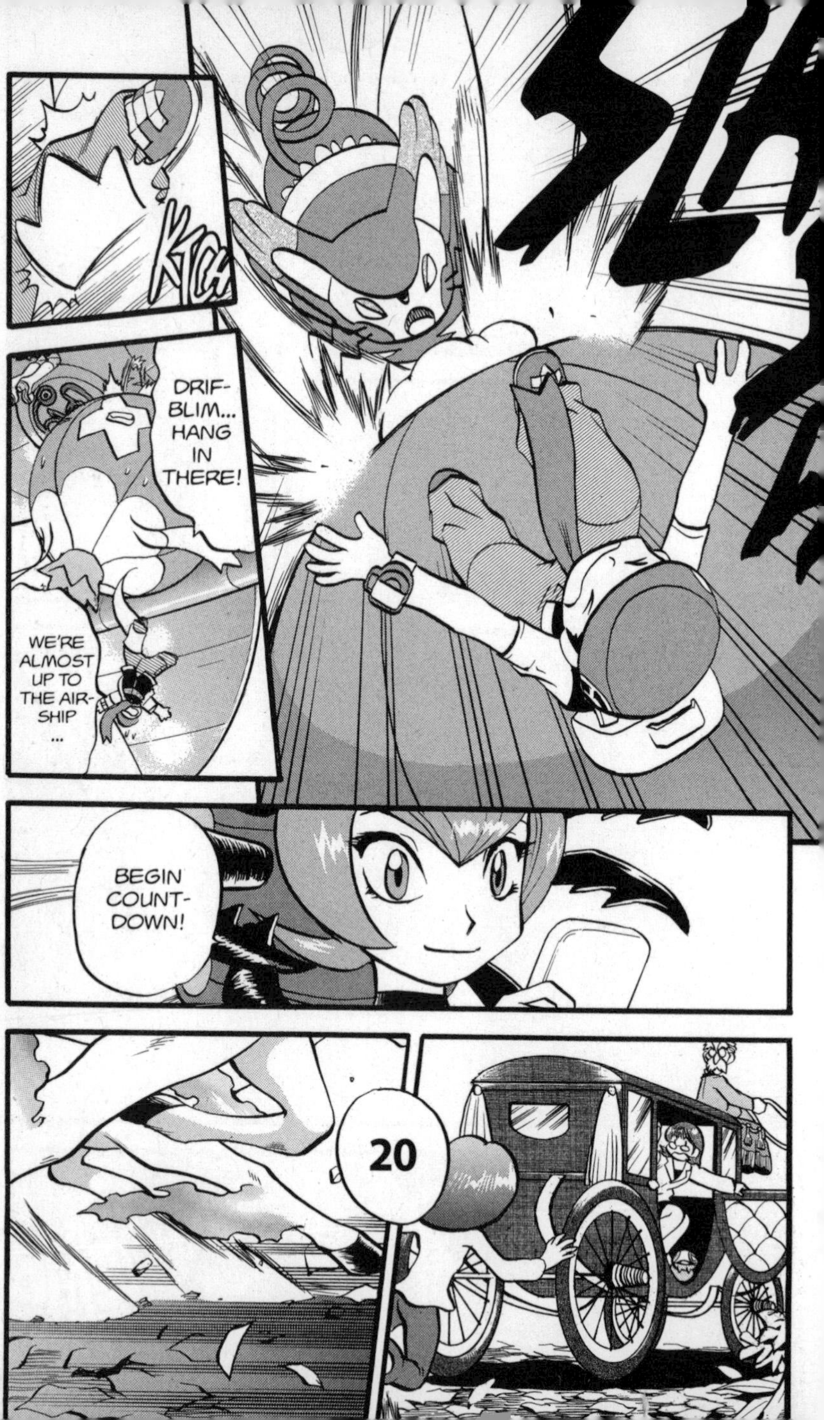
KTCH
DRIF-BLIM... HANG IN THERE!
WE'RE ALMOST UP TO THE AIR-SHIP ...
BEGIN COUNT-DOWN!
20

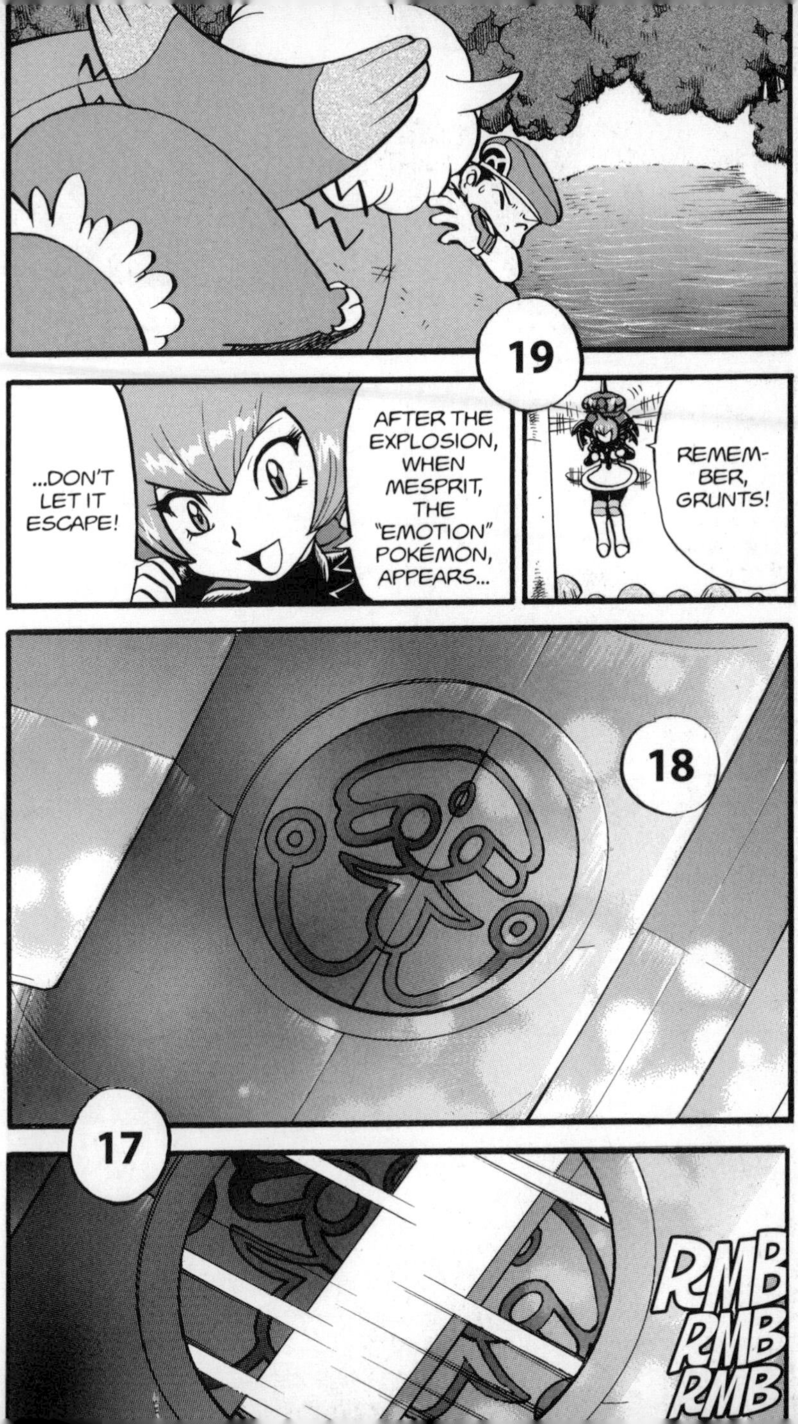
19
REMEMBER, GRUNTS!
AFTER THE EXPLOSION, WHEN MESPRIT, THE "EMOTION" POKÉMON, APPEARS...
...DON'T LET IT ESCAPE!
18
17
RMB
RMB
RMB

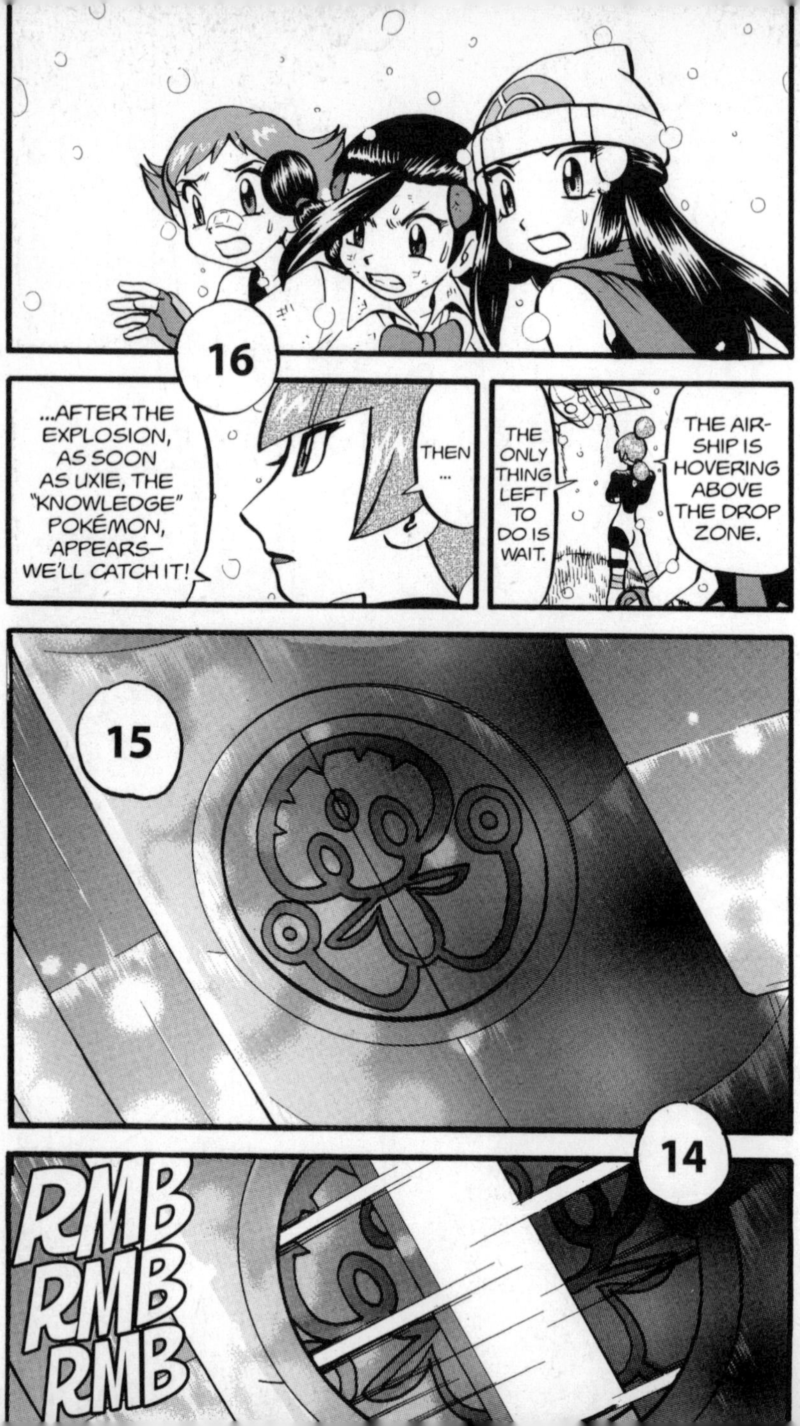
16
THE AIR-SHIP IS HOVERING ABOVE THE DROP ZONE.
THE ONLY THING LEFT TO DO IS WAIT.
THEN...
...AFTER THE EXPLOSION, AS SOON AS UXIE, THE "KNOWLEDGE" POKÉMON, APPEARS—WE'LL CATCH IT!
15
14
RMB
RMB
RMB

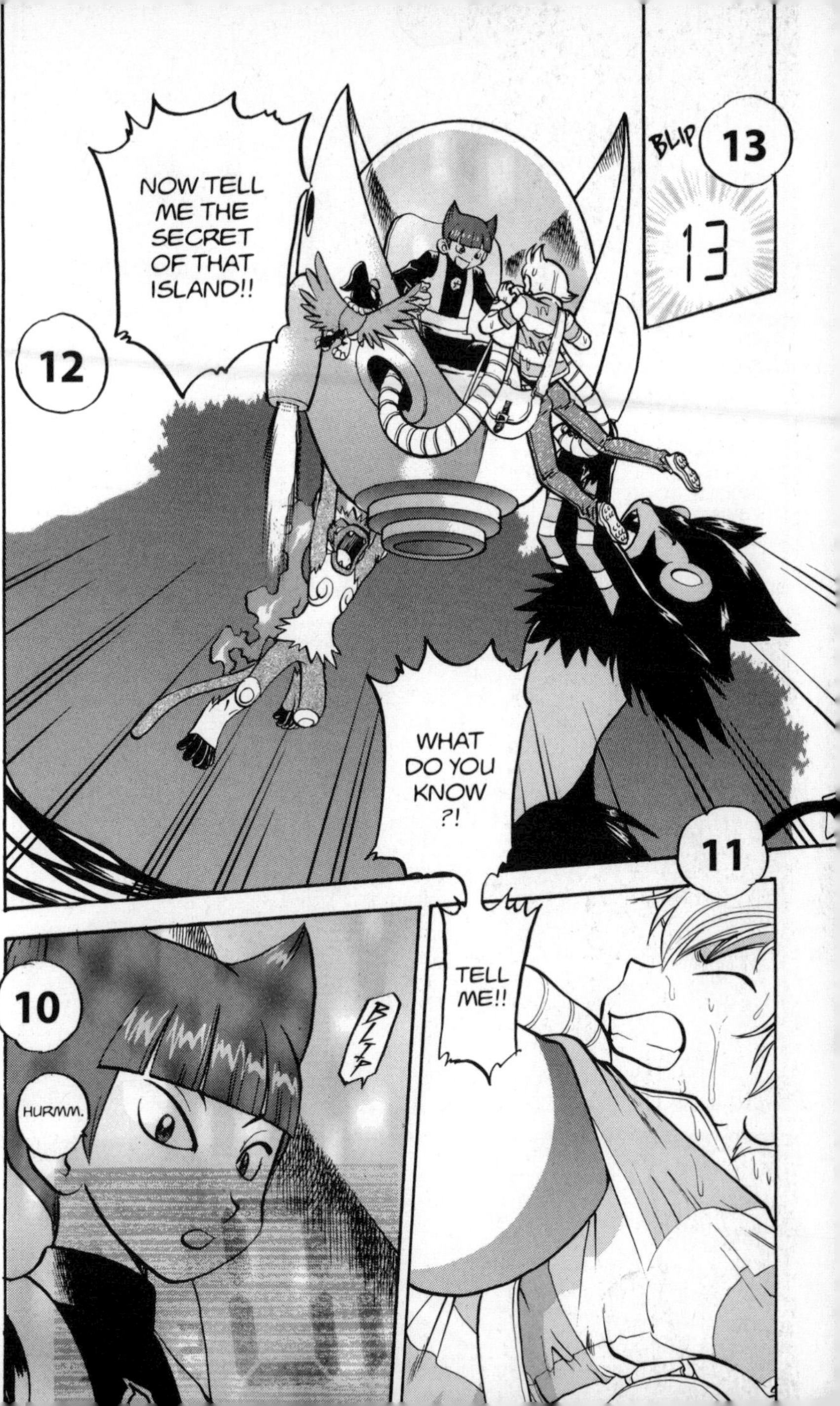
BLIP
13
13
NOW TELL ME THE SECRET OF THAT ISLAND!!
12
WHAT DO YOU KNOW ?!
11
TELL ME!!
10
BLIP
HURMM.

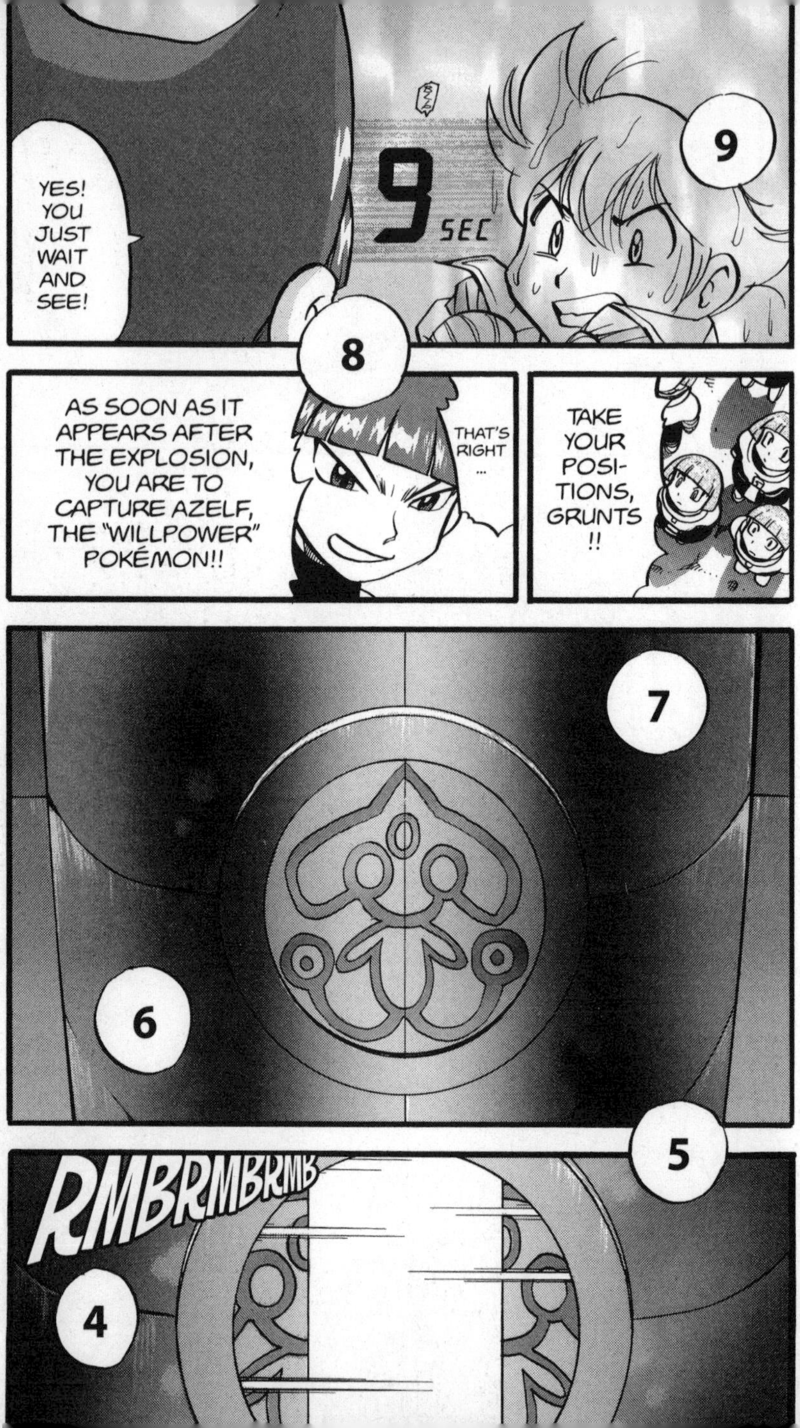
9
9 SEC
YES! YOU JUST WAIT AND SEE!
8
TAKE YOUR POSI-TIONS, GRUNTS!!
THAT'S RIGHT...
AS SOON AS IT APPEARS AFTER THE EXPLOSION, YOU ARE TO CAPTURE AZELF, THE "WILLPOWER" POKÉMON!!
7
6
5
RMBRMBRMB
4

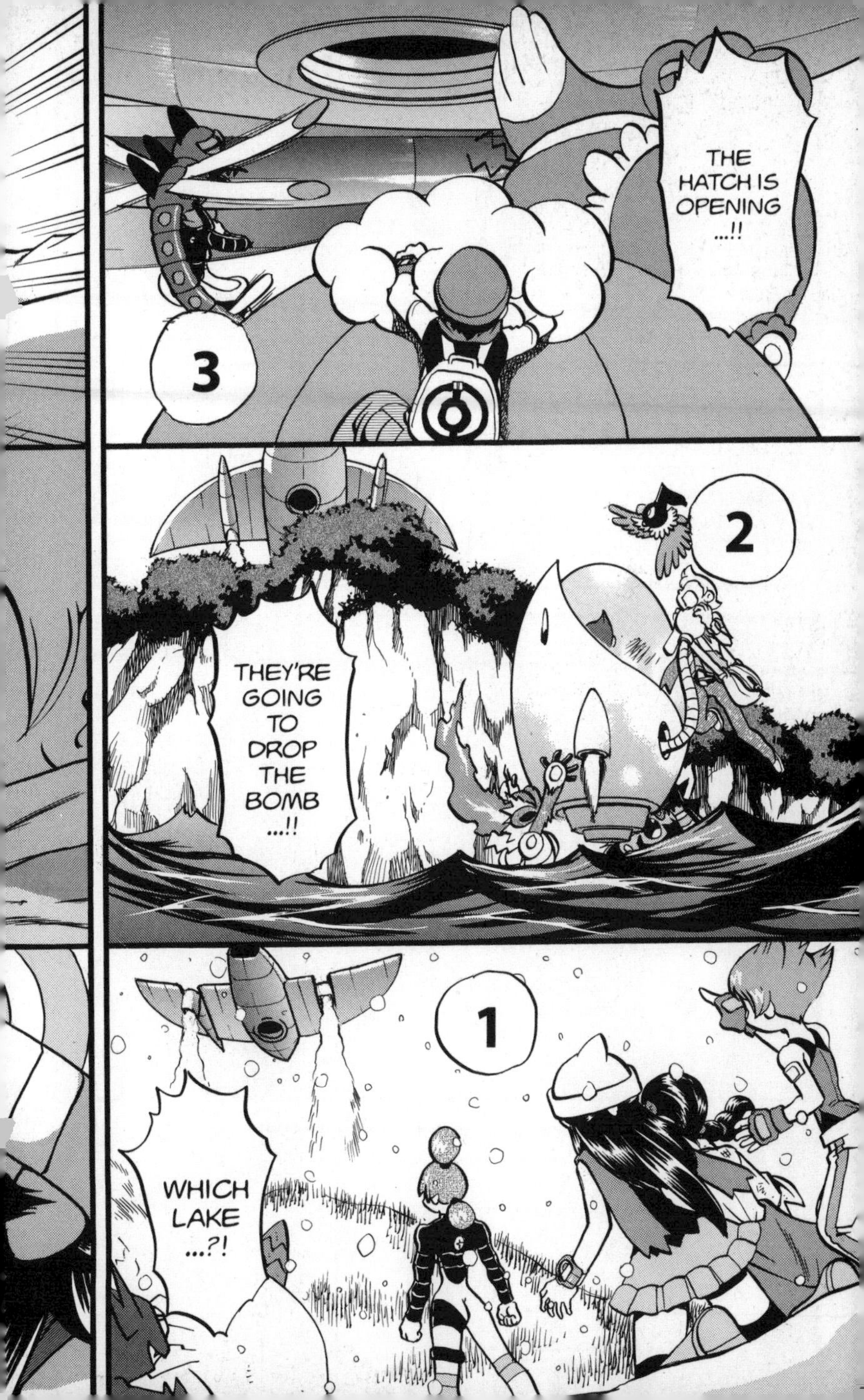
THE HATCH IS OPENING ...!!
3
2
THEY'RE GOING TO DROP THE BOMB ...!!
1
WHICH LAKE ...?!

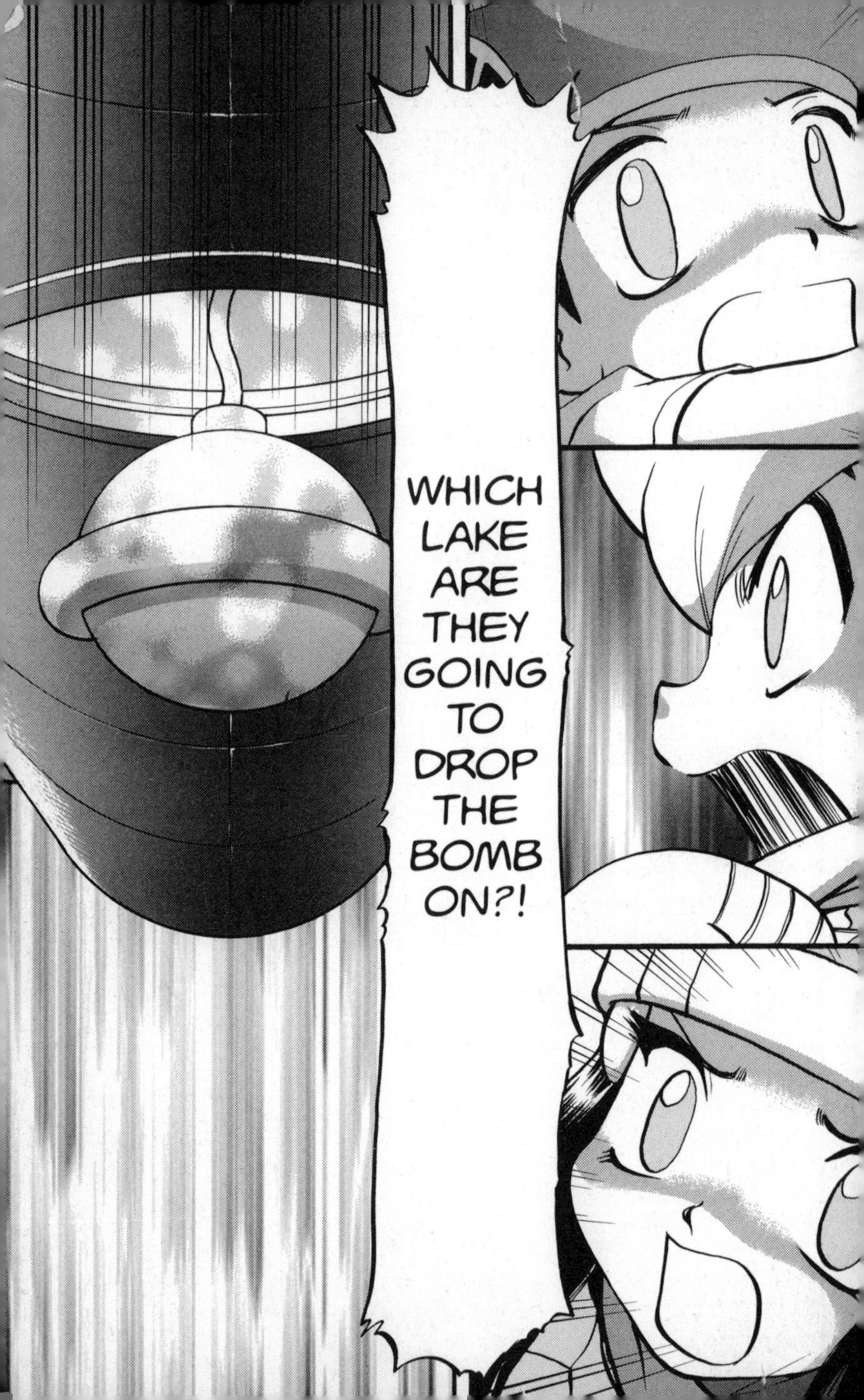
WHICH LAKE ARE THEY GOING TO DROP THE BOMB ON?!

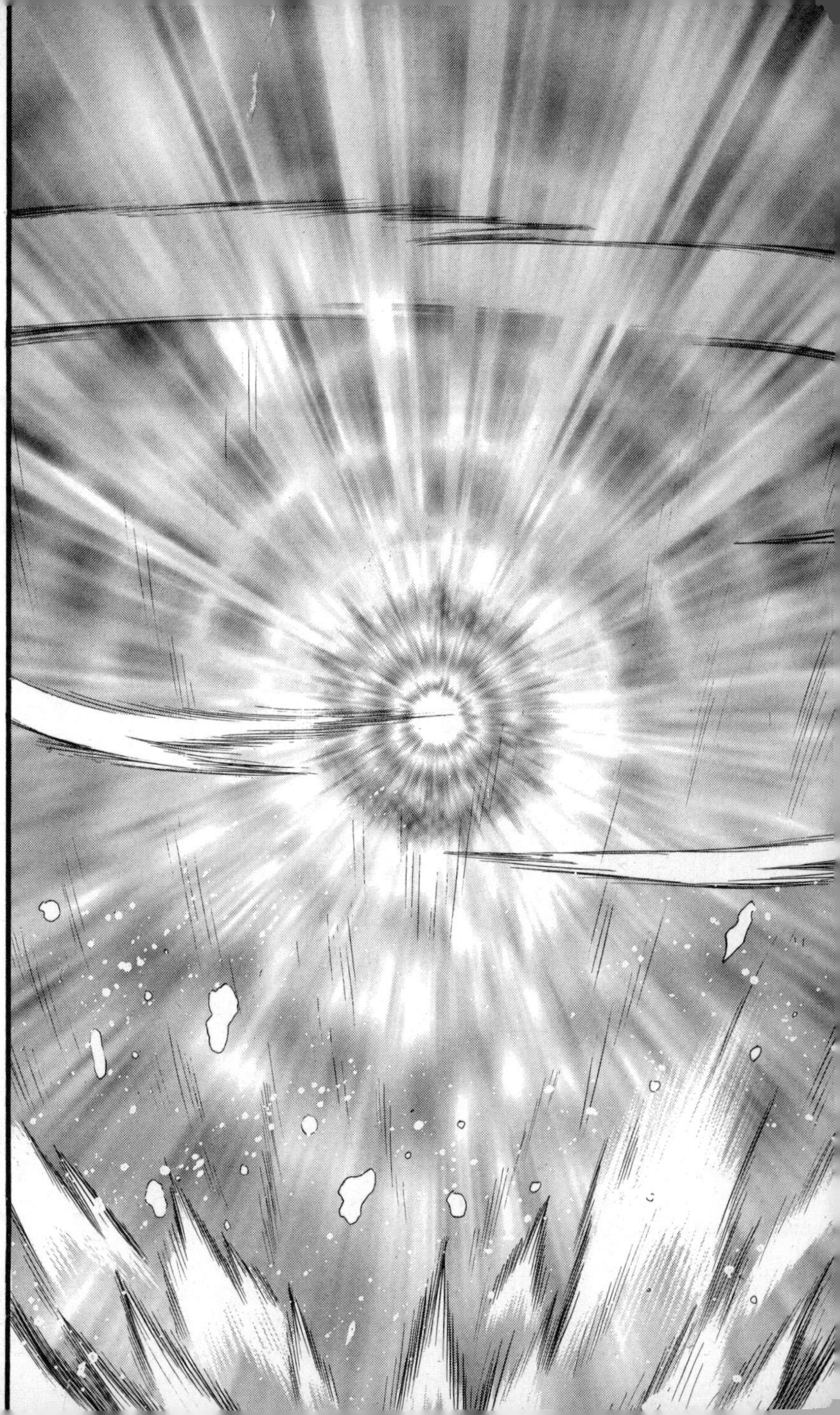

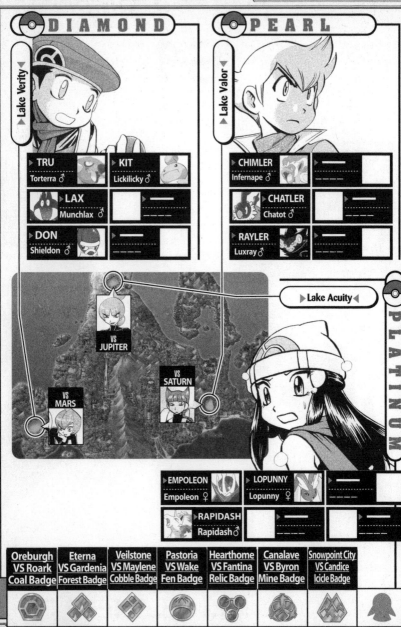

◈ ADVENTURE MAP ◈

◉ DIAMOND

▶ Lake Verity ▼

▶ TRU
Torterra ♂

▶ KIT
Lickilicky ♂

▶ LAX
Munchlax ♂

▶ DON
Shieldon ♂

◉ PEARL

▶ Lake Valor ▼

▶ CHIMLER
Infernape ♂

▶ CHATLER
Chatot ♂

▶ RAYLER
Luxray ♂

▶ Lake Acuity ◀

VS JUPITER

VS SATURN

VS MARS

PLATINUM

▶ EMPOLEON
Empoleon ♀

▶ LOPUNNY
Lopunny ♀

▶ RAPIDASH
Rapidash ♂

Oreburgh VS Roark Coal Badge	Eterna VS Gardenia Forest Badge	Veilstone VS Maylene Cobble Badge	Pastoria VS Wake Fen Badge	Hearthome VS Fantina Relic Badge	Canalave VS Byron Mine Badge	Snowpoint City VS Candice Icicle Badge	

61

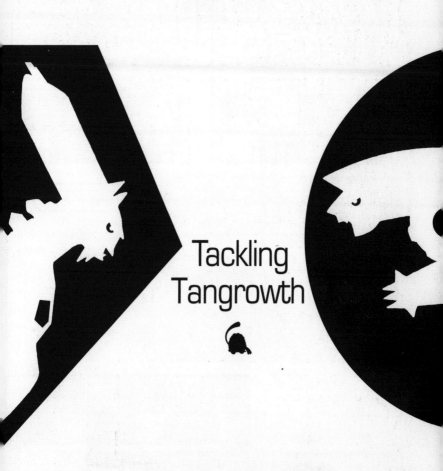

Tackling
Tangrowth

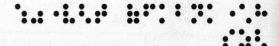

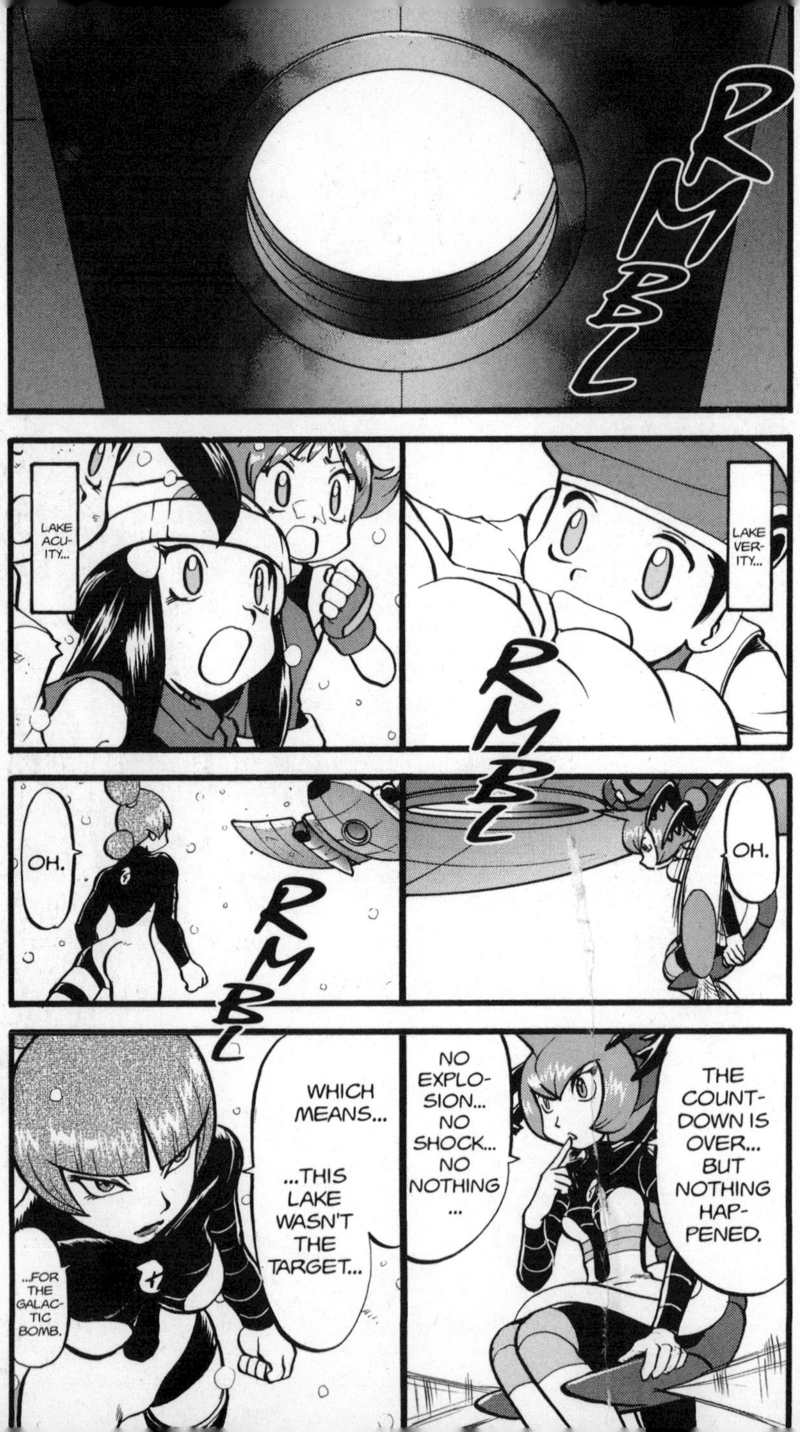
RMBL
LAKE VERITY...
RMBL
LAKE ACUITY...
OH.
RMBL
OH.
RMBL
THE COUNTDOWN IS OVER... BUT NOTHING HAPPENED.
NO EXPLOSION... NO SHOCK... NO NOTHING...
WHICH MEANS...
...THIS LAKE WASN'T THE TARGET...
...FOR THE GALACTIC BOMB.

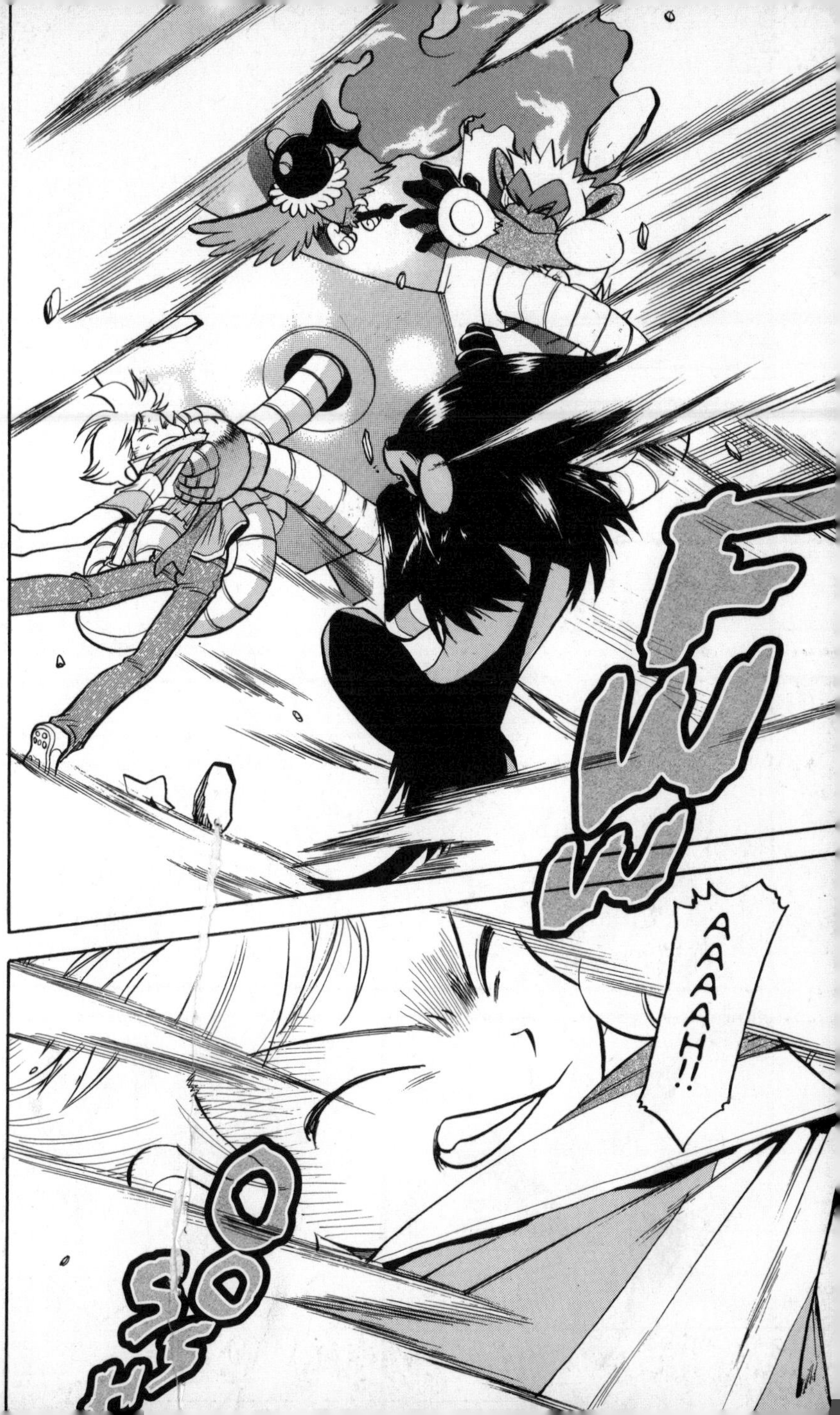
FWW
AAAAAH!!
OOSH

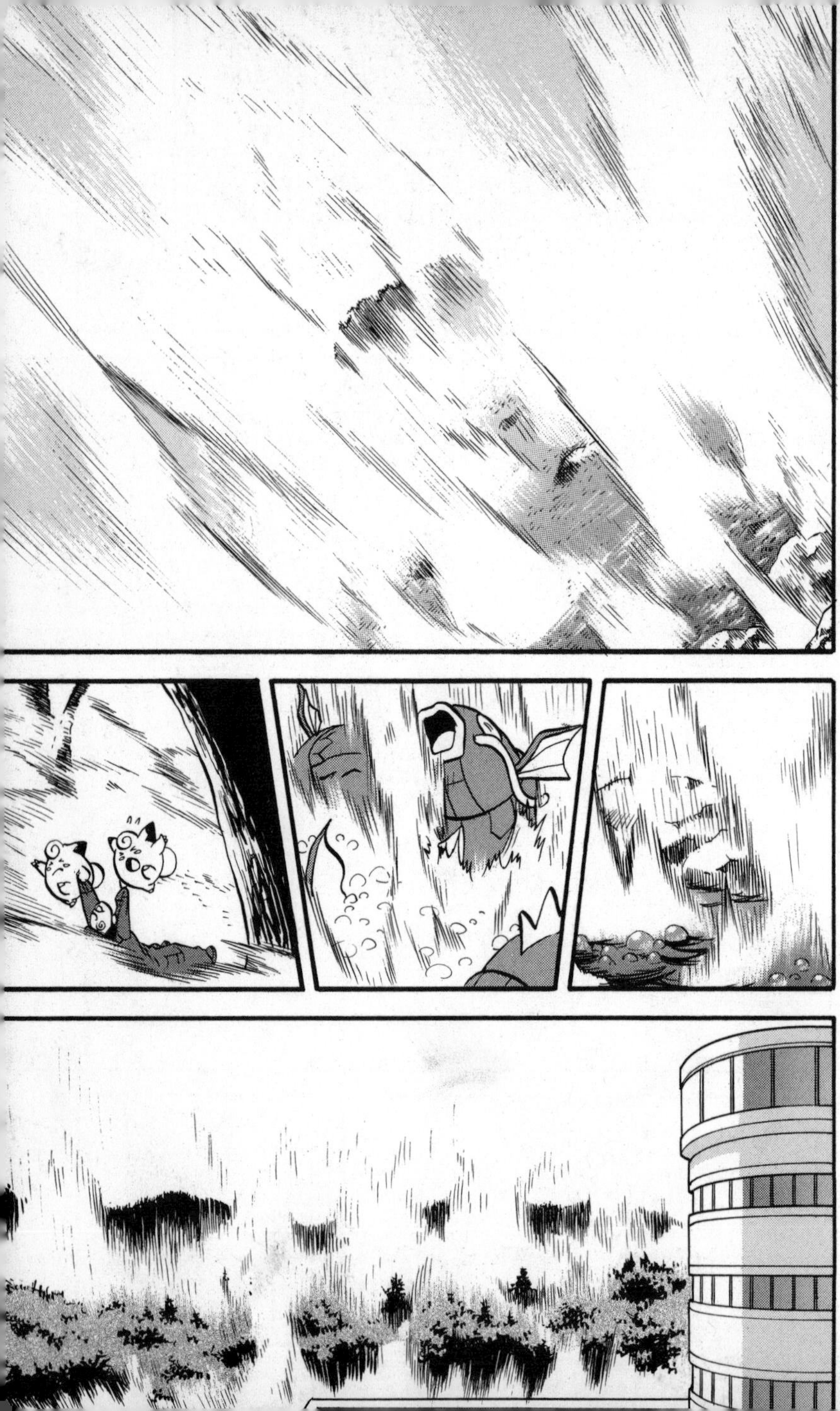

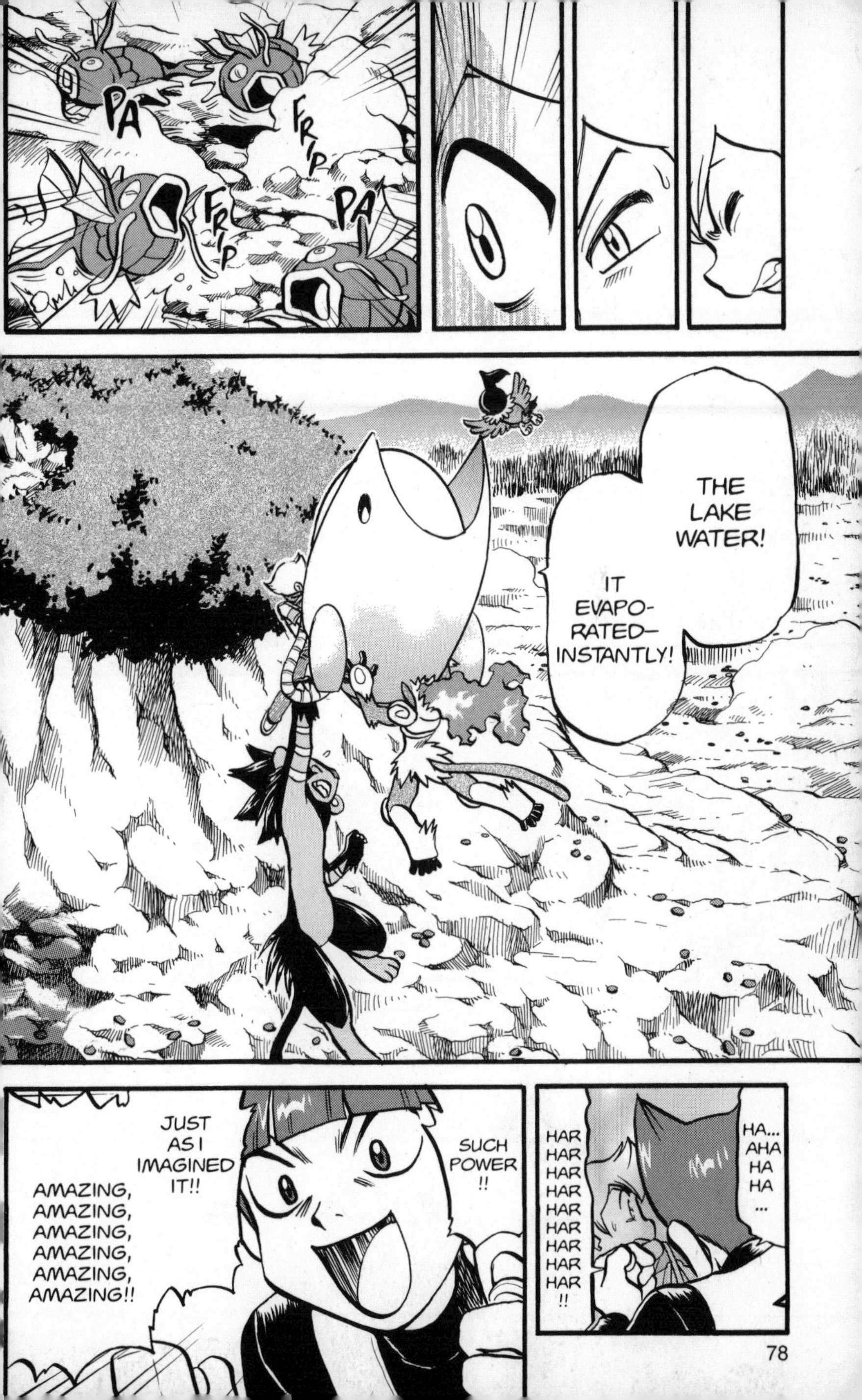

FRIP
PA
PA
FRIP
THE LAKE WATER!
IT EVAPORATED—INSTANTLY!
HA... AHA HA HA ...
HAR HAR HAR HAR HAR HAR HAR HAR HAR !!
SUCH POWER !!
JUST AS I IMAGINED IT!!
AMAZING, AMAZING, AMAZING, AMAZING, AMAZING, AMAZING!!

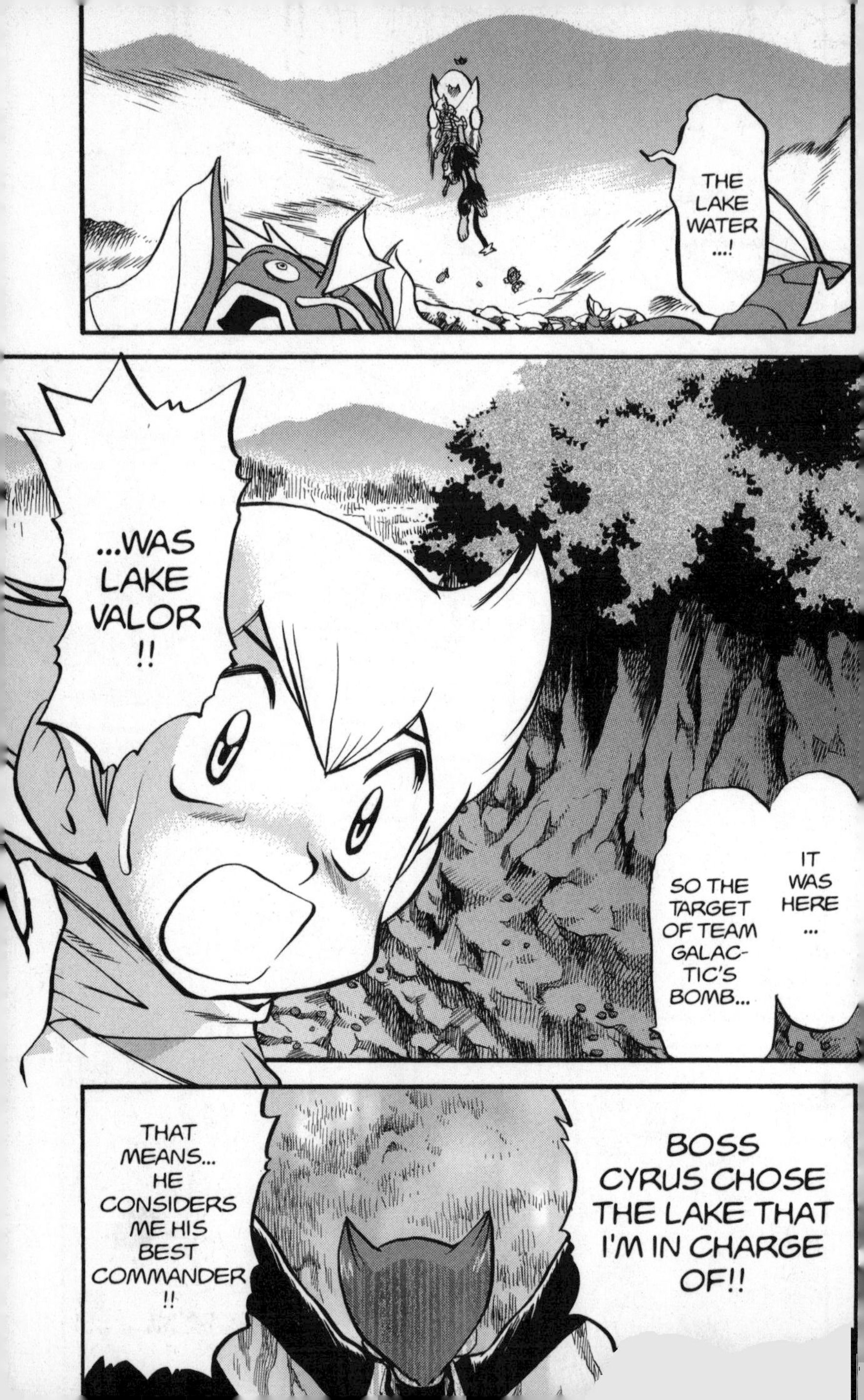
THE LAKE WATER ...!
SO THE TARGET OF TEAM GALAC-TIC'S BOMB...
IT WAS HERE ...
...WAS LAKE VALOR !!
BOSS CYRUS CHOSE THE LAKE THAT I'M IN CHARGE OF!!
THAT MEANS... HE CONSIDERS ME HIS BEST COMMANDER !!

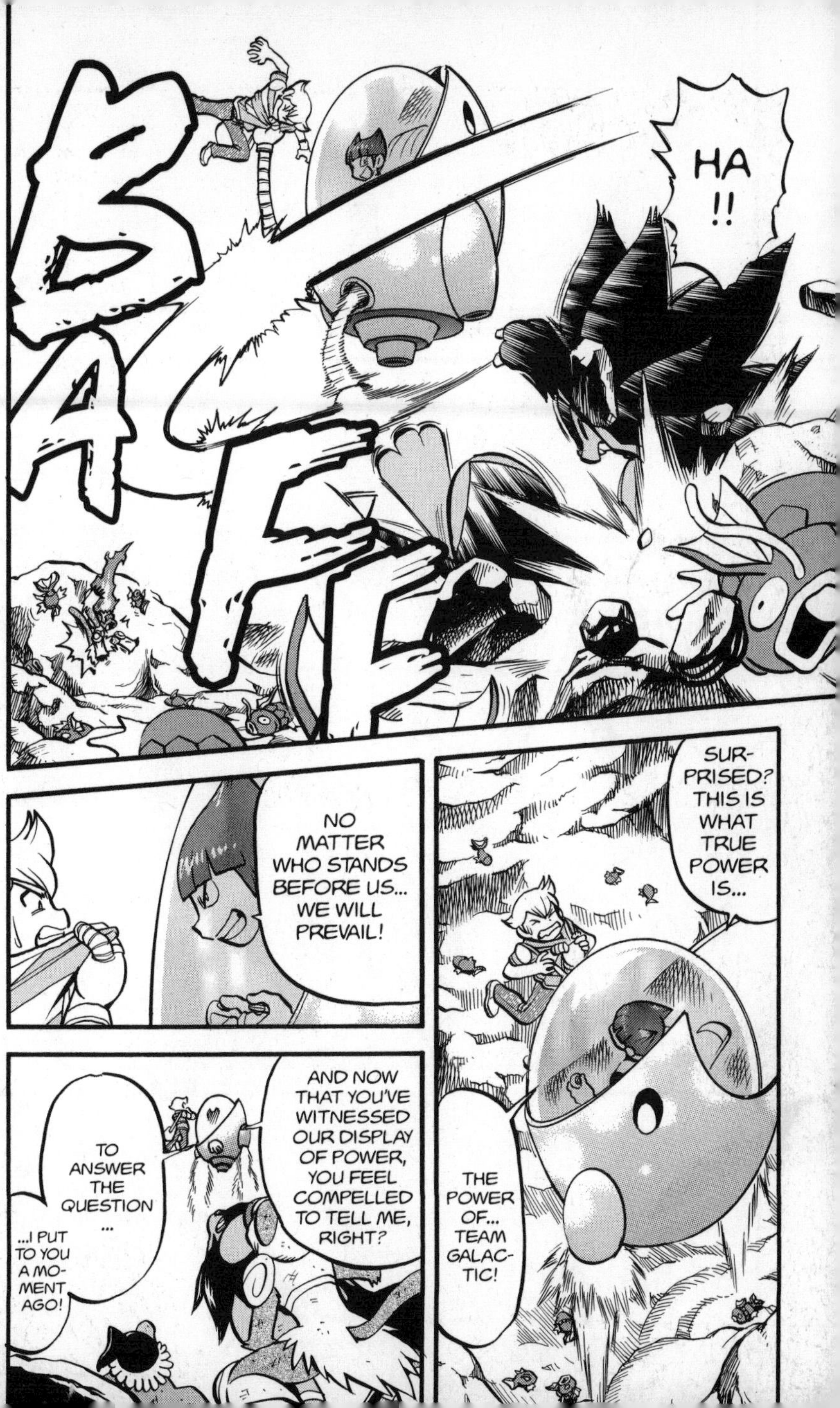
HA !!
BAFF
SUR-PRISED? THIS IS WHAT TRUE POWER IS...
THE POWER OF... TEAM GALAC-TIC!
NO MATTER WHO STANDS BEFORE US... WE WILL PREVAIL!
AND NOW THAT YOU'VE WITNESSED OUR DISPLAY OF POWER, YOU FEEL COMPELLED TO TELL ME, RIGHT?
TO ANSWER THE QUESTION ...
...I PUT TO YOU A MO-MENT AGO!

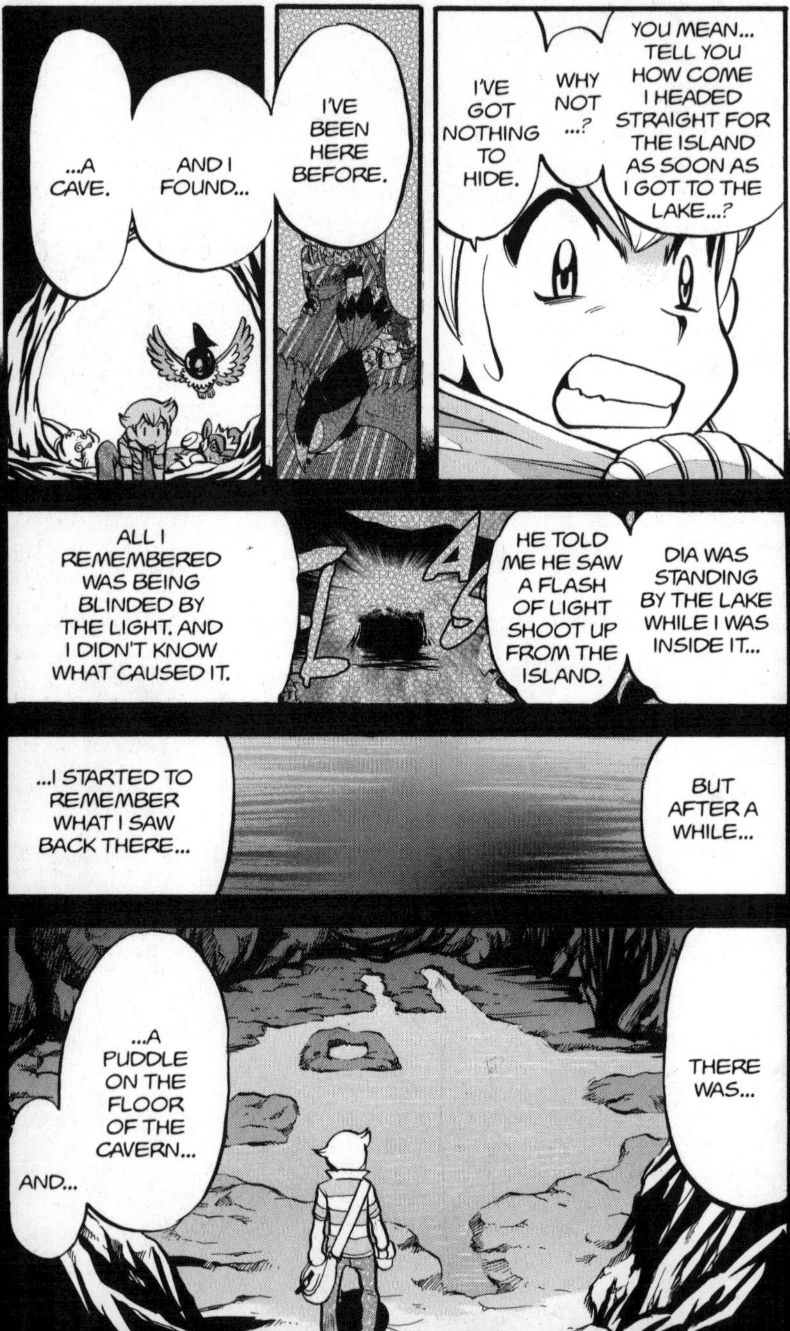
YOU MEAN... TELL YOU HOW COME I HEADED STRAIGHT FOR THE ISLAND AS SOON AS I GOT TO THE LAKE...?
WHY NOT ...?
I'VE GOT NOTHING TO HIDE.
I'VE BEEN HERE BEFORE.
AND I FOUND...
...A CAVE.
DIA WAS STANDING BY THE LAKE WHILE I WAS INSIDE IT...
HE TOLD ME HE SAW A FLASH OF LIGHT SHOOT UP FROM THE ISLAND.
ALL I REMEMBERED WAS BEING BLINDED BY THE LIGHT. AND I DIDN'T KNOW WHAT CAUSED IT.
BUT AFTER A WHILE...
...I STARTED TO REMEMBER WHAT I SAW BACK THERE...
THERE WAS...
...A PUDDLE ON THE FLOOR OF THE CAVERN...
AND...

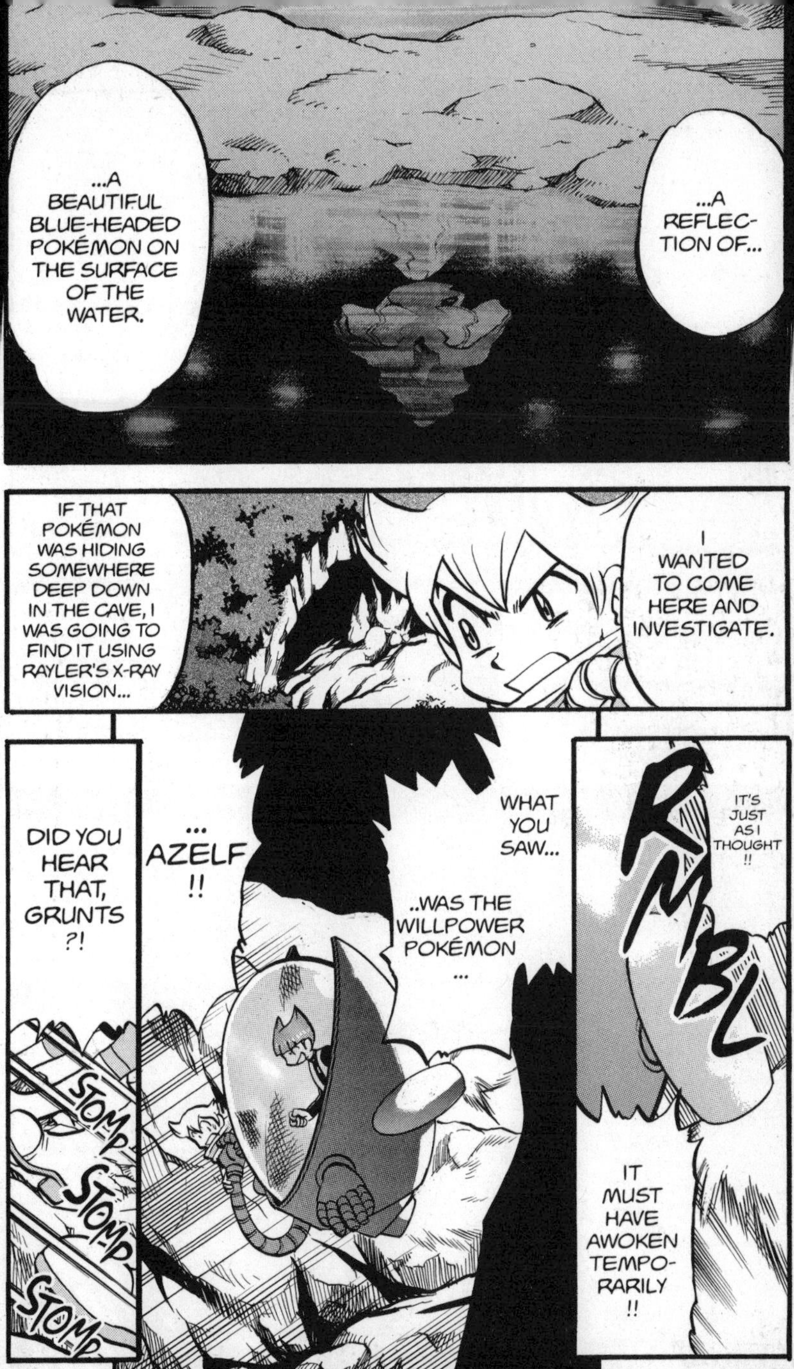
...A REFLEC-TION OF...
...A BEAUTIFUL BLUE-HEADED POKÉMON ON THE SURFACE OF THE WATER.
I WANTED TO COME HERE AND INVESTIGATE.
IF THAT POKÉMON WAS HIDING SOMEWHERE DEEP DOWN IN THE CAVE, I WAS GOING TO FIND IT USING RAYLER'S X-RAY VISION...
IT'S JUST AS I THOUGHT!!
RMBL
WHAT YOU SAW...
..WAS THE WILLPOWER POKÉMON ...
IT MUST HAVE AWOKEN TEMPO-RARILY!!
... AZELF!!
DID YOU HEAR THAT, GRUNTS?!
STOMP
STOMP
STOMP
STOMP

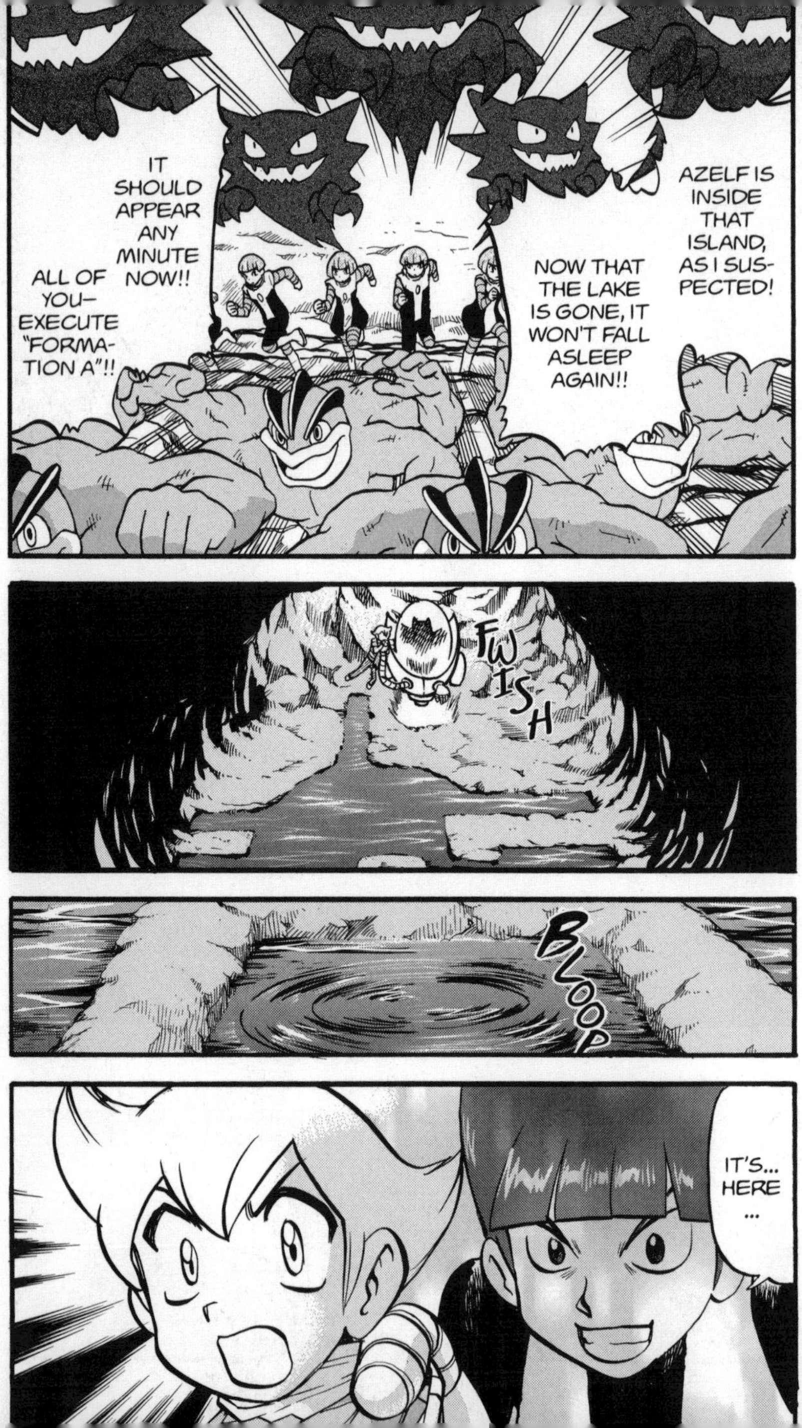
AZELF IS INSIDE THAT ISLAND, AS I SUS-PECTED!
NOW THAT THE LAKE IS GONE, IT WON'T FALL ASLEEP AGAIN!!
IT SHOULD APPEAR ANY MINUTE NOW!!
ALL OF YOU— EXECUTE "FORMA-TION A"!!
FWISH
BLOOP
IT'S... HERE ...

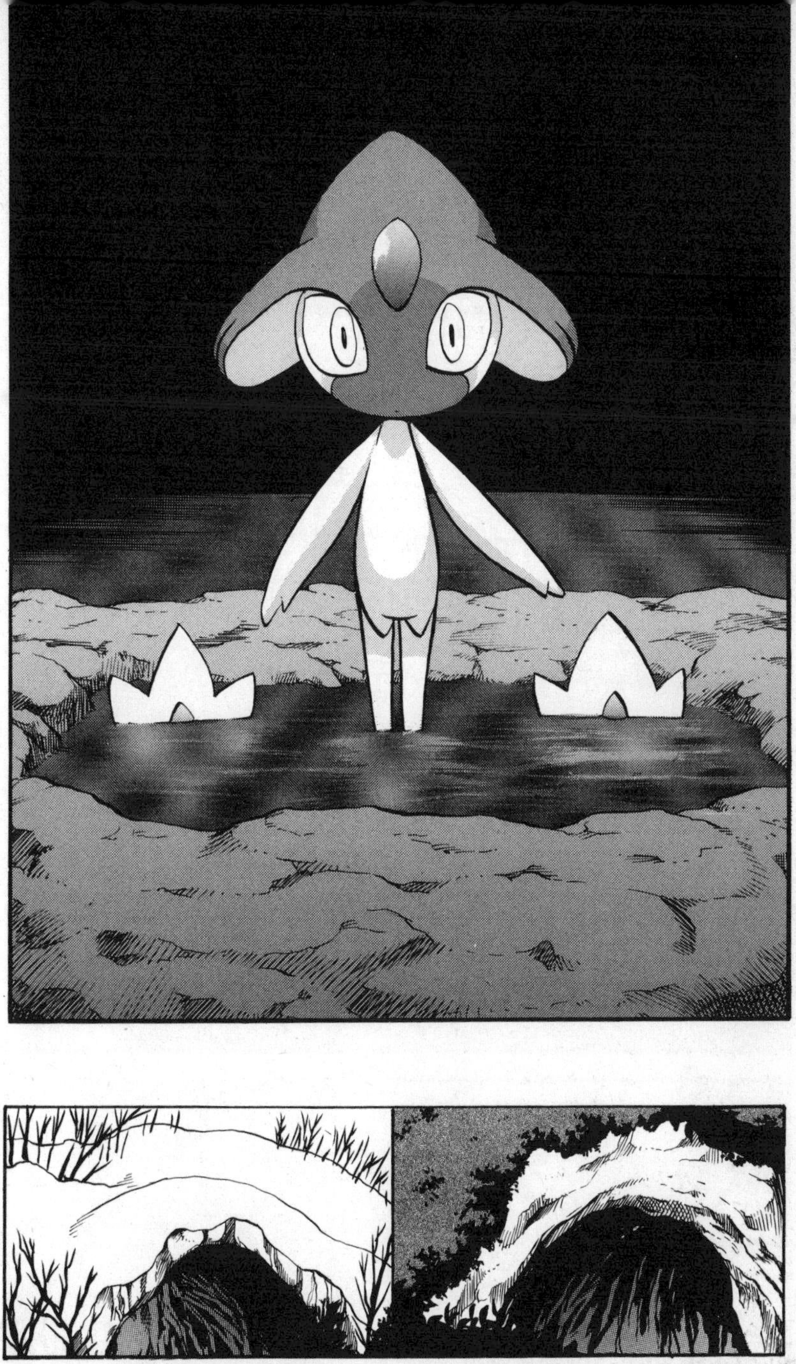

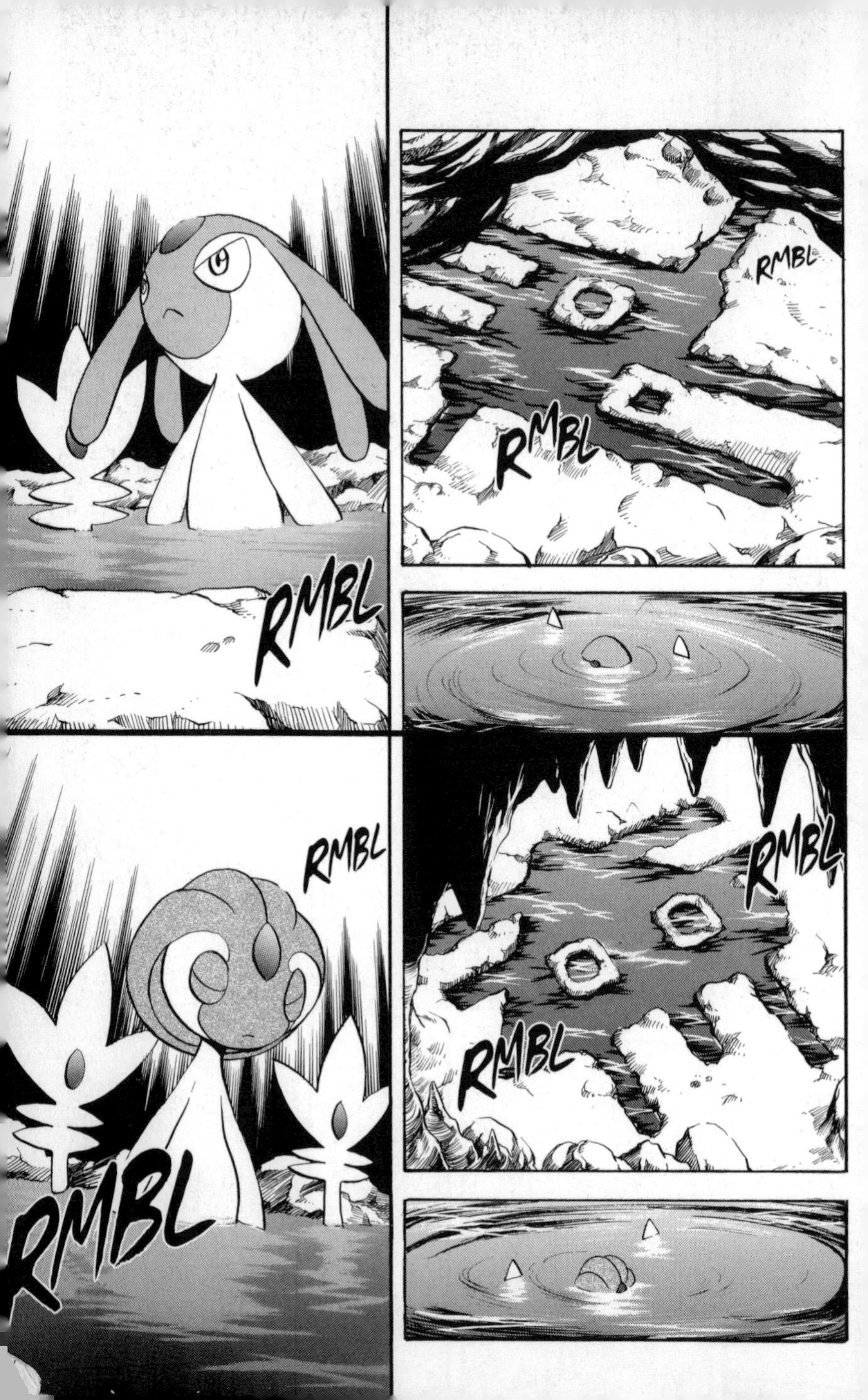
RMBL
RMBL
RMBL
RMBL
RMBL
RMBL
RMBL

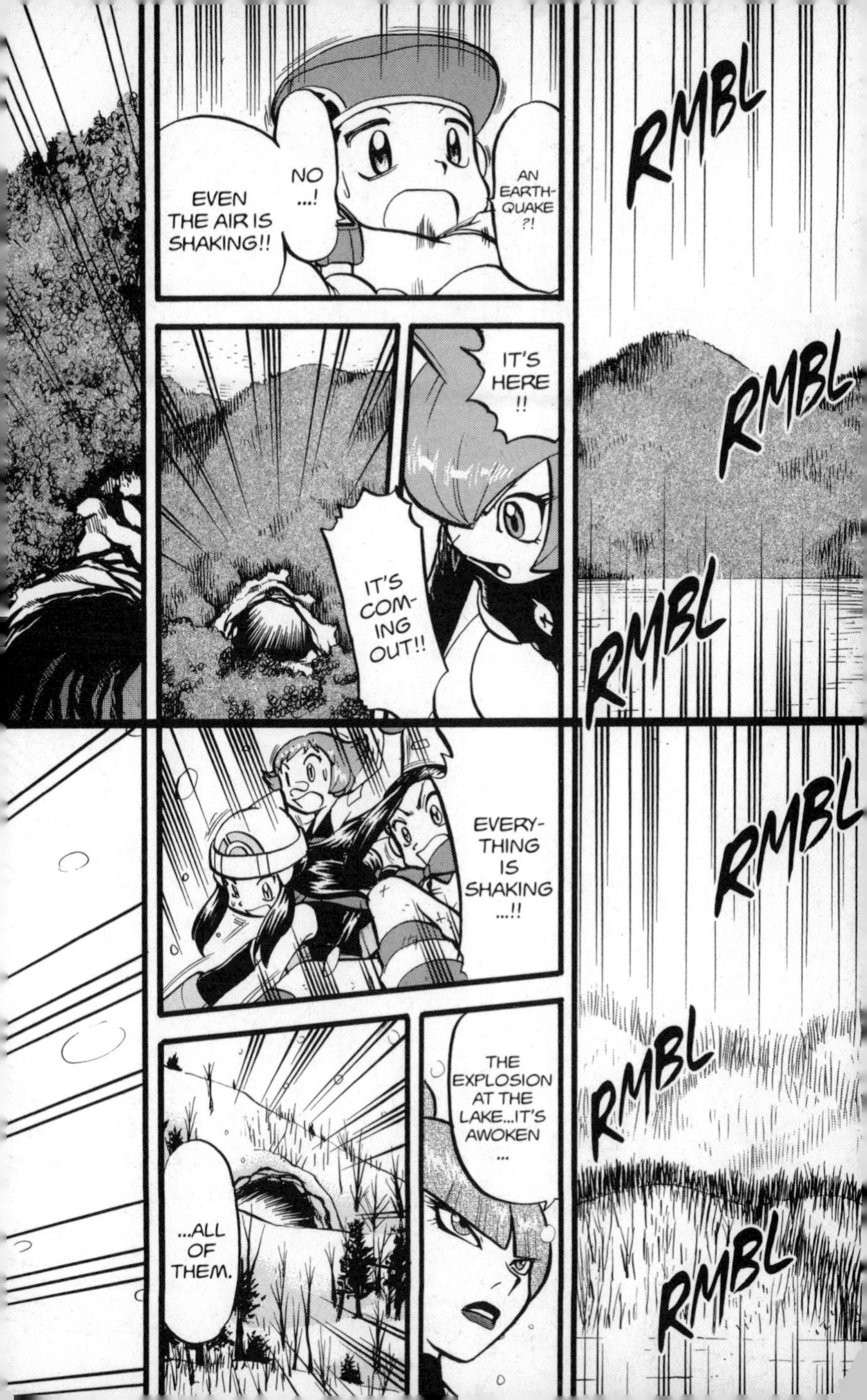
RMBL
AN EARTHQUAKE?!
NO ...!
EVEN THE AIR IS SHAKING!!
RMBL
RMBL
IT'S HERE!!
IT'S COMING OUT!!
RMBL
EVERYTHING IS SHAKING ...!!
RMBL
RMBL
THE EXPLOSION AT THE LAKE...IT'S AWOKEN ...
...ALL OF THEM.

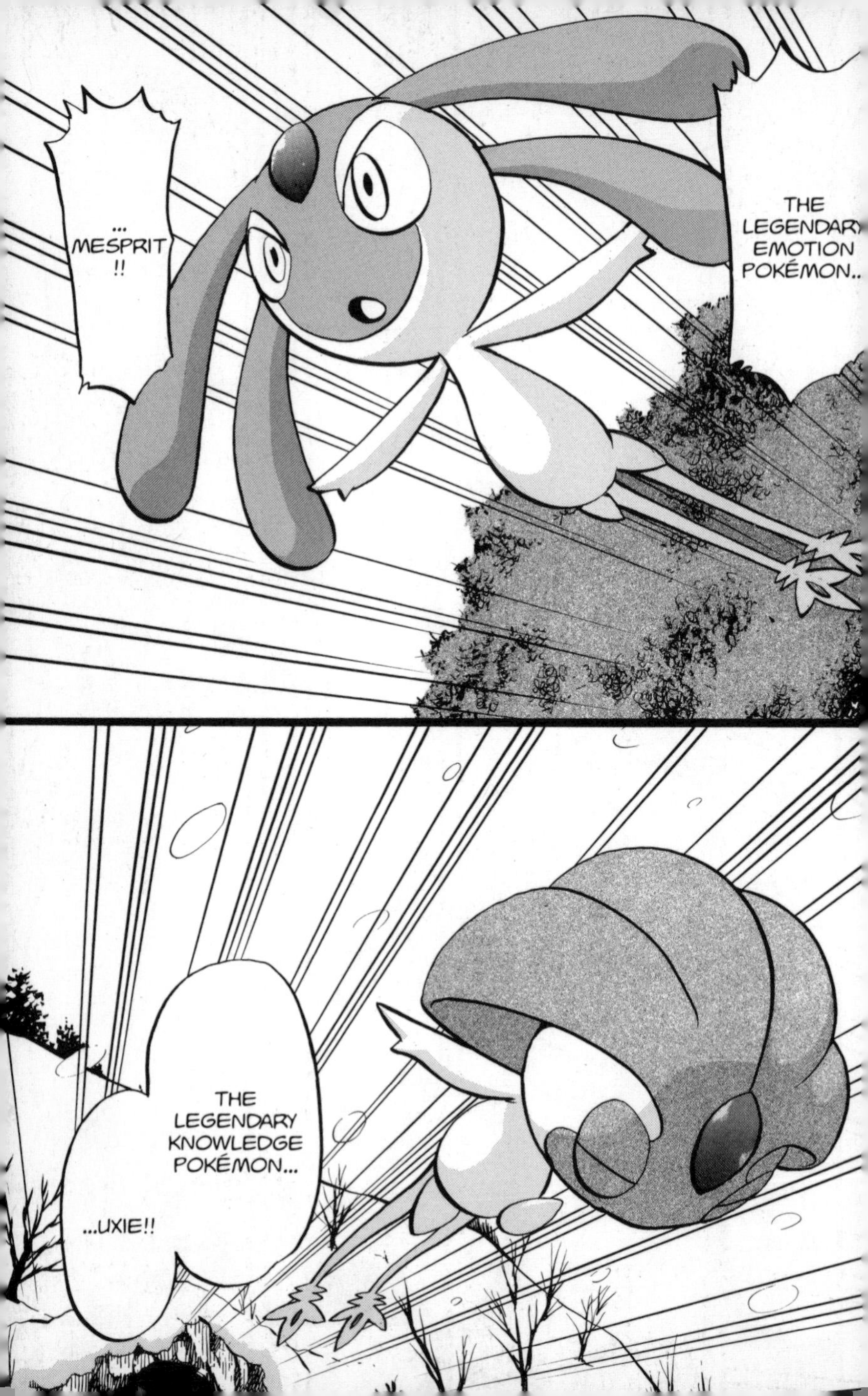
THE LEGENDARY EMOTION POKÉMON...
...MESPRIT!!
THE LEGENDARY KNOWLEDGE POKÉMON...
...UXIE!!

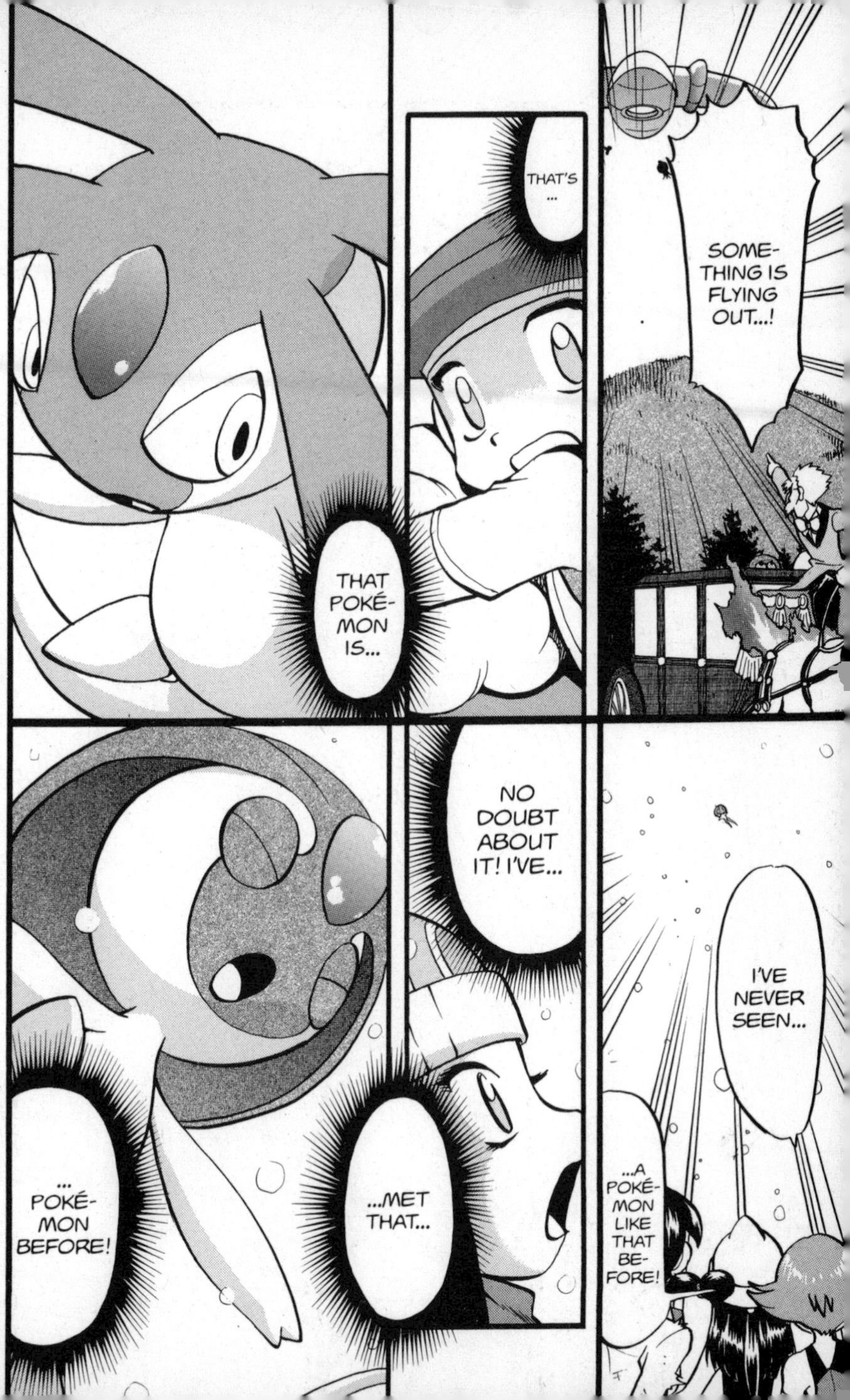
SOMETHING IS FLYING OUT...!
THAT'S ...
THAT POKÉMON IS...
I'VE NEVER SEEN...
...A POKÉMON LIKE THAT BEFORE!
NO DOUBT ABOUT IT! I'VE...
...MET THAT...
... POKÉMON BEFORE!

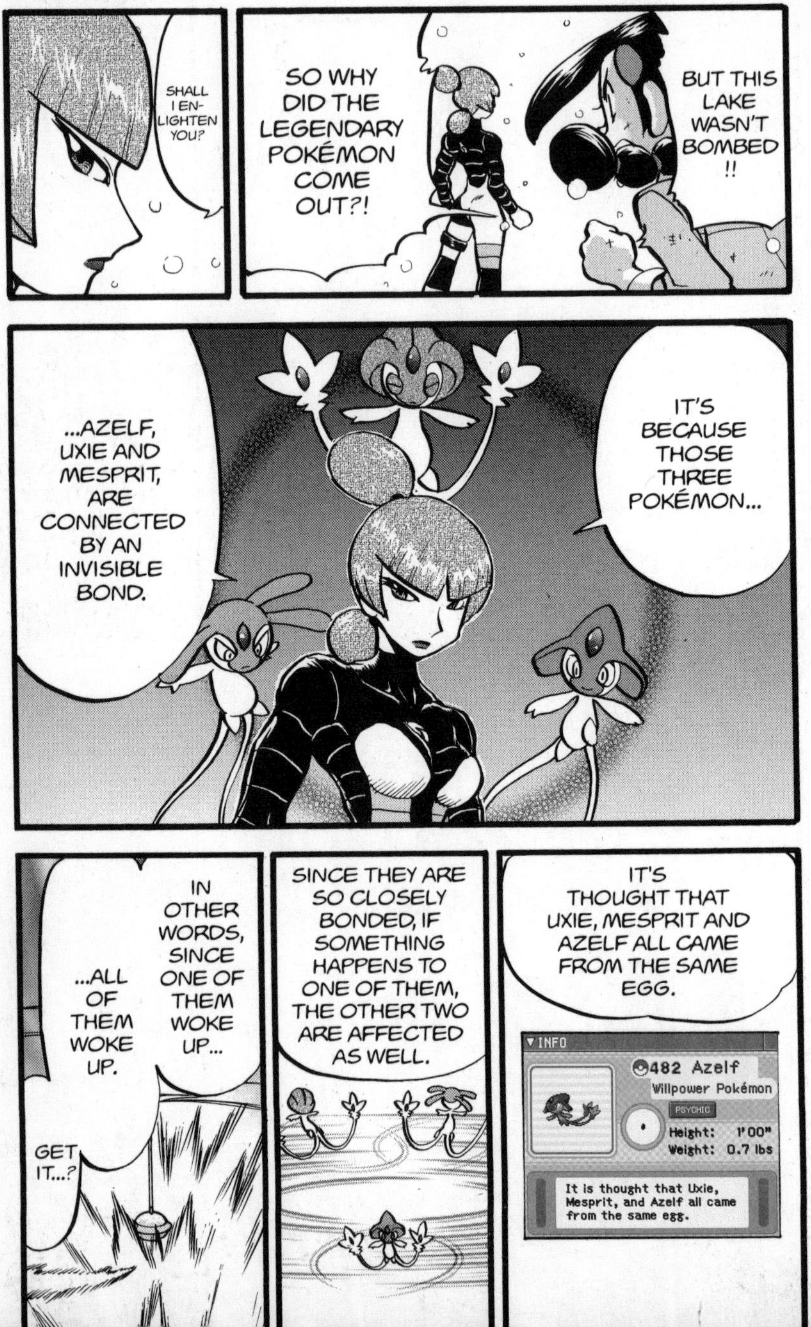
BUT THIS LAKE WASN'T BOMBED!!
SO WHY DID THE LEGENDARY POKÉMON COME OUT?!
SHALL I EN-LIGHTEN YOU?
IT'S BECAUSE THOSE THREE POKÉMON...
...AZELF, UXIE AND MESPRIT, ARE CONNECTED BY AN INVISIBLE BOND.
IT'S THOUGHT THAT UXIE, MESPRIT AND AZELF ALL CAME FROM THE SAME EGG.
INFO
482 Azelf
Willpower Pokémon
PSYCHIC
Height: 1'00"
Weight: 0.7 lbs
It is thought that Uxie, Mesprit, and Azelf all came from the same egg.
SINCE THEY ARE SO CLOSELY BONDED, IF SOMETHING HAPPENS TO ONE OF THEM, THE OTHER TWO ARE AFFECTED AS WELL.
IN OTHER WORDS, SINCE ONE OF THEM WOKE UP...
...ALL OF THEM WOKE UP.
GET IT...?

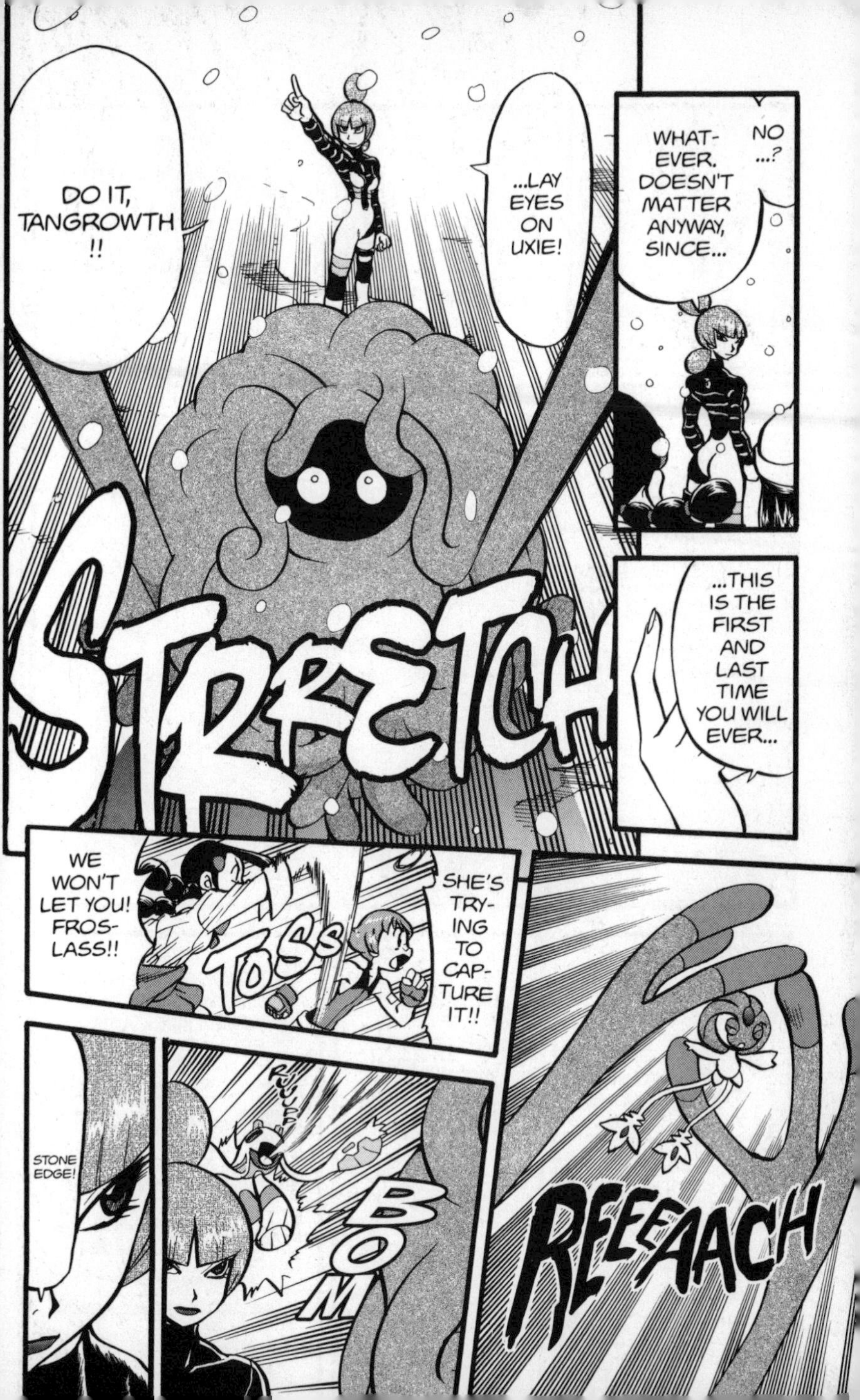
NO ...?
WHAT-EVER. DOESN'T MATTER ANYWAY, SINCE...
...THIS IS THE FIRST AND LAST TIME YOU WILL EVER...
...LAY EYES ON UXIE!
DO IT, TANGROWTH!!
STRETCH
REEEAACH
SHE'S TRY-ING TO CAP-TURE IT!!
WE WON'T LET YOU! FROS-LASS!!
TOSS
BOOM
STONE EDGE!

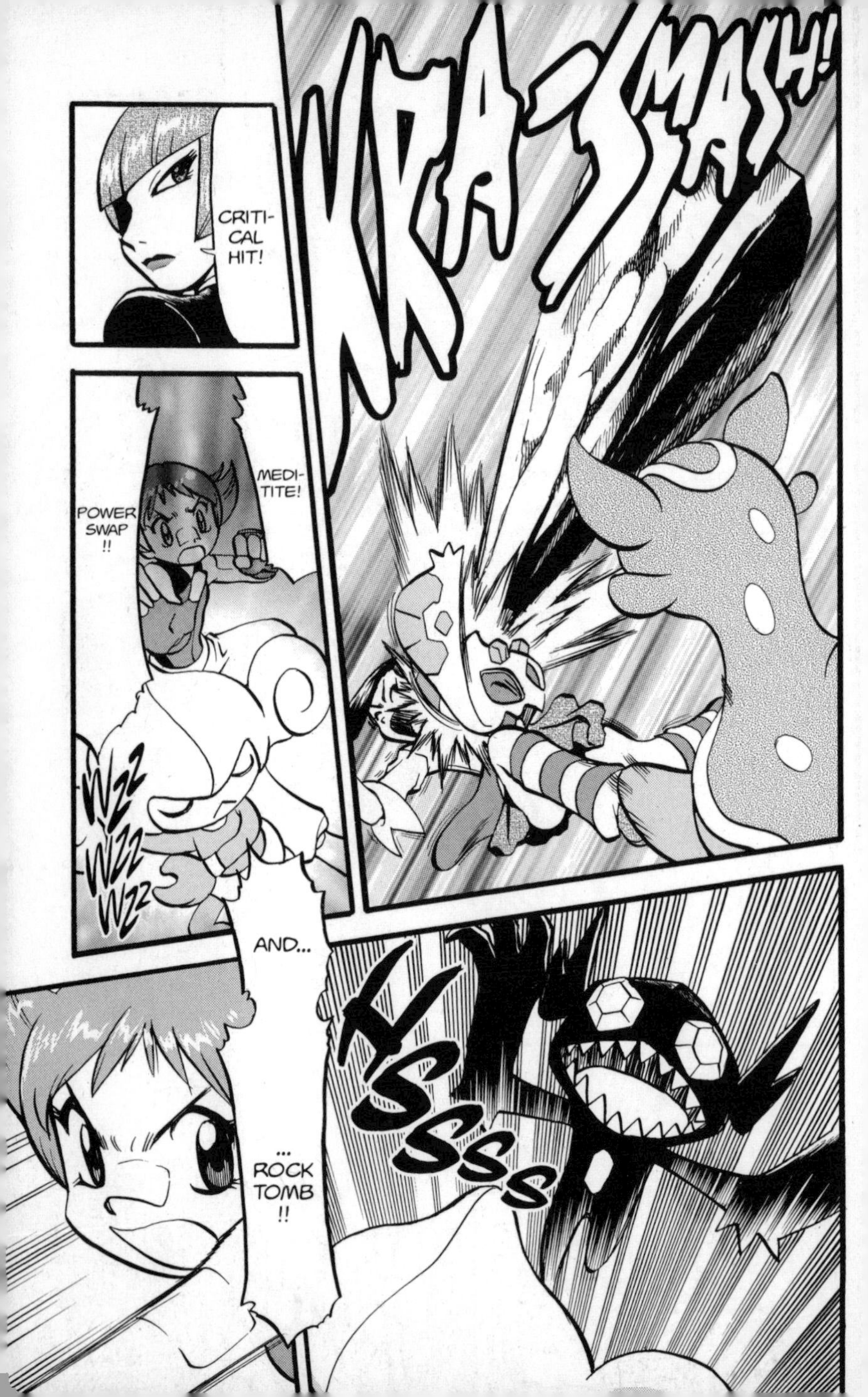
KRA-SMASH!
CRITI-CAL HIT!
MEDI-TITE!
POWER SWAP!!
WZZ WZZ WZZ
AND...
...ROCK TOMB!!
HISSSS

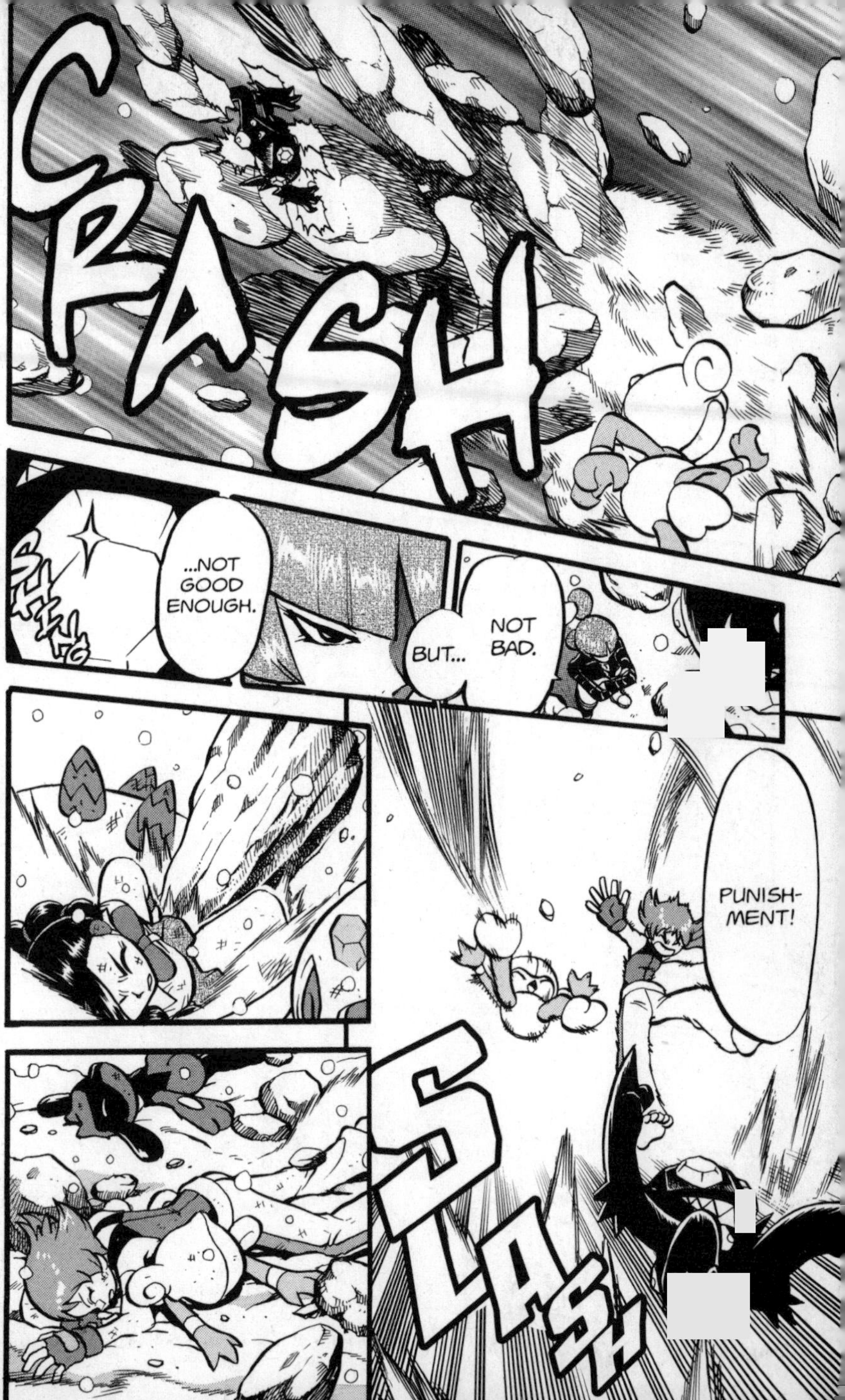
CRASH
NOT BAD.
BUT...
...NOT GOOD ENOUGH.
PUNISH-MENT!
SLASH

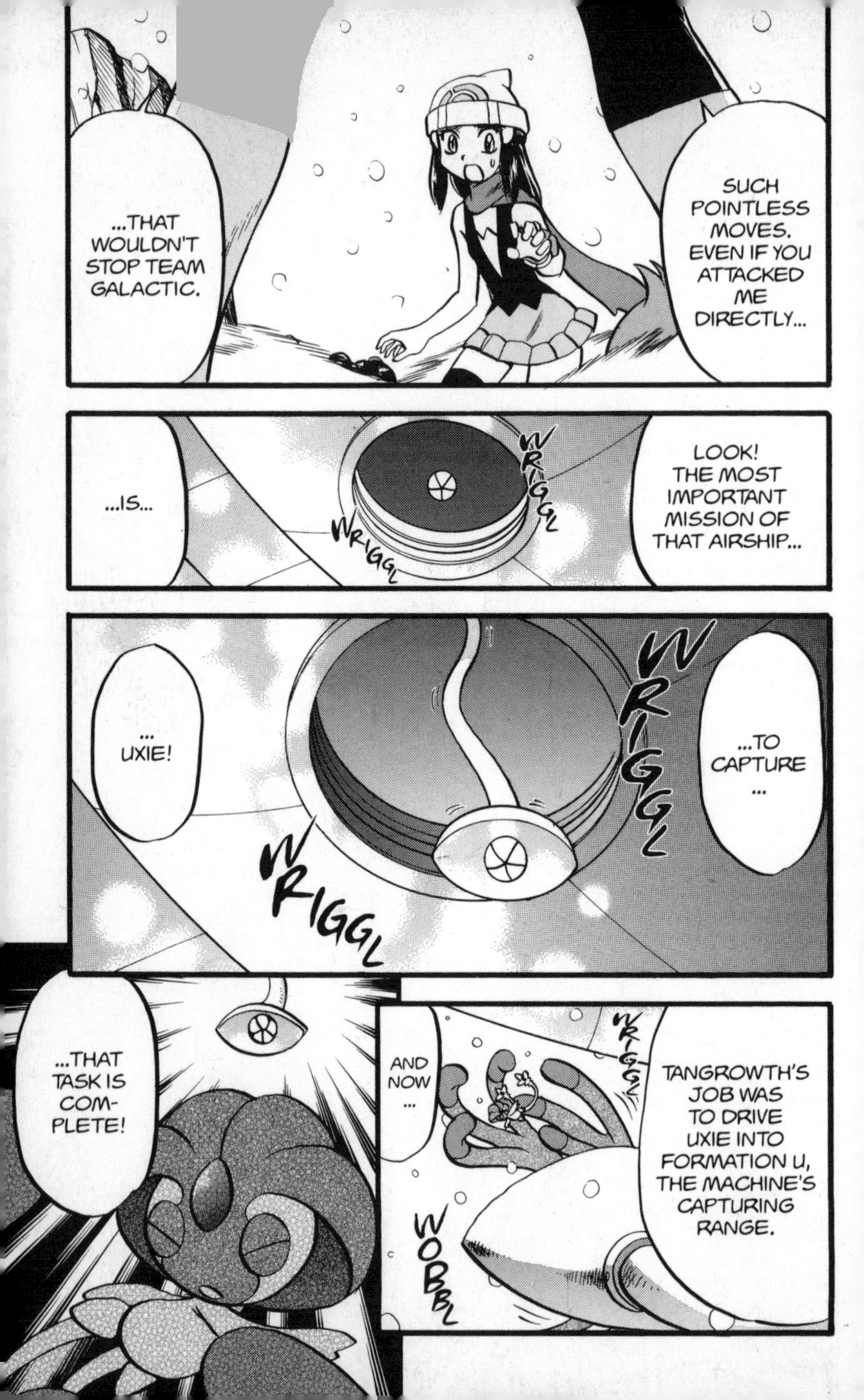
SUCH POINTLESS MOVES. EVEN IF YOU ATTACKED ME DIRECTLY...
...THAT WOULDN'T STOP TEAM GALACTIC.
LOOK! THE MOST IMPORTANT MISSION OF THAT AIRSHIP...
WRIGGL
WRIGGL
...IS...
...TO CAPTURE ...
WRIGGL
... UXIE!
WRIGGL
TANGROWTH'S JOB WAS TO DRIVE UXIE INTO FORMATION U, THE MACHINE'S CAPTURING RANGE.
WRIGGL
AND NOW ...
WOBBL
...THAT TASK IS COM-PLETE!

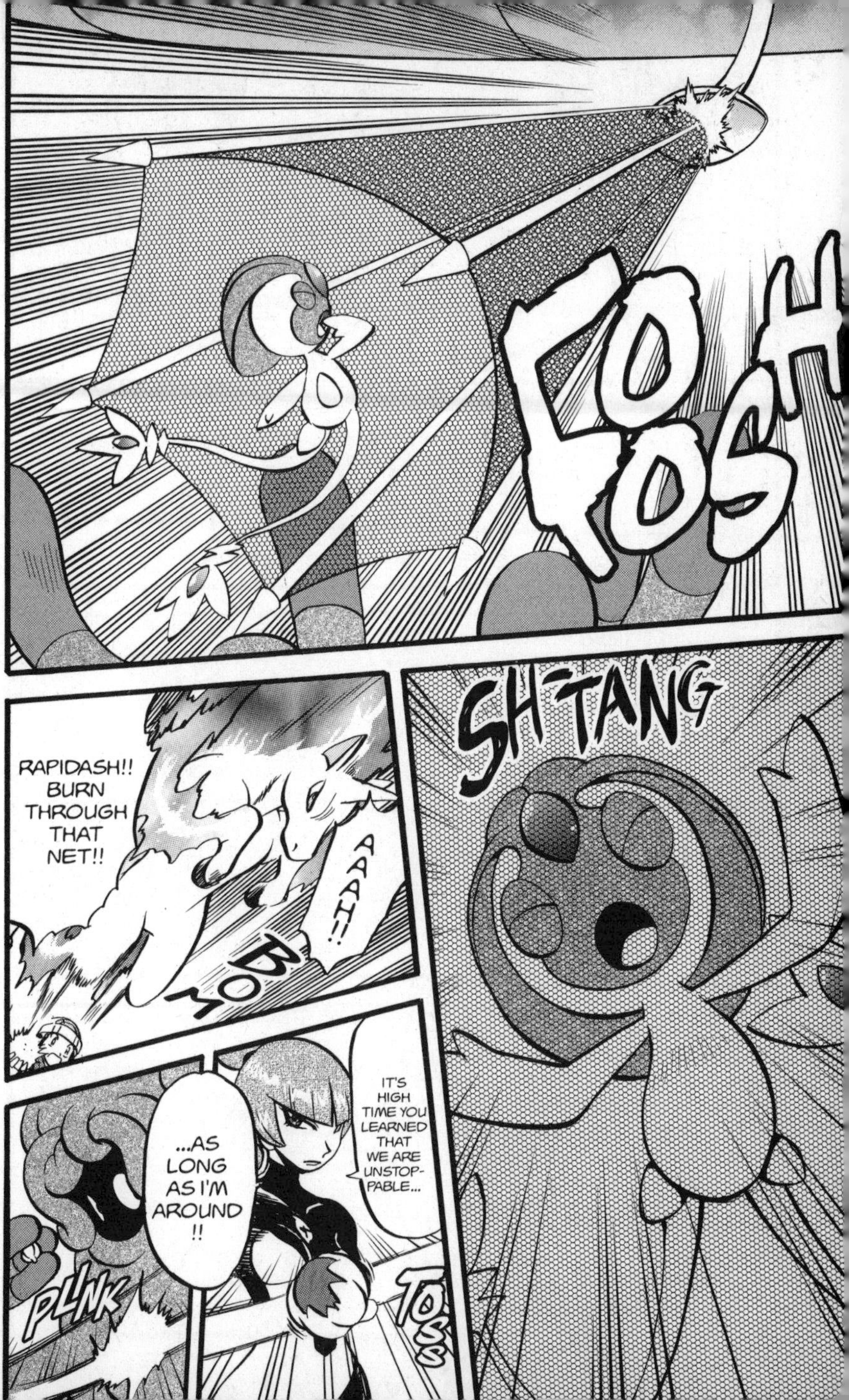
FOOSH
SH-TANG
RAPIDASH!! BURN THROUGH THAT NET!!
AAAAH!!
BOOM
IT'S HIGH TIME YOU LEARNED THAT WE ARE UNSTOP-PABLE...
...AS LONG AS I'M AROUND !!
TOSS
PLINK

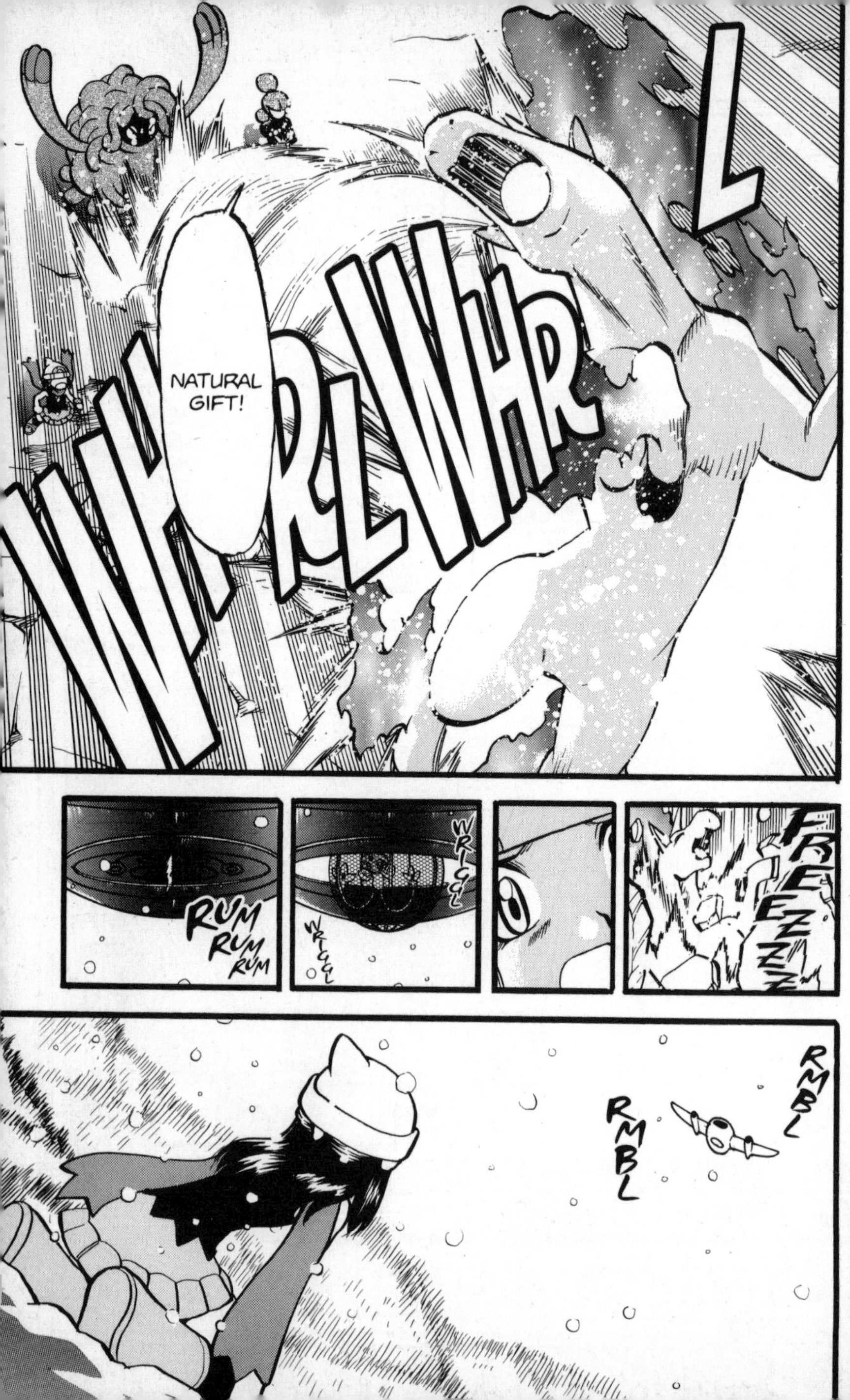
NATURAL GIFT!
FREEZZZ
WRIGGL
WRIGGL
RUM RUM RUM
RMBL
RMBL

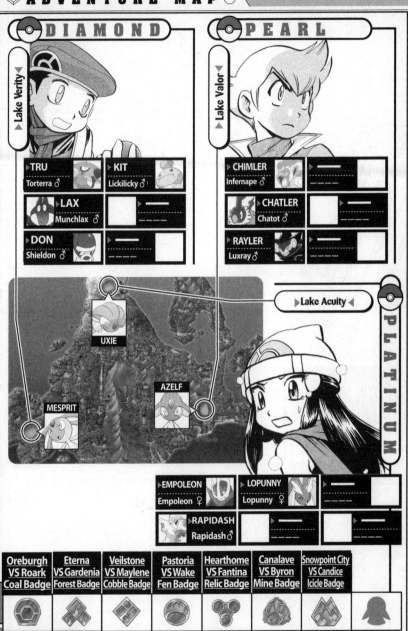

ADVENTURE MAP

DIAMOND

▶ Lake Verity ▼

TRU
Torterra ♂

KIT
Lickilicky ♂

LAX
Munchlax ♂

DON
Shieldon ♂

PEARL

▶ Lake Valor ▼

CHIMLER
Infernape ♂

CHATLER
Chatot ♂

RAYLER
Luxray ♂

▶ Lake Acuity ◀

UXIE

AZELF

MESPRIT

PLATINUM

EMPOLEON
Empoleon ♀

LOPUNNY
Lopunny ♀

RAPIDASH
Rapidash ♂

| Oreburgh VS Roark Coal Badge | Eterna VS Gardenia Forest Badge | Veilstone VS Maylene Cobble Badge | Pastoria VS Wake Fen Badge | Hearthome VS Fantina Relic Badge | Canalave VS Byron Mine Badge | Snowpoint City VS Candice Icicle Badge | |

62

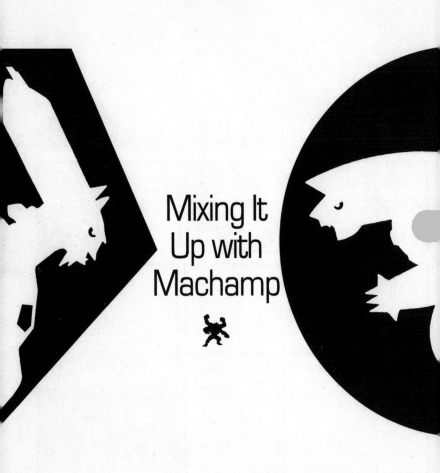

Mixing It
Up with
Machamp

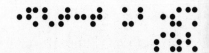

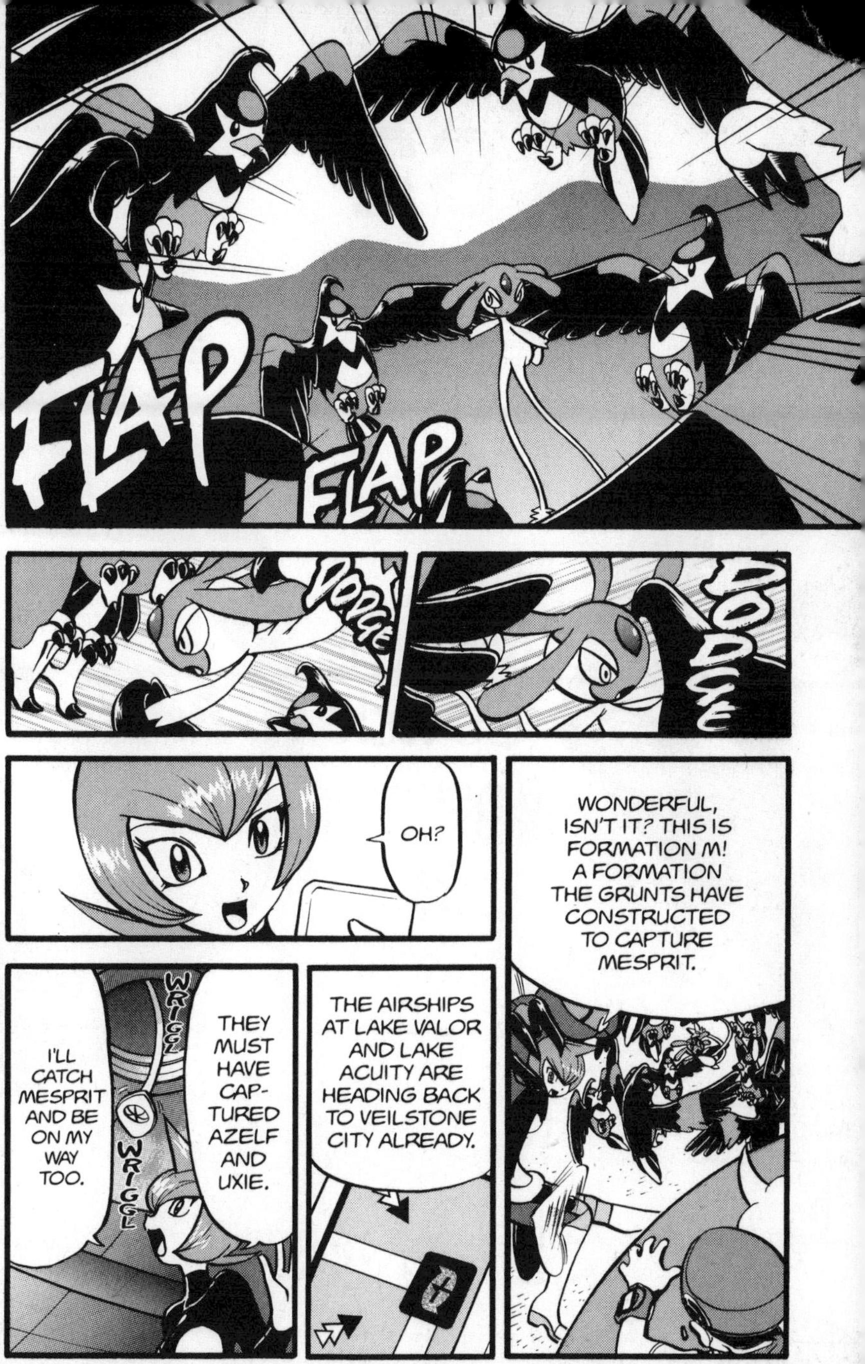
FLAP
FLAP
DODGE
DODGE
DODGE
WONDERFUL, ISN'T IT? THIS IS FORMATION M! A FORMATION THE GRUNTS HAVE CONSTRUCTED TO CAPTURE MESPRIT.
OH?
THE AIRSHIPS AT LAKE VALOR AND LAKE ACUITY ARE HEADING BACK TO VEILSTONE CITY ALREADY.
THEY MUST HAVE CAPTURED AZELF AND UXIE.
WRIGGL
WRIGGL
I'LL CATCH MESPRIT AND BE ON MY WAY TOO.

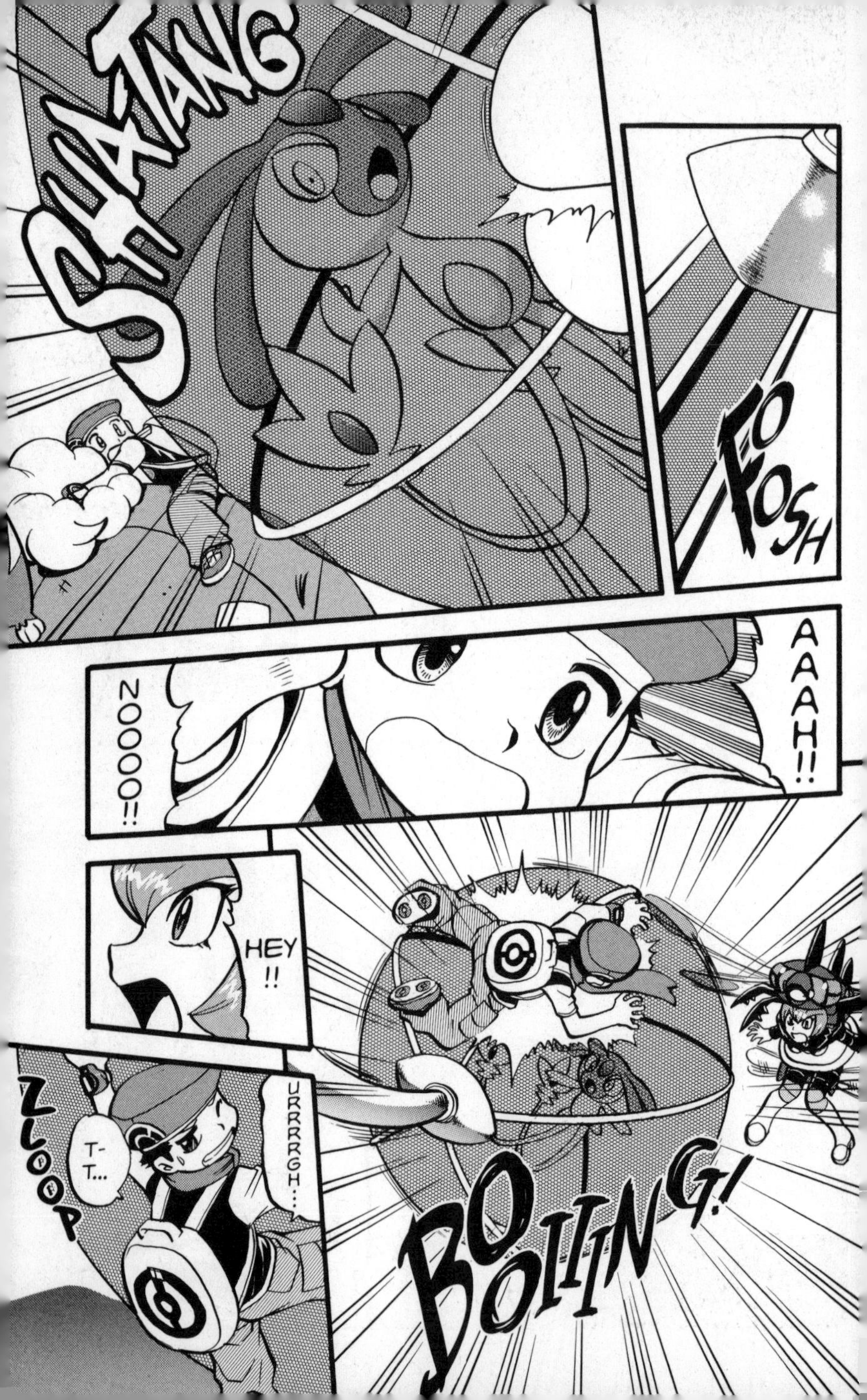
FOOSH
SHATANG
AAAH!!
NOOOOO!!
BOIIING!
HEY!!
URRRGH...
T-T...
ZLOOP

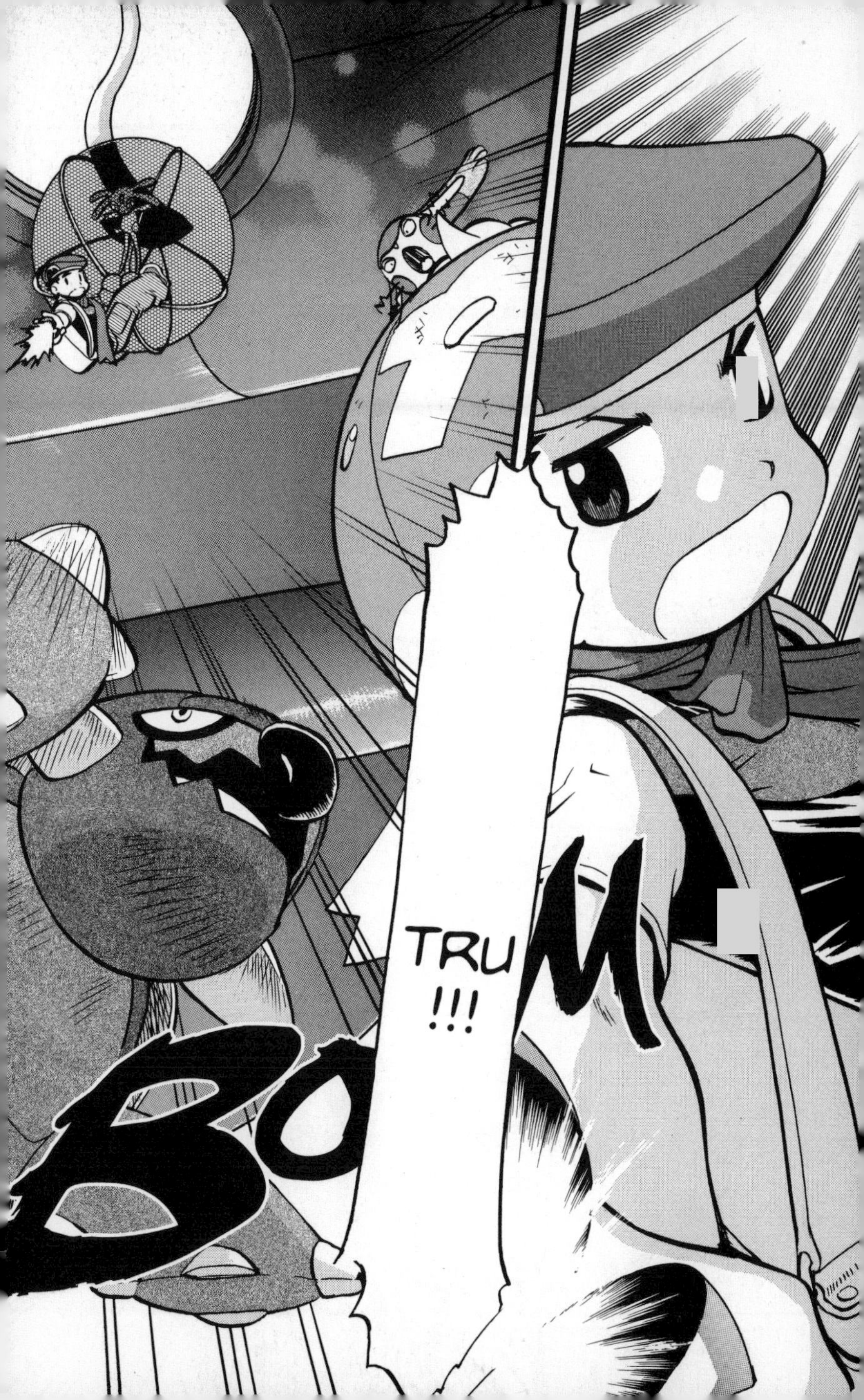
TRU !!!
BOOM

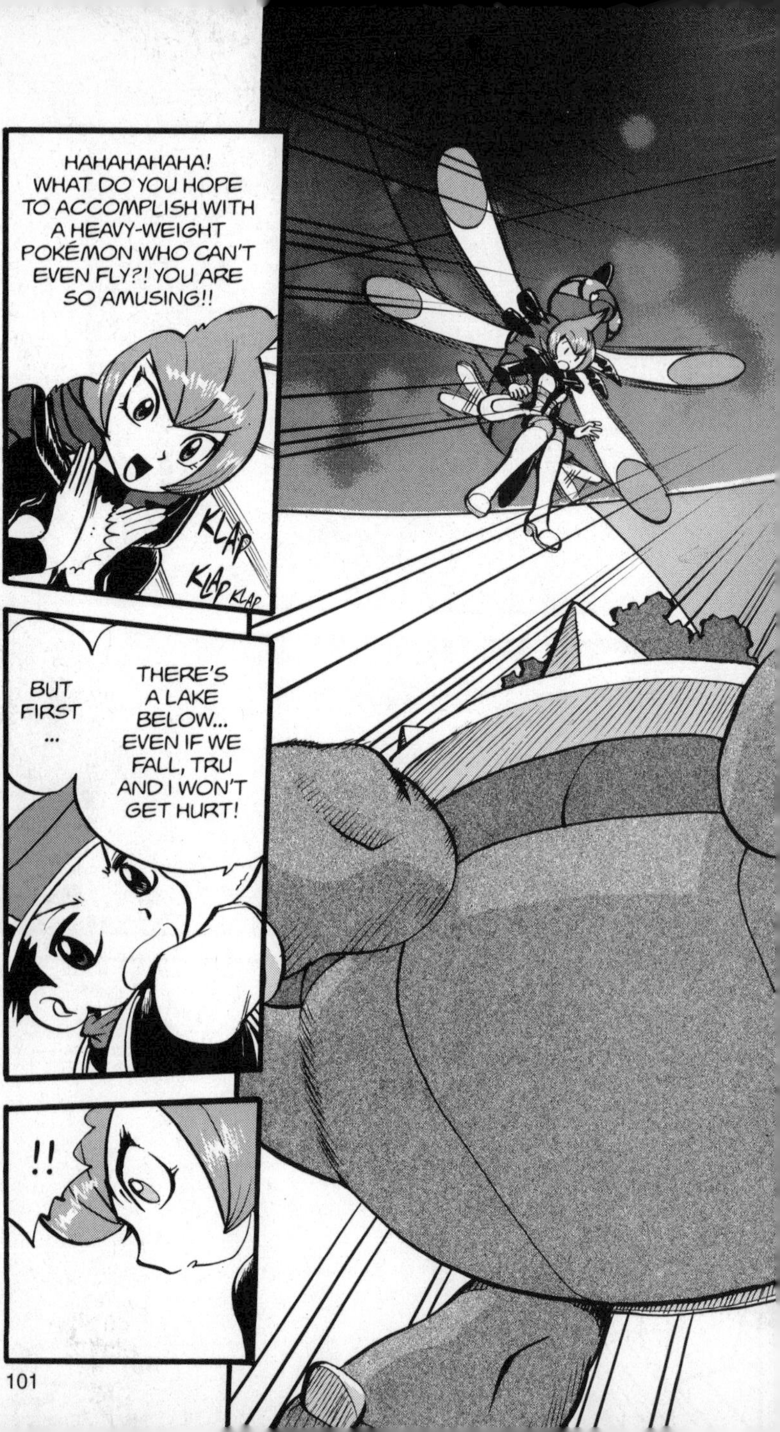
HAHAHAHAHA! WHAT DO YOU HOPE TO ACCOMPLISH WITH A HEAVY-WEIGHT POKÉMON WHO CAN'T EVEN FLY?! YOU ARE SO AMUSING!!
KLAP KLAP KLAP
THERE'S A LAKE BELOW... EVEN IF WE FALL, TRU AND I WON'T GET HURT!
BUT FIRST ...
!!

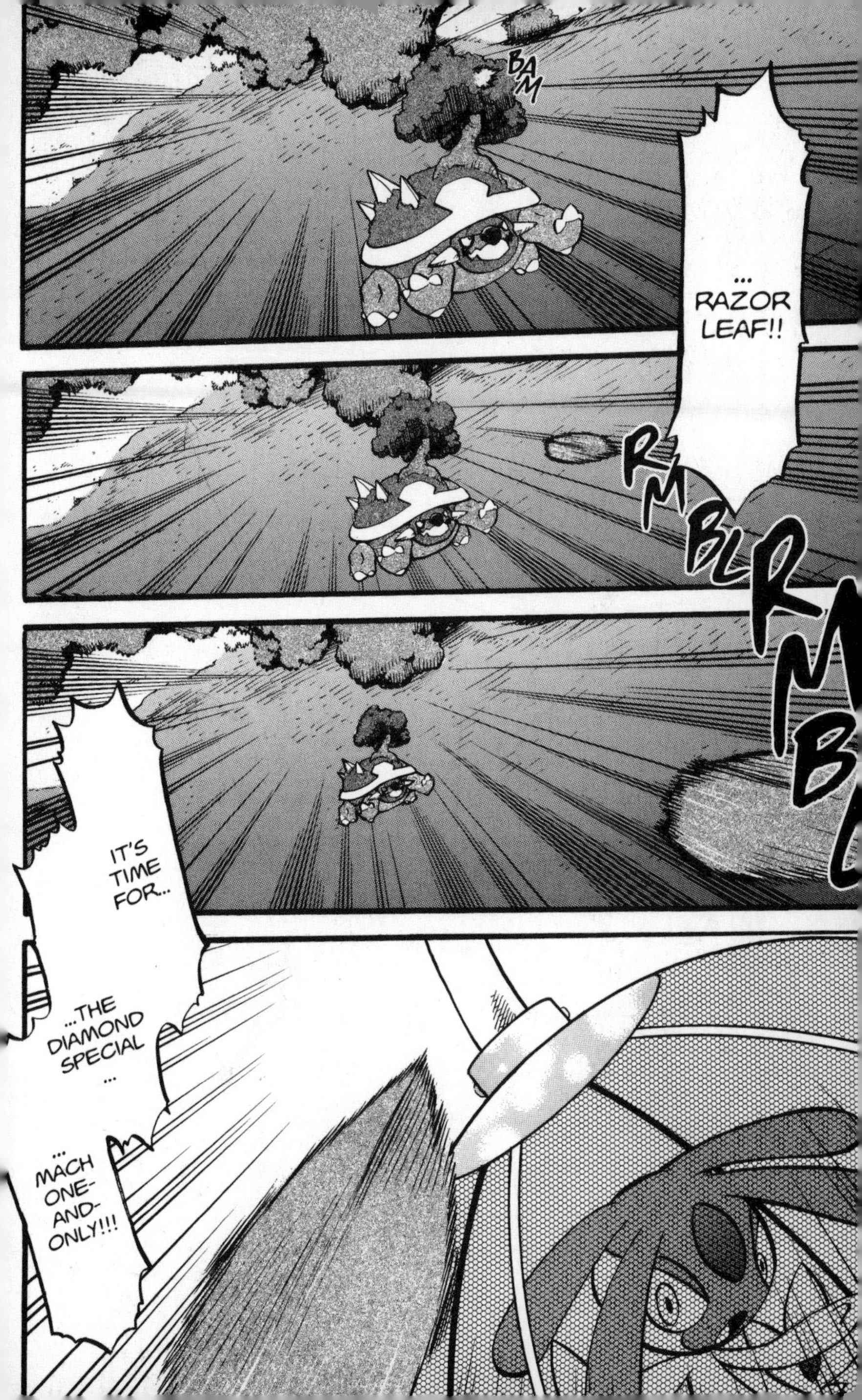
BAM
... RAZOR LEAF!!
RMBL
RMBL
IT'S TIME FOR...
...THE DIAMOND SPECIAL ...
... MACH ONE-AND-ONLY!!!

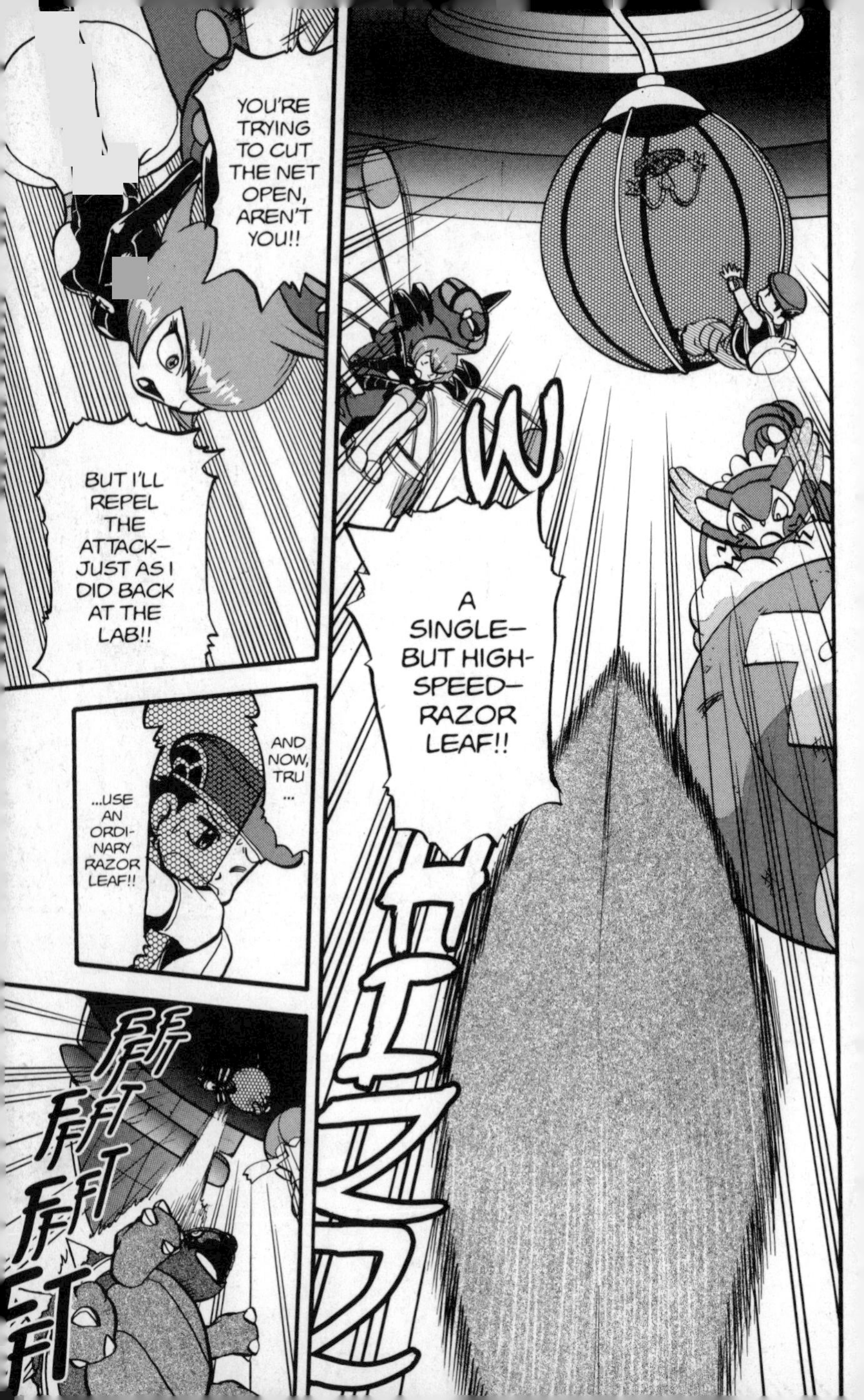
A SINGLE— BUT HIGH-SPEED— RAZOR LEAF!!
YOU'RE TRYING TO CUT THE NET OPEN, AREN'T YOU!!
BUT I'LL REPEL THE ATTACK— JUST AS I DID BACK AT THE LAB!!
AND NOW, TRU...
...USE AN ORDINARY RAZOR LEAF!!
FFFT FFFT FFFT FFFT

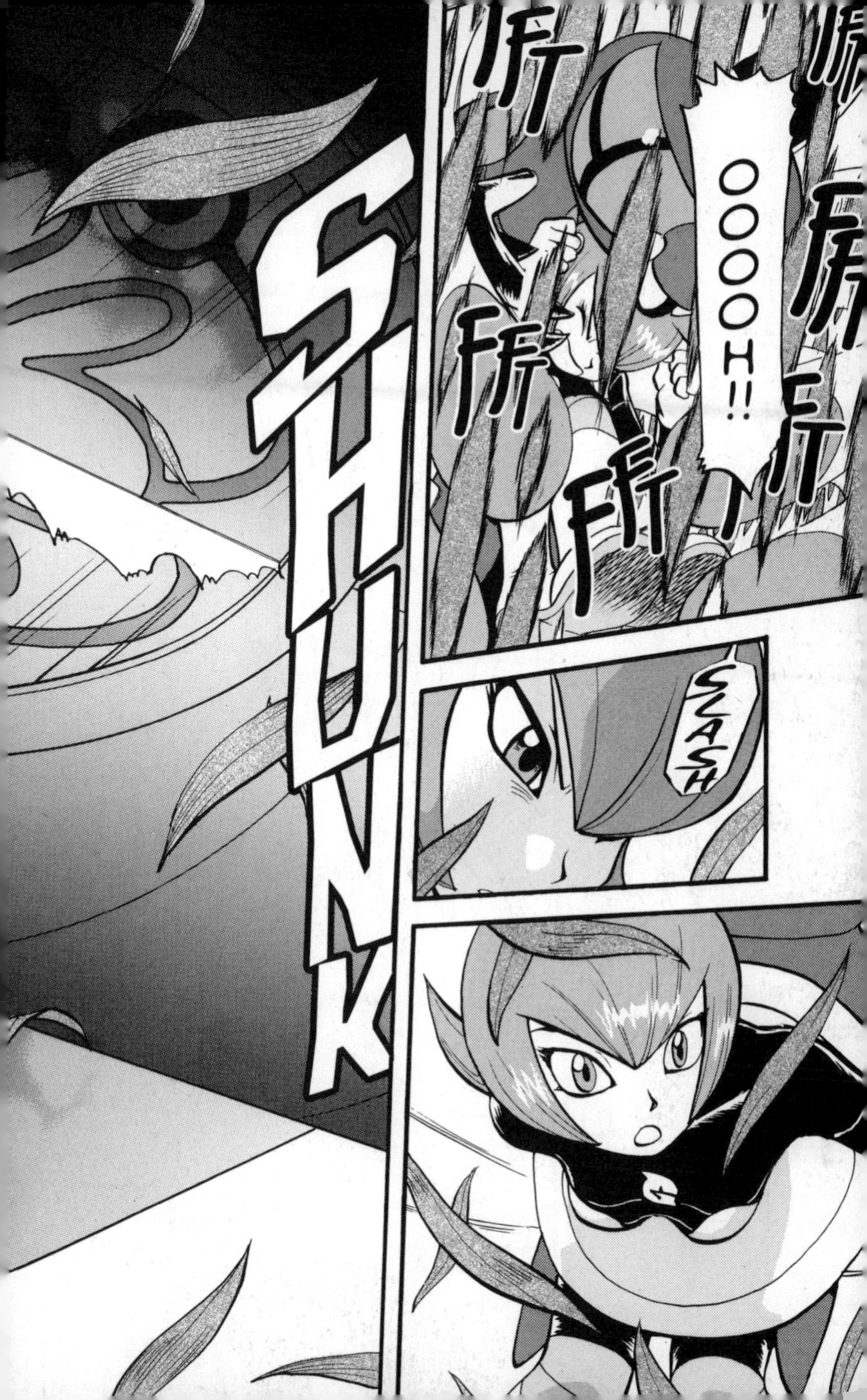

OOOOOH!!
FFFT
FFFT
FFFT
SLASH
SHUNK

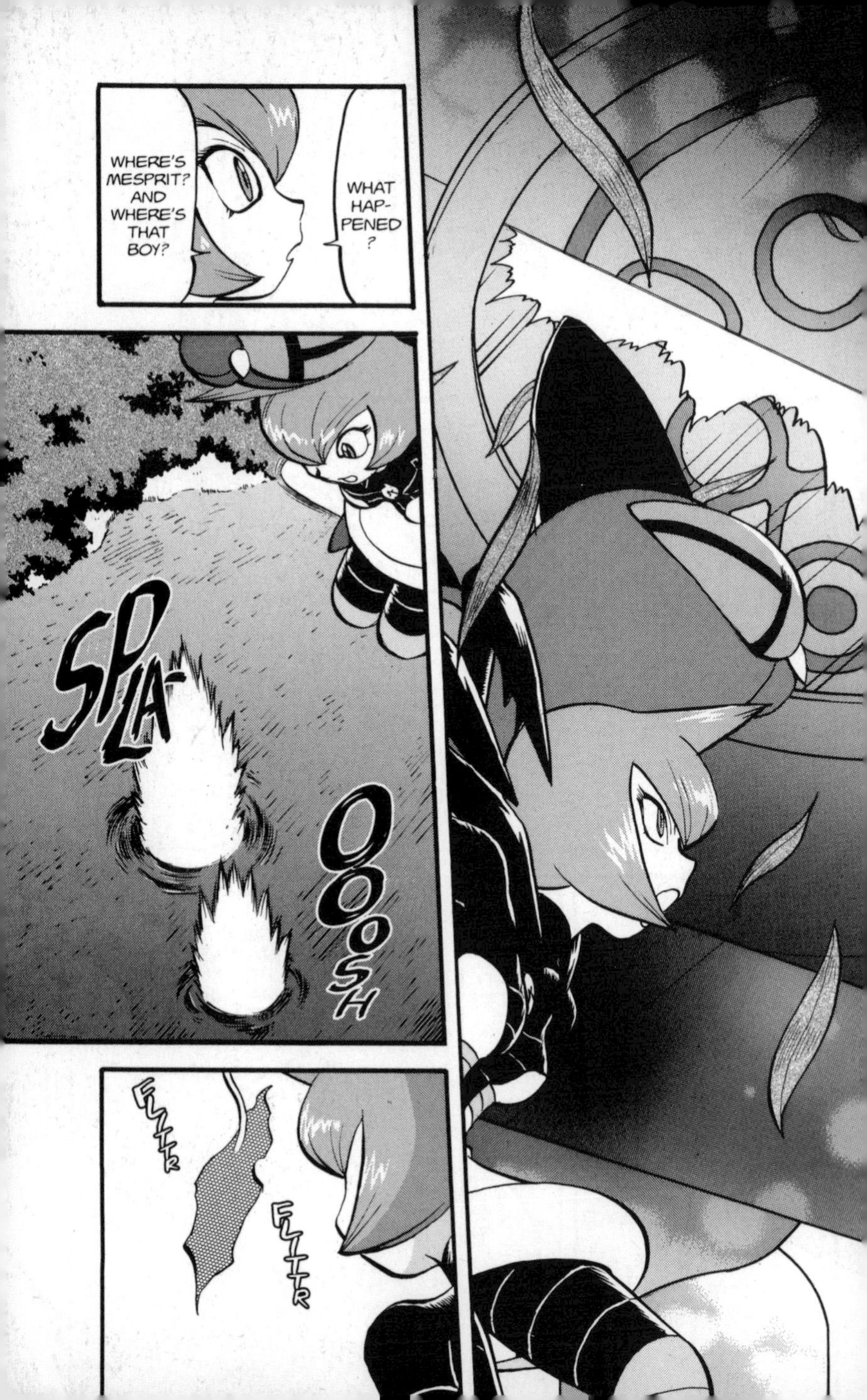
WHAT HAP-PENED?
WHERE'S MESPRIT? AND WHERE'S THAT BOY?
SPLA-
OOOOSH
FLITTR
FLITTR

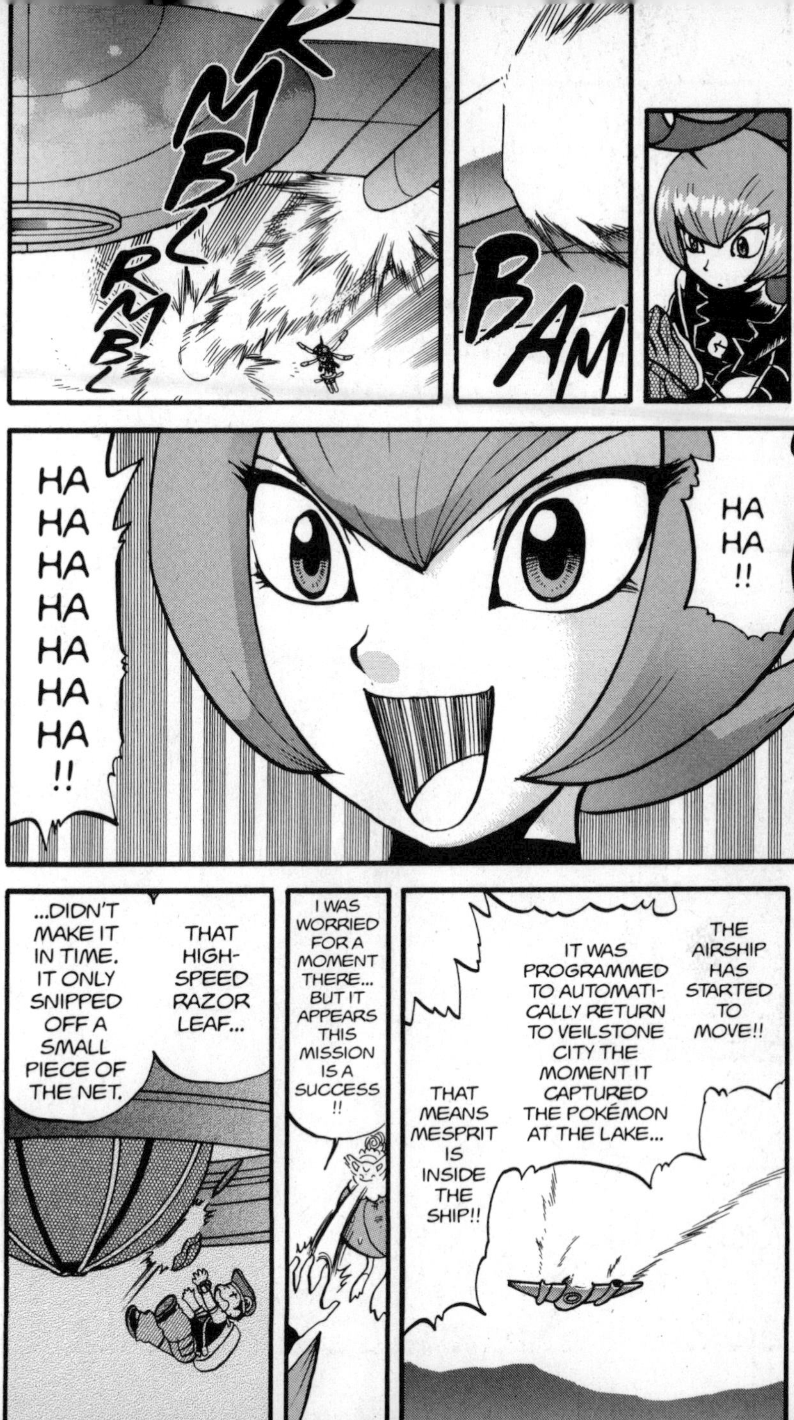
BAM
KMBL
RMBL
HA HA!!
HA HA HA HA HA HA HA!!
THE AIRSHIP HAS STARTED TO MOVE!!
IT WAS PROGRAMMED TO AUTOMATICALLY RETURN TO VEILSTONE CITY THE MOMENT IT CAPTURED THE POKÉMON AT THE LAKE...
THAT MEANS MESPRIT IS INSIDE THE SHIP!!
I WAS WORRIED FOR A MOMENT THERE... BUT IT APPEARS THIS MISSION IS A SUCCESS!!
THAT HIGH-SPEED RAZOR LEAF...
...DIDN'T MAKE IT IN TIME. IT ONLY SNIPPED OFF A SMALL PIECE OF THE NET.

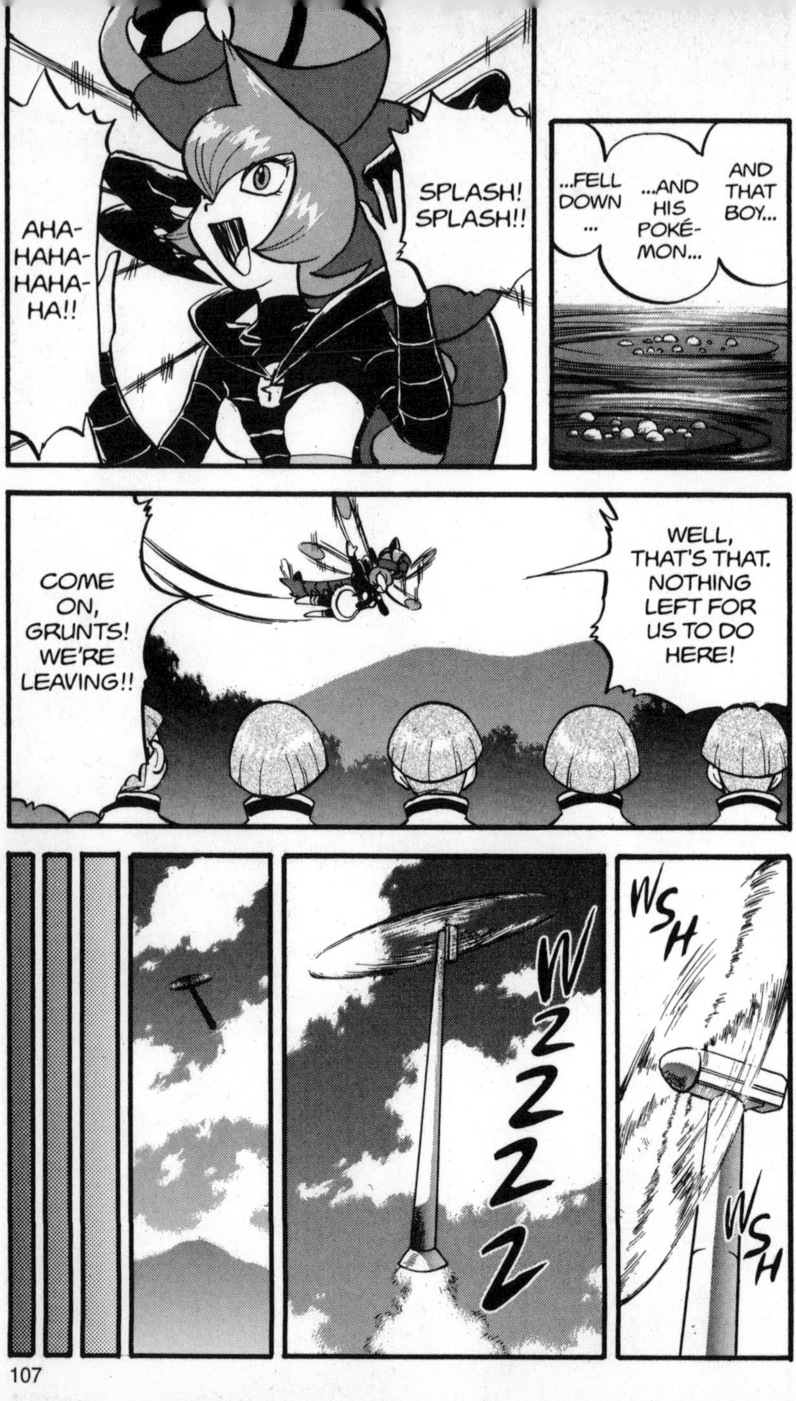
AND THAT BOY...
...AND HIS POKÉMON...
...FELL DOWN ...
SPLASH! SPLASH!!
AHA-HAHA-HAHA-HA!!
WELL, THAT'S THAT. NOTHING LEFT FOR US TO DO HERE!
COME ON, GRUNTS! WE'RE LEAVING!!
WSH
WSH
WZZZZZ

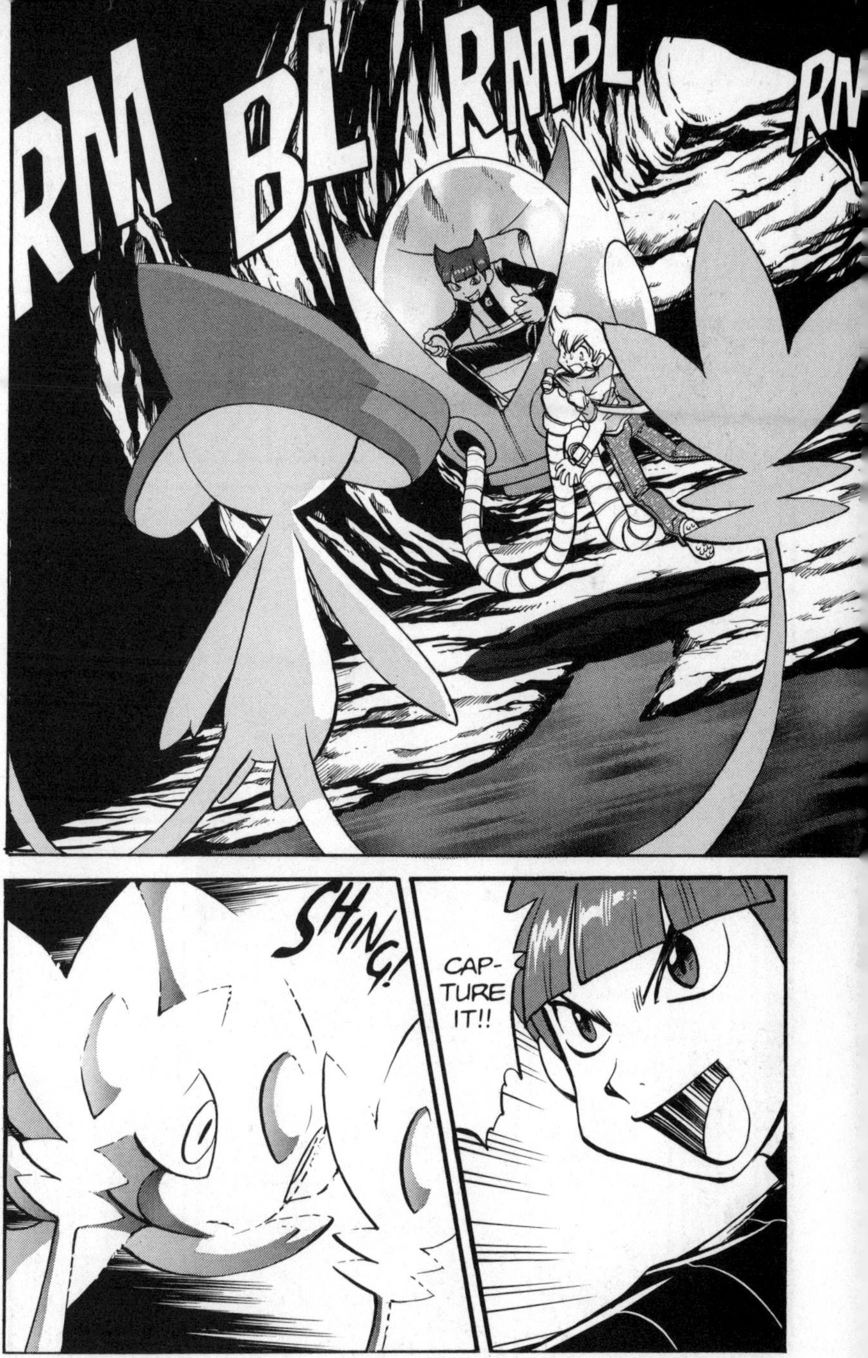
RM BL
RMBL
CAP-TURE IT!!
SHING!

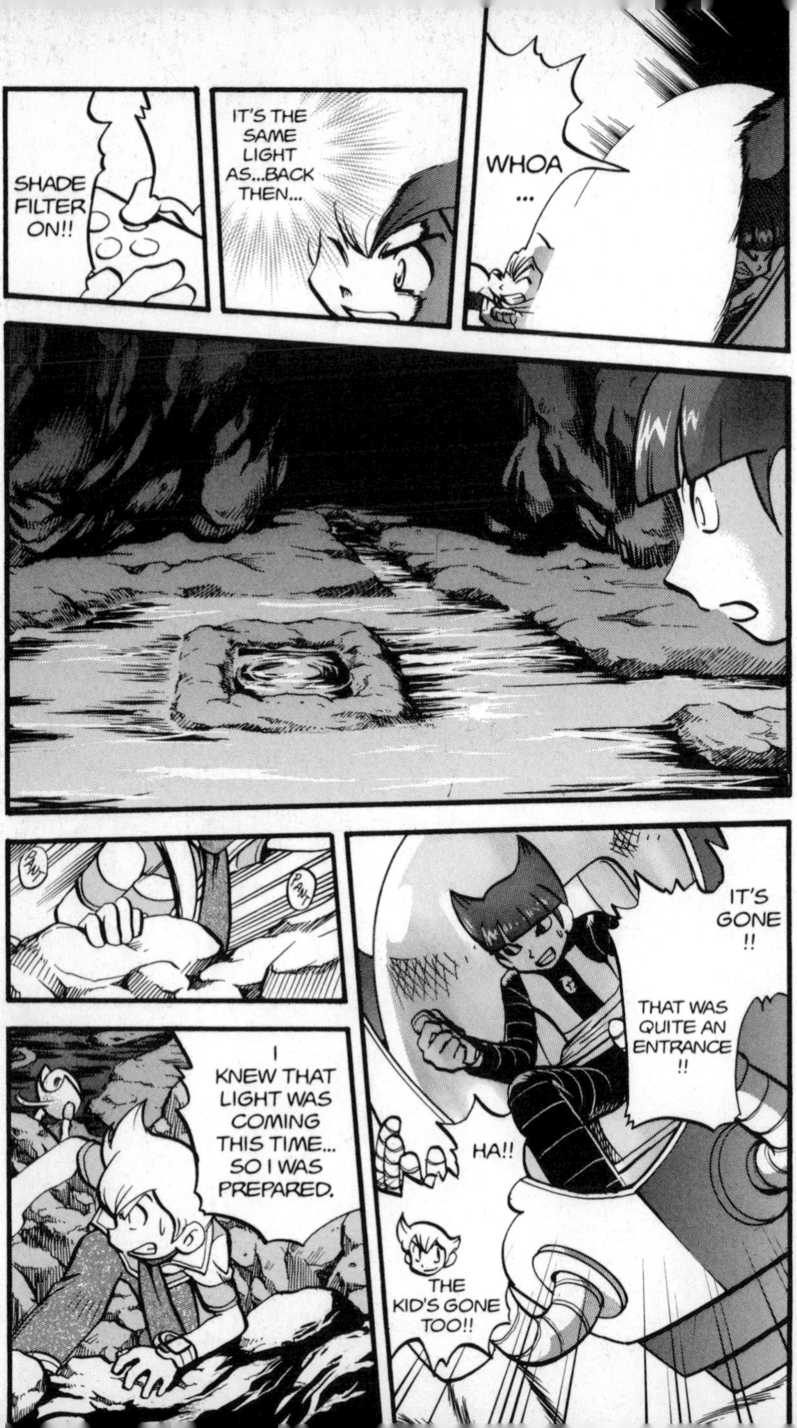
WHOA ...
IT'S THE SAME LIGHT AS...BACK THEN...
SHADE FILTER ON!!
IT'S GONE !!
THAT WAS QUITE AN ENTRANCE !!
HA!!
THE KID'S GONE TOO!!
PANT
PANT
I KNEW THAT LIGHT WAS COMING THIS TIME... SO I WAS PREPARED.

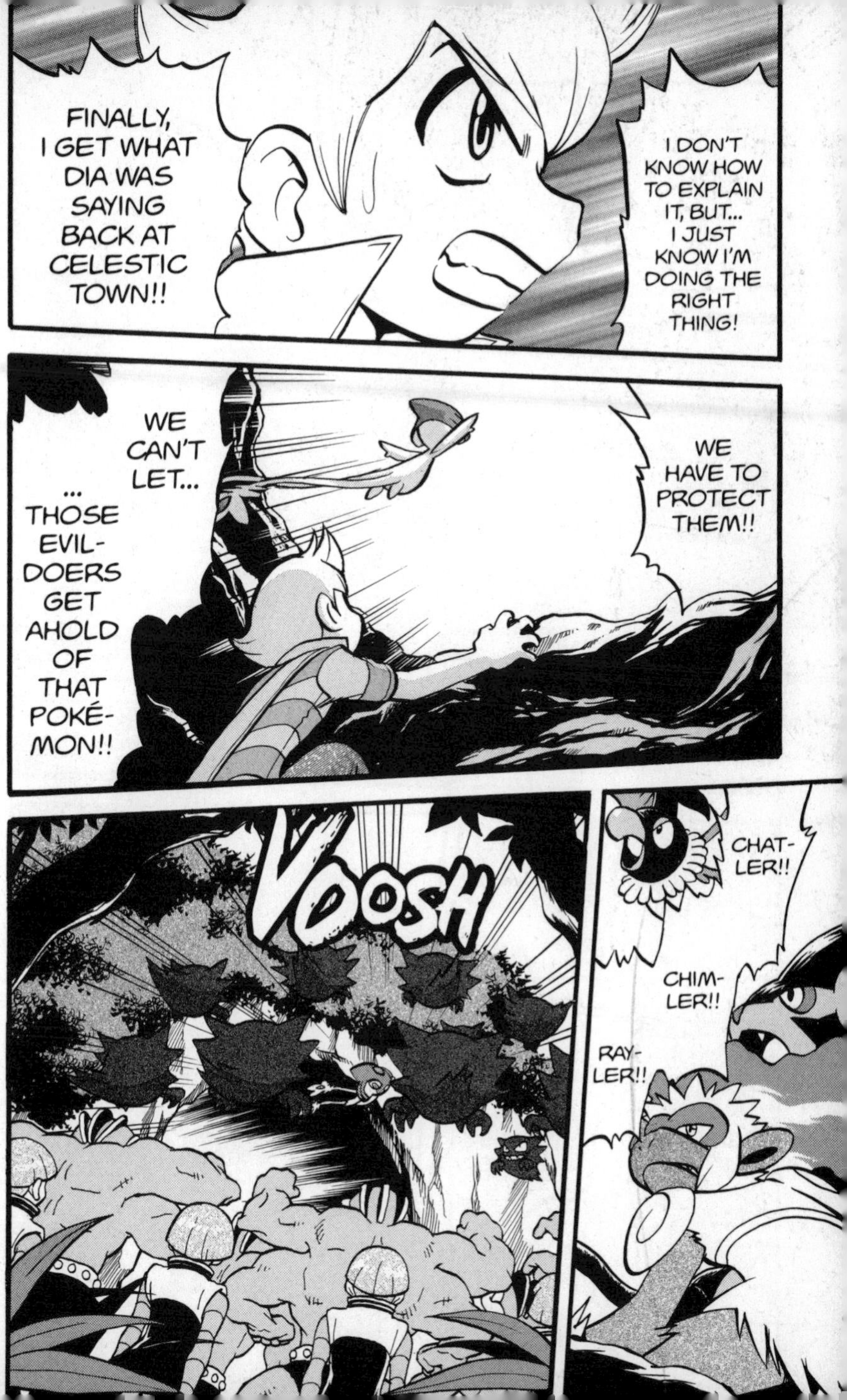
I DON'T KNOW HOW TO EXPLAIN IT, BUT... I JUST KNOW I'M DOING THE RIGHT THING!
FINALLY, I GET WHAT DIA WAS SAYING BACK AT CELESTIC TOWN!!
WE HAVE TO PROTECT THEM!!
WE CAN'T LET...
... THOSE EVIL-DOERS GET AHOLD OF THAT POKÉ-MON!!
CHAT-LER!!
CHIM-LER!!
RAY-LER!!
VOOSH

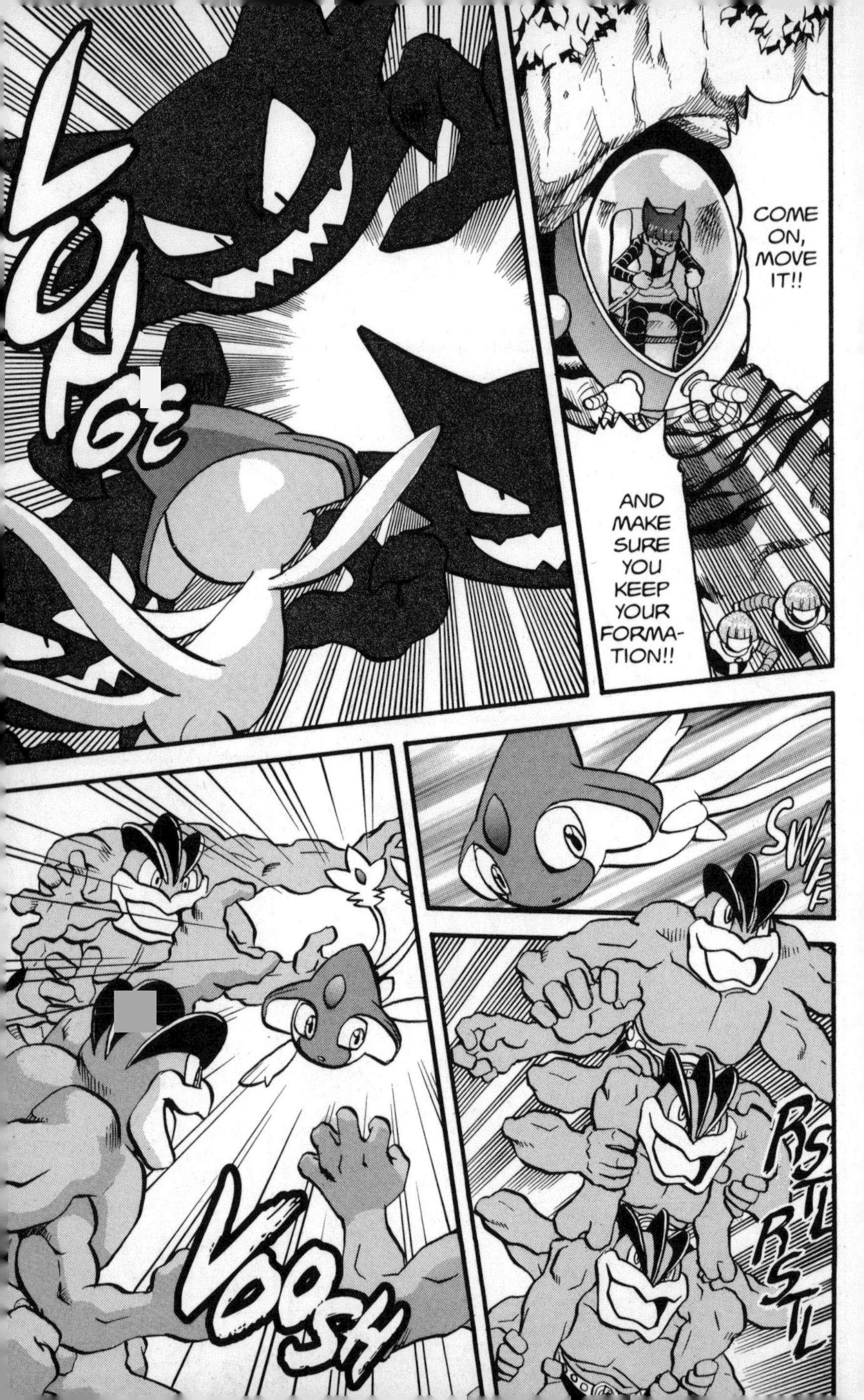
COME ON, MOVE IT!!
AND MAKE SURE YOU KEEP YOUR FORMATION!!
LUNGE
SWFF
RSTL RSTL
VOOSH

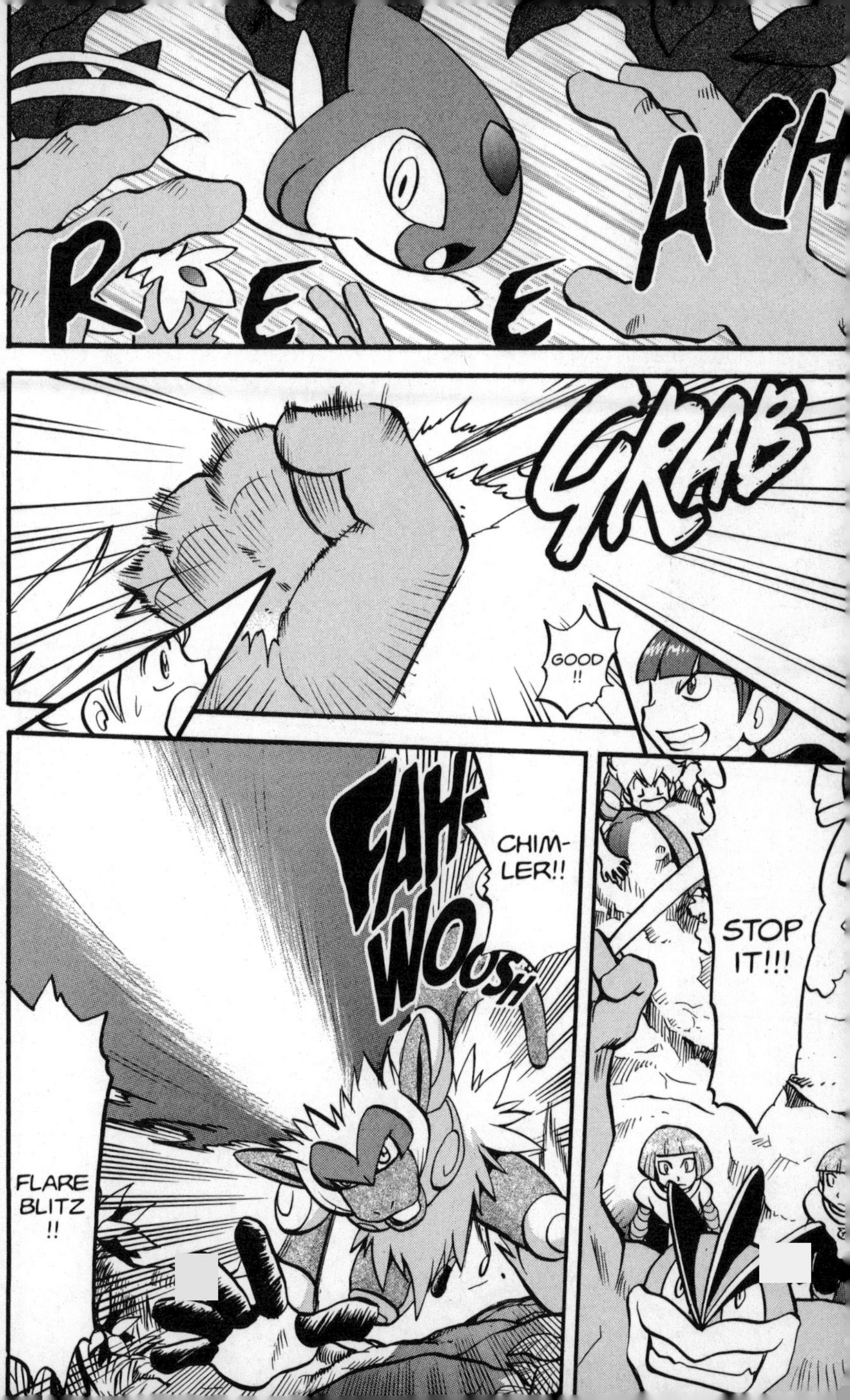
ACH
REE
GRAB
GOOD!!
STOP IT!!!
FAH
CHIM-LER!!
WOOSH
FLARE BLITZ!!

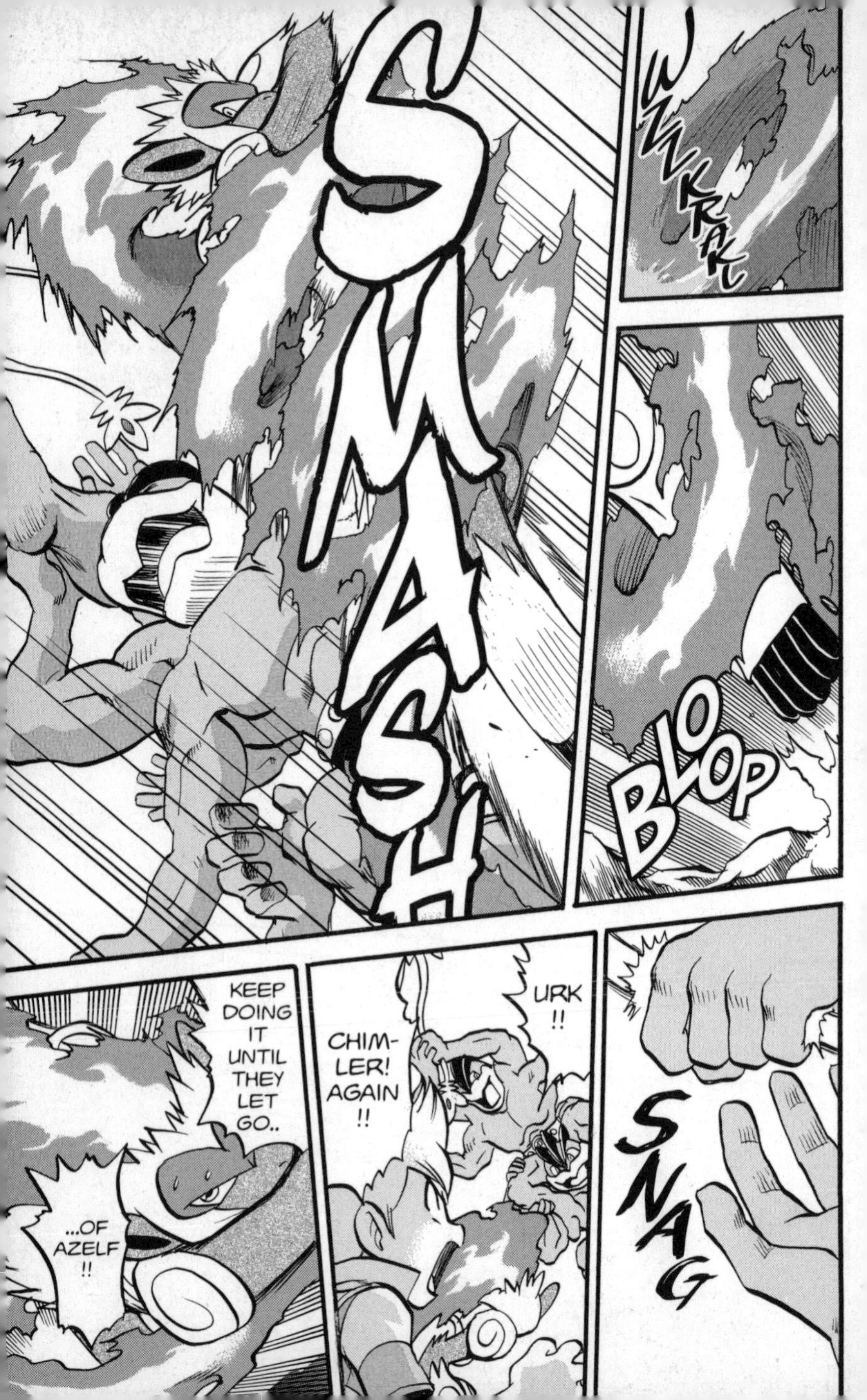
WZZKRAKL
BLOOP
SMASH
SNAG
URK!!
CHIM-LER! AGAIN!!
KEEP DOING IT UNTIL THEY LET GO..
...OF AZELF!!

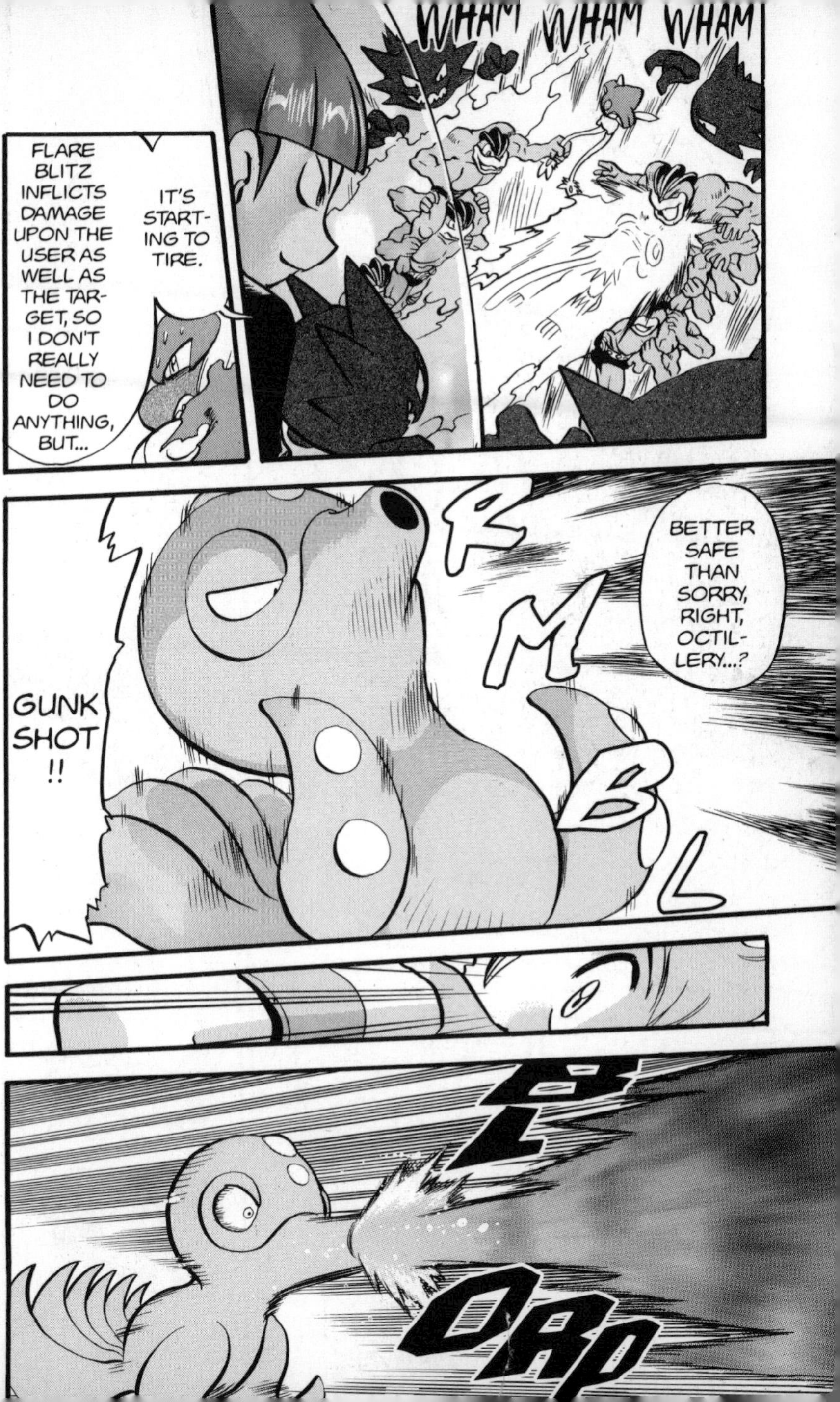
WHAM WHAM WHAM
IT'S START-ING TO TIRE.
FLARE BLITZ INFLICTS DAMAGE UPON THE USER AS WELL AS THE TAR-GET, SO I DON'T REALLY NEED TO DO ANYTHING, BUT...
RMBL
BETTER SAFE THAN SORRY, RIGHT, OCTIL-LERY...?
GUNK SHOT !!
BLORP

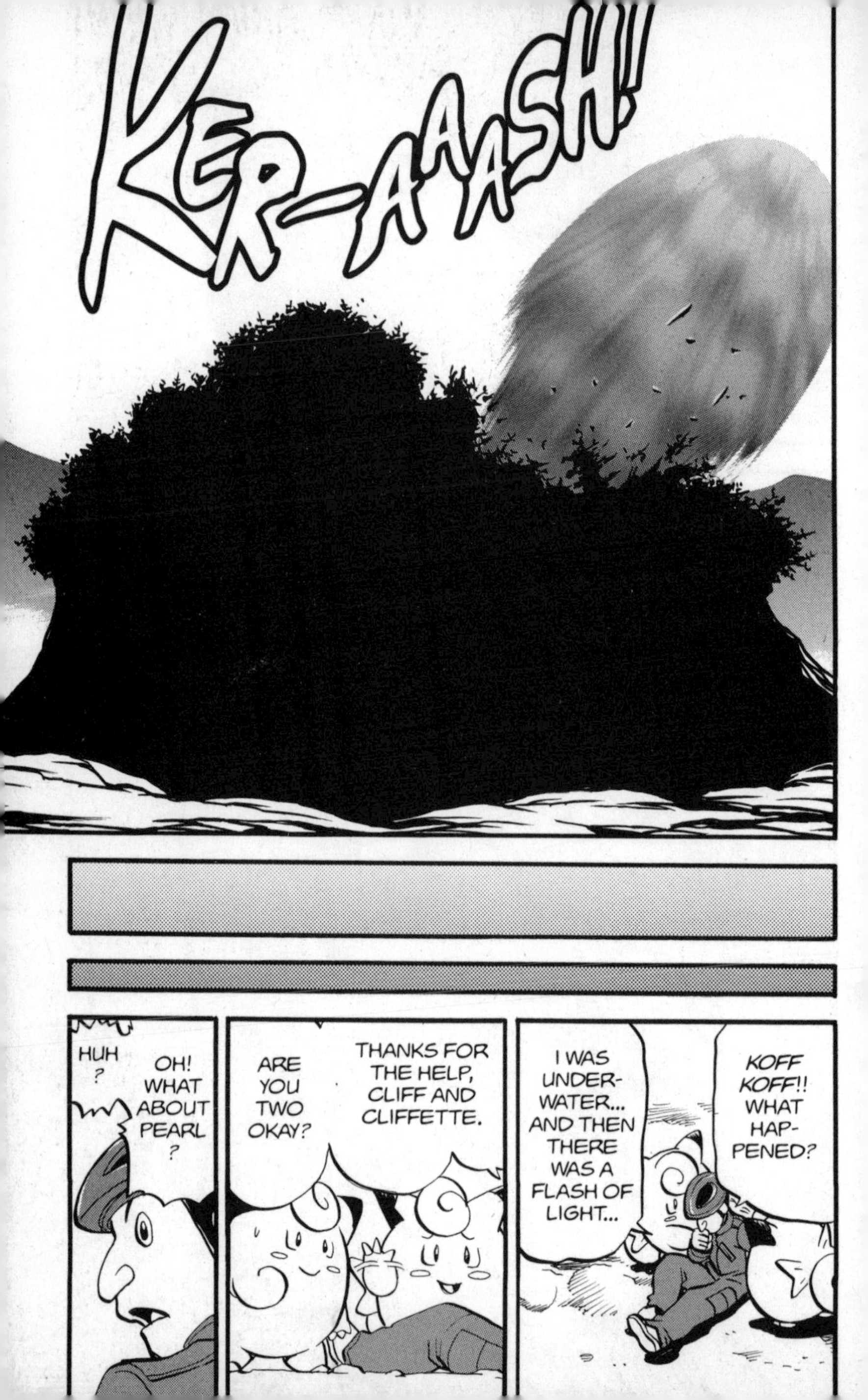
KER-AAASH!!
KOFF KOFF!! WHAT HAP-PENED?
I WAS UNDER-WATER... AND THEN THERE WAS A FLASH OF LIGHT...
THANKS FOR THE HELP, CLIFF AND CLIFFETTE.
ARE YOU TWO OKAY?
OH! WHAT ABOUT PEARL?
HUH?

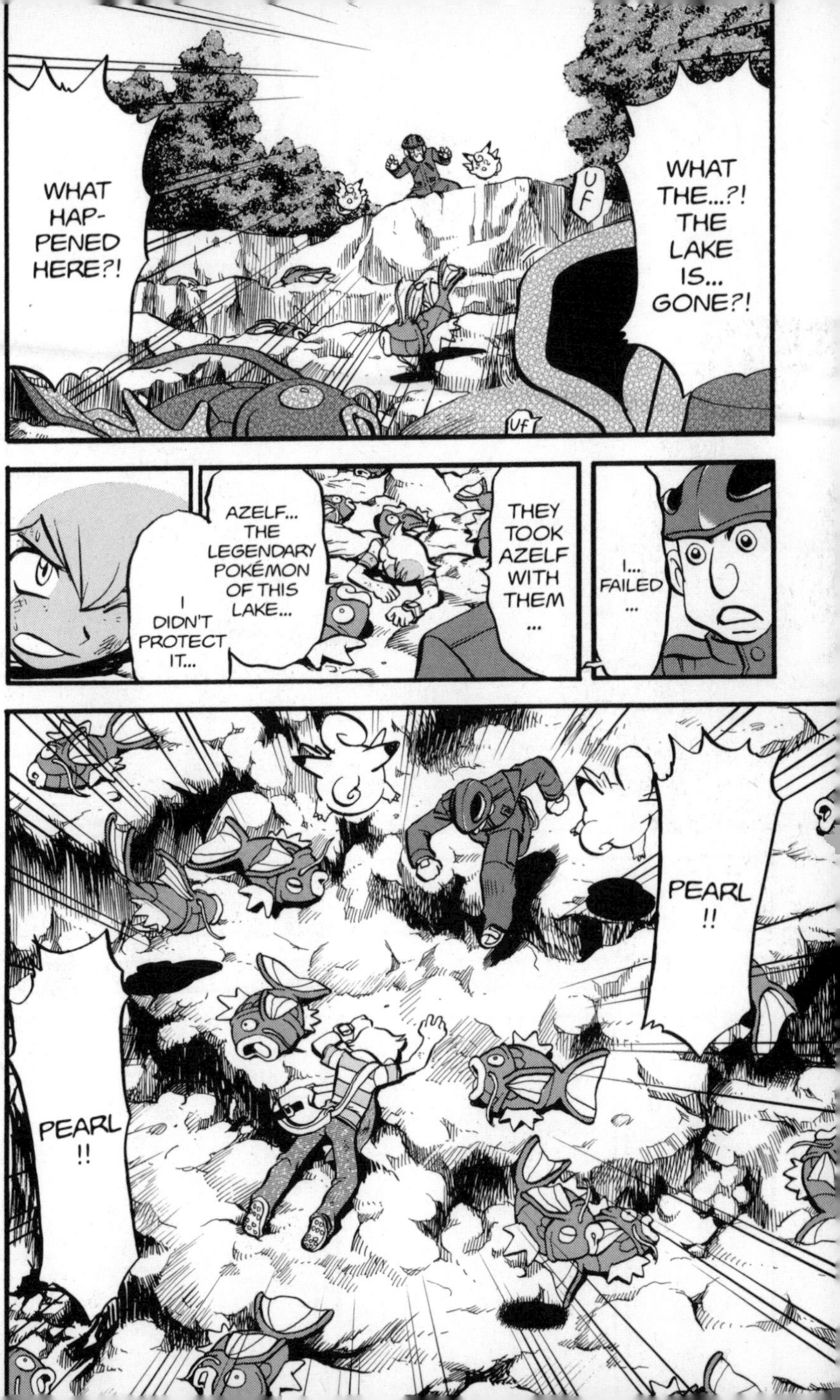
WHAT THE...?! THE LAKE IS... GONE?!
UF
WHAT HAP-PENED HERE?!
UF
I... FAILED ...
THEY TOOK AZELF WITH THEM ...
AZELF... THE LEGENDARY POKÉMON OF THIS LAKE...
I DIDN'T PROTECT IT...
PEARL !!
PEARL !!

63

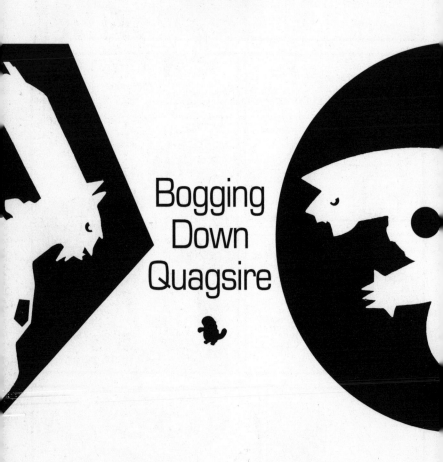

Bogging
Down
Quagsire

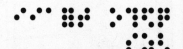

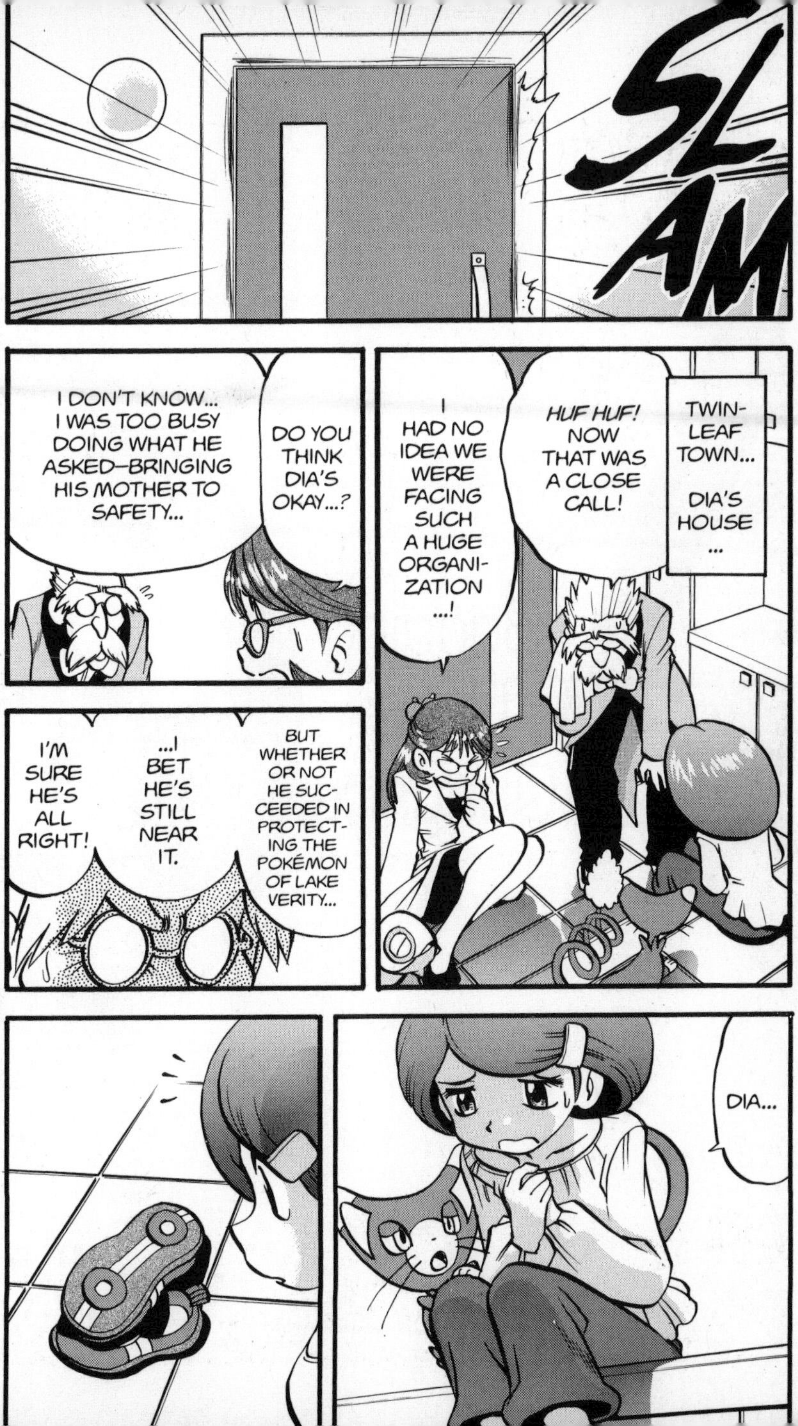
SLAM
TWINLEAF TOWN... DIA'S HOUSE...
HUF HUF! NOW THAT WAS A CLOSE CALL!
I HAD NO IDEA WE WERE FACING SUCH A HUGE ORGANIZATION...!
DO YOU THINK DIA'S OKAY...?
I DON'T KNOW... I WAS TOO BUSY DOING WHAT HE ASKED—BRINGING HIS MOTHER TO SAFETY...
BUT WHETHER OR NOT HE SUCCEEDED IN PROTECTING THE POKÉMON OF LAKE VERITY...
...I BET HE'S STILL NEAR IT.
I'M SURE HE'S ALL RIGHT!
DIA...

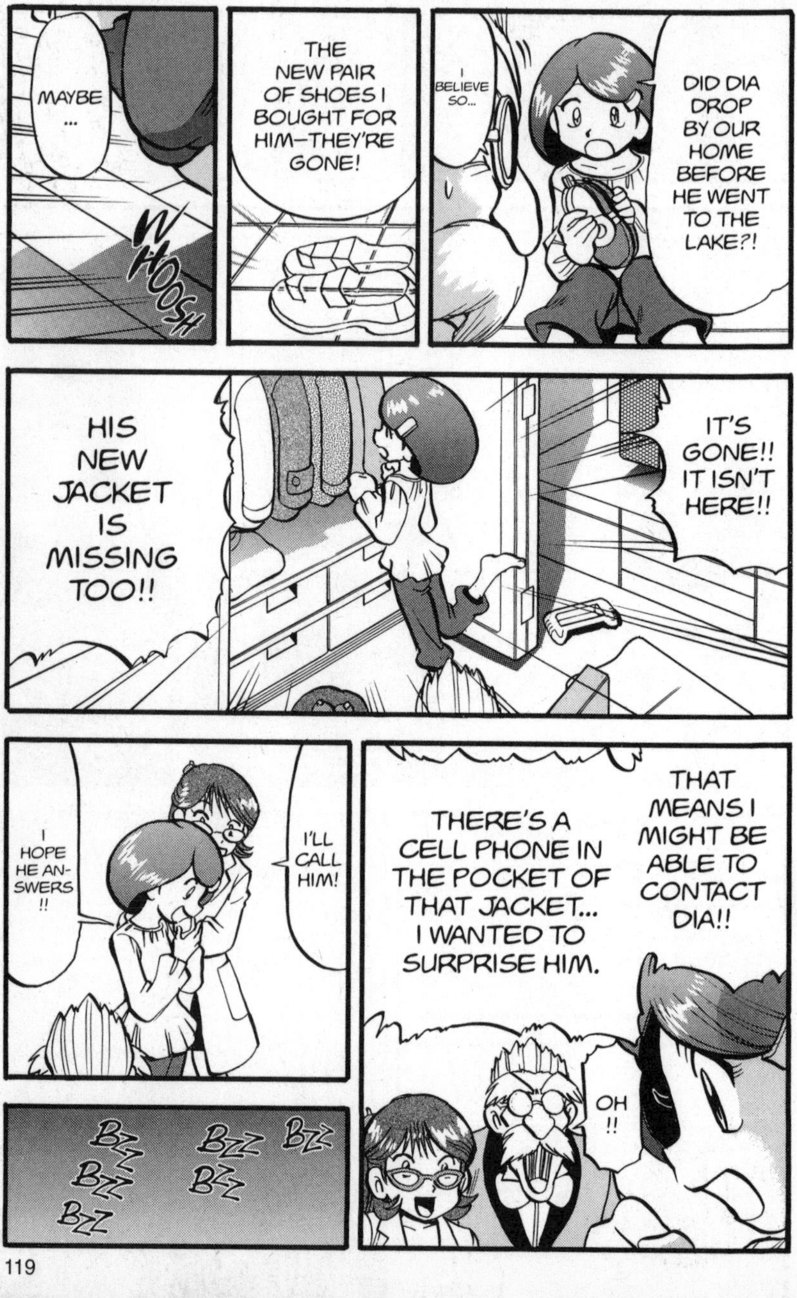
DID DIA DROP BY OUR HOME BEFORE HE WENT TO THE LAKE?!
I BELIEVE SO...
THE NEW PAIR OF SHOES I BOUGHT FOR HIM—THEY'RE GONE!
MAYBE ...
WHOOSH
IT'S GONE!! IT ISN'T HERE!!
HIS NEW JACKET IS MISSING TOO!!
THAT MEANS I MIGHT BE ABLE TO CONTACT DIA!!
THERE'S A CELL PHONE IN THE POCKET OF THAT JACKET... I WANTED TO SURPRISE HIM.
OH !!
I'LL CALL HIM!
I HOPE HE AN-SWERS !!
BZZ BZZ BZZ BZZ BZZ BZZ

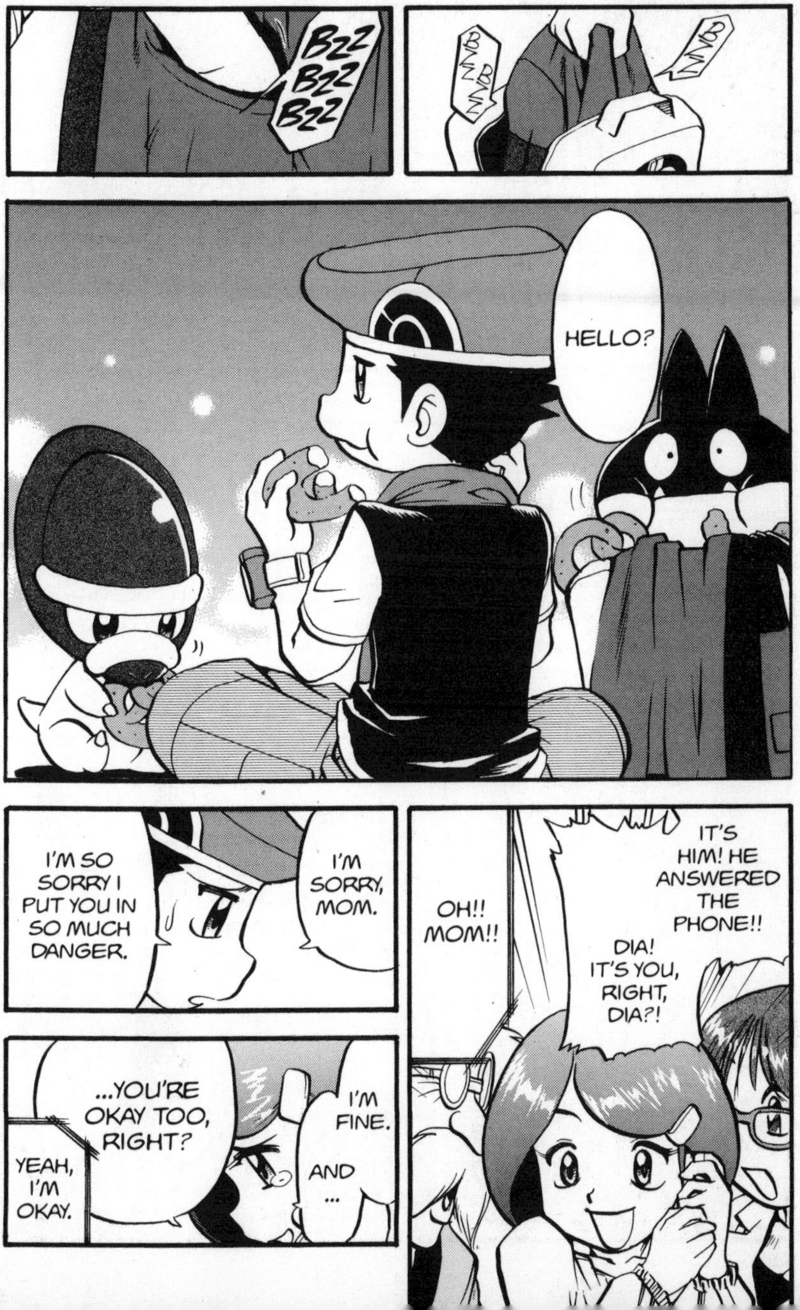
BZZ
BZZ
BZZ BZZ BZZ
HELLO?
IT'S HIM! HE ANSWERED THE PHONE!!
OH!! MOM!!
DIA! IT'S YOU, RIGHT, DIA?!
I'M SORRY, MOM.
I'M SO SORRY I PUT YOU IN SO MUCH DANGER.
I'M FINE.
AND ...
...YOU'RE OKAY TOO, RIGHT?
YEAH, I'M OKAY.

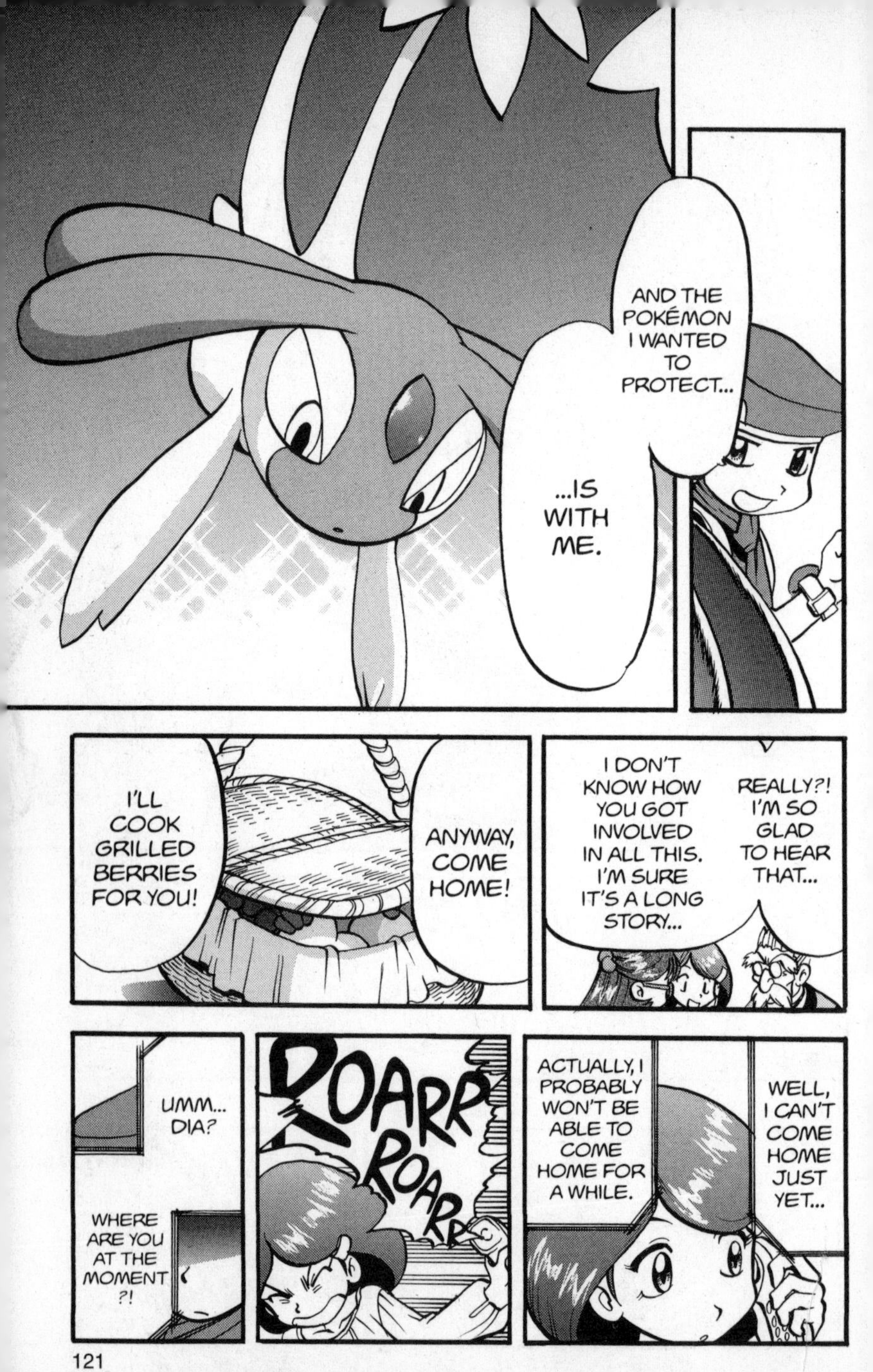
AND THE POKÉMON I WANTED TO PROTECT...
...IS WITH ME.
REALLY?! I'M SO GLAD TO HEAR THAT...
I DON'T KNOW HOW YOU GOT INVOLVED IN ALL THIS. I'M SURE IT'S A LONG STORY...
ANYWAY, COME HOME!
I'LL COOK GRILLED BERRIES FOR YOU!
WELL, I CAN'T COME HOME JUST YET...
ACTUALLY, I PROBABLY WON'T BE ABLE TO COME HOME FOR A WHILE.
ROARR
ROARR
UMM... DIA?
WHERE ARE YOU AT THE MOMENT?!

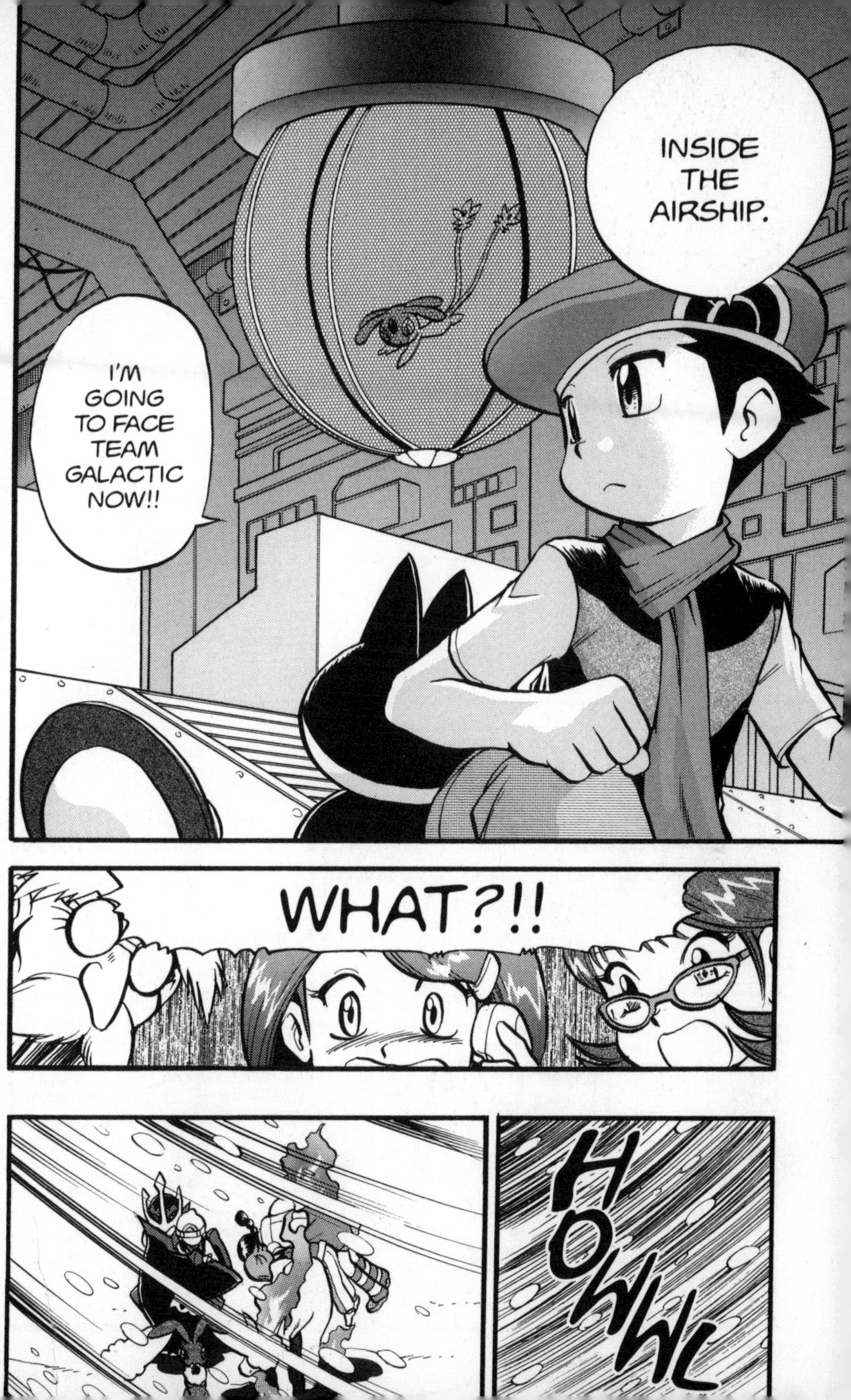
INSIDE THE AIRSHIP.
I'M GOING TO FACE TEAM GALACTIC NOW!!
WHAT?!!
HOWWL

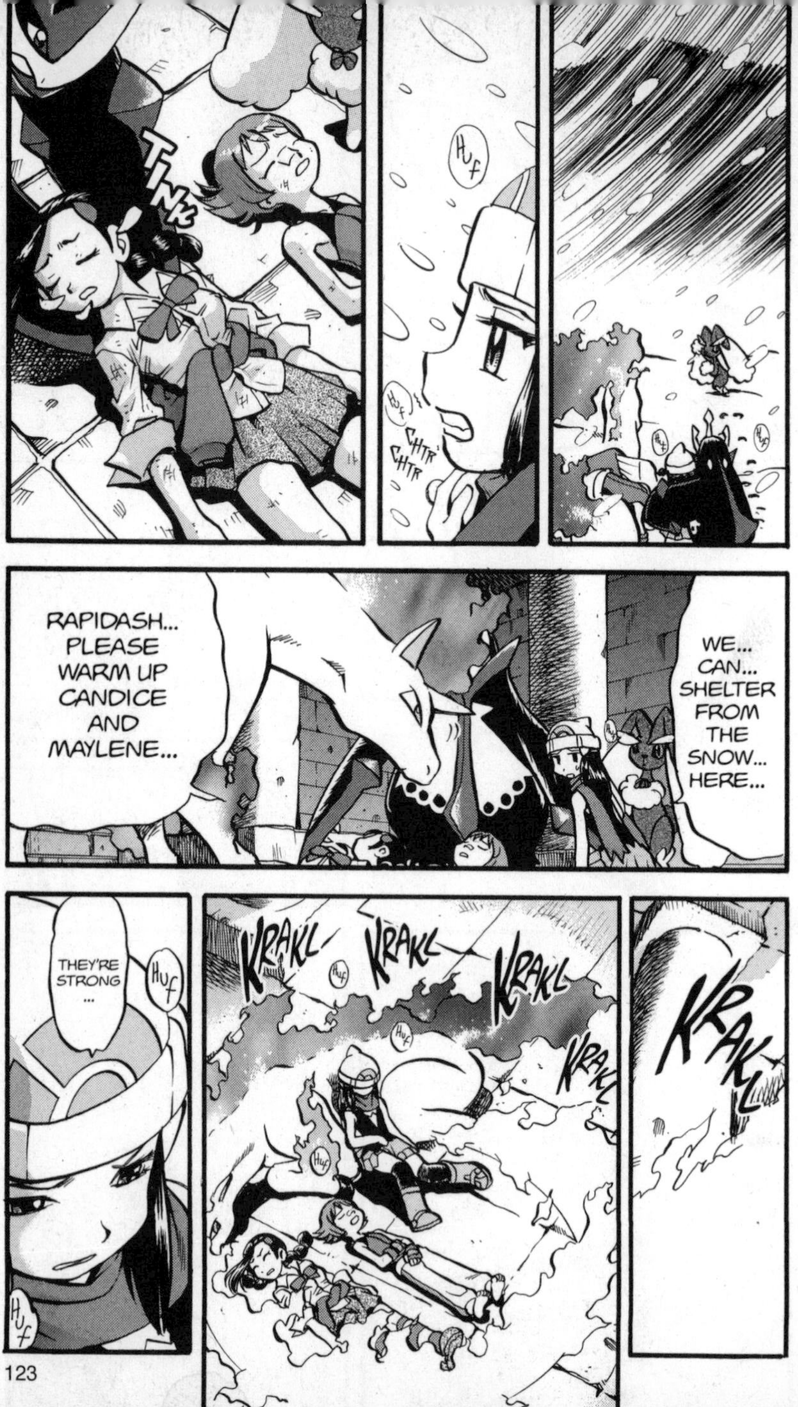
HUF
HUF
HUF
HUF
CHTR CHTR
TINK
WE... CAN... SHELTER FROM THE SNOW... HERE...
RAPIDASH... PLEASE WARM UP CANDICE AND MAYLENE...
KRAKL
KRAKL
HUF
KRAKL
HUF
KRAKL
HUF
KRAKL
THEY'RE STRONG ...
HUF
HUF

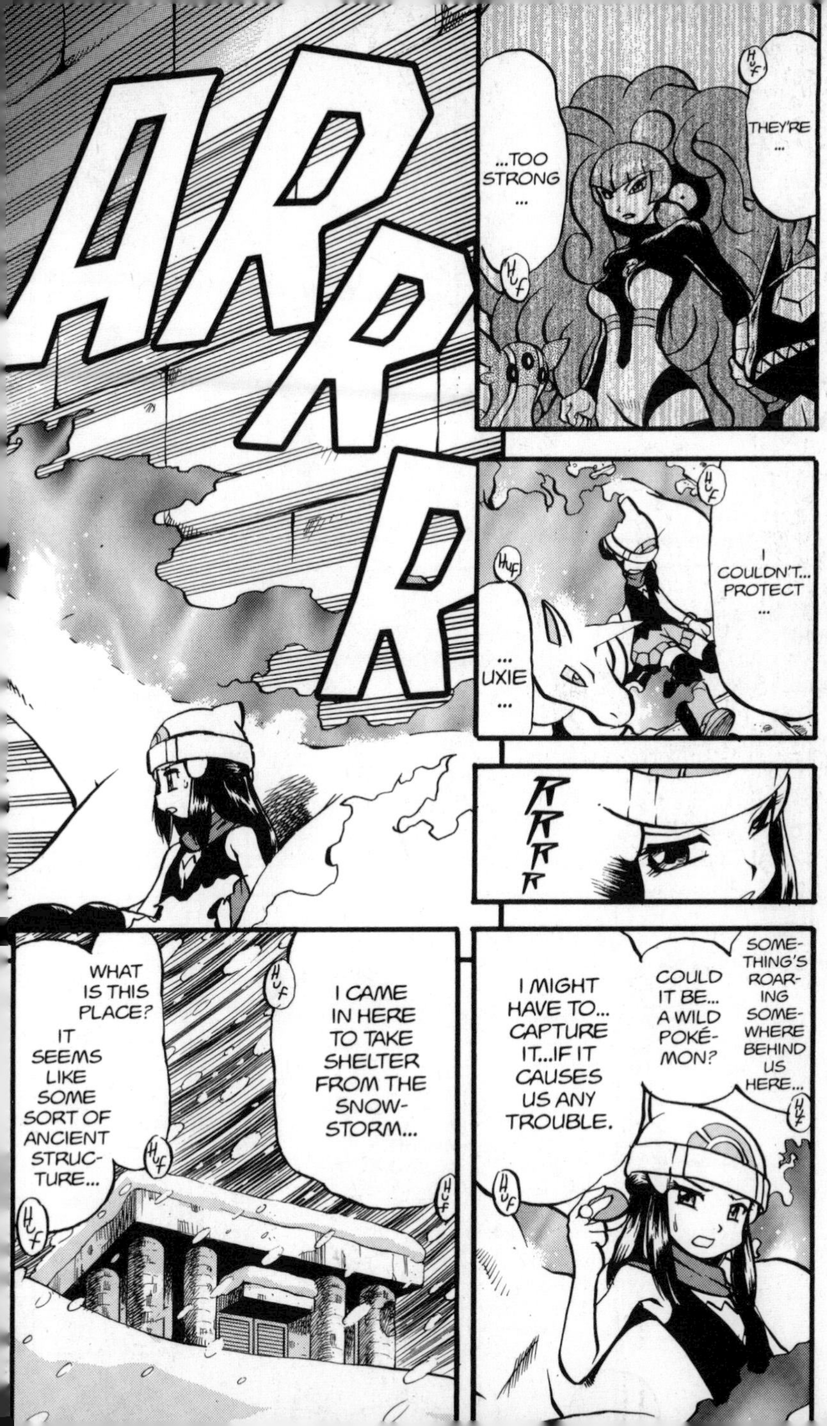
HUF
THEY'RE...
...TOO STRONG...
HUF
HUF
I COULDN'T... PROTECT...
HUF
...UXIE...
RRRR
ARRR
SOME-THING'S ROAR-ING SOME-WHERE BEHIND US HERE...
COULD IT BE... A WILD POKÉ-MON?
I MIGHT HAVE TO... CAPTURE IT...IF IT CAUSES US ANY TROUBLE.
HUF
HUF
I CAME IN HERE TO TAKE SHELTER FROM THE SNOW-STORM...
HUF
WHAT IS THIS PLACE?
IT SEEMS LIKE SOME SORT OF ANCIENT STRUC-TURE...
HUF
HUF

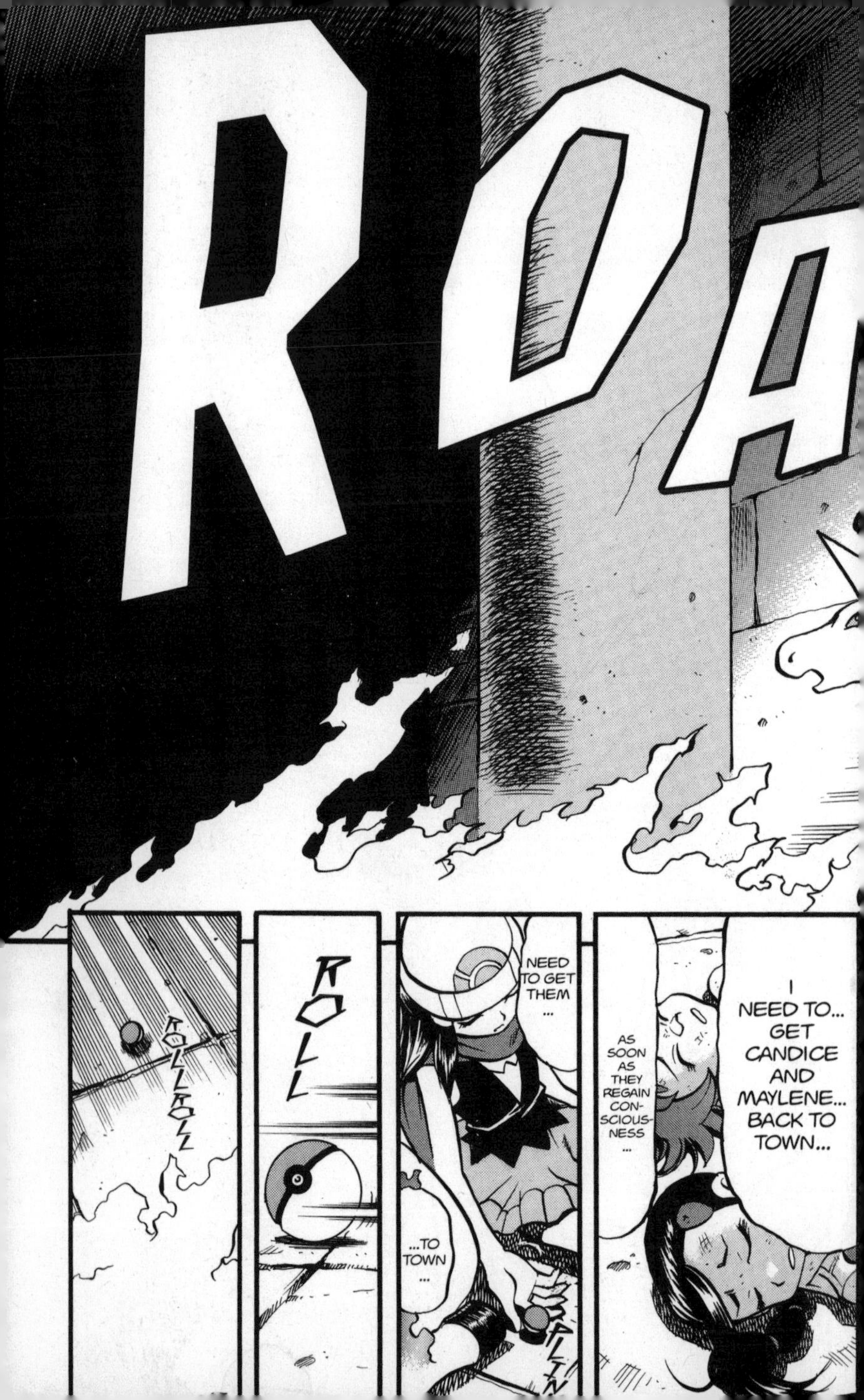
ROA
I NEED TO... GET CANDICE AND MAYLENE... BACK TO TOWN...
AS SOON AS THEY REGAIN CONSCIOUSNESS ...
NEED TO GET THEM ...
...TO TOWN ...
ROLL
ROLLROLL

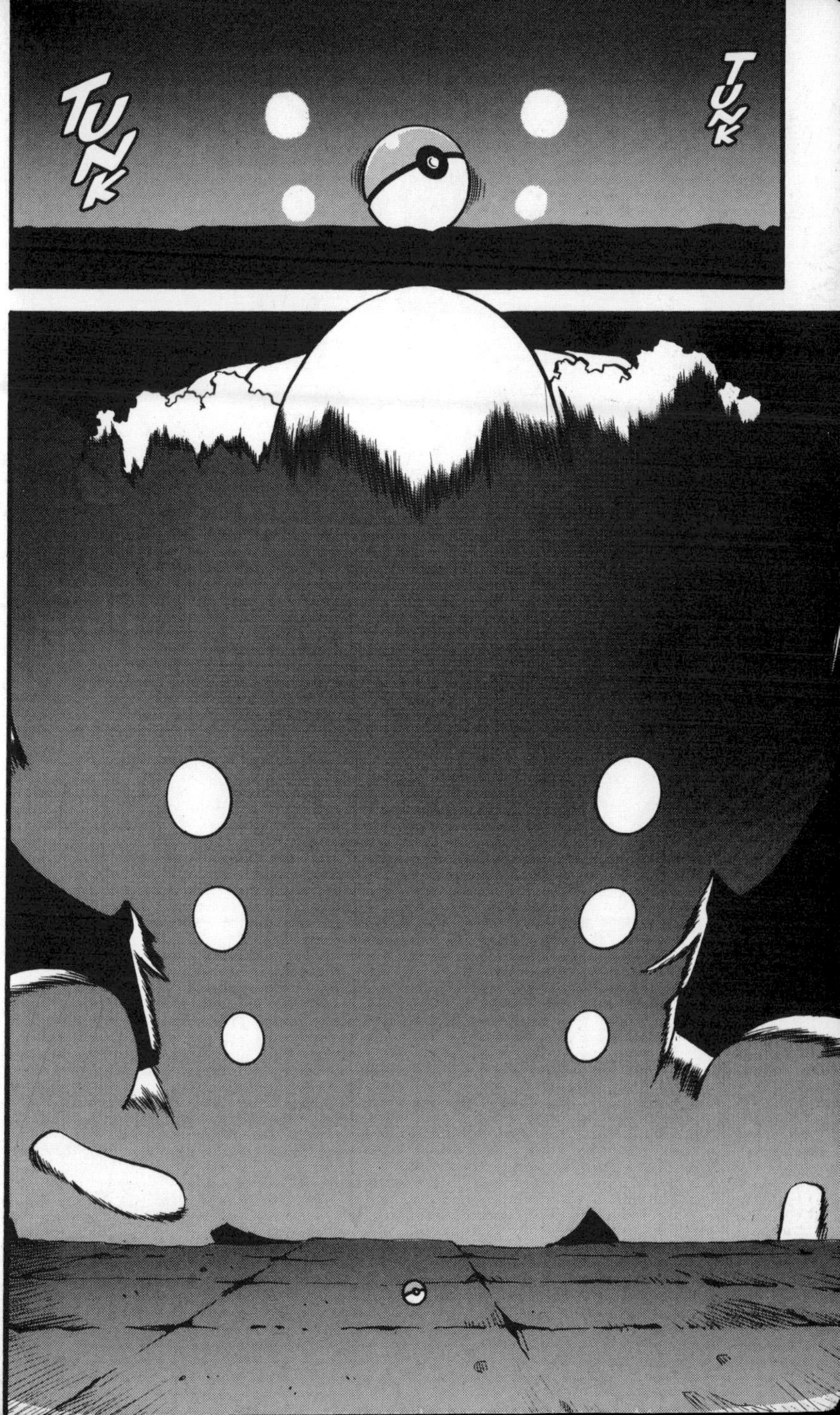
TUNK
TUNK

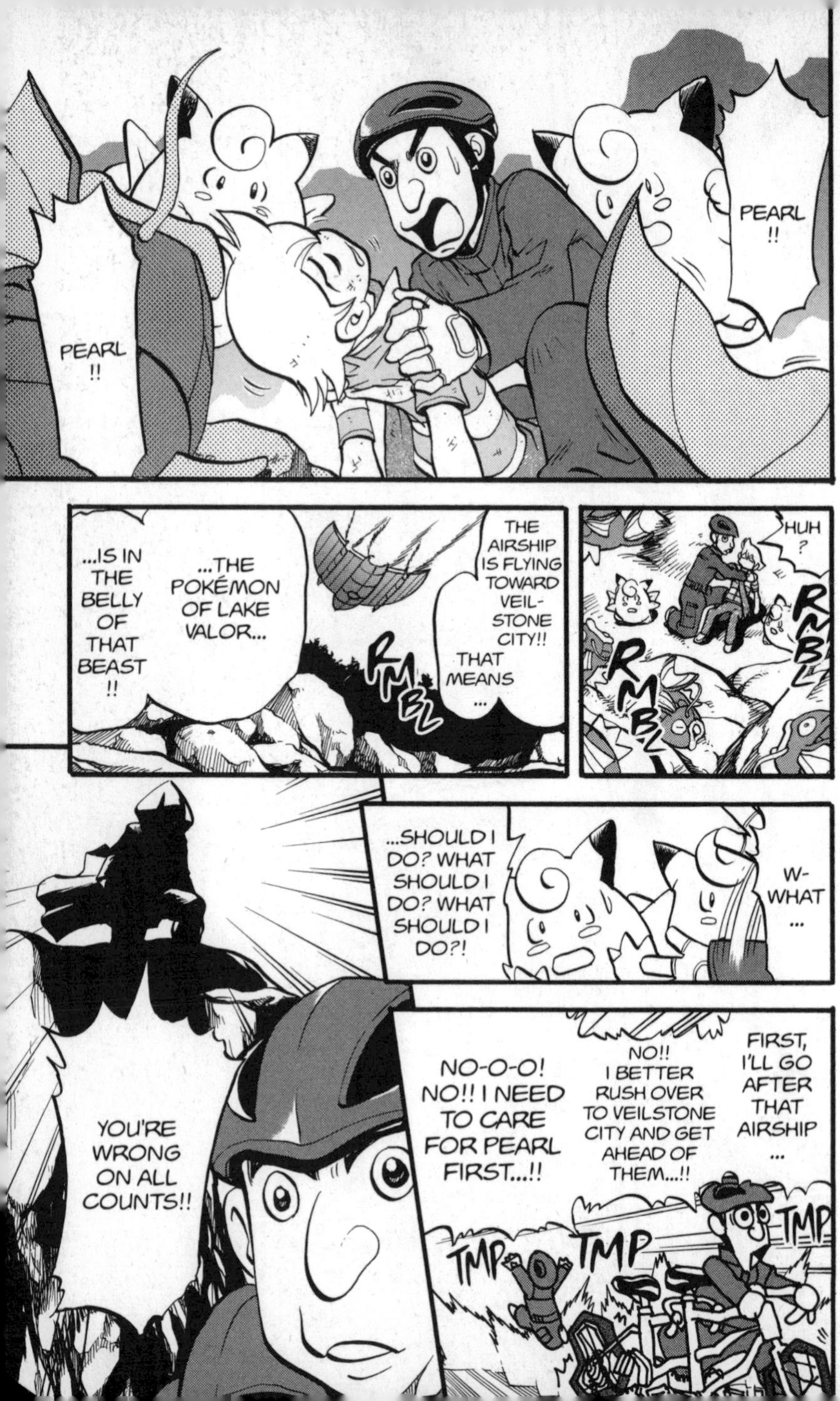
PEARL !!
PEARL !!
HUH ?
RMBL
RMBL
THE AIRSHIP IS FLYING TOWARD VEIL-STONE CITY!!
THAT MEANS ...
...THE POKÉMON OF LAKE VALOR...
...IS IN THE BELLY OF THAT BEAST !!
RMBL
W-WHAT ...
...SHOULD I DO? WHAT SHOULD I DO? WHAT SHOULD I DO?!
FIRST, I'LL GO AFTER THAT AIRSHIP ...
NO!! I BETTER RUSH OVER TO VEILSTONE CITY AND GET AHEAD OF THEM...!!
NO-O-O! NO!! I NEED TO CARE FOR PEARL FIRST...!!
TMP
TMP
TMP
YOU'RE WRONG ON ALL COUNTS!!

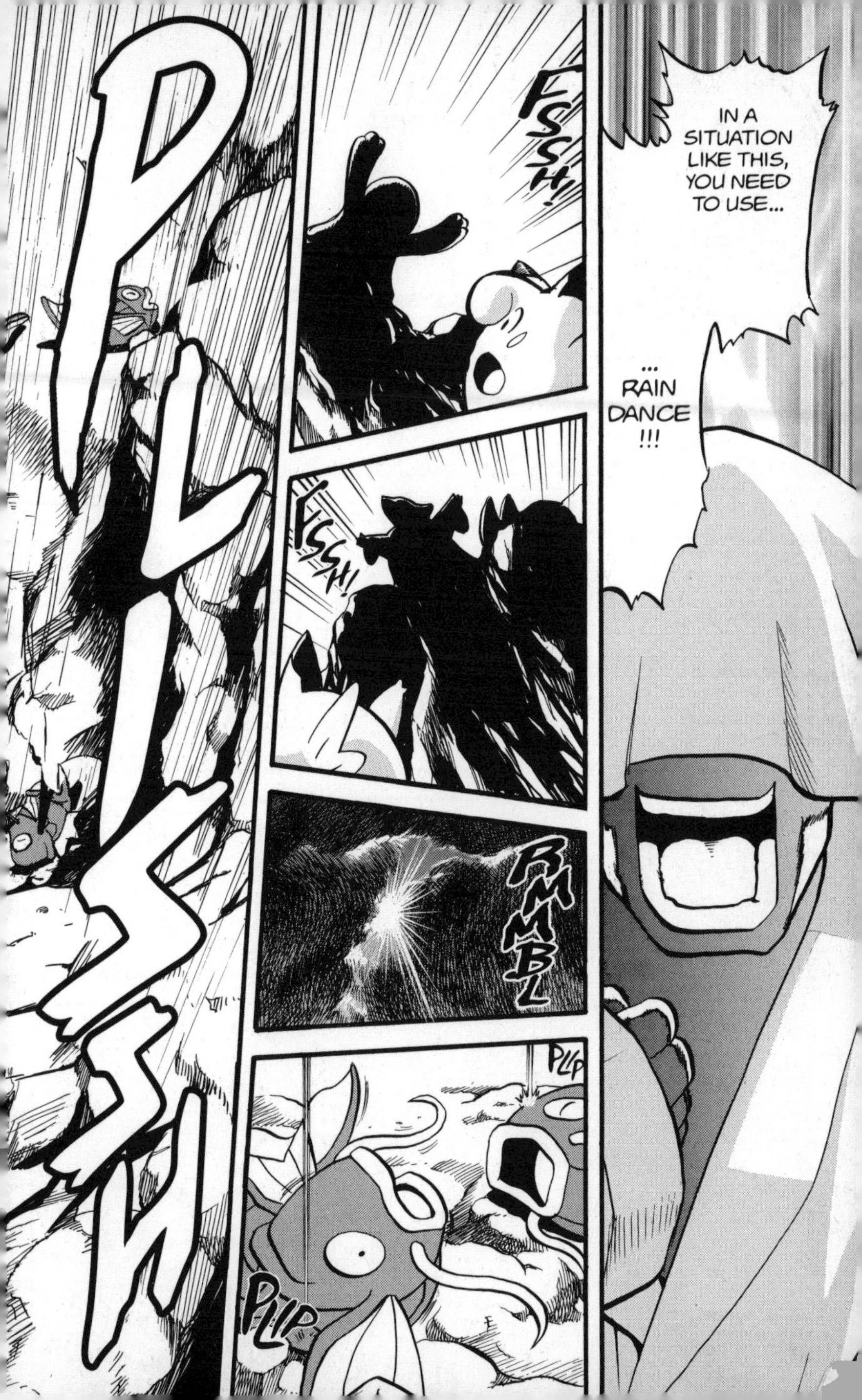
IN A SITUATION LIKE THIS, YOU NEED TO USE...
...RAIN DANCE!!!
FSSH!
FSSH!
RMMBL
PLIP
PLIP
PLISSH

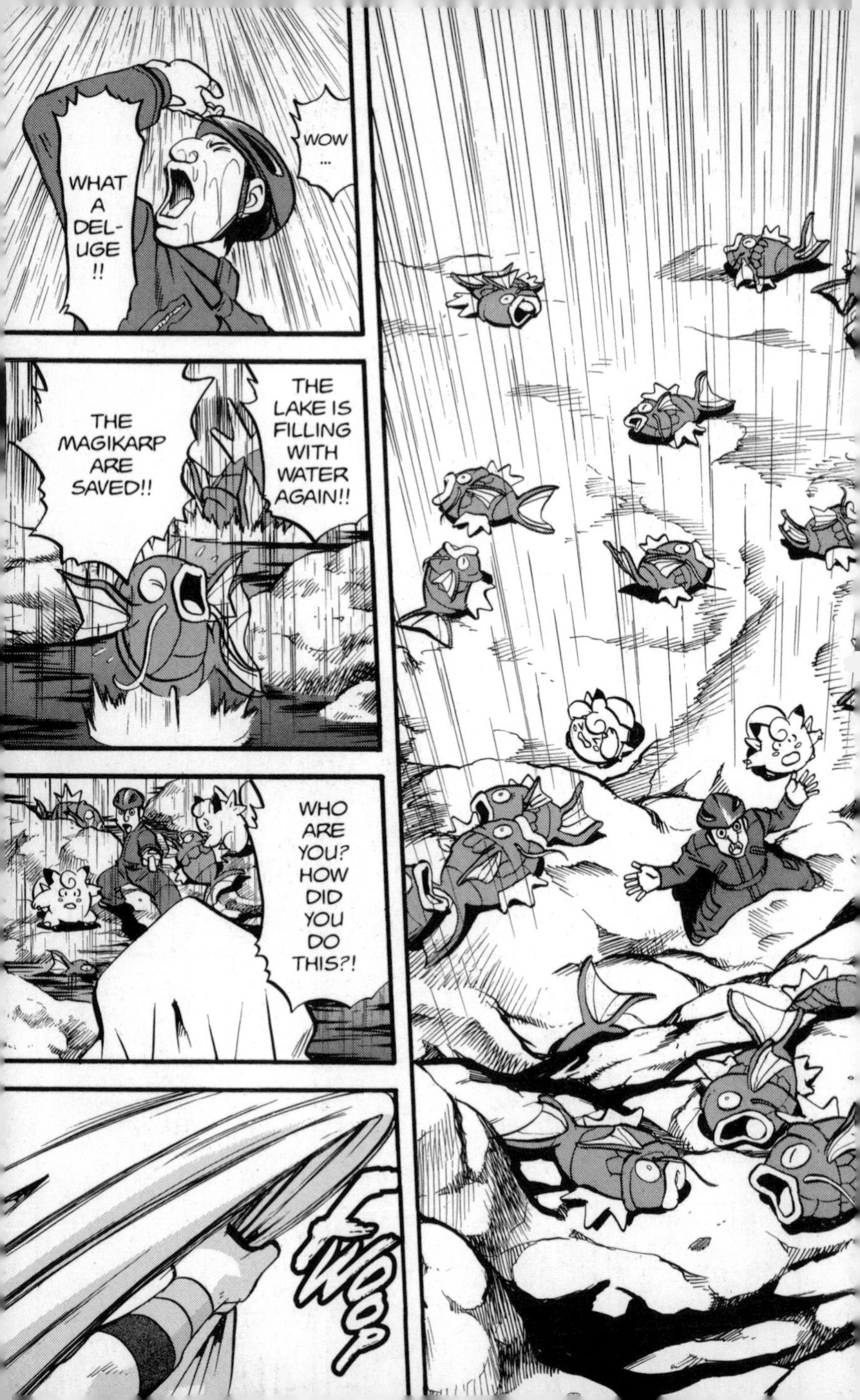
WOW ...
WHAT A DEL-UGE !!
THE LAKE IS FILLING WITH WATER AGAIN!!
THE MAGIKARP ARE SAVED!!
WHO ARE YOU? HOW DID YOU DO THIS?!
WHOOP

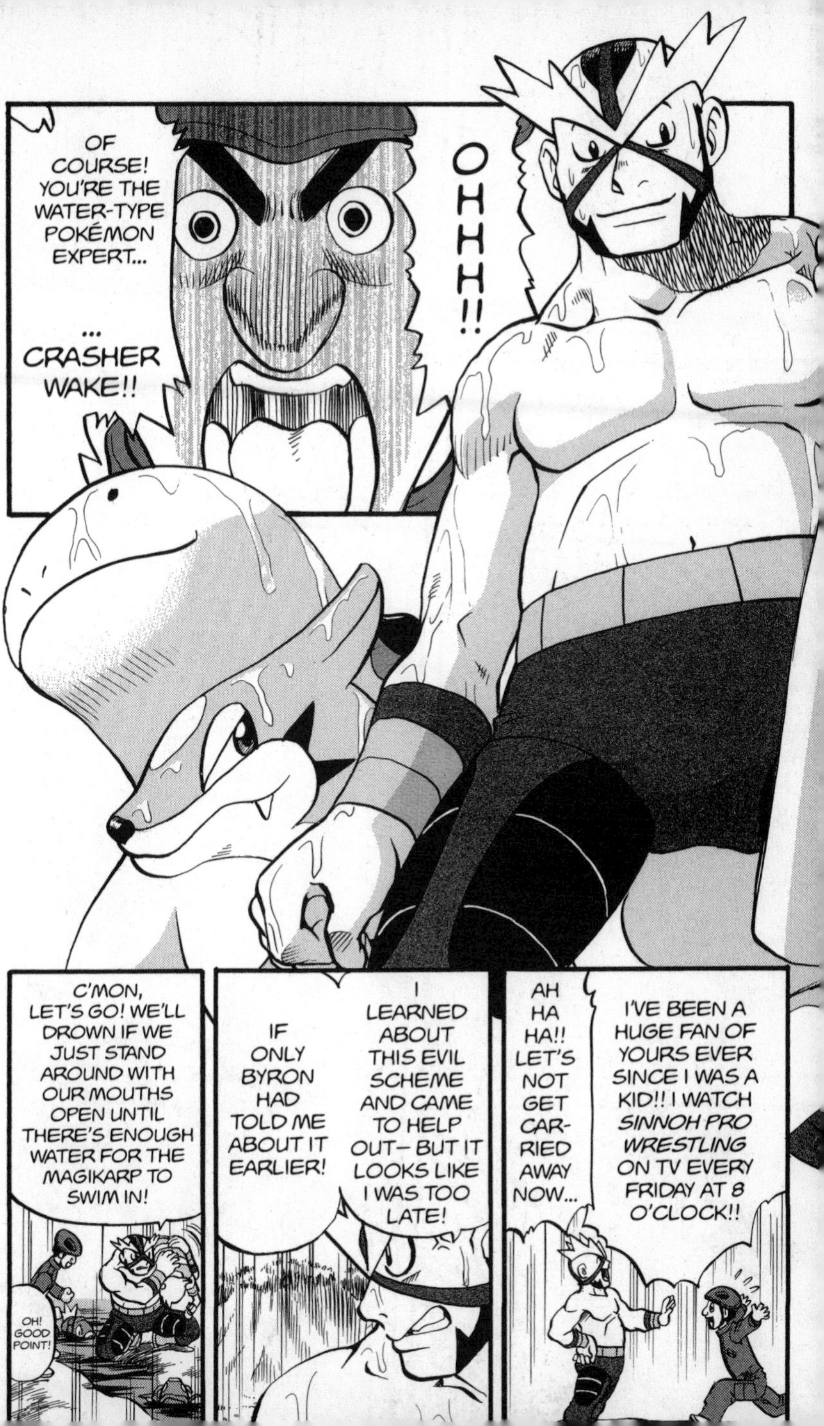
OHHHH!!
OF COURSE! YOU'RE THE WATER-TYPE POKÉMON EXPERT...
... CRASHER WAKE!!
I'VE BEEN A HUGE FAN OF YOURS EVER SINCE I WAS A KID!! I WATCH *SINNOH PRO WRESTLING* ON TV EVERY FRIDAY AT 8 O'CLOCK!!
AH HA HA!! LET'S NOT GET CAR-RIED AWAY NOW...
I LEARNED ABOUT THIS EVIL SCHEME AND CAME TO HELP OUT—BUT IT LOOKS LIKE I WAS TOO LATE!
IF ONLY BYRON HAD TOLD ME ABOUT IT EARLIER!
C'MON, LET'S GO! WE'LL DROWN IF WE JUST STAND AROUND WITH OUR MOUTHS OPEN UNTIL THERE'S ENOUGH WATER FOR THE MAGIKARP TO SWIM IN!
OH! GOOD POINT!

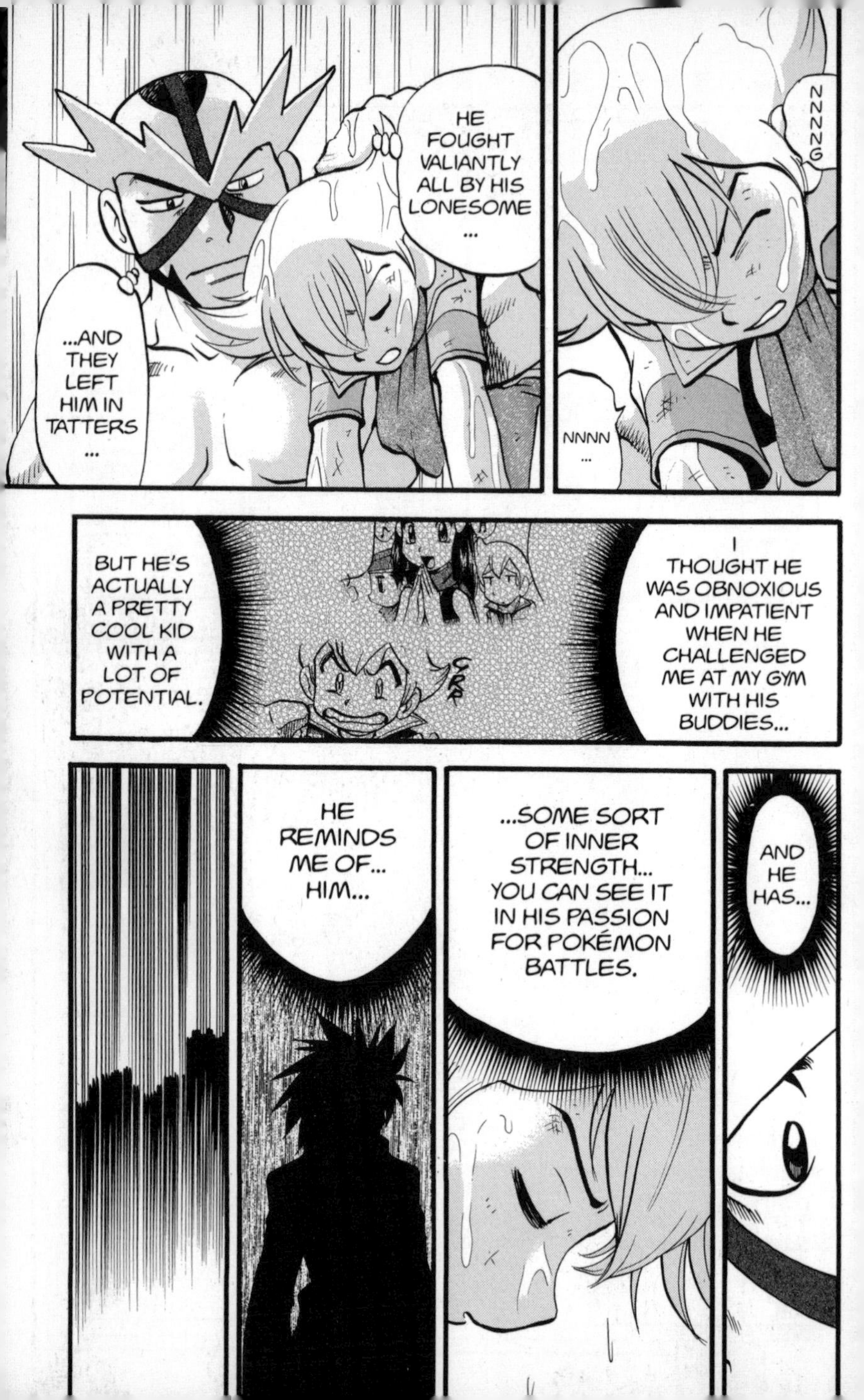
NNNNG
NNNN ...
HE FOUGHT VALIANTLY ALL BY HIS LONESOME ...
...AND THEY LEFT HIM IN TATTERS ...
I THOUGHT HE WAS OBNOXIOUS AND IMPATIENT WHEN HE CHALLENGED ME AT MY GYM WITH HIS BUDDIES...
BUT HE'S ACTUALLY A PRETTY COOL KID WITH A LOT OF POTENTIAL.
GRR
AND HE HAS...
...SOME SORT OF INNER STRENGTH... YOU CAN SEE IT IN HIS PASSION FOR POKÉMON BATTLES.
HE REMINDS ME OF... HIM...

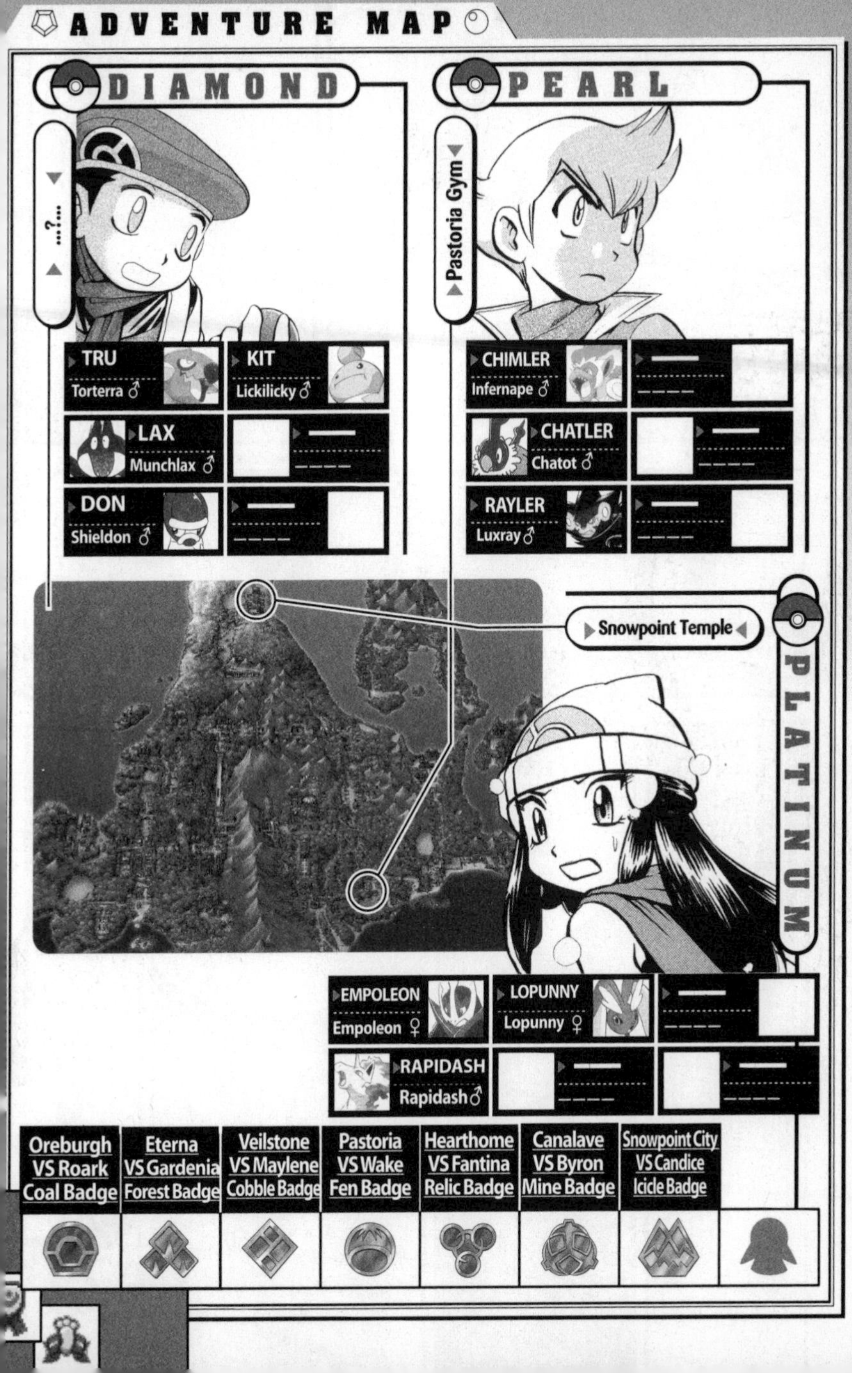
ADVENTURE MAP
DIAMOND
...?...
TRU
Torterra ♂
KIT
Lickilicky ♂
LAX
Munchlax ♂
DON
Shieldon ♂
PEARL
Pastoria Gym
CHIMLER
Infernape ♂
CHATLER
Chatot ♂
RAYLER
Luxray ♂
Snowpoint Temple
PLATINUM
EMPOLEON
Empoleon ♀
LOPUNNY
Lopunny ♀
RAPIDASH
Rapidash ♂
Oreburgh
VS Roark
Coal Badge
Eterna
VS Gardenia
Forest Badge
Veilstone
VS Maylene
Cobble Badge
Pastoria
VS Wake
Fen Badge
Hearthome
VS Fantina
Relic Badge
Canalave
VS Byron
Mine Badge
Snowpoint City
VS Candice
Icicle Badge

64

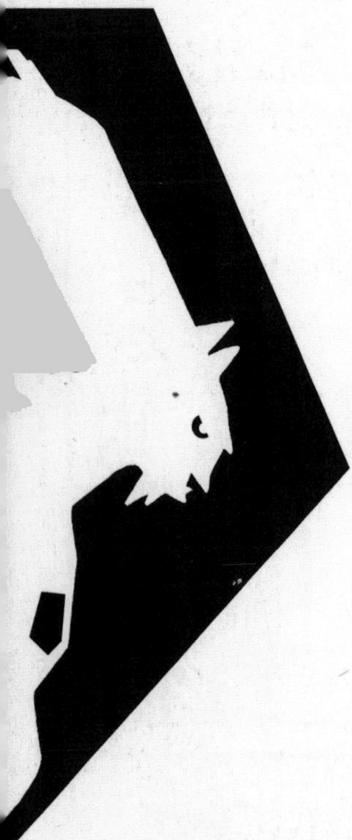

Besting Buizel I

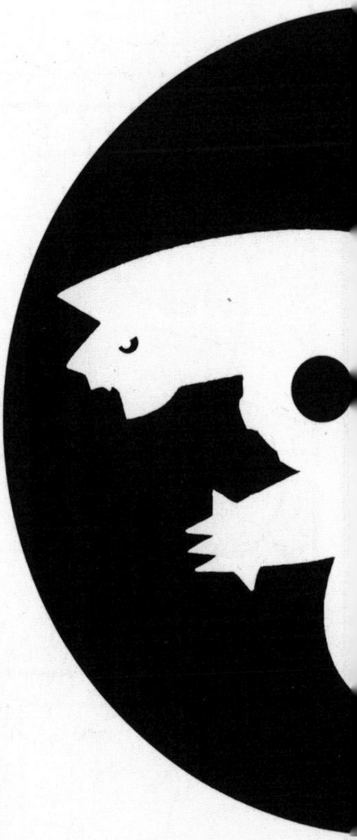

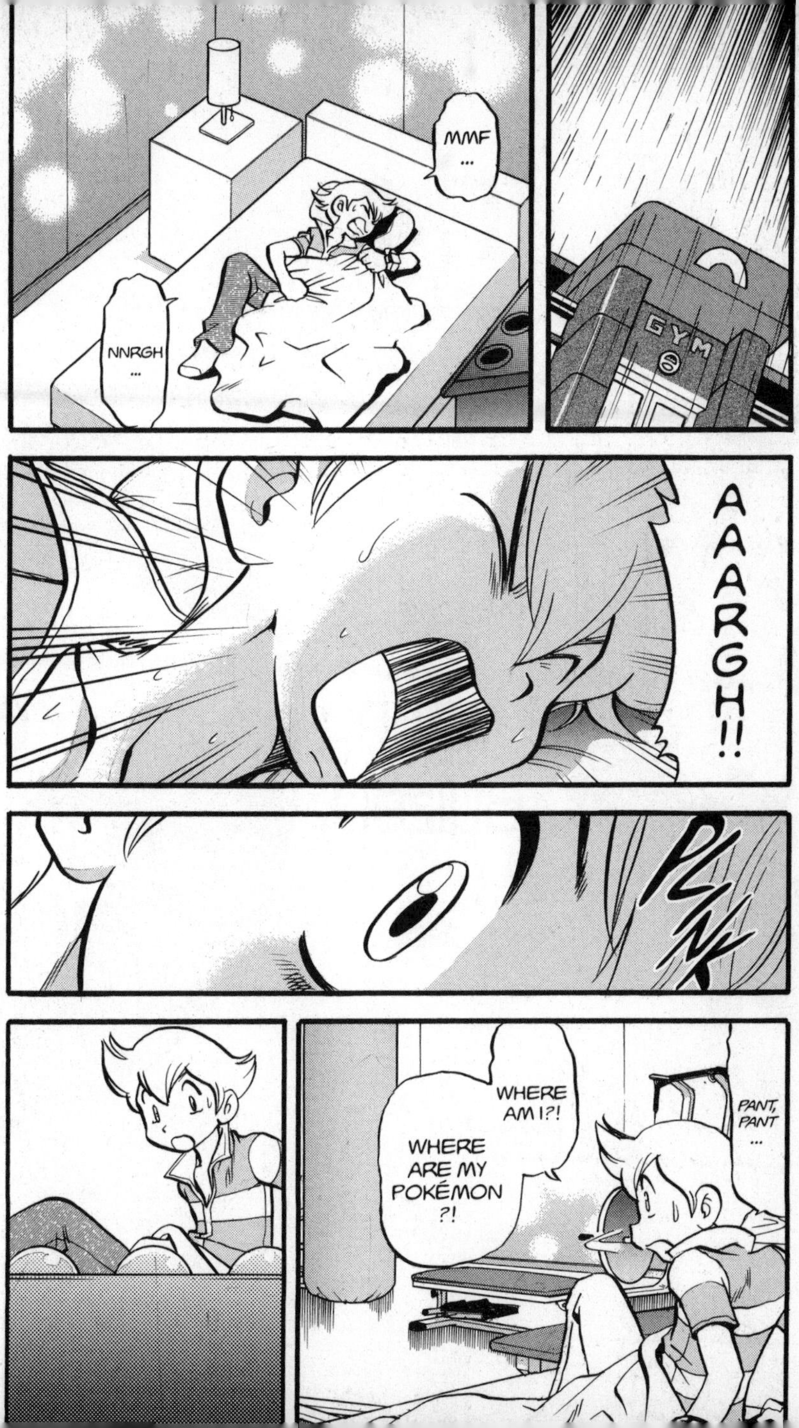
MMF ...
NNRGH ...
AAAARGH!!
PLINK
PANT, PANT ...
WHERE AM I?!
WHERE ARE MY POKÉMON ?!

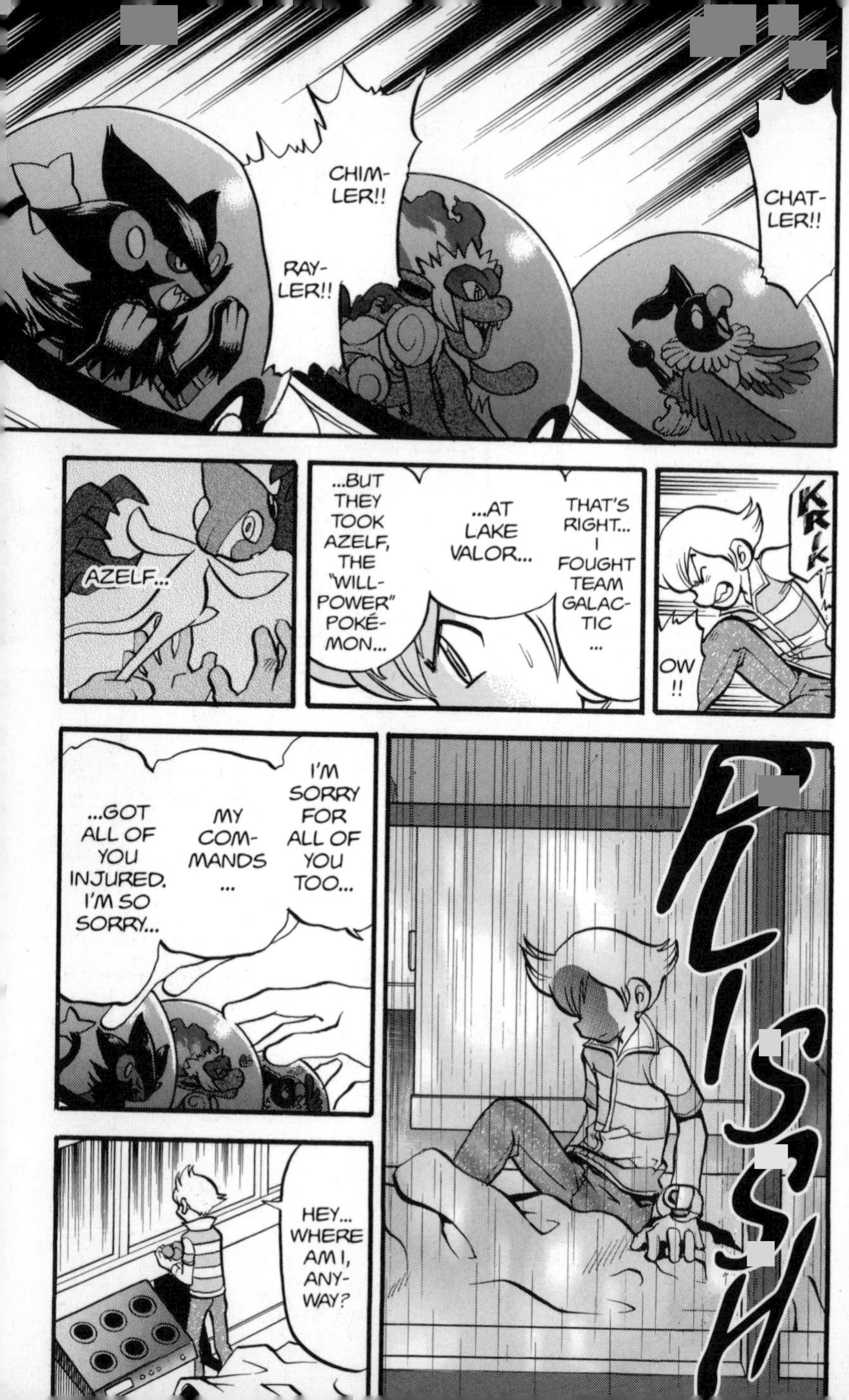
CHAT-LER!!
CHIM-LER!!
RAY-LER!!
KRIK
OW!!
THAT'S RIGHT... I FOUGHT TEAM GALACTIC...
...AT LAKE VALOR...
...BUT THEY TOOK AZELF, THE "WILL-POWER" POKÉMON...
AZELF...
FLISSH
I'M SORRY FOR ALL OF YOU TOO...
MY COMMANDS...
...GOT ALL OF YOU INJURED. I'M SO SORRY...
HEY... WHERE AM I, ANYWAY?

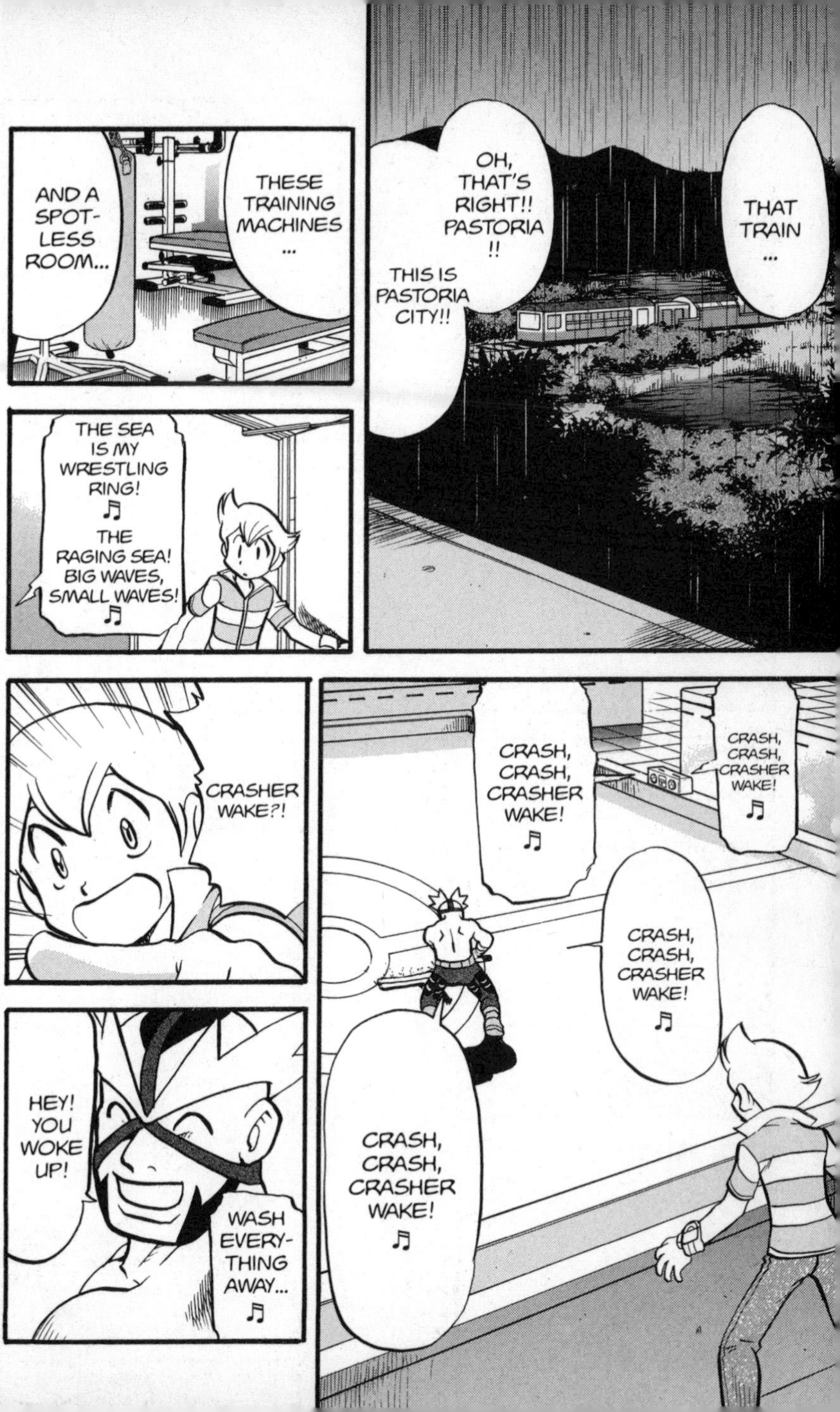
THAT TRAIN ...
OH, THAT'S RIGHT!! PASTORIA !!
THIS IS PASTORIA CITY!!
THESE TRAINING MACHINES ...
AND A SPOT-LESS ROOM...
THE SEA IS MY WRESTLING RING! ♬ THE RAGING SEA! BIG WAVES, SMALL WAVES! ♬
CRASH, CRASH, CRASHER WAKE! ♬
CRASH, CRASH, CRASHER WAKE! ♬
CRASH, CRASH, CRASHER WAKE! ♬
CRASH, CRASH, CRASHER WAKE! ♬
CRASHER WAKE?!
HEY! YOU WOKE UP!
WASH EVERY-THING AWAY... ♬

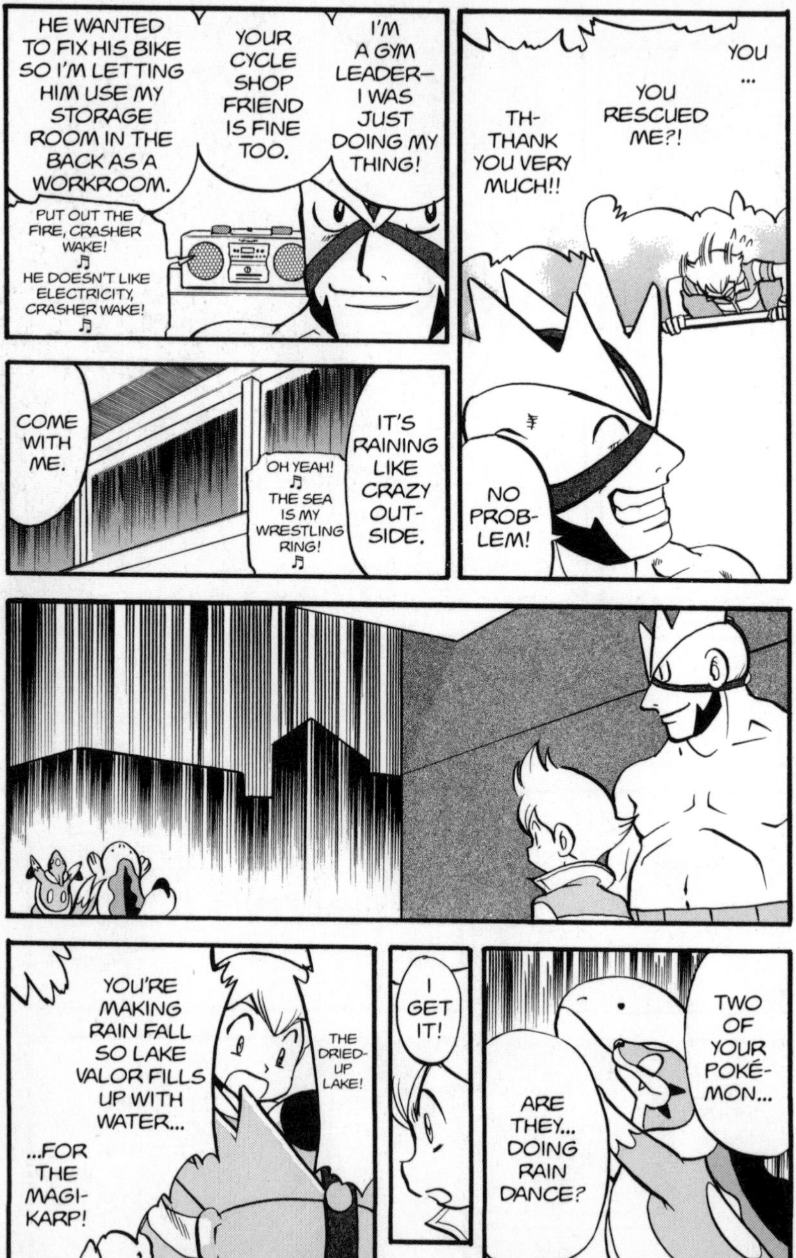
YOU ...
YOU RESCUED ME?!
TH-THANK YOU VERY MUCH!!
NO PROB-LEM!
I'M A GYM LEADER— I WAS JUST DOING MY THING!
YOUR CYCLE SHOP FRIEND IS FINE TOO.
HE WANTED TO FIX HIS BIKE SO I'M LETTING HIM USE MY STORAGE ROOM IN THE BACK AS A WORKROOM.
PUT OUT THE FIRE, CRASHER WAKE! ♬ HE DOESN'T LIKE ELECTRICITY, CRASHER WAKE! ♬
IT'S RAINING LIKE CRAZY OUT-SIDE.
OH YEAH! ♬ THE SEA IS MY WRESTLING RING! ♬
COME WITH ME.
TWO OF YOUR POKÉ-MON...
ARE THEY... DOING RAIN DANCE?
I GET IT!
THE DRIED-UP LAKE!
YOU'RE MAKING RAIN FALL SO LAKE VALOR FILLS UP WITH WATER...
...FOR THE MAGI-KARP!

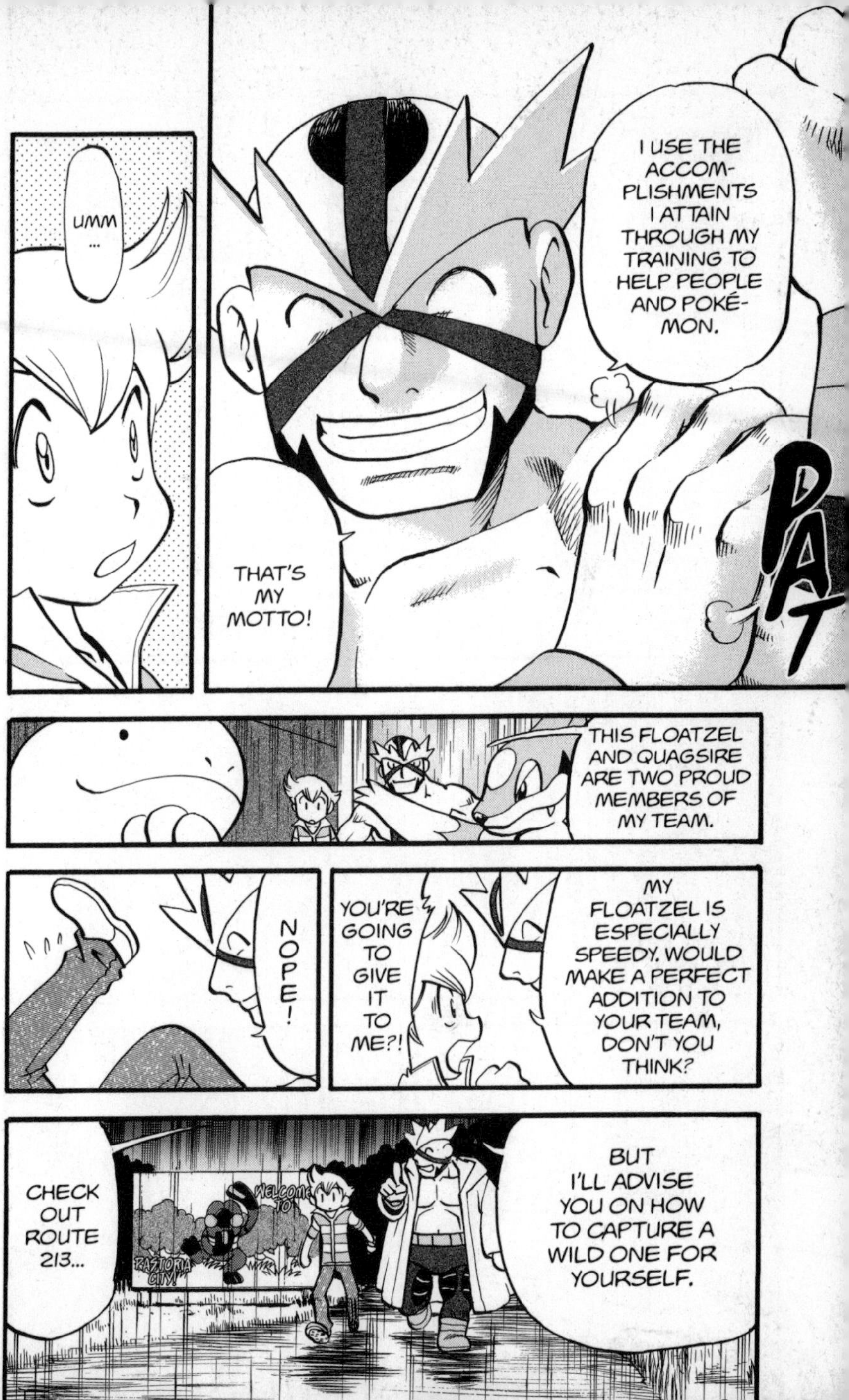
I USE THE ACCOMPLISHMENTS I ATTAIN THROUGH MY TRAINING TO HELP PEOPLE AND POKÉMON.
PAT
THAT'S MY MOTTO!
UMM ...
THIS FLOATZEL AND QUAGSIRE ARE TWO PROUD MEMBERS OF MY TEAM.
MY FLOATZEL IS ESPECIALLY SPEEDY. WOULD MAKE A PERFECT ADDITION TO YOUR TEAM, DON'T YOU THINK?
YOU'RE GOING TO GIVE IT TO ME?!
NOPE!
BUT I'LL ADVISE YOU ON HOW TO CAPTURE A WILD ONE FOR YOURSELF.
WELCOME TO
PASTORIA CITY!
CHECK OUT ROUTE 213...

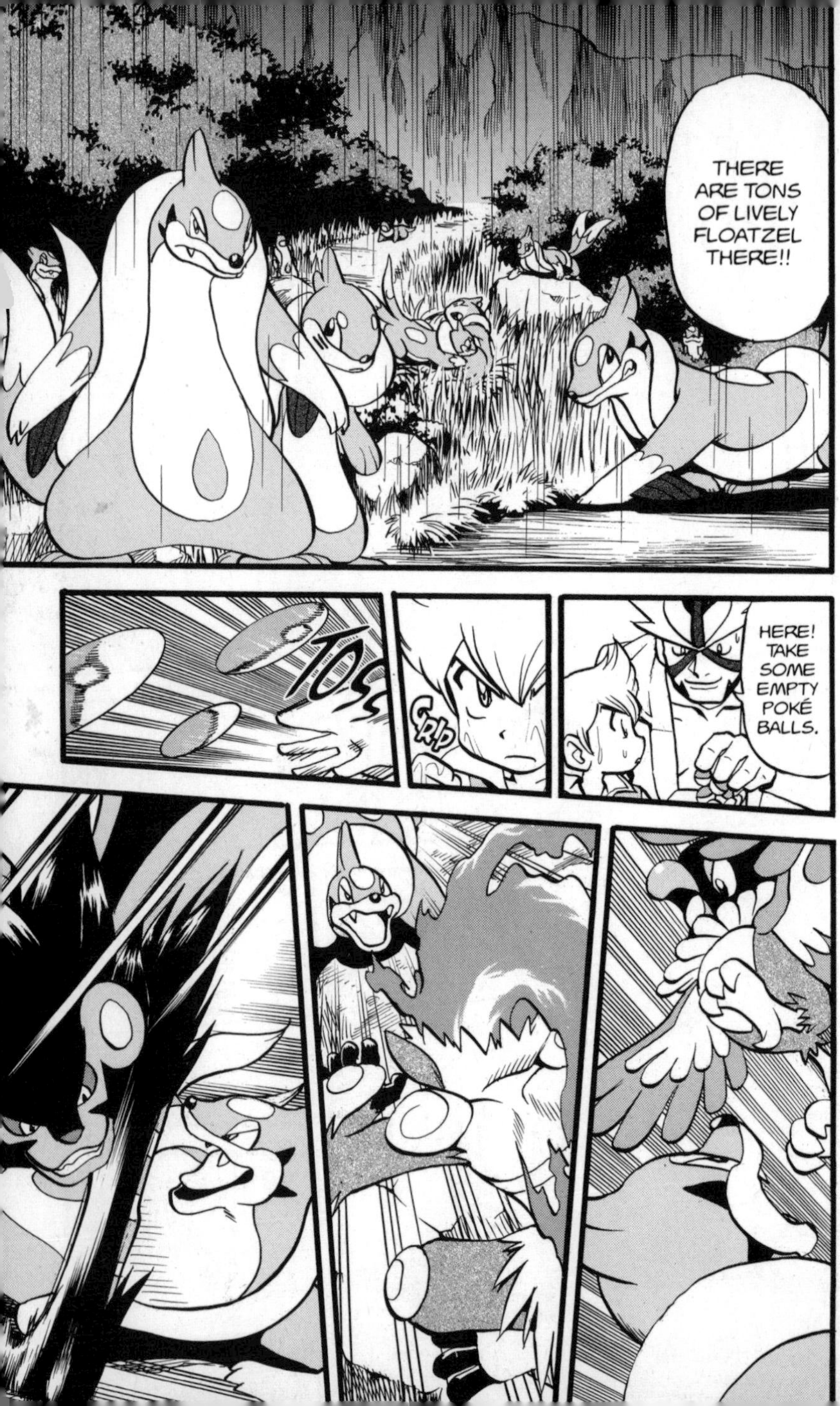
THERE ARE TONS OF LIVELY FLOATZEL THERE!!
HERE! TAKE SOME EMPTY POKÉ BALLS.
GRIP
TOSS

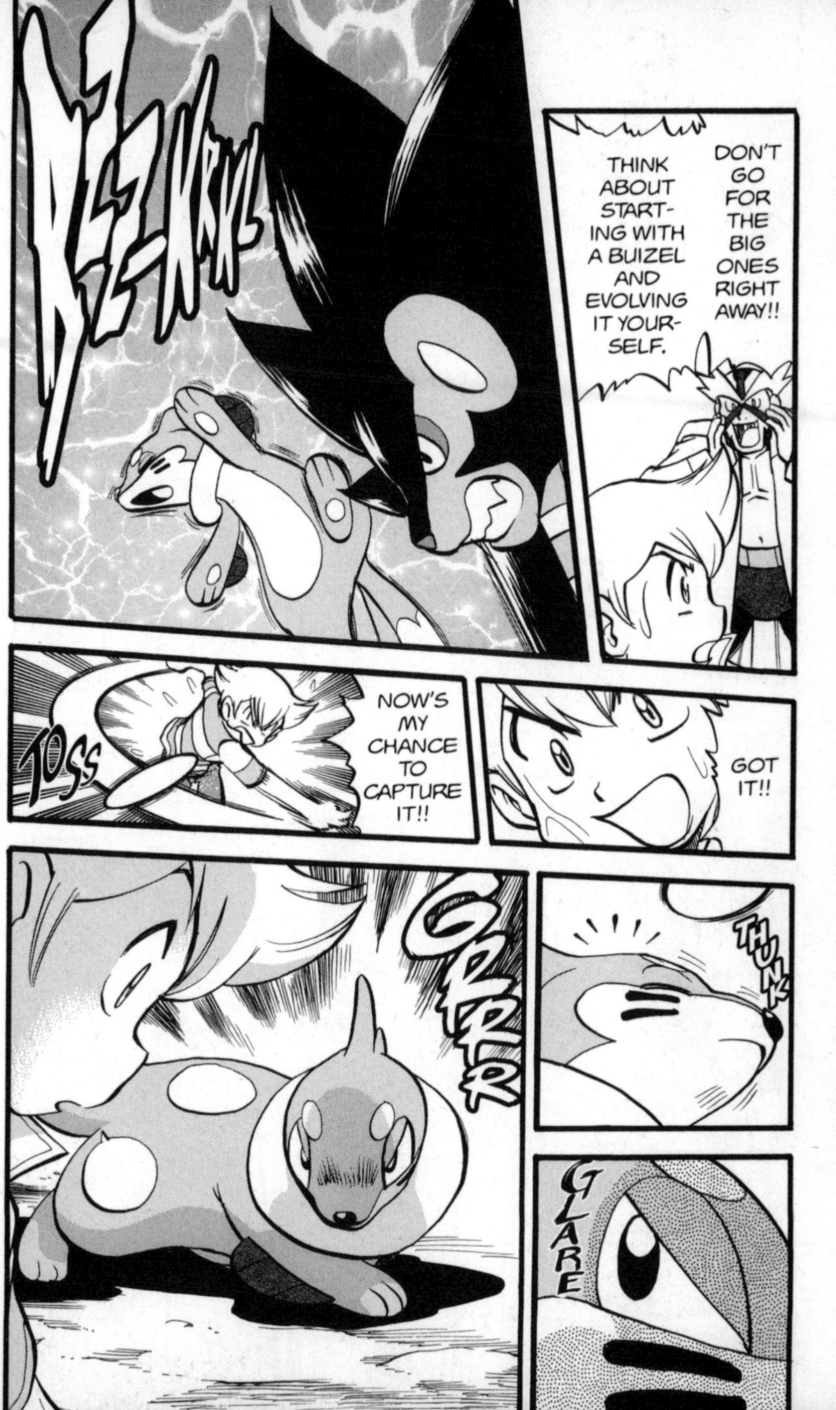
DON'T GO FOR THE BIG ONES RIGHT AWAY!!
THINK ABOUT START-ING WITH A BUIZEL AND EVOLVING IT YOUR-SELF.
GOT IT!!
NOW'S MY CHANCE TO CAPTURE IT!!
TOSS
THUNK
GLARE
GRRRR

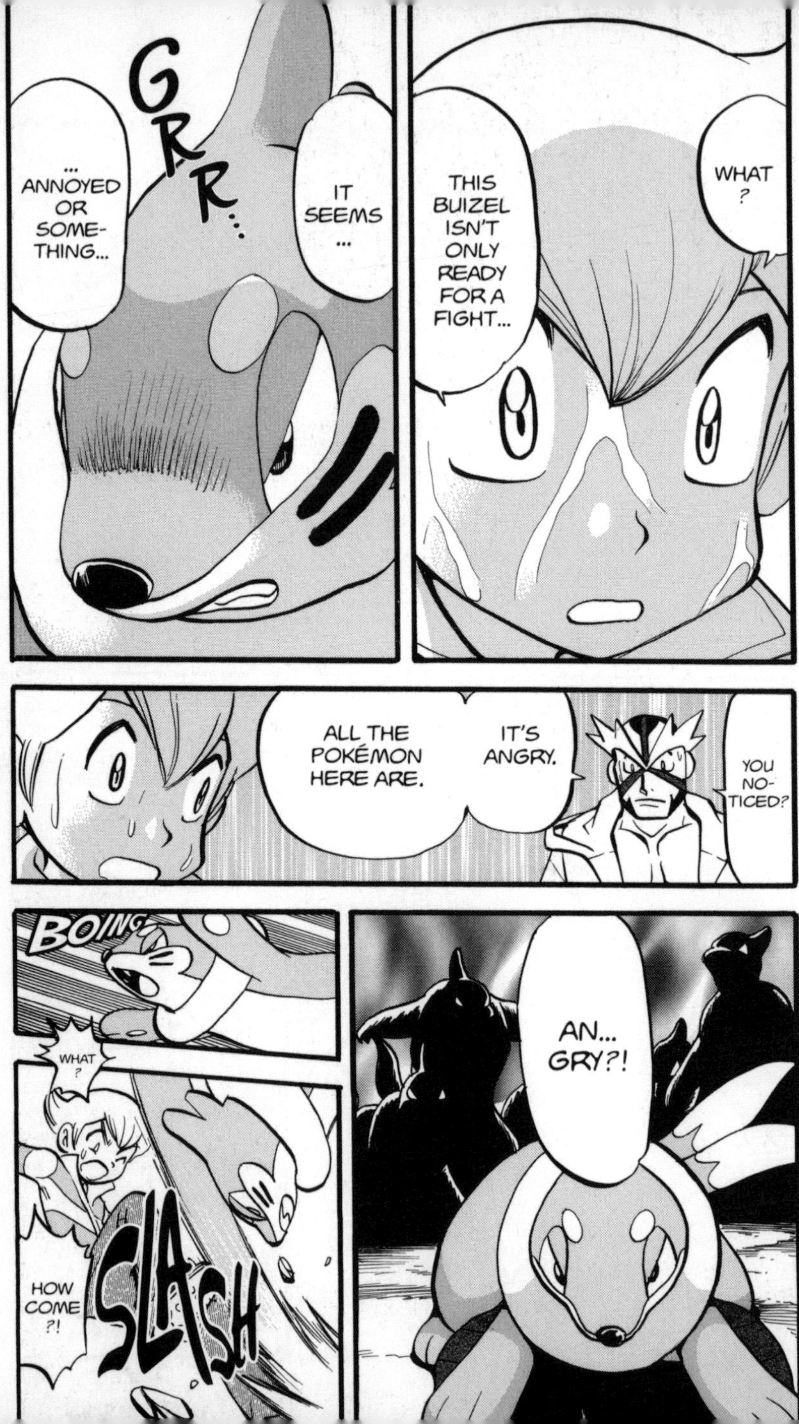
WHAT?
THIS BUIZEL ISN'T ONLY READY FOR A FIGHT...
IT SEEMS...
GRR...
...ANNOYED OR SOME-THING...
YOU NO-TICED?
IT'S ANGRY.
ALL THE POKÉMON HERE ARE.
AN... GRY?!
BOING
WHAT?
SLASH
HOW COME?!

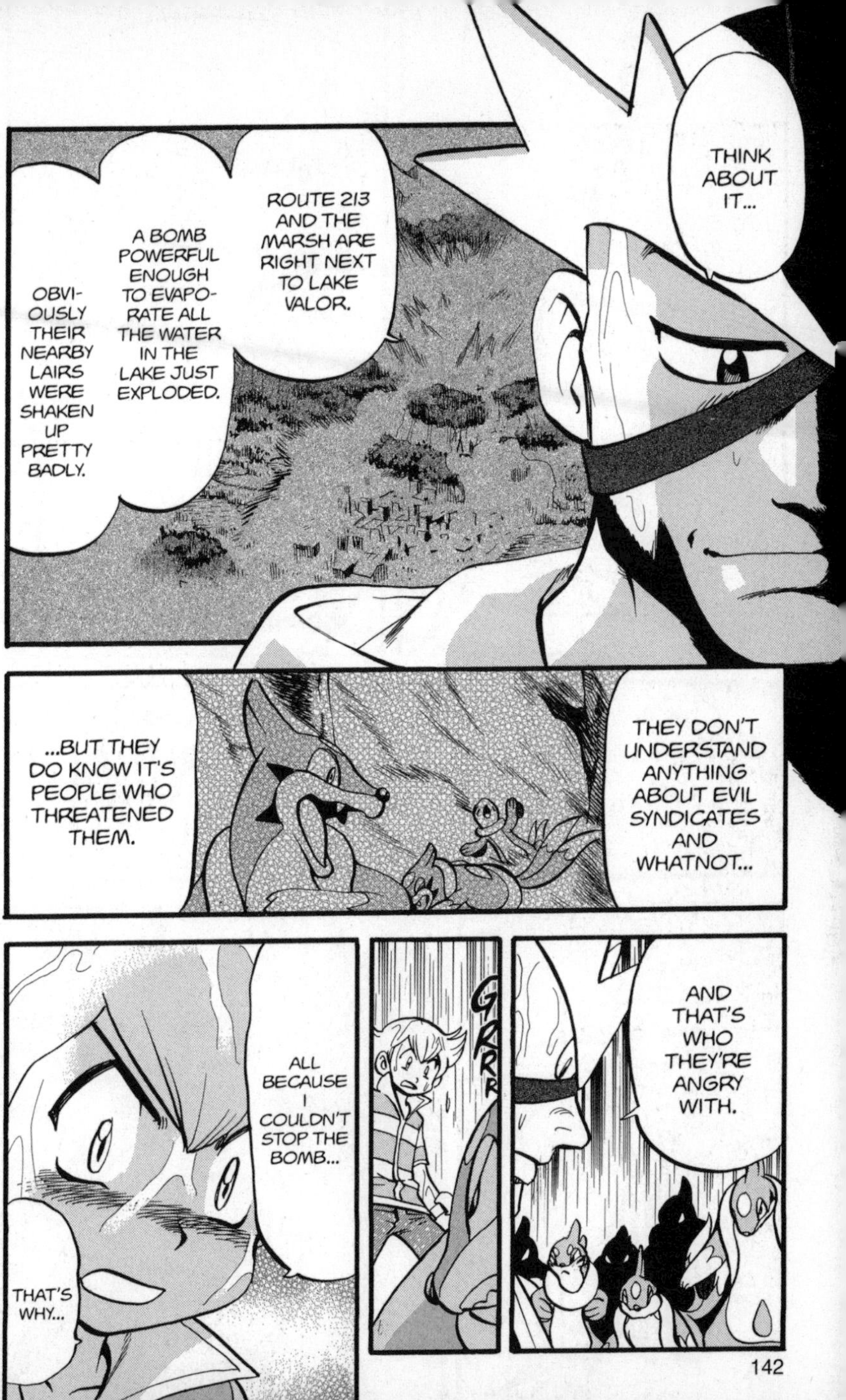
THINK ABOUT IT...
ROUTE 213 AND THE MARSH ARE RIGHT NEXT TO LAKE VALOR.
A BOMB POWERFUL ENOUGH TO EVAPORATE ALL THE WATER IN THE LAKE JUST EXPLODED.
OBVIOUSLY THEIR NEARBY LAIRS WERE SHAKEN UP PRETTY BADLY.
THEY DON'T UNDERSTAND ANYTHING ABOUT EVIL SYNDICATES AND WHATNOT...
...BUT THEY DO KNOW IT'S PEOPLE WHO THREATENED THEM.
AND THAT'S WHO THEY'RE ANGRY WITH.
GRRR
ALL BECAUSE I COULDN'T STOP THE BOMB...
THAT'S WHY...

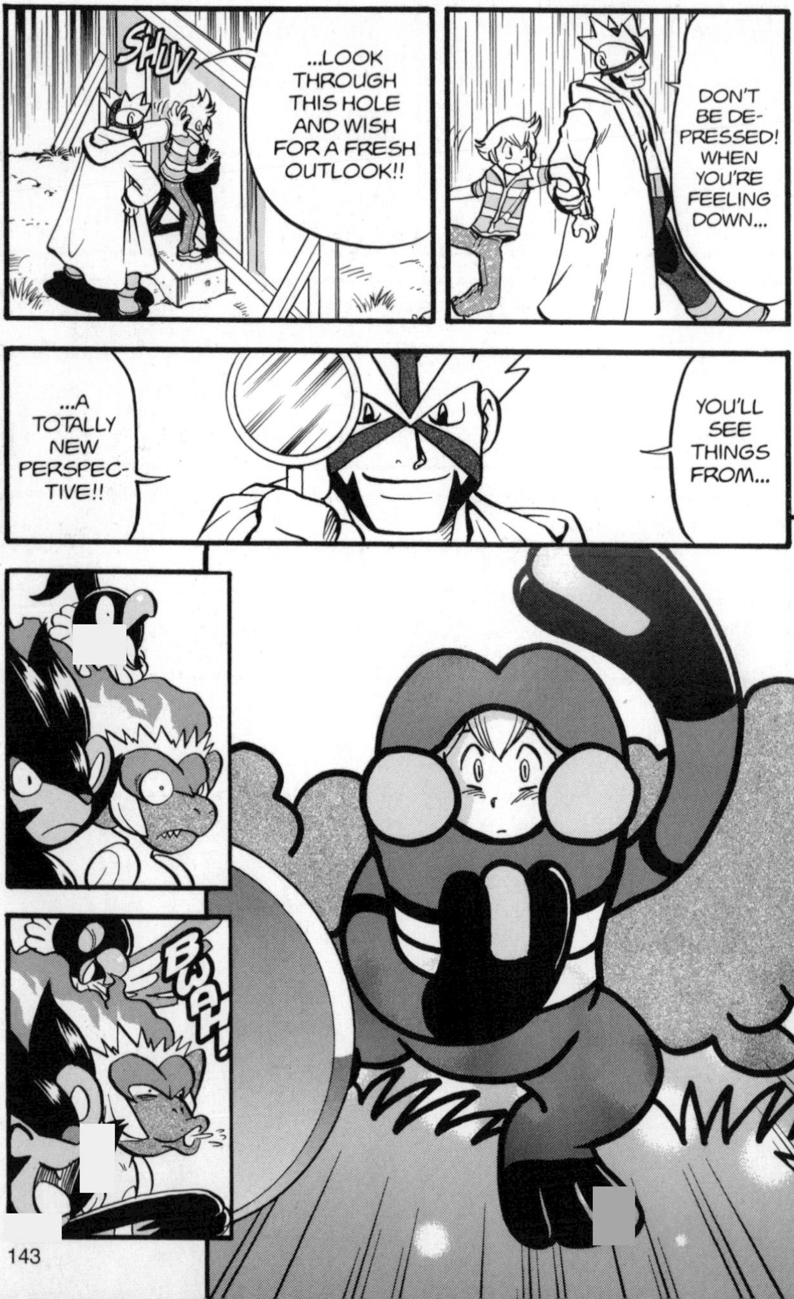
DON'T BE DE-PRESSED! WHEN YOU'RE FEELING DOWN...
SHUV
...LOOK THROUGH THIS HOLE AND WISH FOR A FRESH OUTLOOK!!
YOU'LL SEE THINGS FROM...
...A TOTALLY NEW PERSPEC-TIVE!!
BWAH!

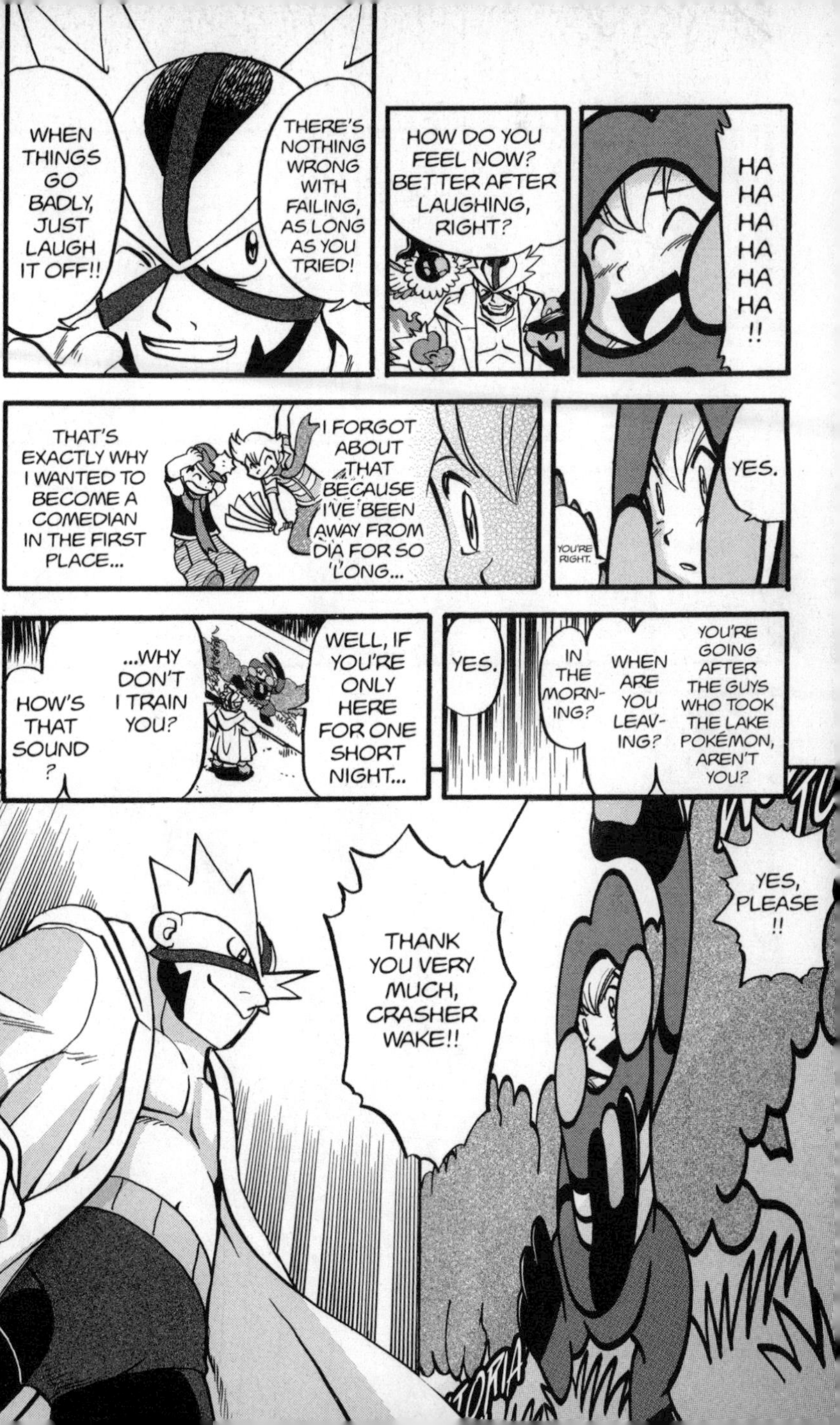

HA HA HA HA HA HA!!
HOW DO YOU FEEL NOW? BETTER AFTER LAUGHING, RIGHT?
THERE'S NOTHING WRONG WITH FAILING, AS LONG AS YOU TRIED!
WHEN THINGS GO BADLY, JUST LAUGH IT OFF!!
YES.
YOU'RE RIGHT.
I FORGOT ABOUT THAT BECAUSE I'VE BEEN AWAY FROM DIA FOR SO LONG...
THAT'S EXACTLY WHY I WANTED TO BECOME A COMEDIAN IN THE FIRST PLACE...
YOU'RE GOING AFTER THE GUYS WHO TOOK THE LAKE POKÉMON, AREN'T YOU?
WHEN ARE YOU LEAVING?
IN THE MORNING?
YES.
WELL, IF YOU'RE ONLY HERE FOR ONE SHORT NIGHT...
...WHY DON'T I TRAIN YOU?
HOW'S THAT SOUND?
YES, PLEASE!!
THANK YOU VERY MUCH, CRASHER WAKE!!

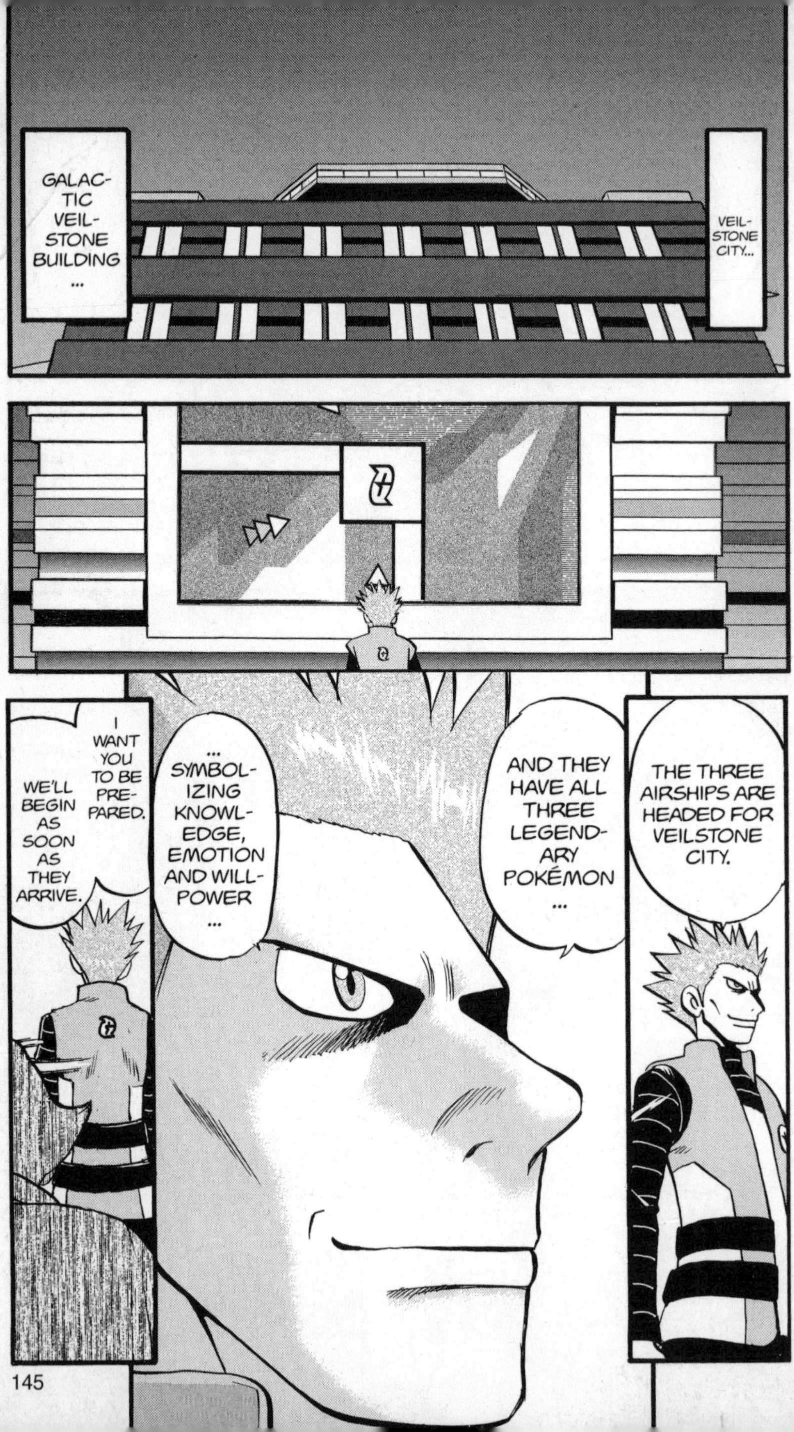
VEIL-STONE CITY...
GALAC-TIC VEIL-STONE BUILDING ...
THE THREE AIRSHIPS ARE HEADED FOR VEILSTONE CITY.
AND THEY HAVE ALL THREE LEGEND-ARY POKÉMON ...
... SYMBOL-IZING KNOWL-EDGE, EMOTION AND WILL-POWER ...
I WANT YOU TO BE PRE-PARED.
WE'LL BEGIN AS SOON AS THEY ARRIVE.

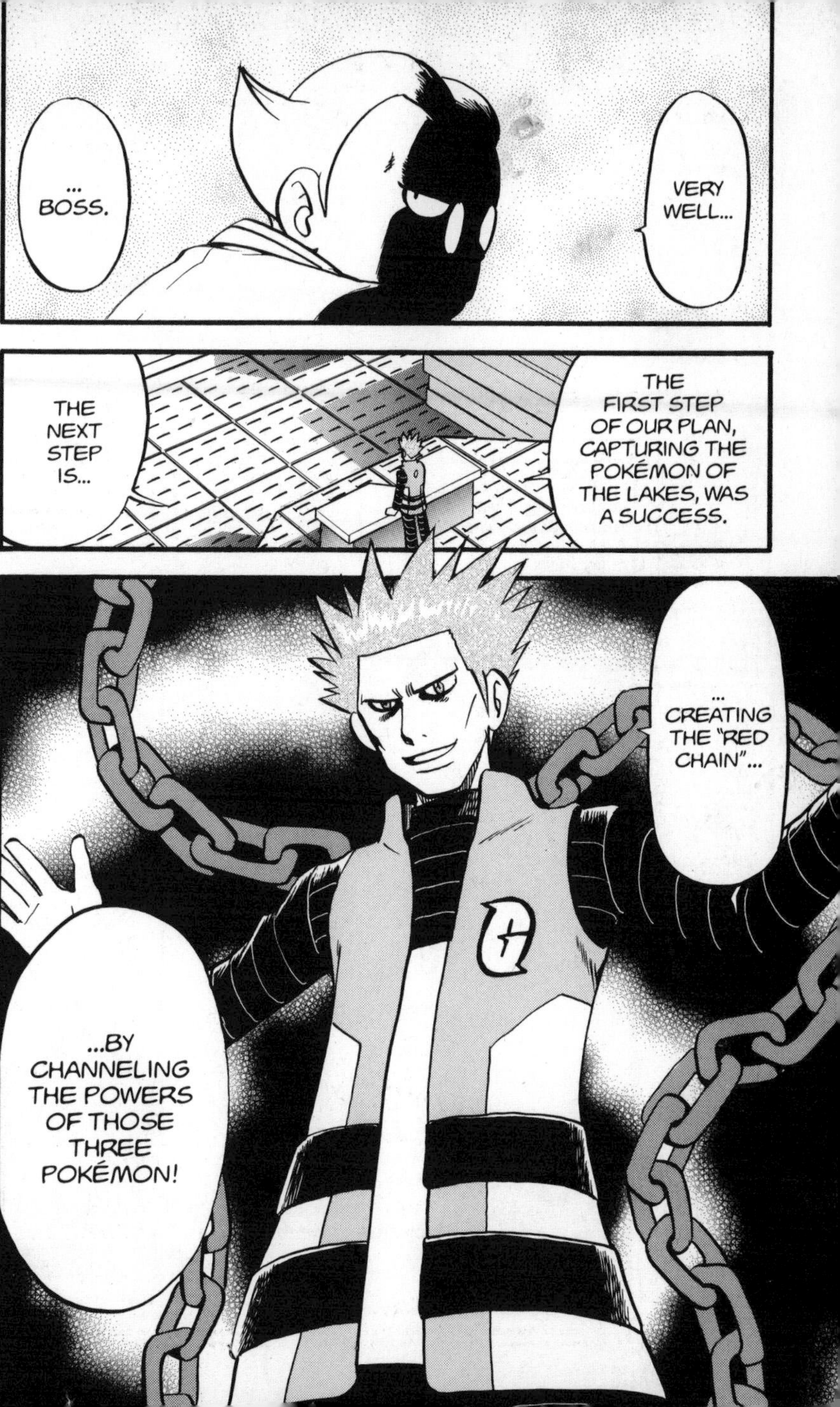
VERY WELL...
... BOSS.
THE FIRST STEP OF OUR PLAN, CAPTURING THE POKÉMON OF THE LAKES, WAS A SUCCESS.
THE NEXT STEP IS...
... CREATING THE "RED CHAIN"...
...BY CHANNELING THE POWERS OF THOSE THREE POKÉMON!

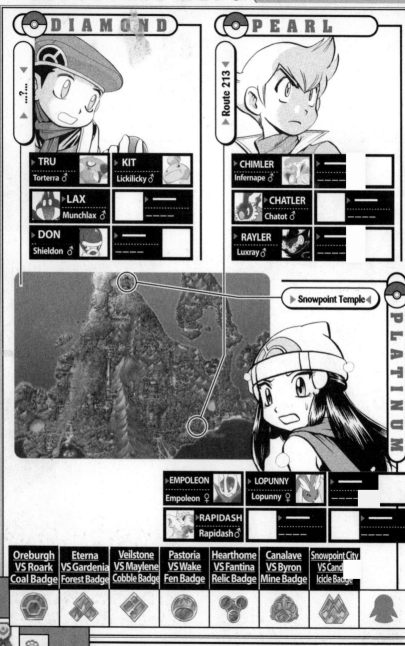

DIAMOND

PEARL

▲ Route 213 ▼

TRU
Torterra ♂

KIT
Lickilicky ♂

LAX
Munchlax ♂

DON
Shieldon ♂

CHIMLER
Infernape ♂

CHATLER
Chatot ♂

RAYLER
Luxray ♂

▶ Snowpoint Temple ◀

PLATINUM

EMPOLEON
Empoleon ♀

LOPUNNY
Lopunny ♀

RAPIDASH
Rapidash ♂

Oreburgh VS Roark Coal Badge	Eterna VS Gardenia Forest Badge	Veilstone VS Maylene Cobble Badge	Pastoria VS Wake Fen Badge	Hearthome VS Fantina Relic Badge	Canalave VS Byron Mine Badge	Snowpoint City VS Cand Icicle Badge	

65

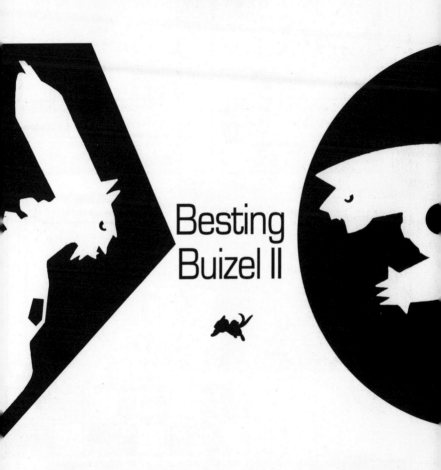

Besting
Buizel II

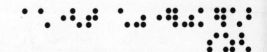

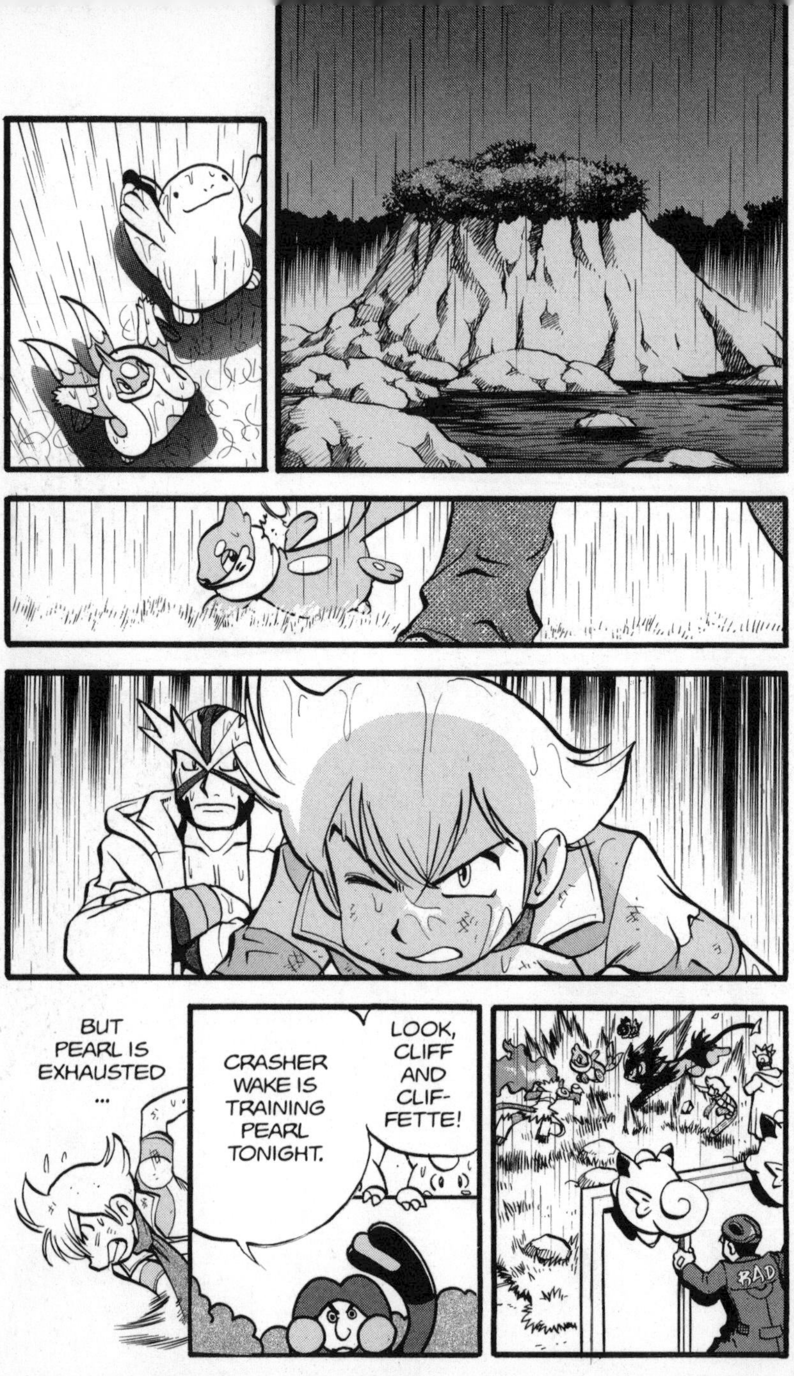
LOOK, CLIFF AND CLIF-FETTE!
CRASHER WAKE IS TRAINING PEARL TONIGHT.
BUT PEARL IS EXHAUSTED ...
RAD

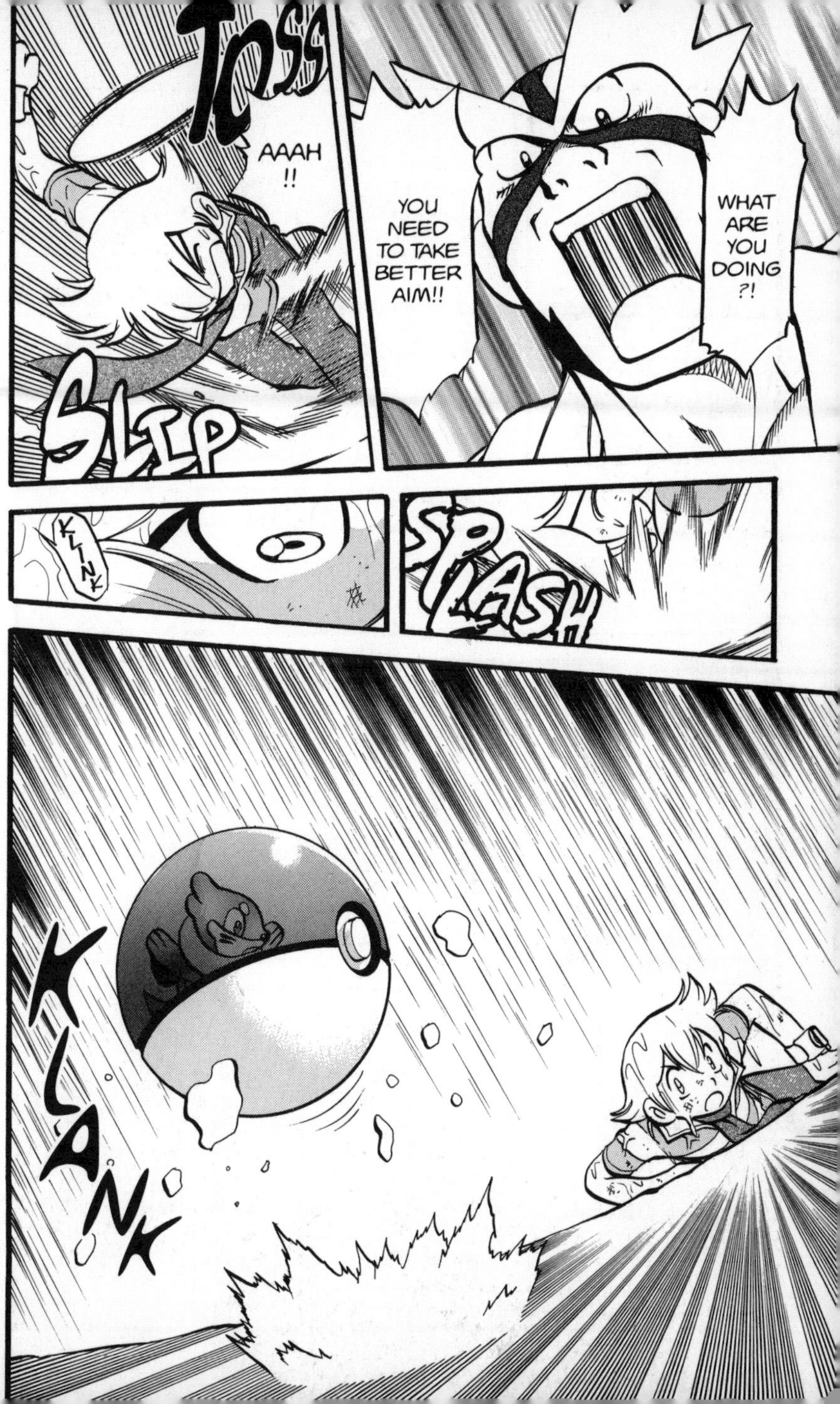
WHAT ARE YOU DOING?!
YOU NEED TO TAKE BETTER AIM!!
TOSS
AAAH!!
SLIP
SPLASH
KLINK
KLANK

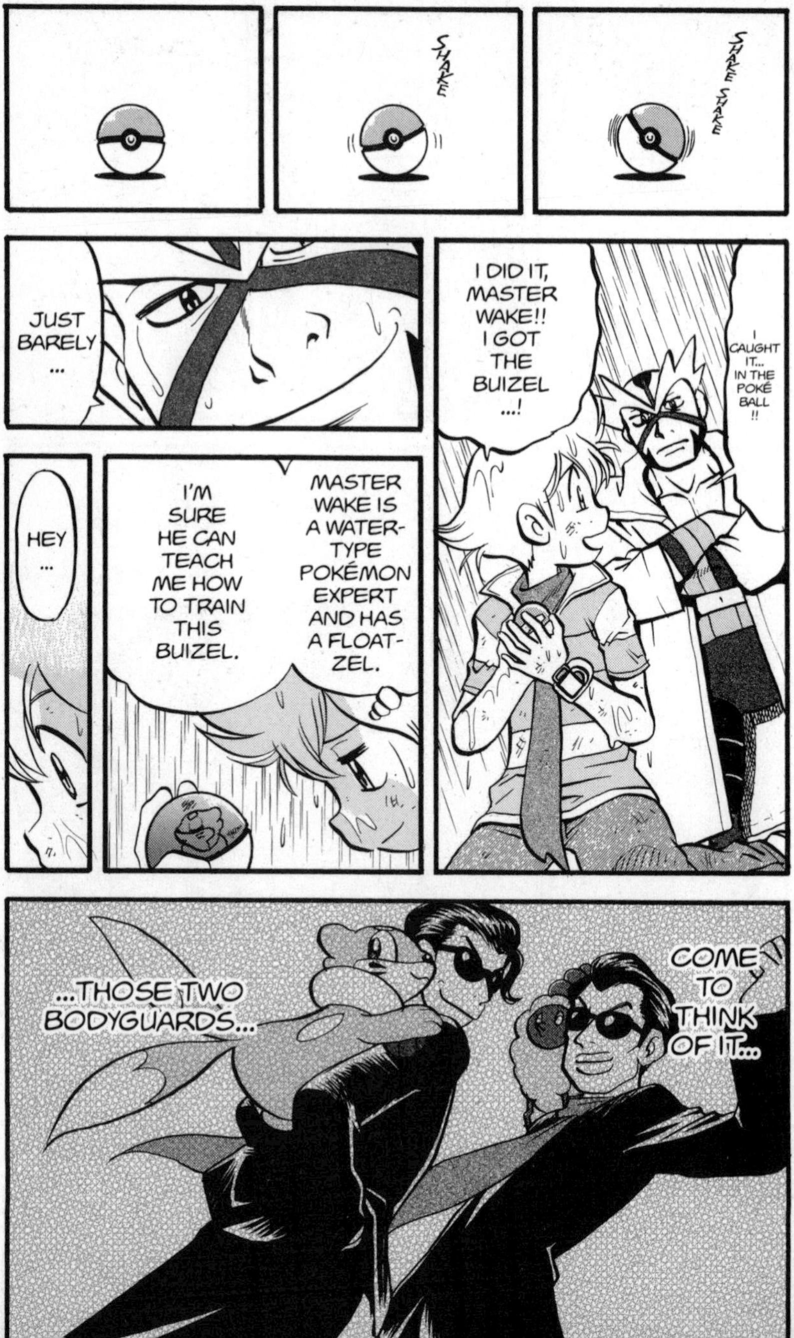
SHAKE SHAKE
SHAKE
I DID IT, MASTER WAKE!! I GOT THE BUIZEL ...!
I CAUGHT IT... IN THE POKÉ BALL !!
JUST BARELY ...
MASTER WAKE IS A WATER-TYPE POKÉMON EXPERT AND HAS A FLOAT-ZEL.
I'M SURE HE CAN TEACH ME HOW TO TRAIN THIS BUIZEL.
HEY ...
COME TO THINK OF IT...
...THOSE TWO BODYGUARDS...

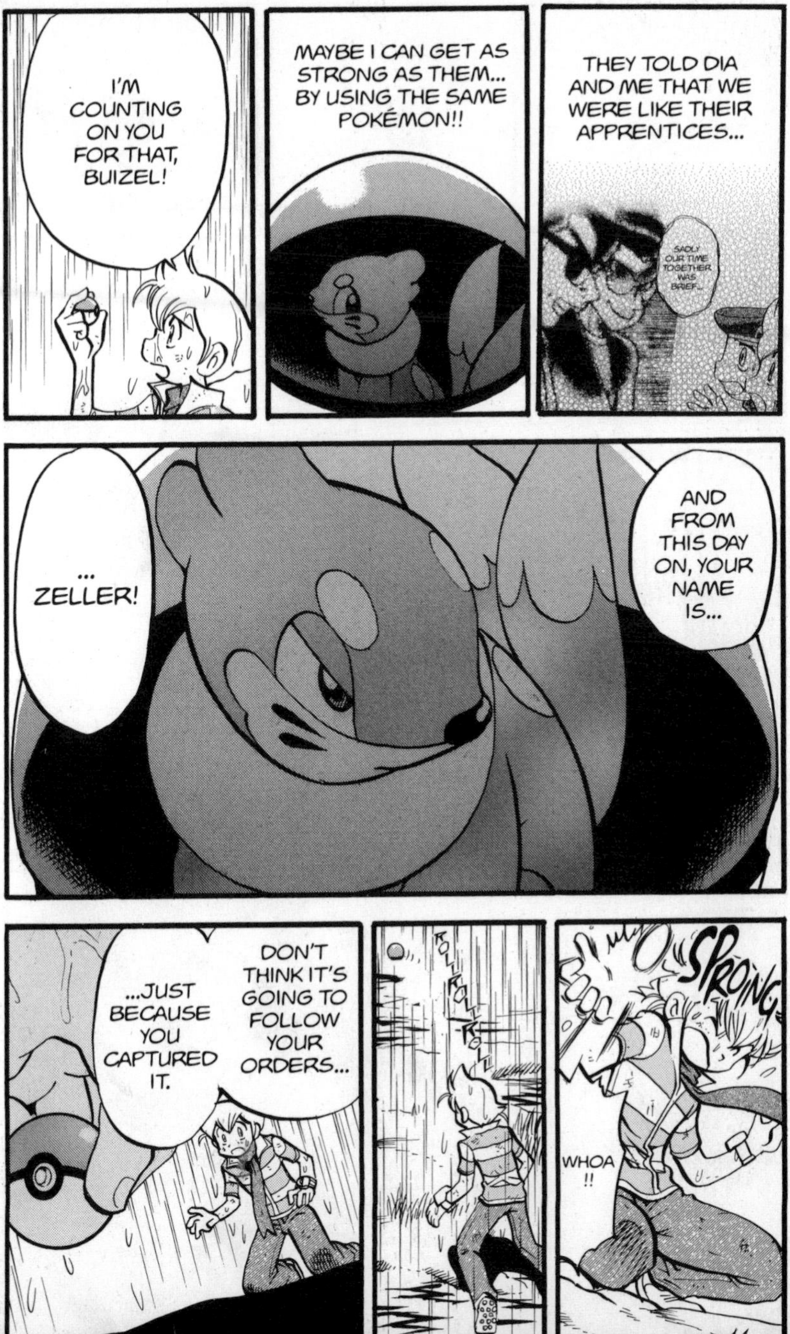
THEY TOLD DIA AND ME THAT WE WERE LIKE THEIR APPRENTICES...
SADLY OUR TIME TOGETHER WAS BRIEF...
MAYBE I CAN GET AS STRONG AS THEM... BY USING THE SAME POKÉMON!!
I'M COUNTING ON YOU FOR THAT, BUIZEL!
AND FROM THIS DAY ON, YOUR NAME IS...
... ZELLER!
SPRONG
WHOA !!
ROLL ROLL ROLL
DON'T THINK IT'S GOING TO FOLLOW YOUR ORDERS...
...JUST BECAUSE YOU CAPTURED IT.

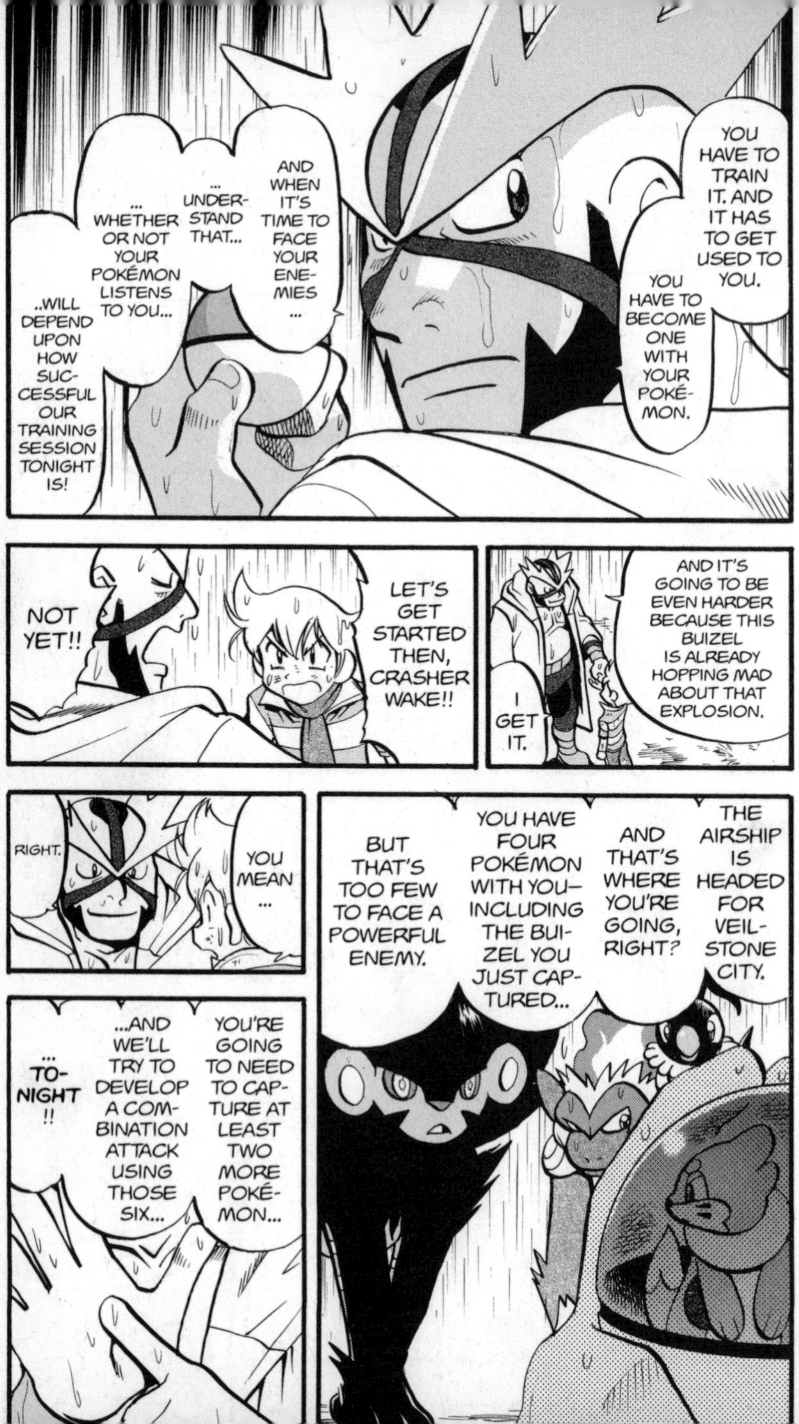
YOU HAVE TO TRAIN IT. AND IT HAS TO GET USED TO YOU.
YOU HAVE TO BECOME ONE WITH YOUR POKÉMON.
AND WHEN IT'S TIME TO FACE YOUR ENEMIES...
...UNDERSTAND THAT...
...WHETHER OR NOT YOUR POKÉMON LISTENS TO YOU...
..WILL DEPEND UPON HOW SUCCESSFUL OUR TRAINING SESSION TONIGHT IS!
AND IT'S GOING TO BE EVEN HARDER BECAUSE THIS BUIZEL IS ALREADY HOPPING MAD ABOUT THAT EXPLOSION.
I GET IT.
LET'S GET STARTED THEN, CRASHER WAKE!!
NOT YET!!
THE AIRSHIP IS HEADED FOR VEILSTONE CITY.
AND THAT'S WHERE YOU'RE GOING, RIGHT?
YOU HAVE FOUR POKÉMON WITH YOU—INCLUDING THE BUIZEL YOU JUST CAPTURED...
BUT THAT'S TOO FEW TO FACE A POWERFUL ENEMY.
YOU MEAN...
RIGHT.
YOU'RE GOING TO NEED TO CAPTURE AT LEAST TWO MORE POKÉMON...
...AND WE'LL TRY TO DEVELOP A COMBINATION ATTACK USING THOSE SIX...
...TONIGHT!!

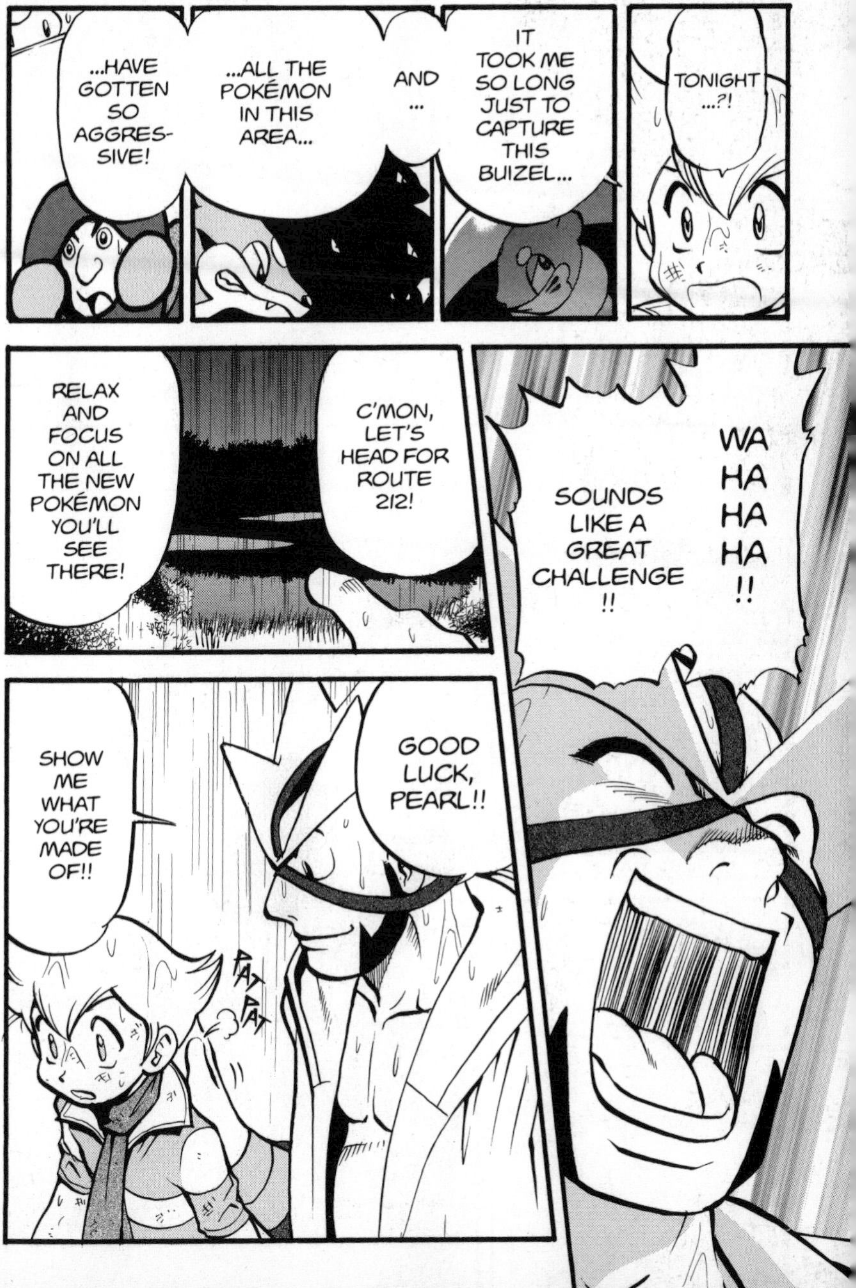
TONIGHT ...?!
IT TOOK ME SO LONG JUST TO CAPTURE THIS BUIZEL...
AND ...
...ALL THE POKÉMON IN THIS AREA...
...HAVE GOTTEN SO AGGRES-SIVE!
WA HA HA HA!!
SOUNDS LIKE A GREAT CHALLENGE!!
C'MON, LET'S HEAD FOR ROUTE 212!
RELAX AND FOCUS ON ALL THE NEW POKÉMON YOU'LL SEE THERE!
GOOD LUCK, PEARL!!
SHOW ME WHAT YOU'RE MADE OF!!
PAT PAT

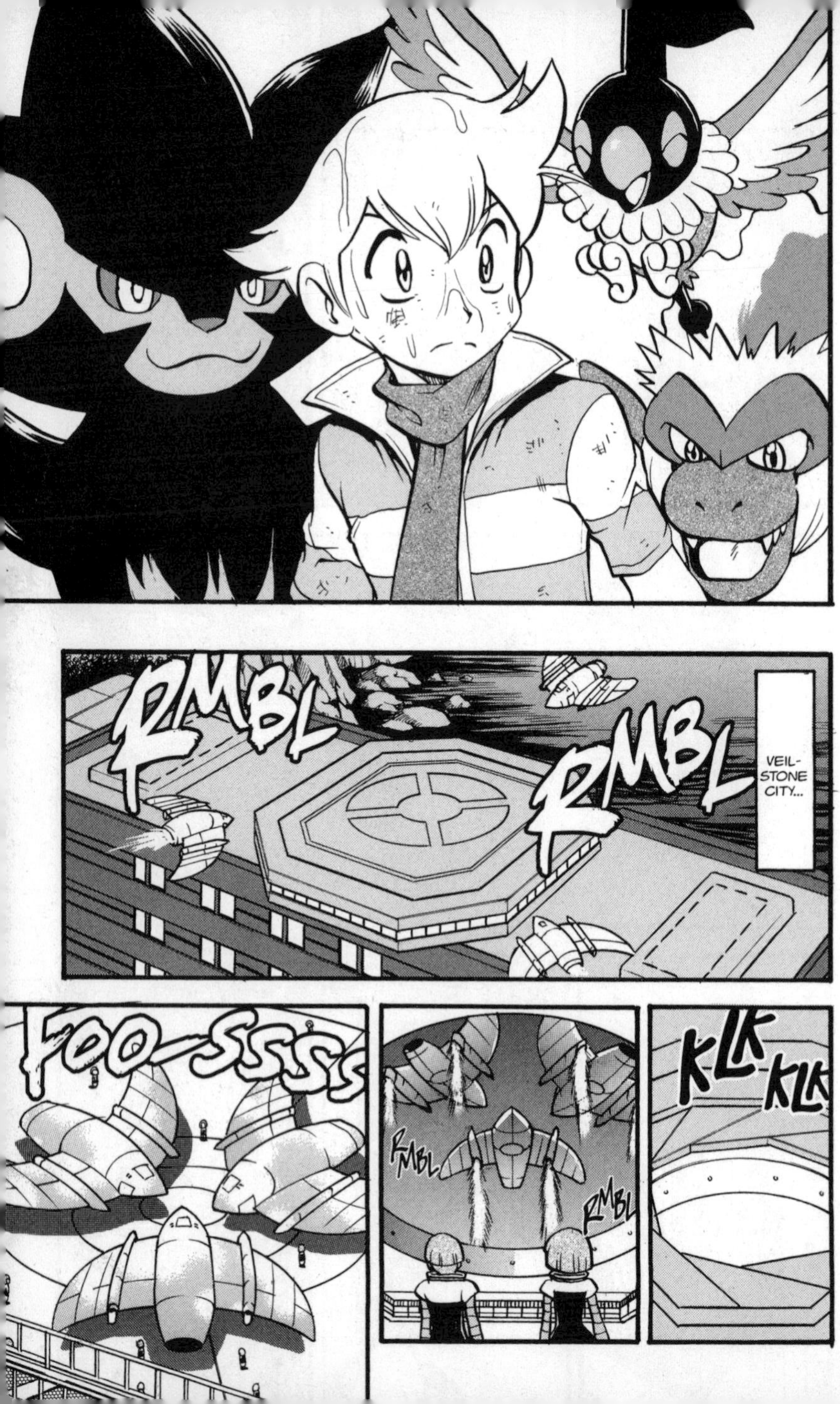
VEIL-STONE CITY...
RMBL
RMBL
KLK
KLK
RMBL
RMBL
FOO-SSSSS

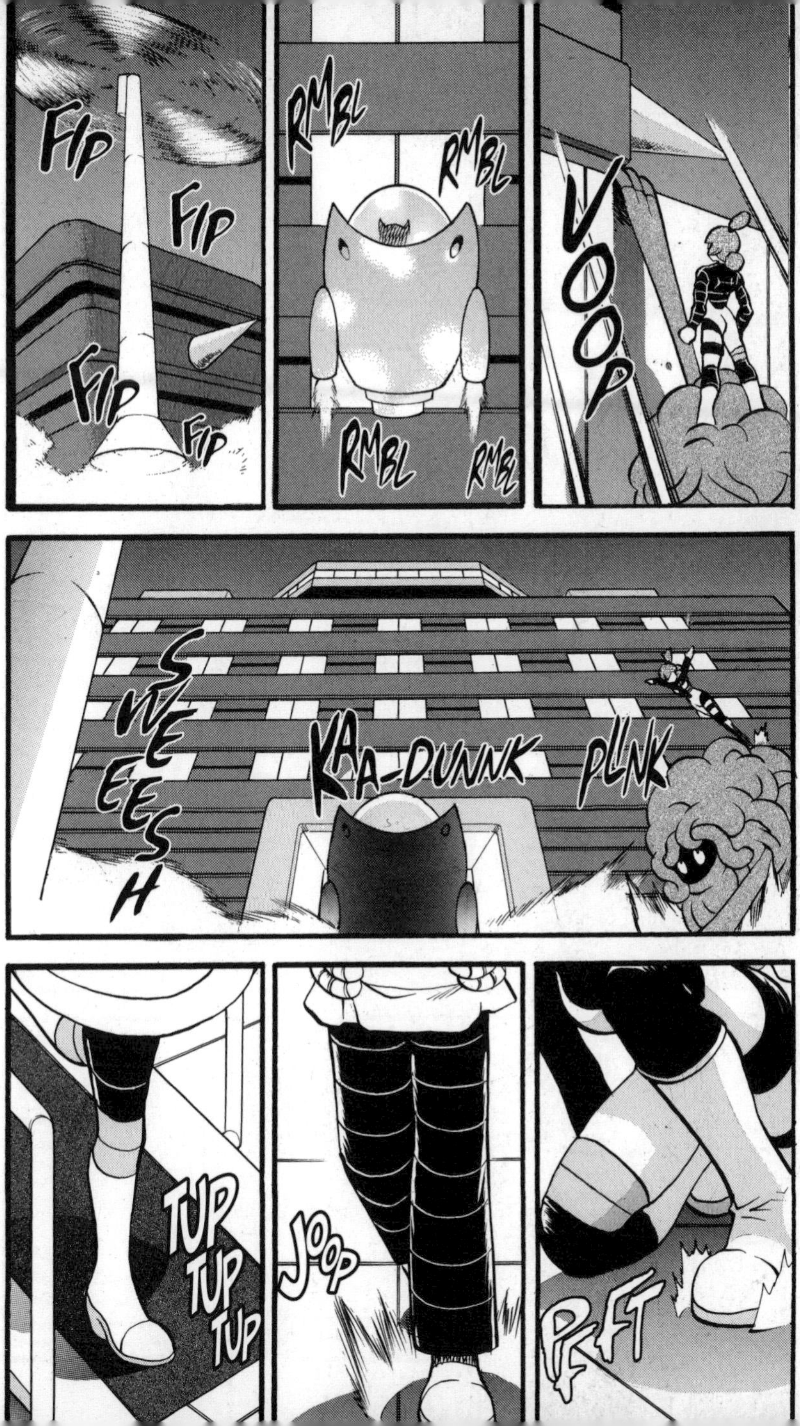
VOOOP
RMBL
RMBL
RMBL
RMBL
FIP
FIP
FIP
FIP
PLINK
KA-DUNNK
SWEEESH
PFFT
JOOP
TUP
TUP
TUP

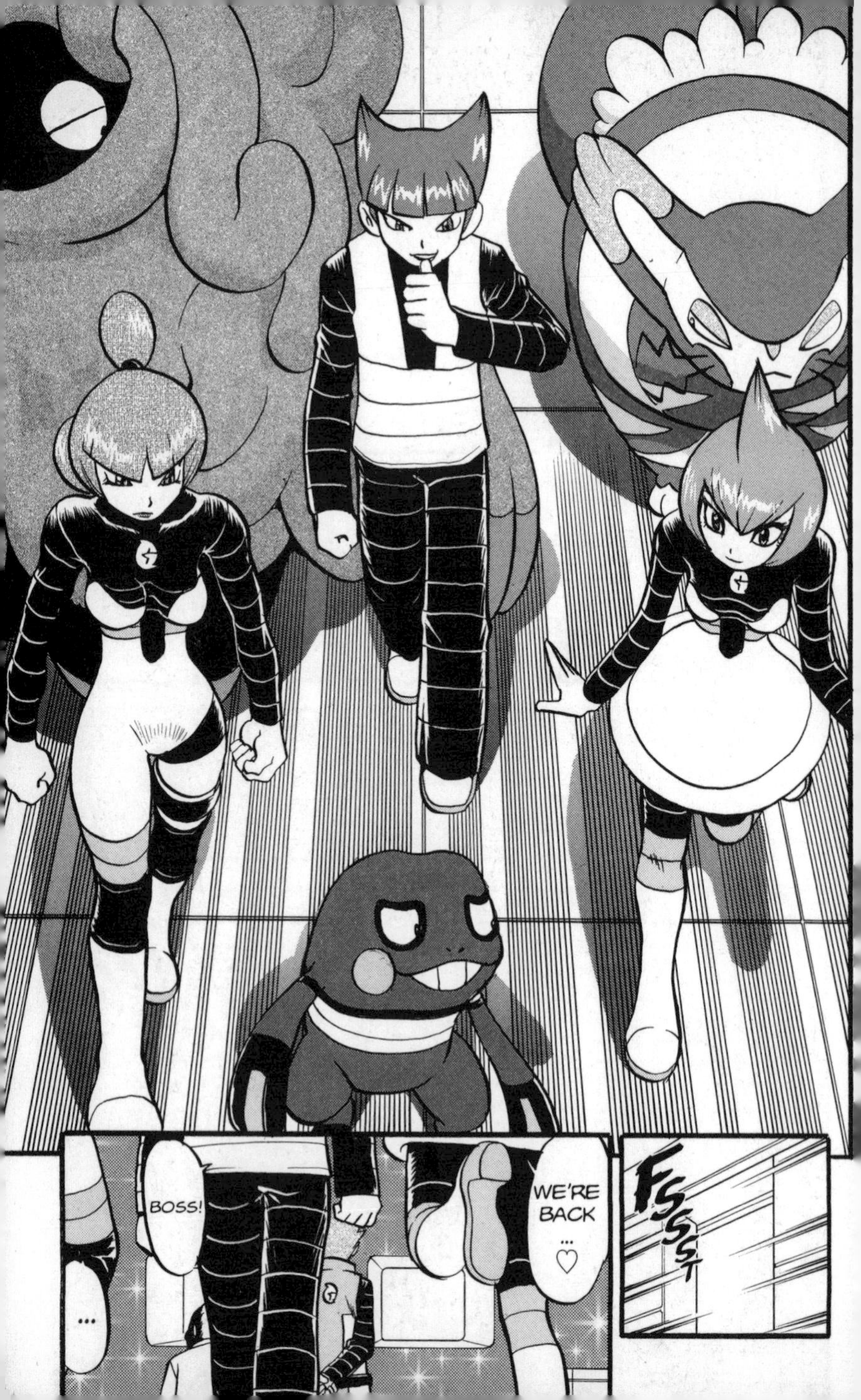
FSSST
WE'RE BACK ... ♡
BOSS!
...

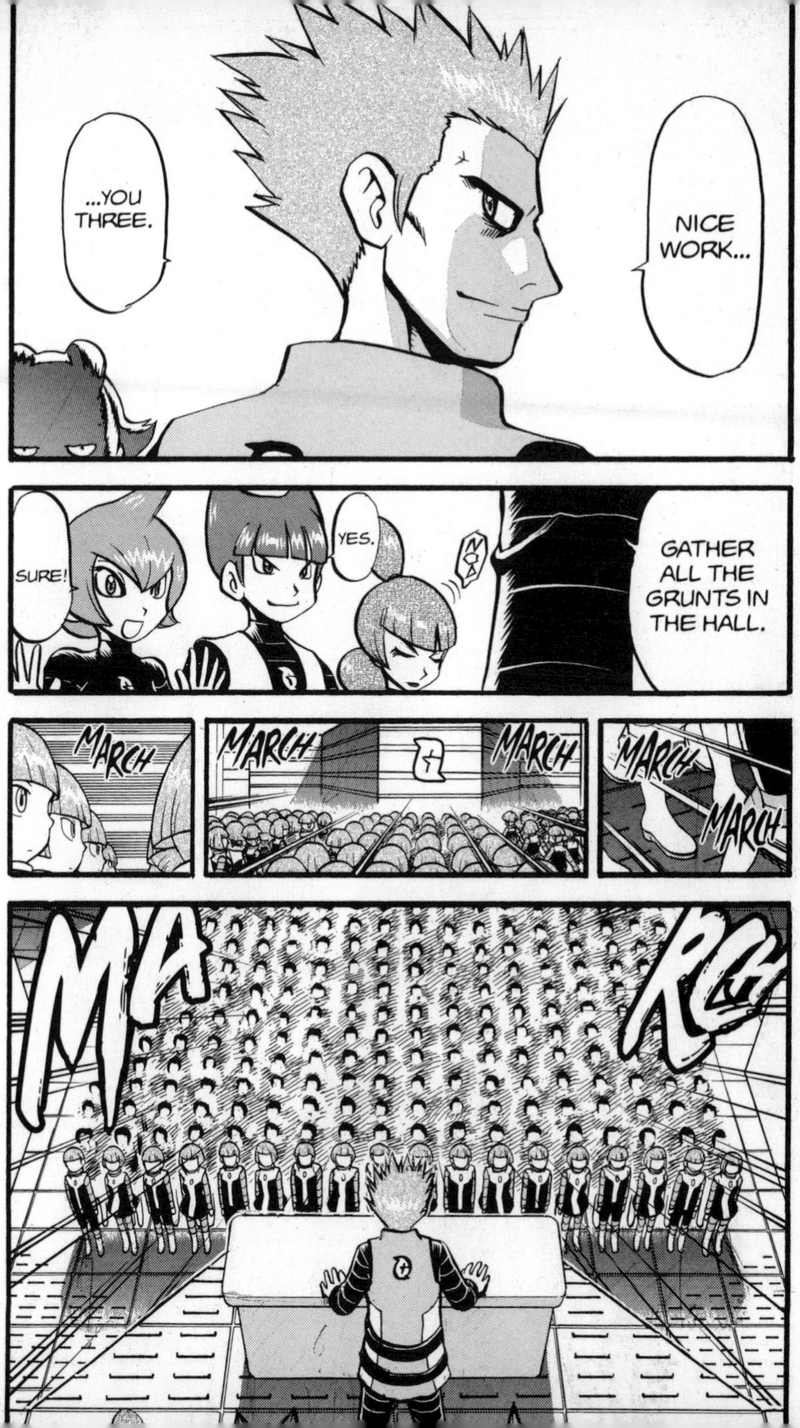
NICE WORK...
...YOU THREE.
GATHER ALL THE GRUNTS IN THE HALL.
NOD
YES.
SURE!
MARCH
MARCH
MARCH
MARCH
MARCH
MA
RCH

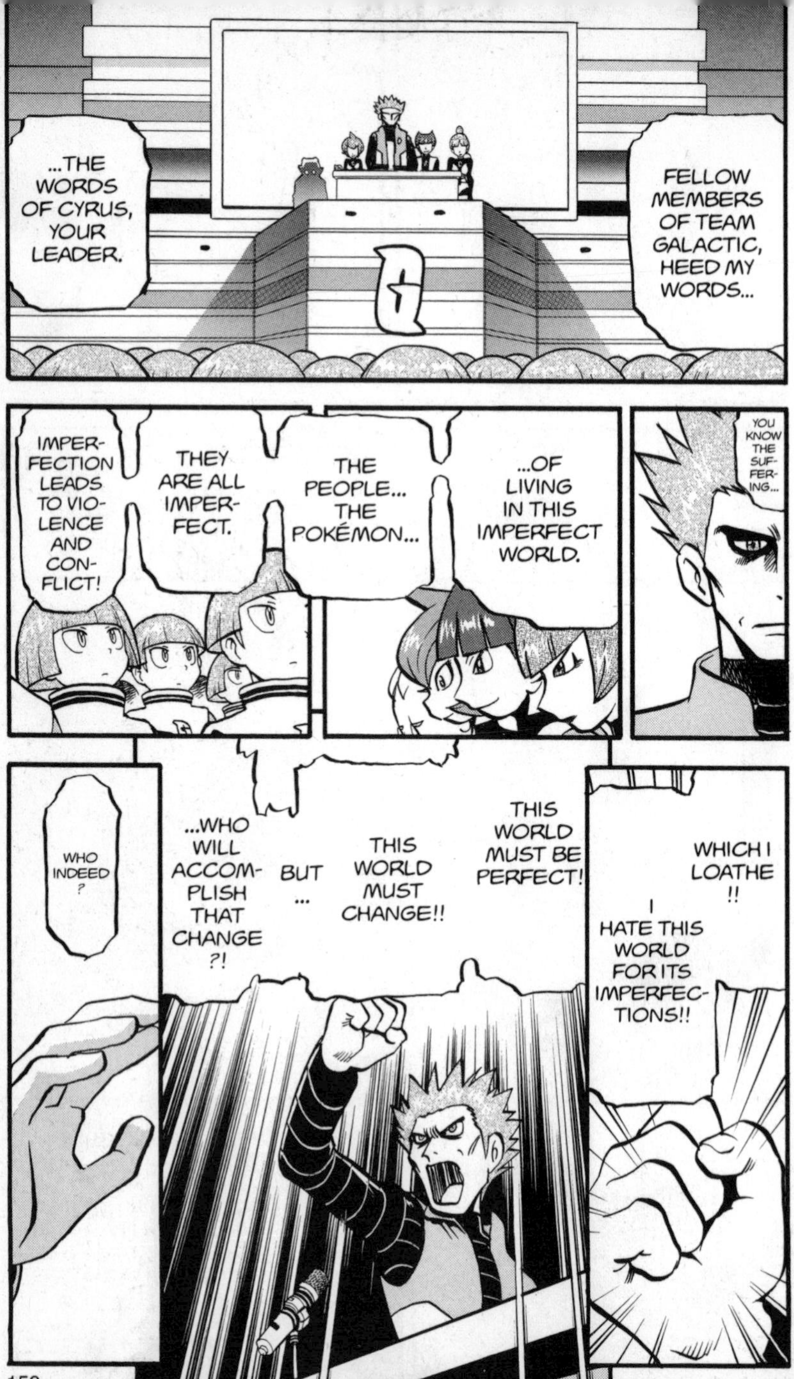
FELLOW MEMBERS OF TEAM GALACTIC, HEED MY WORDS...
...THE WORDS OF CYRUS, YOUR LEADER.
YOU KNOW THE SUF-FER-ING...
...OF LIVING IN THIS IMPERFECT WORLD.
THE PEOPLE... THE POKÉMON...
THEY ARE ALL IMPER-FECT.
IMPER-FECTION LEADS TO VIO-LENCE AND CON-FLICT!
WHICH I LOATHE!!
I HATE THIS WORLD FOR ITS IMPERFEC-TIONS!!
THIS WORLD MUST BE PERFECT!
THIS WORLD MUST CHANGE!!
BUT ...
...WHO WILL ACCOM-PLISH THAT CHANGE ?!
WHO INDEED ?

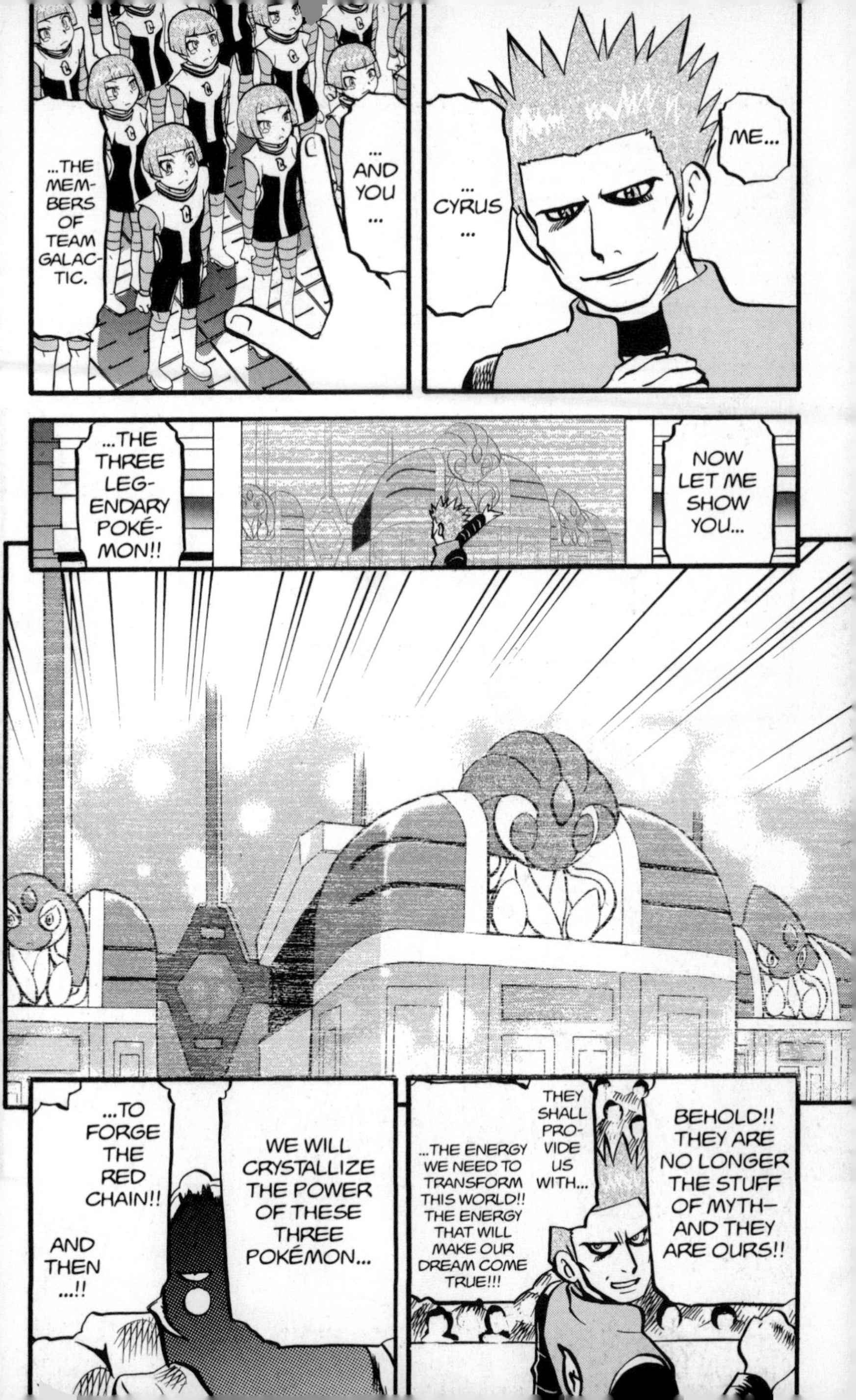
ME...
...CYRUS...
...AND YOU...
...THE MEMBERS OF TEAM GALACTIC.
NOW LET ME SHOW YOU...
...THE THREE LEGENDARY POKÉMON!!
BEHOLD!! THEY ARE NO LONGER THE STUFF OF MYTH— AND THEY ARE OURS!!
THEY SHALL PROVIDE US WITH...
...THE ENERGY WE NEED TO TRANSFORM THIS WORLD!! THE ENERGY THAT WILL MAKE OUR DREAM COME TRUE!!!
WE WILL CRYSTALLIZE THE POWER OF THESE THREE POKÉMON...
...TO FORGE THE RED CHAIN!!
AND THEN ...!!

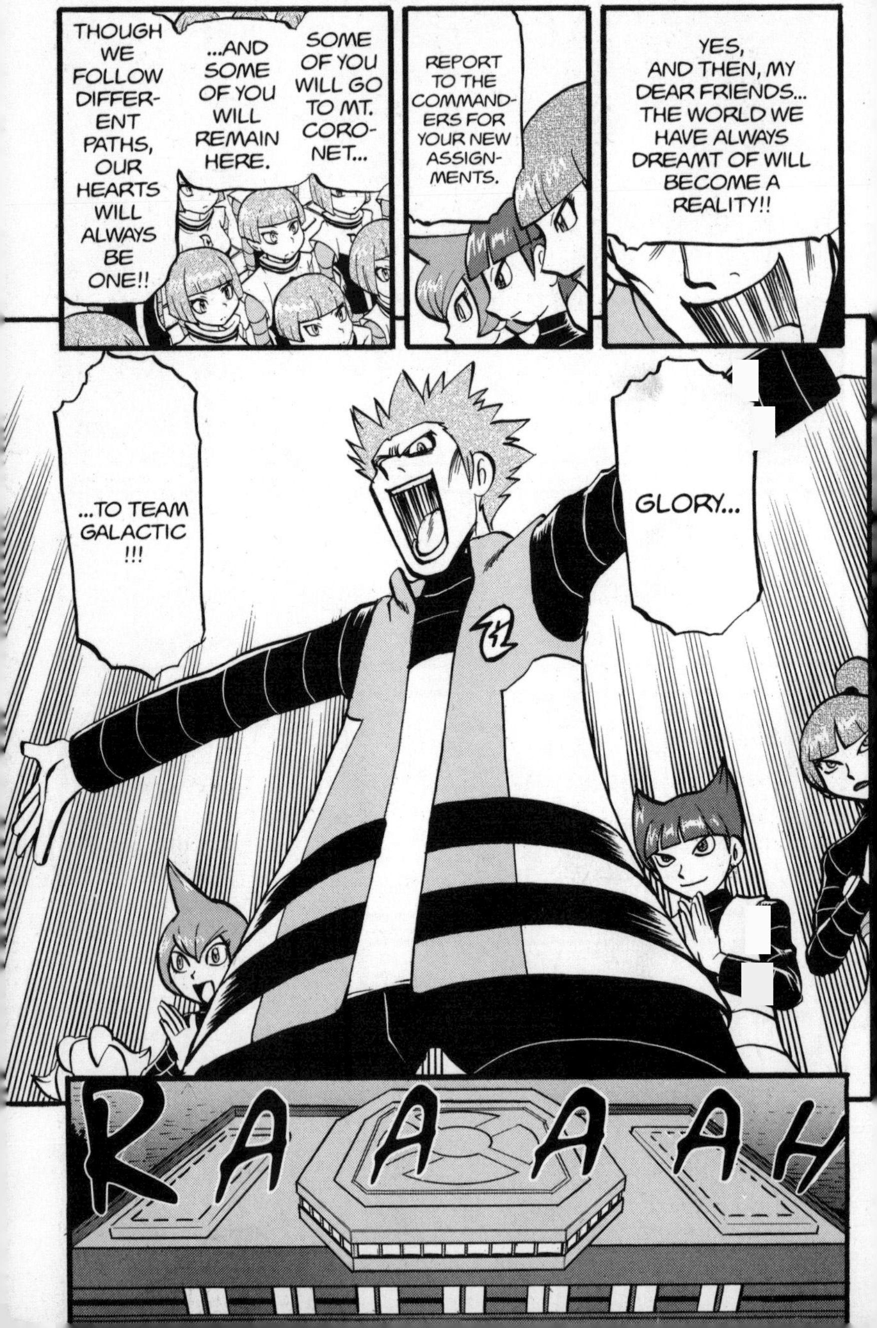

YES, AND THEN, MY DEAR FRIENDS... THE WORLD WE HAVE ALWAYS DREAMT OF WILL BECOME A REALITY!!
REPORT TO THE COMMANDERS FOR YOUR NEW ASSIGNMENTS.
SOME OF YOU WILL GO TO MT. CORONET...
...AND SOME OF YOU WILL REMAIN HERE.
THOUGH WE FOLLOW DIFFERENT PATHS, OUR HEARTS WILL ALWAYS BE ONE!!
GLORY...
...TO TEAM GALACTIC!!!
RAAAAH

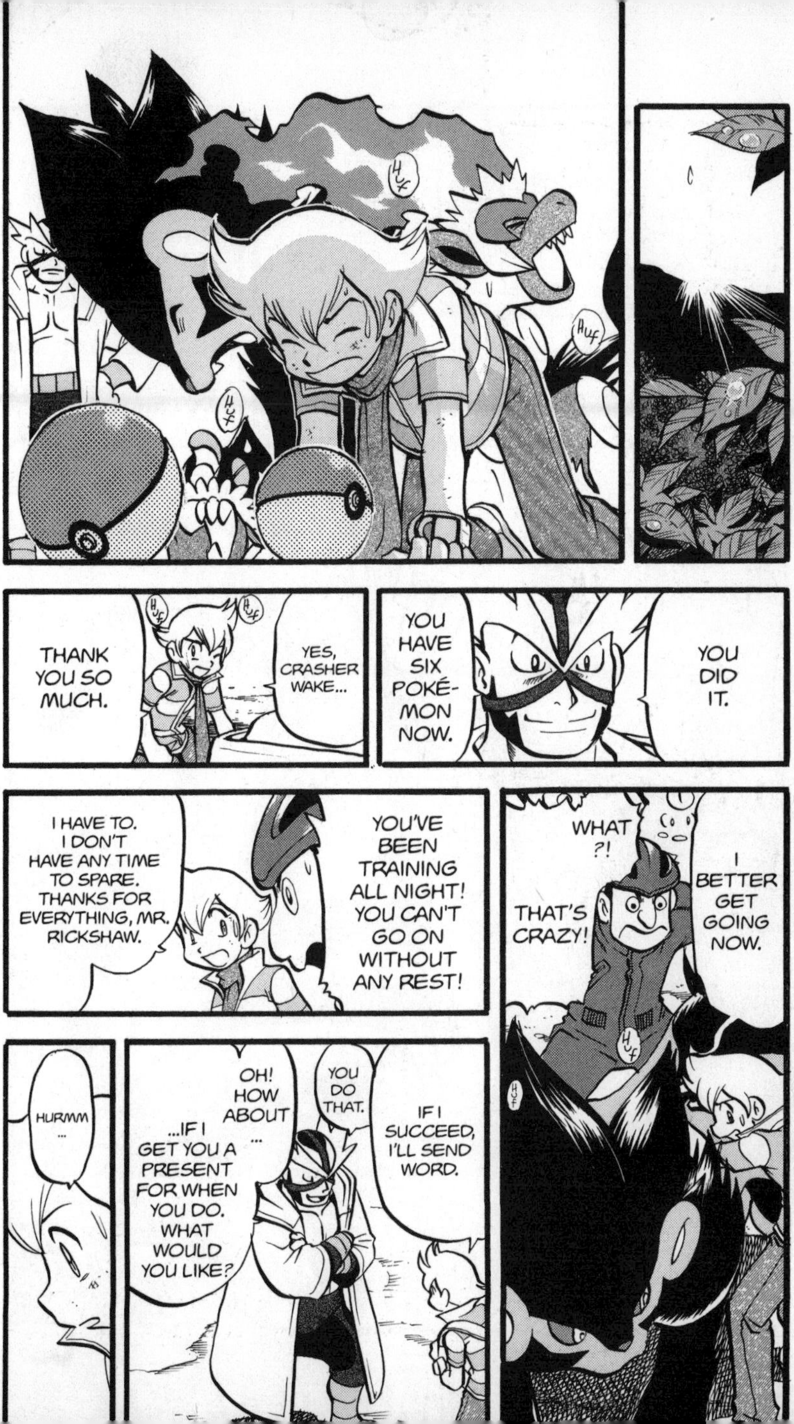
Huf
Huf
Huf
YOU DID IT.
YOU HAVE SIX POKÉ-MON NOW.
YES, CRASHER WAKE...
THANK YOU SO MUCH.
Huf
Huf
I BETTER GET GOING NOW.
WHAT ?!
THAT'S CRAZY!
Huf
Huf
YOU'VE BEEN TRAINING ALL NIGHT! YOU CAN'T GO ON WITHOUT ANY REST!
I HAVE TO. I DON'T HAVE ANY TIME TO SPARE. THANKS FOR EVERYTHING, MR. RICKSHAW.
IF I SUCCEED, I'LL SEND WORD.
YOU DO THAT.
OH! HOW ABOUT ...
...IF I GET YOU A PRESENT FOR WHEN YOU DO. WHAT WOULD YOU LIKE?
HURMM ...

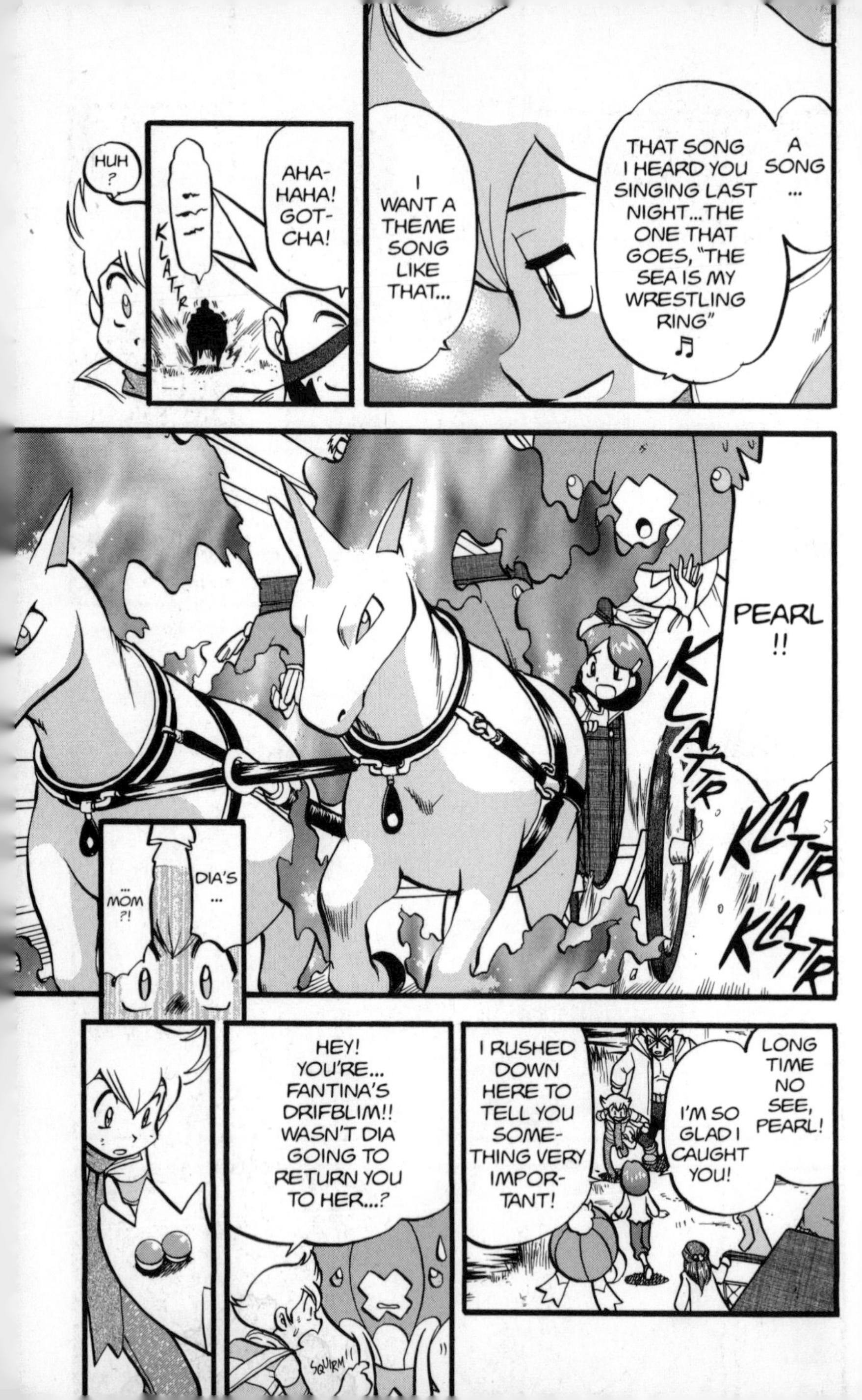

A SONG ...
THAT SONG I HEARD YOU SINGING LAST NIGHT...THE ONE THAT GOES, "THE SEA IS MY WRESTLING RING" ♫
I WANT A THEME SONG LIKE THAT...
AHA-HAHA! GOT-CHA!
KLATTR
HUH ?
PEARL !!
KLATTR
KLATTR
KLATTR
DIA'S ...
... MOM ?!
LONG TIME NO SEE, PEARL!
I'M SO GLAD I CAUGHT YOU!
I RUSHED DOWN HERE TO TELL YOU SOME-THING VERY IMPOR-TANT!
HEY! YOU'RE... FANTINA'S DRIFBLIM!! WASN'T DIA GOING TO RETURN YOU TO HER...?
SQUIRM

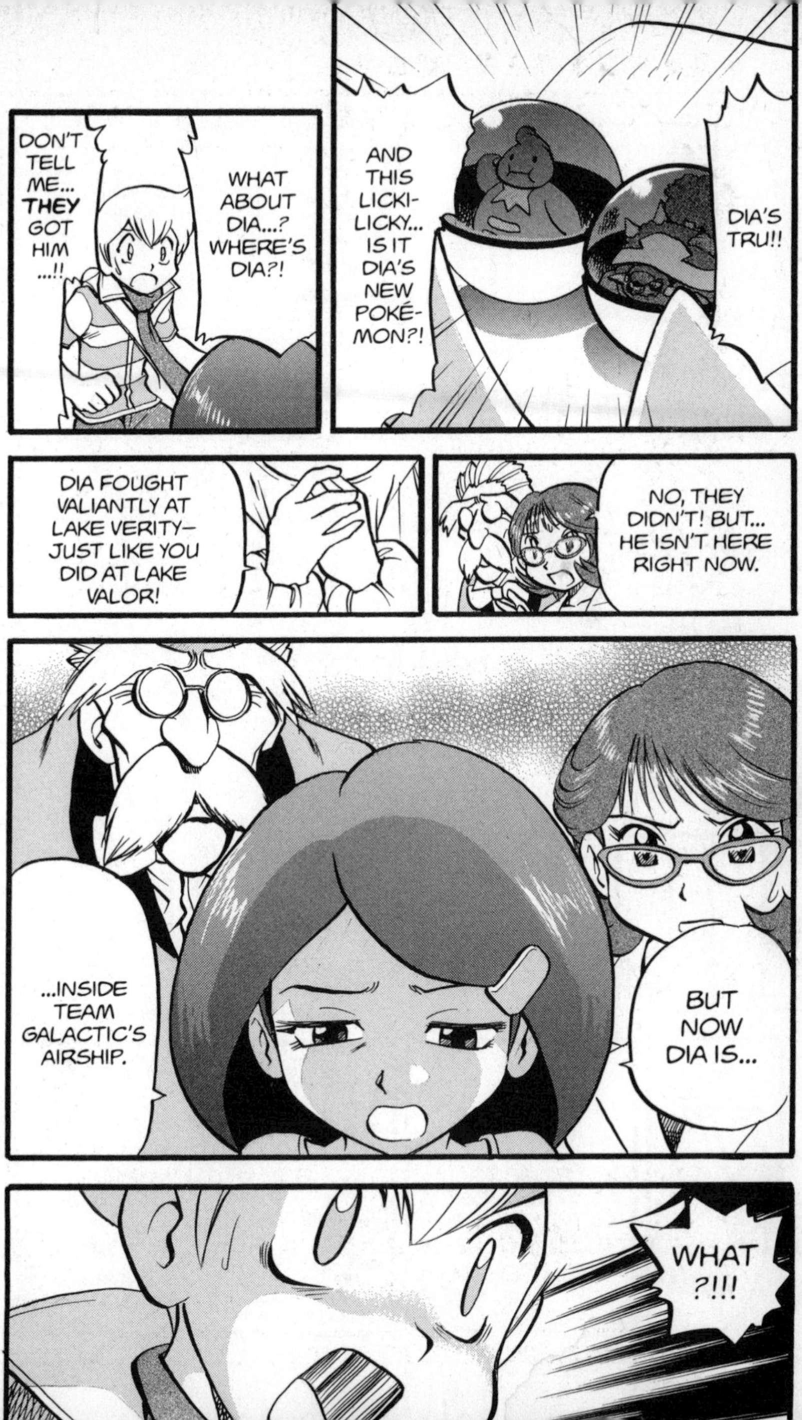
DIA'S TRU!!
AND THIS LICKI-LICKY... IS IT DIA'S NEW POKÉ-MON?!
WHAT ABOUT DIA...? WHERE'S DIA?!
DON'T TELL ME... **THEY** GOT HIM ...!!
NO, THEY DIDN'T! BUT... HE ISN'T HERE RIGHT NOW.
DIA FOUGHT VALIANTLY AT LAKE VERITY– JUST LIKE YOU DID AT LAKE VALOR!
BUT NOW DIA IS...
...INSIDE TEAM GALACTIC'S AIRSHIP.
WHAT ?!!!

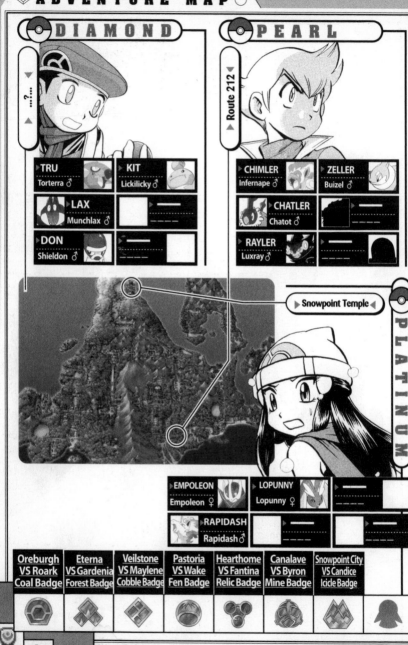

DIAMOND

TRU Torterra ♂
KIT Lickilicky ♂
LAX Munchlax ♂
DON Shieldon ♂

PEARL

CHIMLER Infernape ♂
ZELLER Buizel ♂
CHATLER Chatot ♂
RAYLER Luxray ♂

▲ Route 212 ◀

▶ Snowpoint Temple ◀

PLATINUM

EMPOLEON Empoleon ♀
LOPUNNY Lopunny ♀
RAPIDASH Rapidash ♂

Oreburgh VS Roark Coal Badge	Eterna VS Gardenia Forest Badge	Veilstone VS Maylene Cobble Badge	Pastoria VS Wake Fen Badge	Hearthome VS Fantina Relic Badge	Canalave VS Byron Mine Badge	Snowpoint City VS Candice Icicle Badge

66

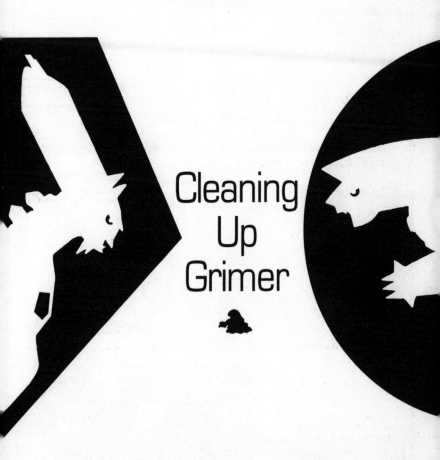

Cleaning
Up
Grimer

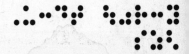

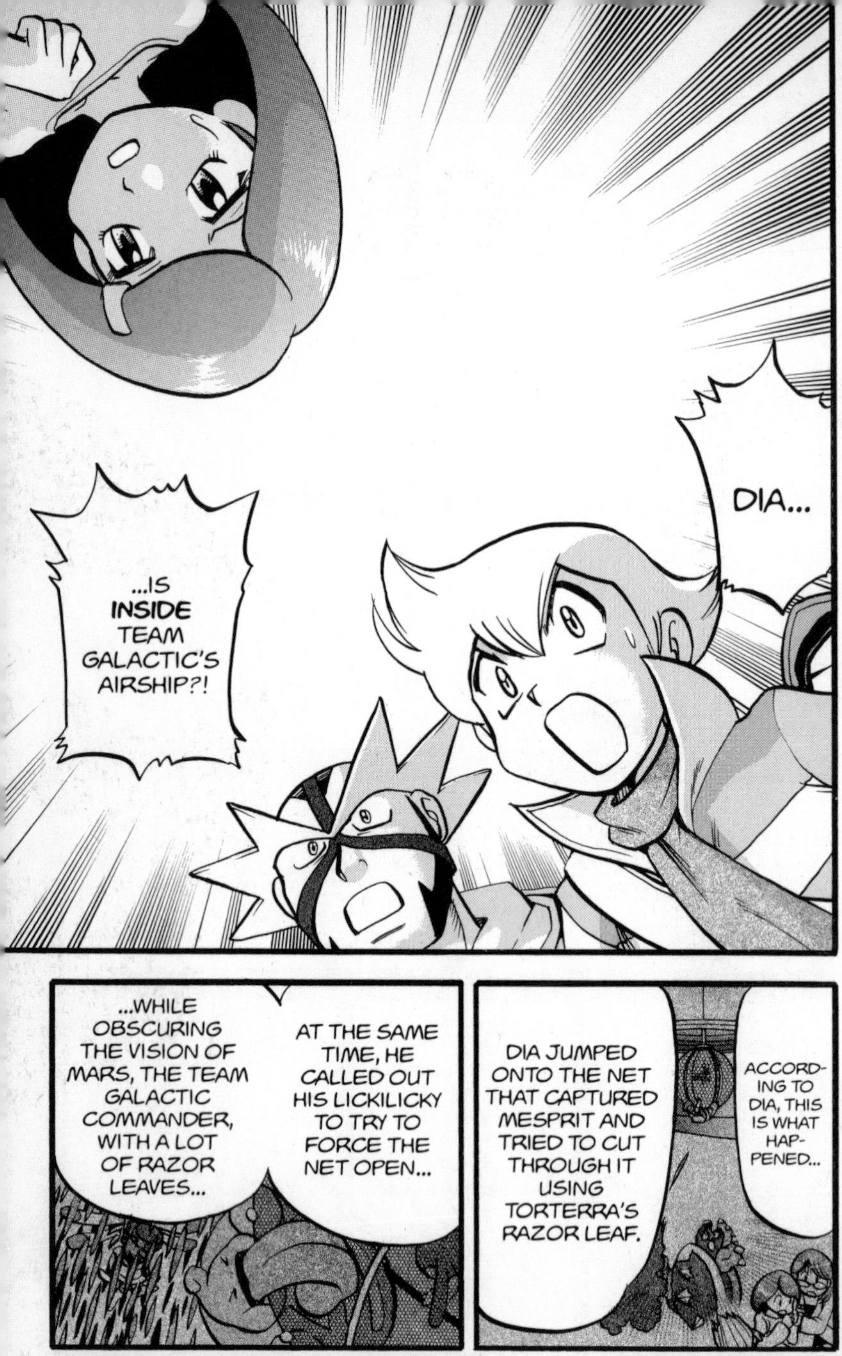
DIA...
...IS **INSIDE** TEAM GALACTIC'S AIRSHIP?!
ACCORD-ING TO DIA, THIS IS WHAT HAP-PENED...
DIA JUMPED ONTO THE NET THAT CAPTURED MESPRIT AND TRIED TO CUT THROUGH IT USING TORTERRA'S RAZOR LEAF.
AT THE SAME TIME, HE CALLED OUT HIS LICKILICKY TO TRY TO FORCE THE NET OPEN...
...WHILE OBSCURING THE VISION OF MARS, THE TEAM GALACTIC COMMANDER, WITH A LOT OF RAZOR LEAVES...

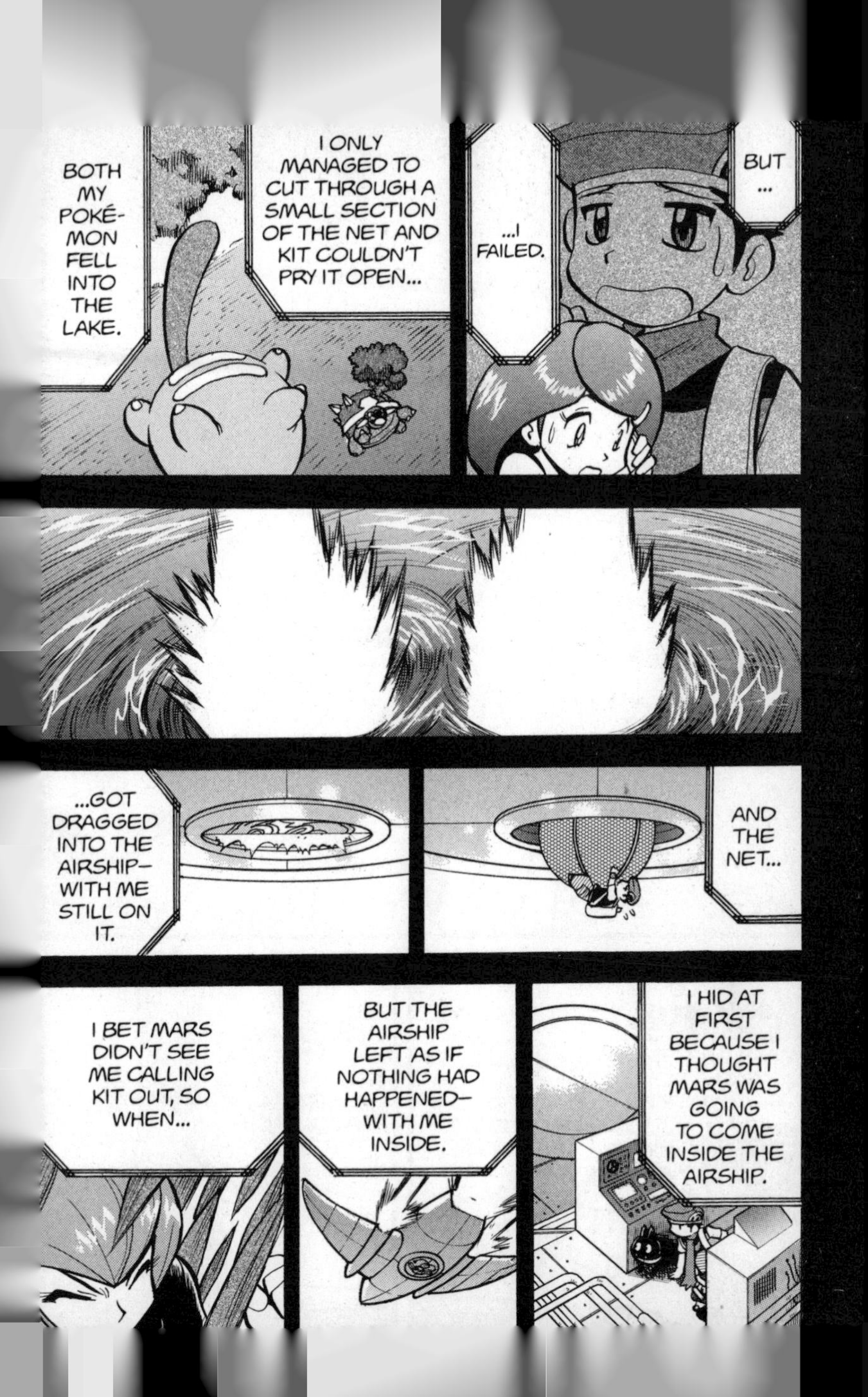
BUT ...
...I FAILED.
I ONLY MANAGED TO CUT THROUGH A SMALL SECTION OF THE NET AND KIT COULDN'T PRY IT OPEN...
BOTH MY POKÉ-MON FELL INTO THE LAKE.
AND THE NET...
...GOT DRAGGED INTO THE AIRSHIP—WITH ME STILL ON IT.
I HID AT FIRST BECAUSE I THOUGHT MARS WAS GOING TO COME INSIDE THE AIRSHIP.
BUT THE AIRSHIP LEFT AS IF NOTHING HAD HAPPENED—WITH ME INSIDE.
I BET MARS DIDN'T SEE ME CALLING KIT OUT, SO WHEN...

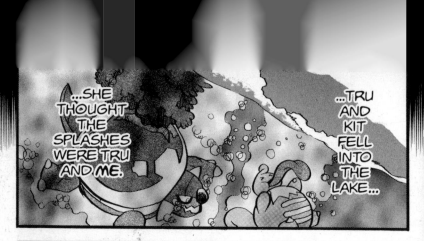

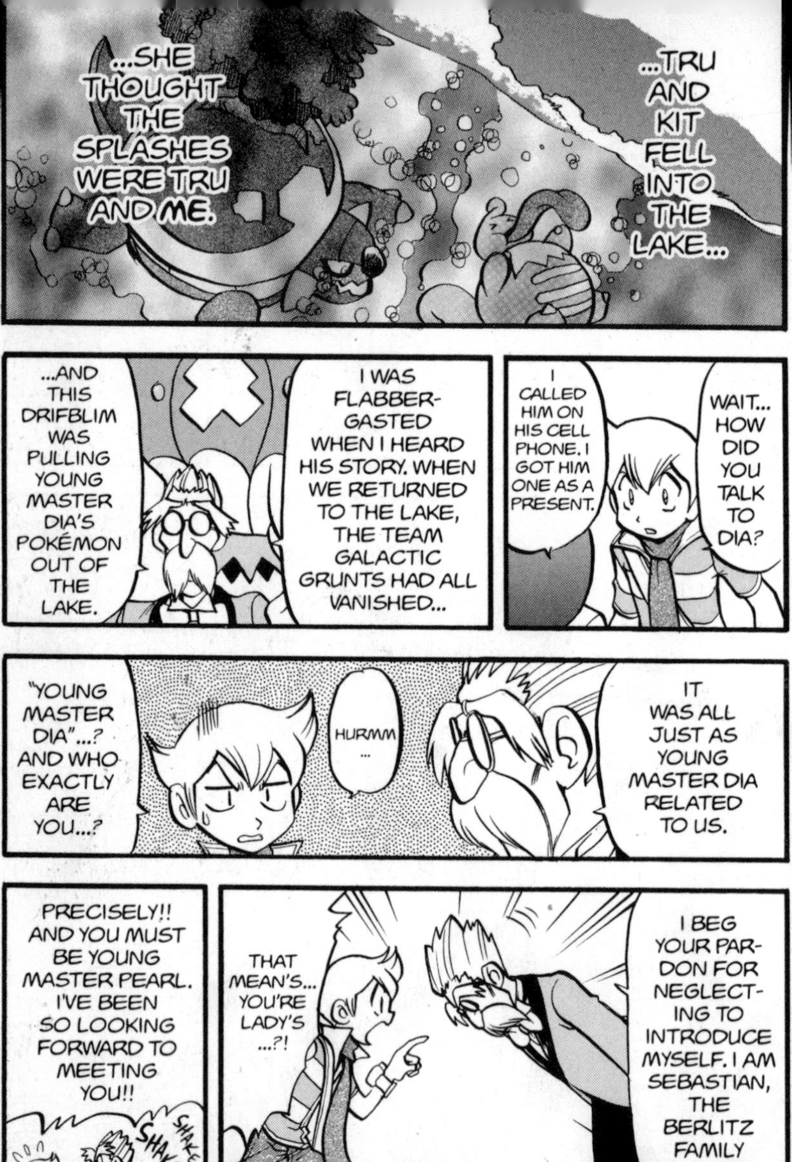
...TRU AND KIT FELL INTO THE LAKE...
...SHE THOUGHT THE SPLASHES WERE TRU AND ME.
WAIT... HOW DID YOU TALK TO DIA?
I CALLED HIM ON HIS CELL PHONE. I GOT HIM ONE AS A PRESENT.
I WAS FLABBER-GASTED WHEN I HEARD HIS STORY. WHEN WE RETURNED TO THE LAKE, THE TEAM GALACTIC GRUNTS HAD ALL VANISHED...
...AND THIS DRIFBLIM WAS PULLING YOUNG MASTER DIA'S POKÉMON OUT OF THE LAKE.
IT WAS ALL JUST AS YOUNG MASTER DIA RELATED TO US.
HURMM...
"YOUNG MASTER DIA"...? AND WHO EXACTLY ARE YOU...?
I BEG YOUR PAR-DON FOR NEGLECT-ING TO INTRODUCE MYSELF. I AM SEBASTIAN, THE BERLITZ FAMILY BUTLER.
THAT MEAN'S... YOU'RE LADY'S ...?!
PRECISELY!! AND YOU MUST BE YOUNG MASTER PEARL. I'VE BEEN SO LOOKING FORWARD TO MEETING YOU!!
SHAKE SHAKE

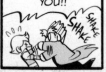

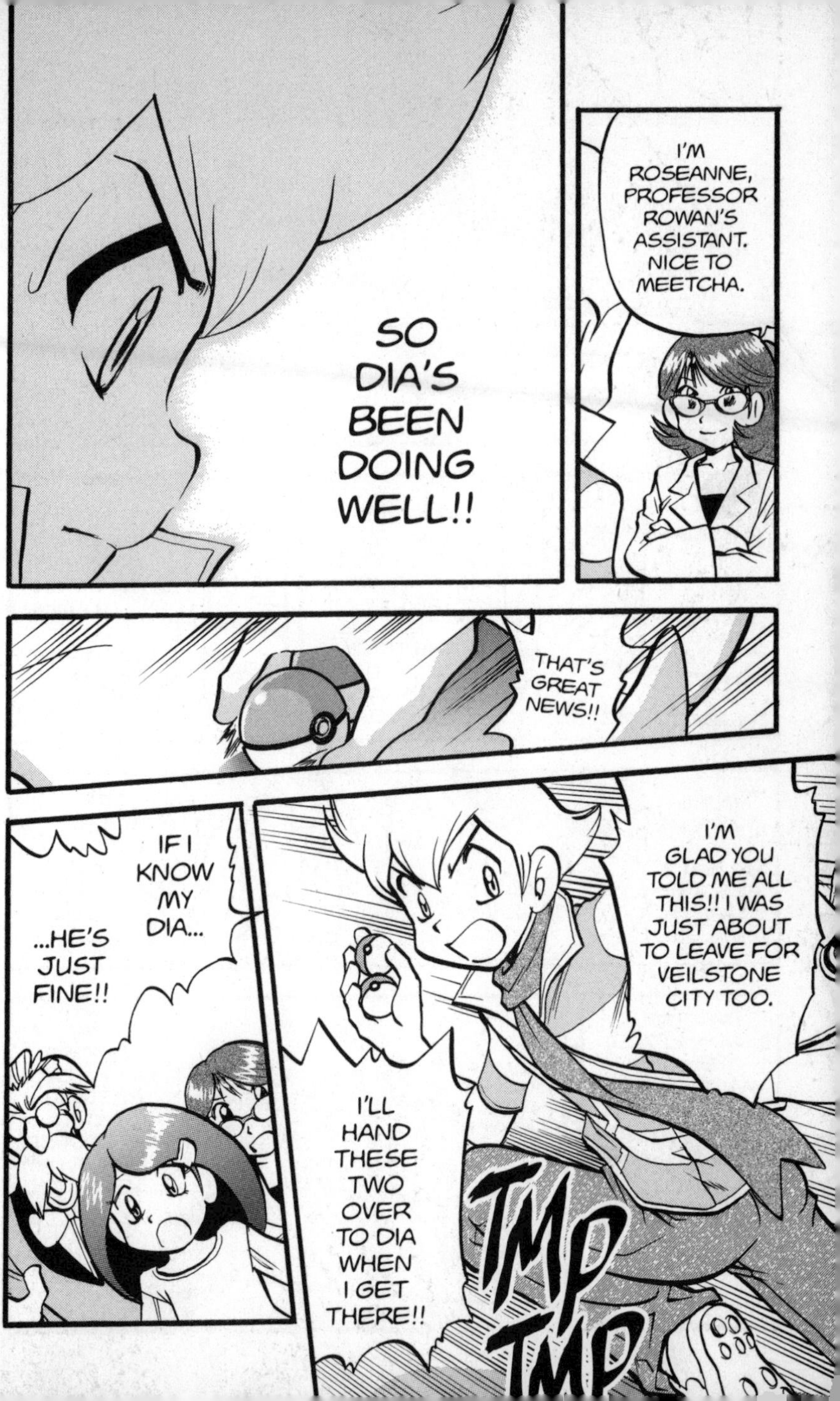
I'M ROSEANNE, PROFESSOR ROWAN'S ASSISTANT. NICE TO MEETCHA.
SO DIA'S BEEN DOING WELL!!
THAT'S GREAT NEWS!!
I'M GLAD YOU TOLD ME ALL THIS!! I WAS JUST ABOUT TO LEAVE FOR VEILSTONE CITY TOO.
I'LL HAND THESE TWO OVER TO DIA WHEN I GET THERE!!
TMP TMP
IF I KNOW MY DIA...
...HE'S JUST FINE!!

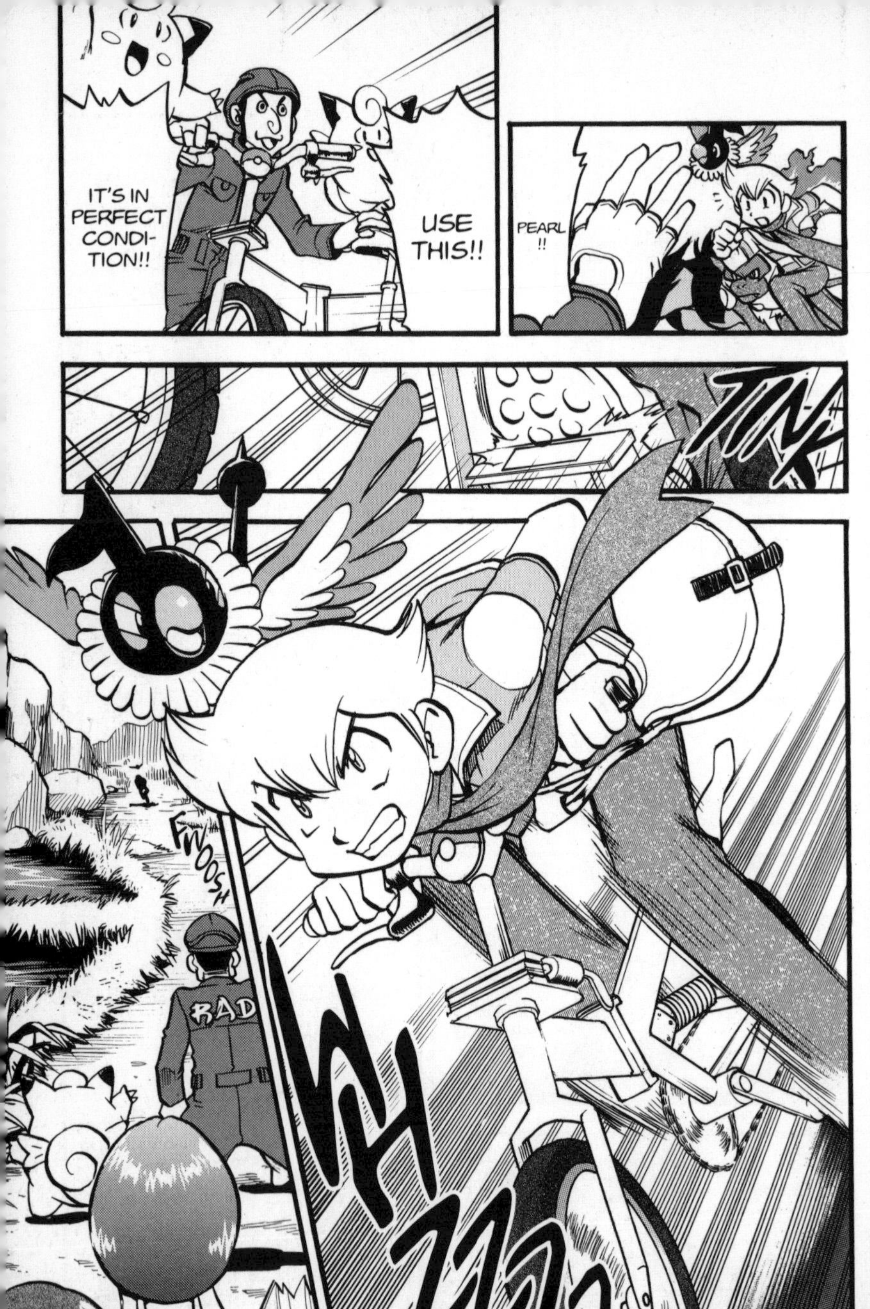
PEARL !!
USE THIS!!
IT'S IN PERFECT CONDITION!!
TINK
FWOOSH
RAD

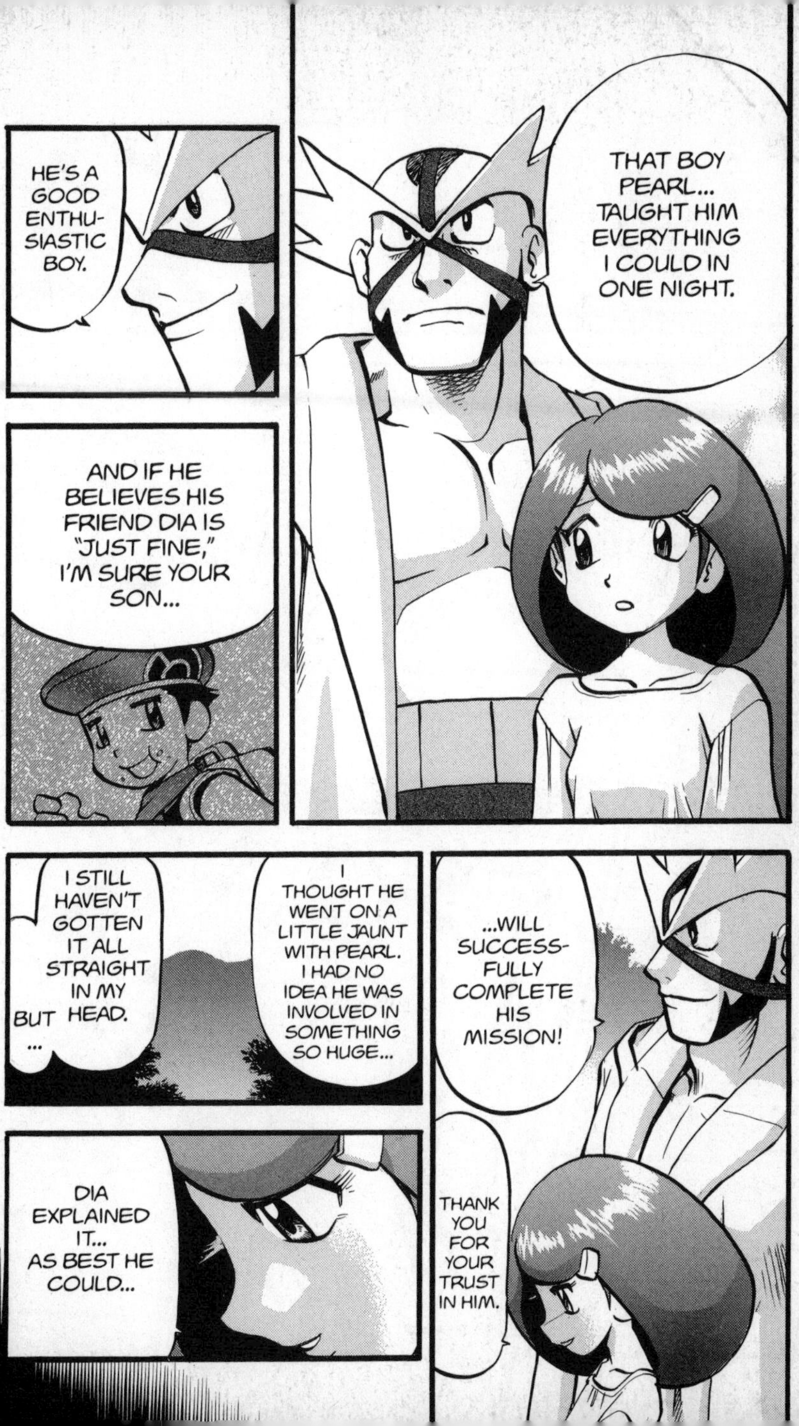

THAT BOY PEARL... TAUGHT HIM EVERYTHING I COULD IN ONE NIGHT.
HE'S A GOOD ENTHU-SIASTIC BOY.
AND IF HE BELIEVES HIS FRIEND DIA IS "JUST FINE," I'M SURE YOUR SON...
...WILL SUCCESS-FULLY COMPLETE HIS MISSION!
THANK YOU FOR YOUR TRUST IN HIM.
I THOUGHT HE WENT ON A LITTLE JAUNT WITH PEARL. I HAD NO IDEA HE WAS INVOLVED IN SOMETHING SO HUGE...
I STILL HAVEN'T GOTTEN IT ALL STRAIGHT IN MY HEAD.
BUT ...
DIA EXPLAINED IT... AS BEST HE COULD...

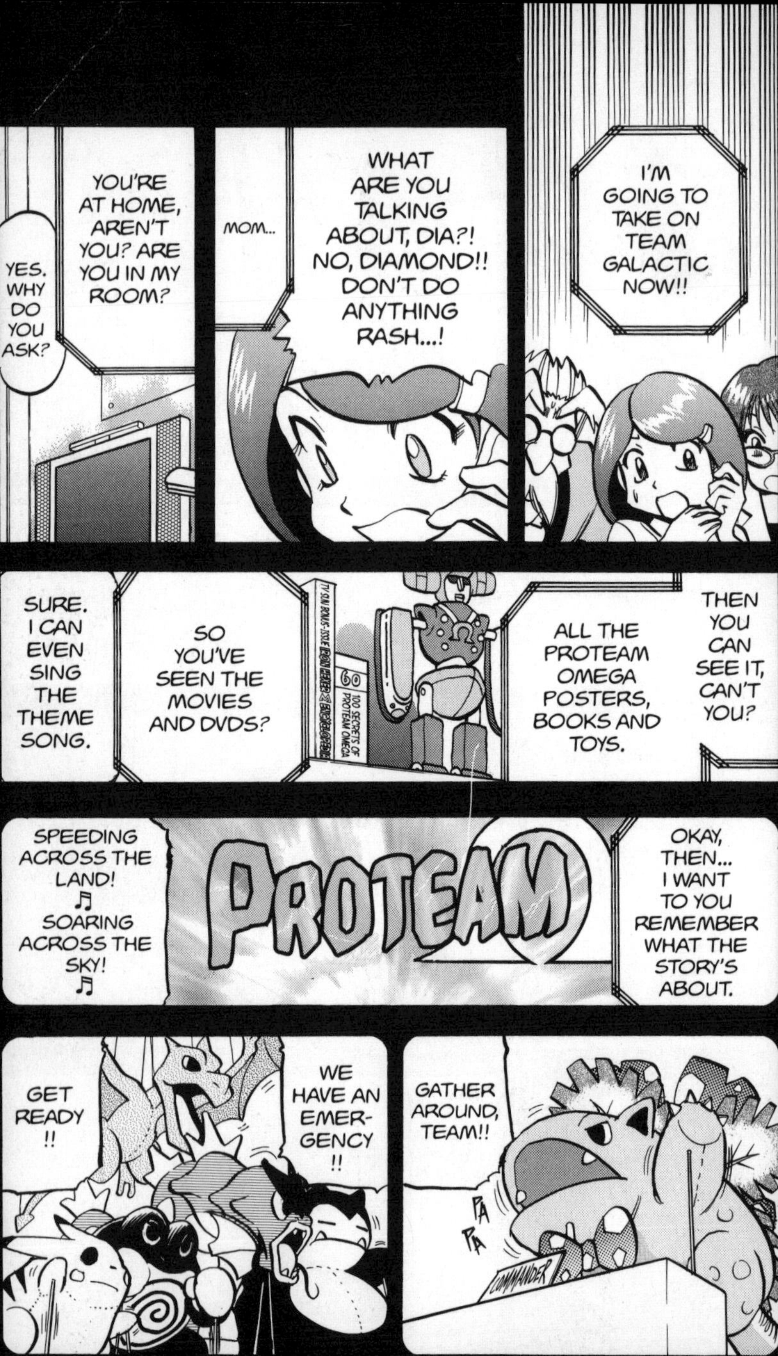
I'M GOING TO TAKE ON TEAM GALACTIC NOW!!
WHAT ARE YOU TALKING ABOUT, DIA?! NO, DIAMOND!! DON'T DO ANYTHING RASH...!
MOM...
YOU'RE AT HOME, AREN'T YOU? ARE YOU IN MY ROOM?
YES. WHY DO YOU ASK?
THEN YOU CAN SEE IT, CAN'T YOU?
ALL THE PROTEAM OMEGA POSTERS, BOOKS AND TOYS.
60
100 SECRETS OF PROTEAM OMEGA
SO YOU'VE SEEN THE MOVIES AND DVDS?
SURE. I CAN EVEN SING THE THEME SONG.
OKAY, THEN... I WANT TO YOU REMEMBER WHAT THE STORY'S ABOUT.
PROTEAM
SPEEDING ACROSS THE LAND! ♫ SOARING ACROSS THE SKY! ♫
GATHER AROUND, TEAM!!
PA PA
COMMANDER
WE HAVE AN EMERGENCY !!
GET READY !!

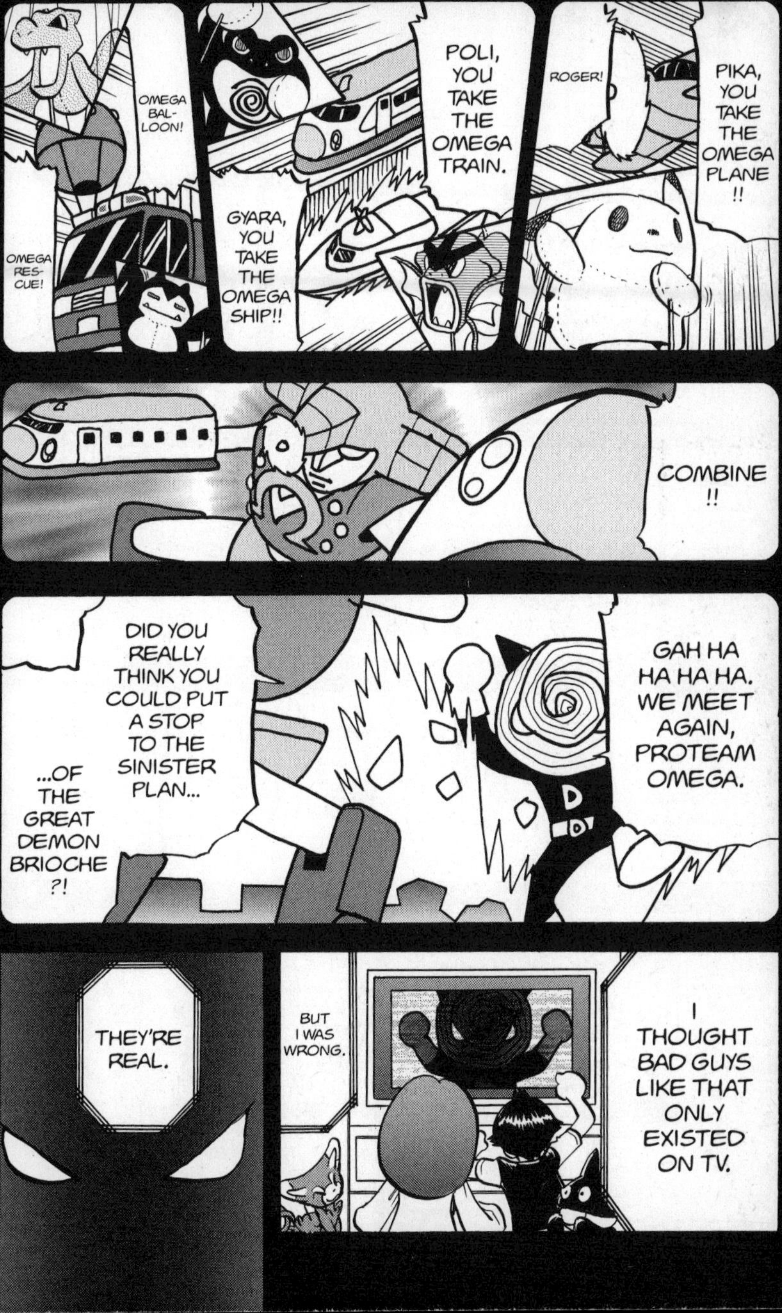
PIKA, YOU TAKE THE OMEGA PLANE!!
ROGER!
POLI, YOU TAKE THE OMEGA TRAIN.
GYARA, YOU TAKE THE OMEGA SHIP!!
OMEGA BALLOON!
OMEGA RESCUE!
COMBINE!!
GAH HA HA HA HA. WE MEET AGAIN, PROTEAM OMEGA.
DID YOU REALLY THINK YOU COULD PUT A STOP TO THE SINISTER PLAN...
...OF THE GREAT DEMON BRIOCHE?!
I THOUGHT BAD GUYS LIKE THAT ONLY EXISTED ON TV.
BUT I WAS WRONG.
THEY'RE REAL.

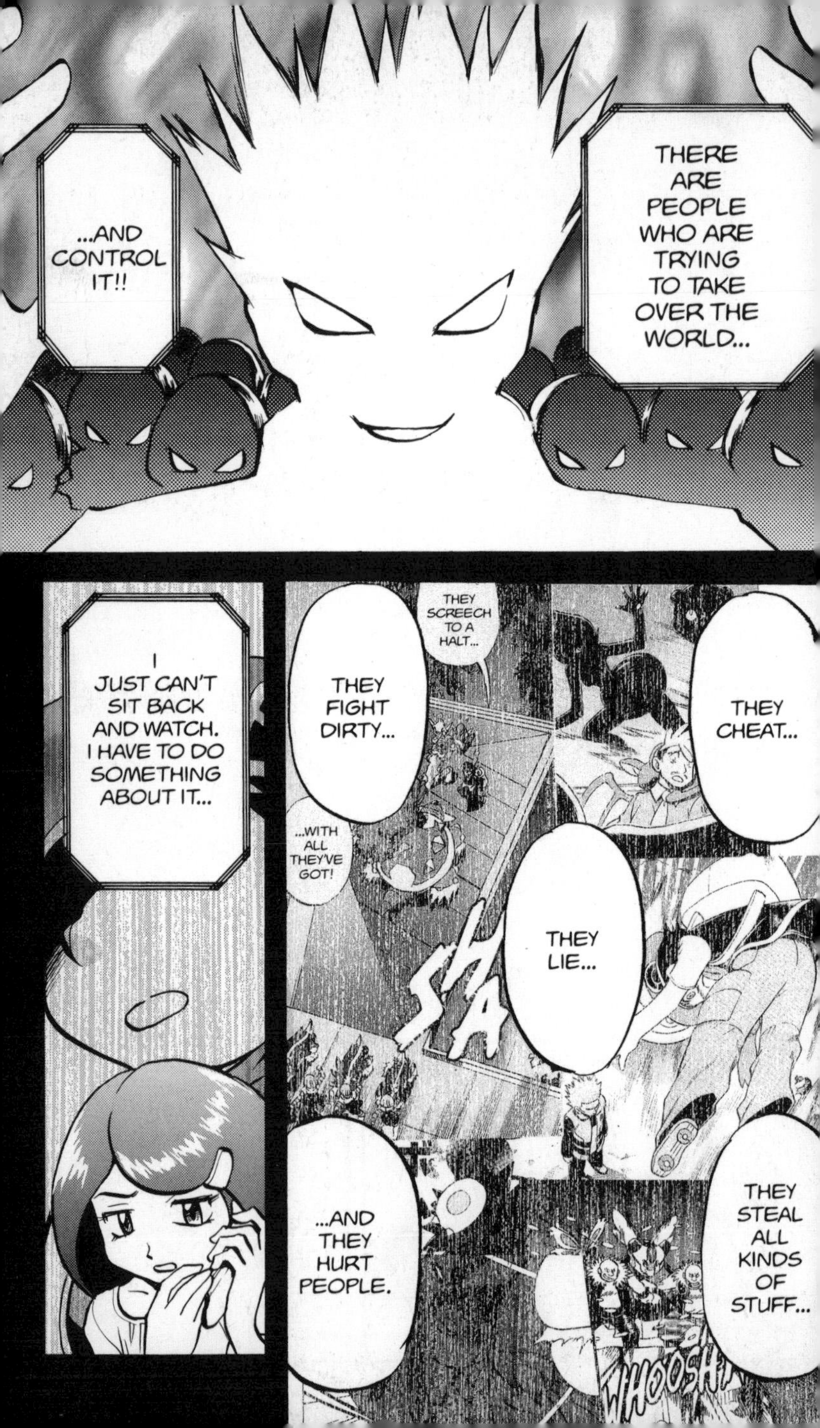
THERE ARE PEOPLE WHO ARE TRYING TO TAKE OVER THE WORLD...
...AND CONTROL IT!!
THEY CHEAT...
THEY SCREECH TO A HALT...
THEY FIGHT DIRTY...
...WITH ALL THEY'VE GOT!
THEY LIE...
SHA
THEY STEAL ALL KINDS OF STUFF...
WHOOSH
...AND THEY HURT PEOPLE.
I JUST CAN'T SIT BACK AND WATCH. I HAVE TO DO SOMETHING ABOUT IT...

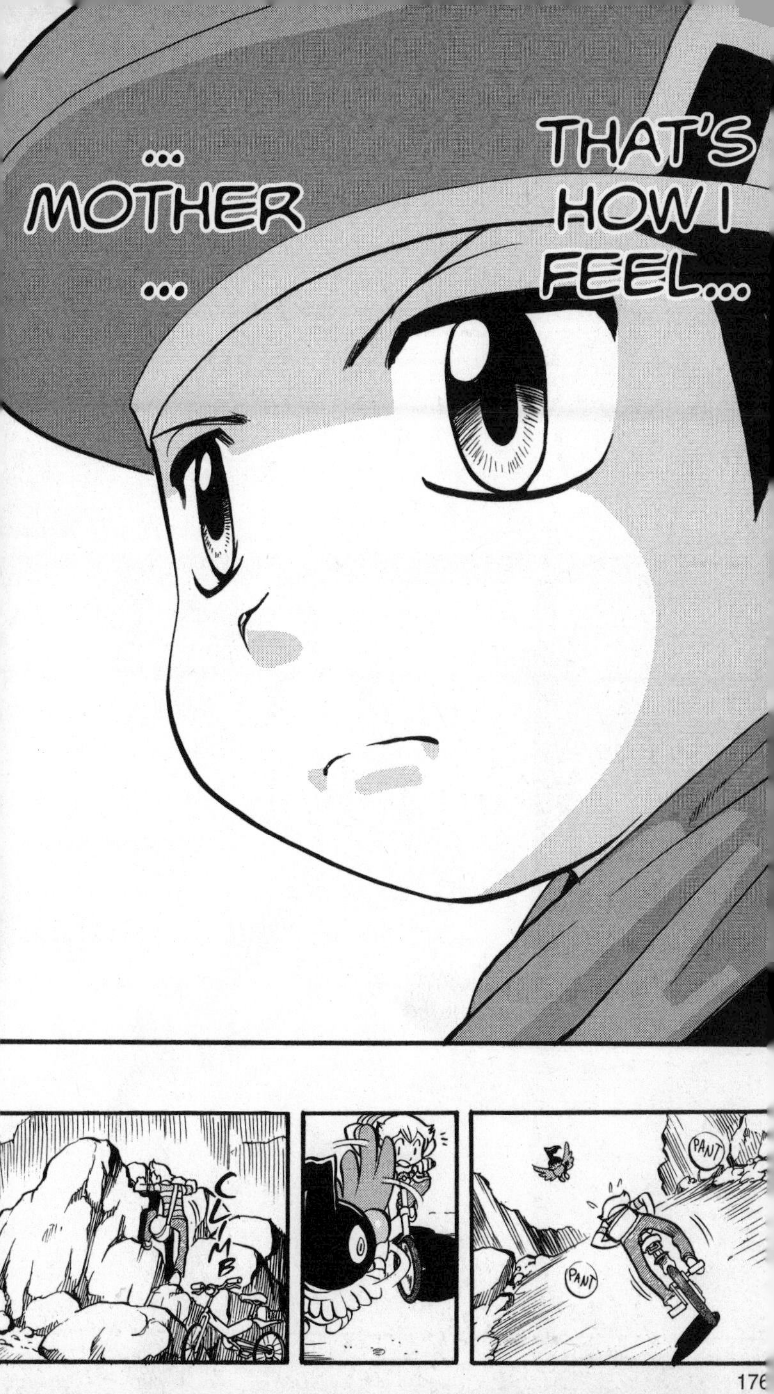
THAT'S HOW I FEEL...
...MOTHER...
PANT
PANT
CLIMB

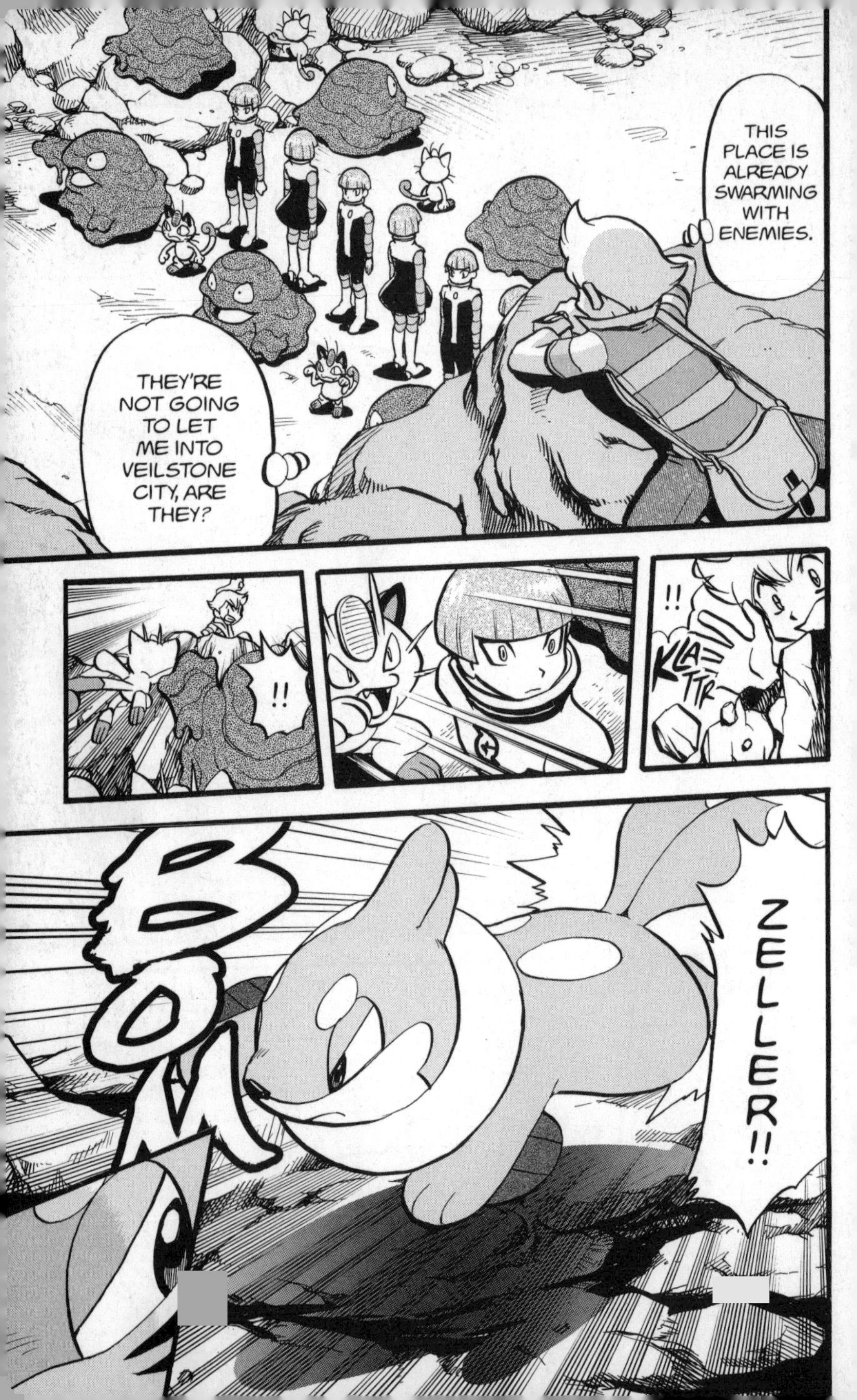
THIS PLACE IS ALREADY SWARMING WITH ENEMIES.
THEY'RE NOT GOING TO LET ME INTO VEILSTONE CITY, ARE THEY?
!!
KLATTR
!!
ZELLER!!
BOM

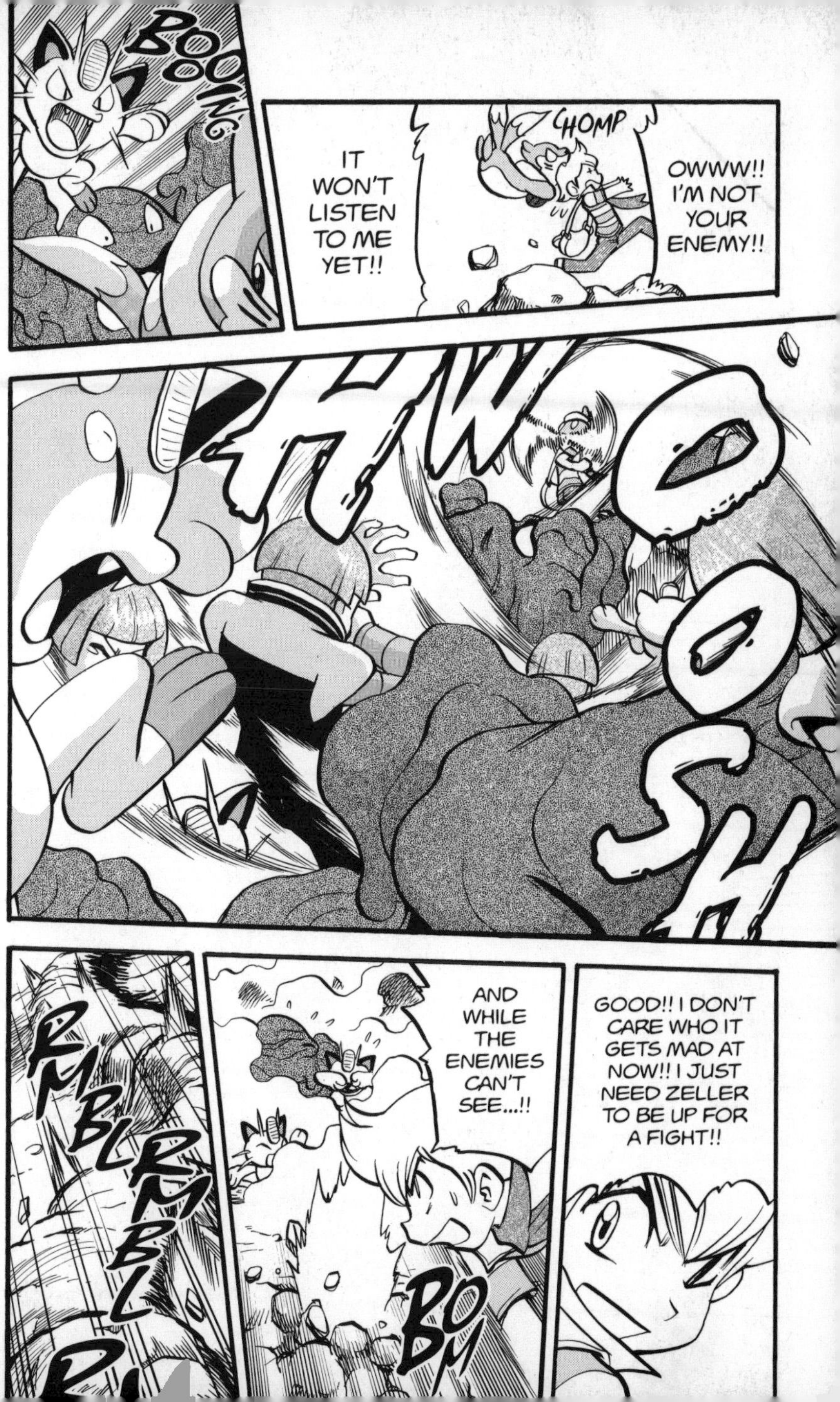

CHOMP
OWWW!! I'M NOT YOUR ENEMY!!
IT WON'T LISTEN TO ME YET!!
BOOOING
FWOOSH
GOOD!! I DON'T CARE WHO IT GETS MAD AT NOW!! I JUST NEED ZELLER TO BE UP FOR A FIGHT!!
AND WHILE THE ENEMIES CAN'T SEE...!!
BOOM
RMBL RMBL

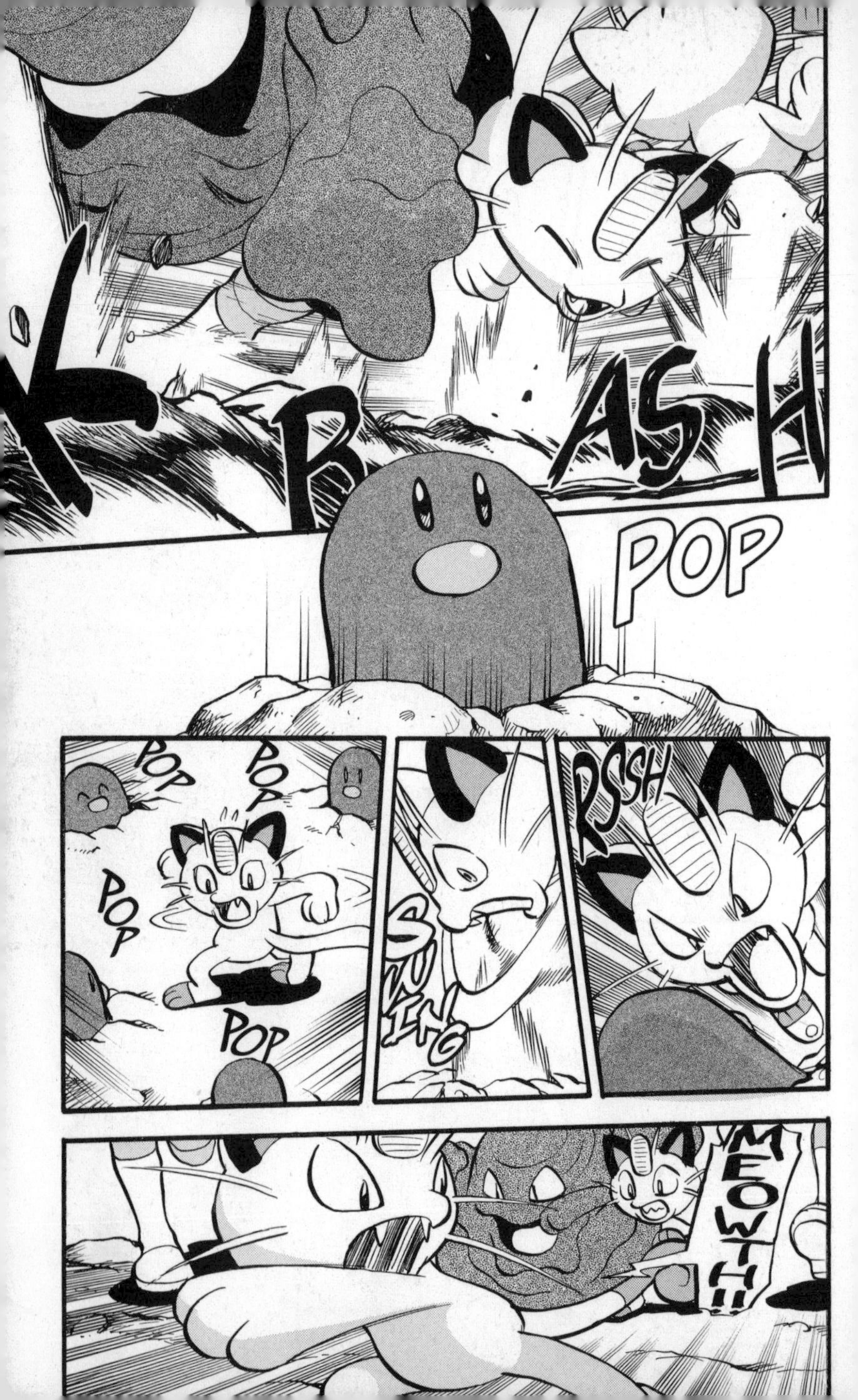
K-BASH
POP
RSSH
SWING
POP
POP
POP
POP
MEOWTH!!

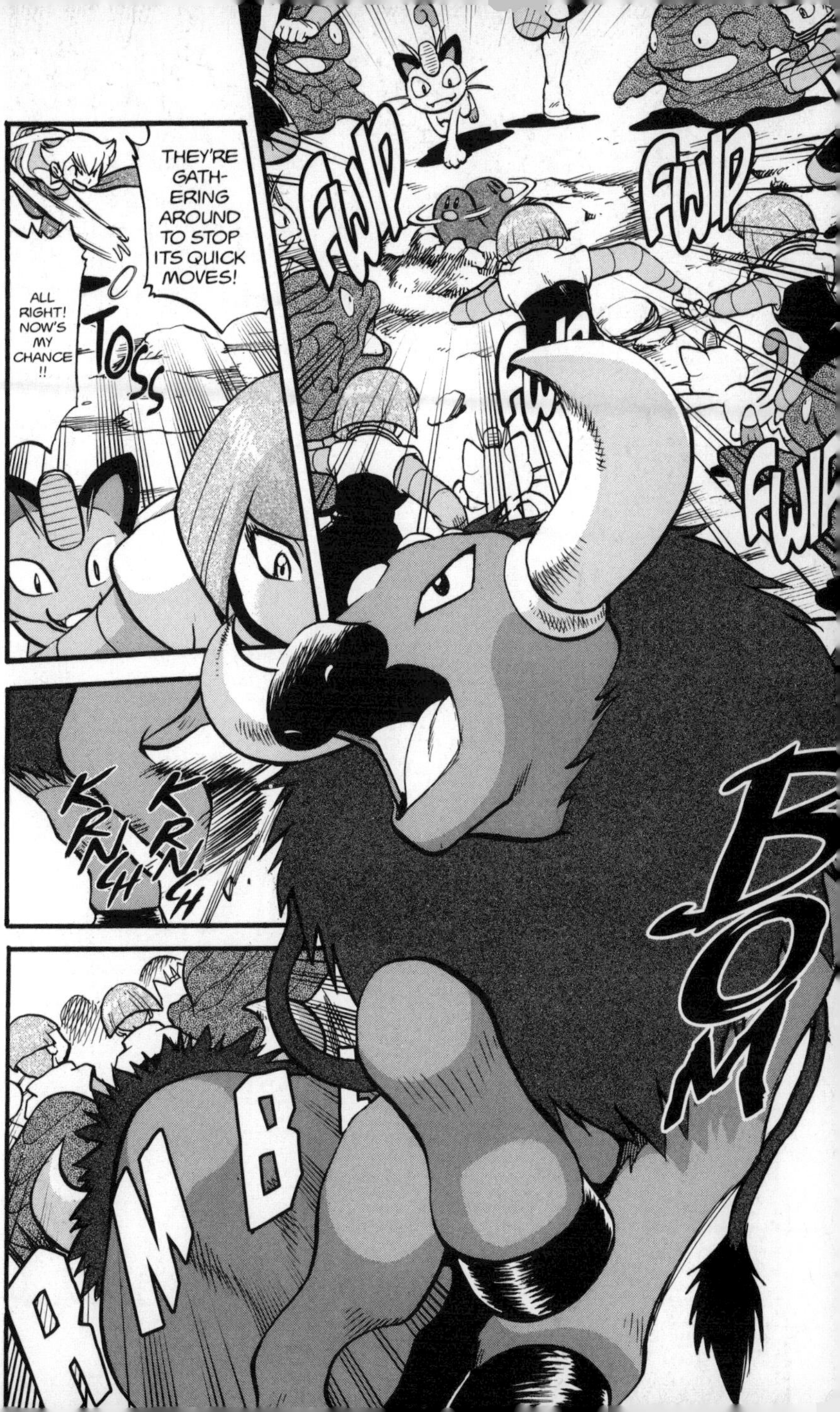
FWIP
FWIP
FWIP
FWIP
THEY'RE GATHERING AROUND TO STOP ITS QUICK MOVES!
ALL RIGHT! NOW'S MY CHANCE!!
TOSS
BOOM
KRNCH KRNCH
B
RAM

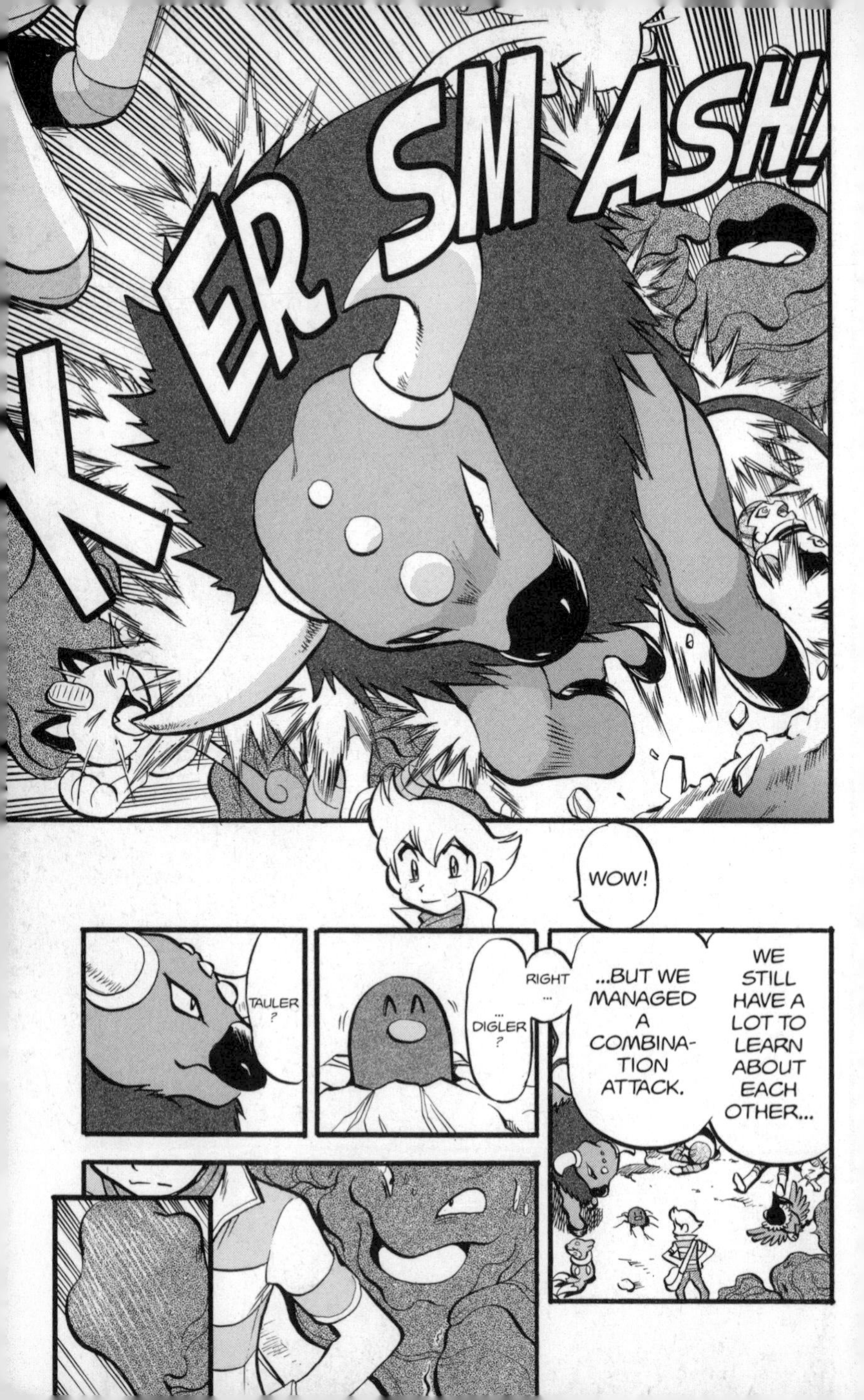

KER SMASH!
WOW!
WE STILL HAVE A LOT TO LEARN ABOUT EACH OTHER...
...BUT WE MANAGED A COMBINATION ATTACK.
RIGHT...
...DIGLER?
TAULER?

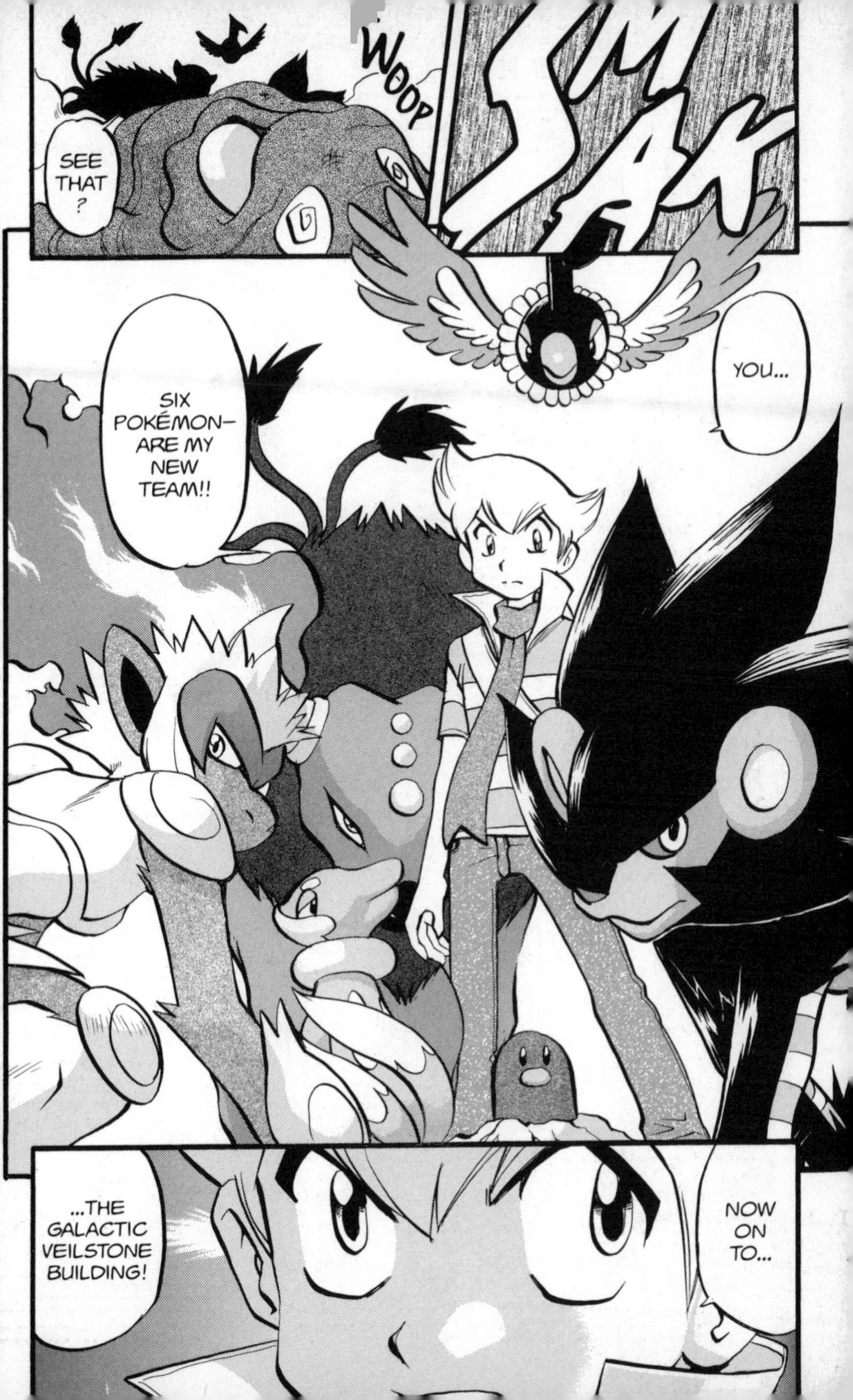
WOOP
SEE THAT?
YOU...
SIX POKÉMON— ARE MY NEW TEAM!!
NOW ON TO...
...THE GALACTIC VEILSTONE BUILDING!

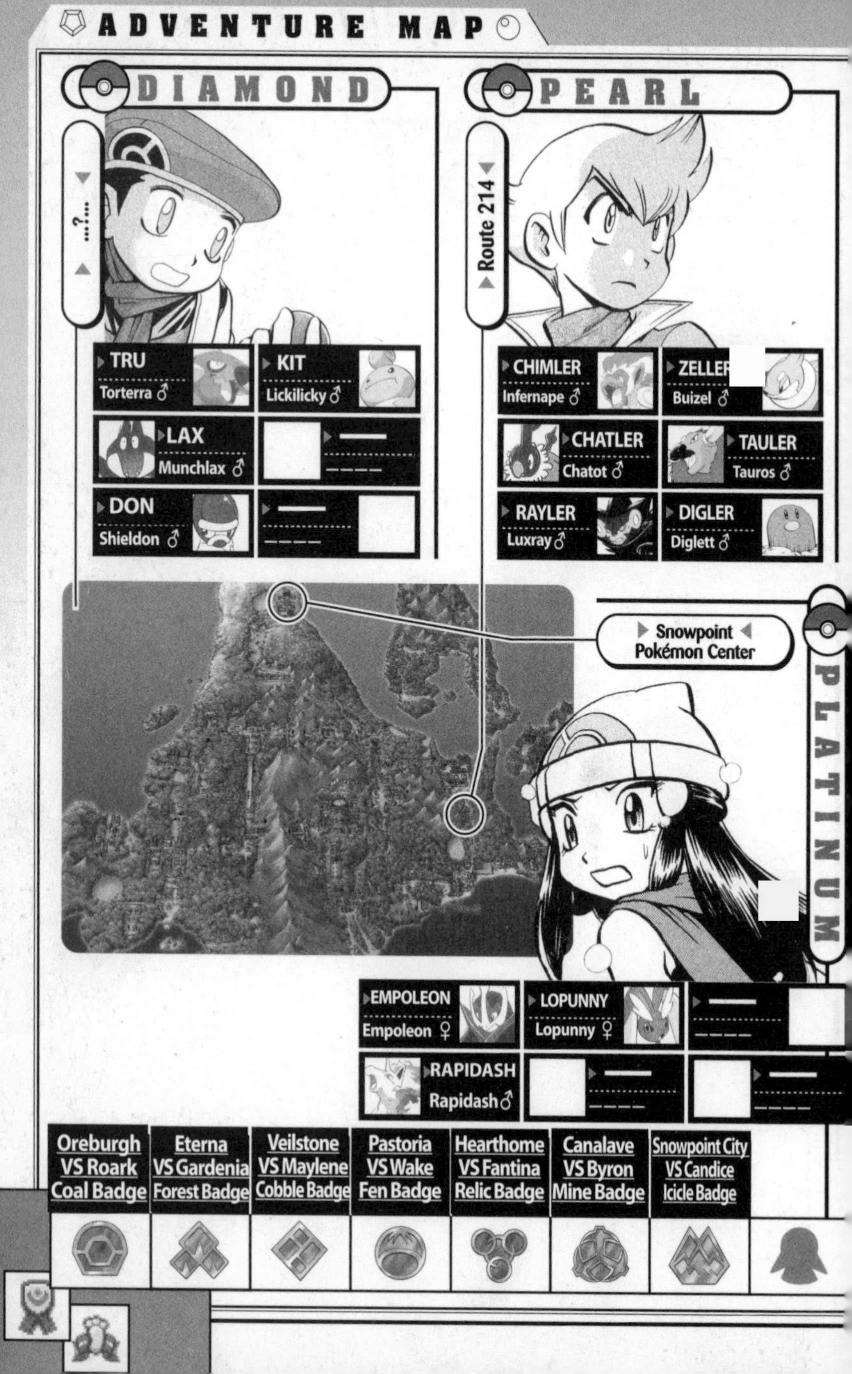
ADVENTURE MAP
DIAMOND
...?...
TRU
Torterra ♂
KIT
Lickilicky ♂
LAX
Munchlax ♂
DON
Shieldon ♂
PEARL
Route 214
CHIMLER
Infernape ♂
ZELLER
Buizel ♂
CHATLER
Chatot ♂
TAULER
Tauros ♂
RAYLER
Luxray ♂
DIGLER
Diglett ♂
Snowpoint
Pokémon Center
PLATINUM
EMPOLEON
Empoleon ♀
LOPUNNY
Lopunny ♀
RAPIDASH
Rapidash ♂
Oreburgh
VS Roark
Coal Badge
Eterna
VS Gardenia
Forest Badge
Veilstone
VS Maylene
Cobble Badge
Pastoria
VS Wake
Fen Badge
Hearthome
VS Fantina
Relic Badge
Canalave
VS Byron
Mine Badge
Snowpoint City
VS Candice
Icicle Badge

67

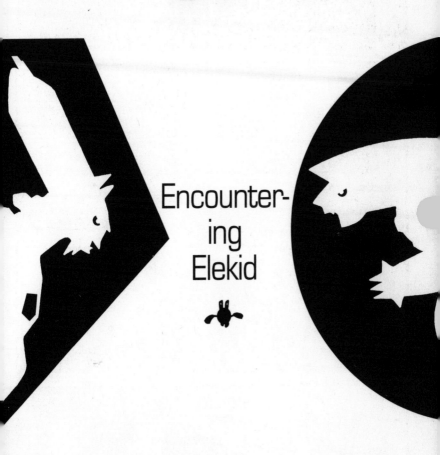

Encounter-
ing
Elekid

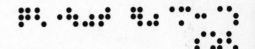

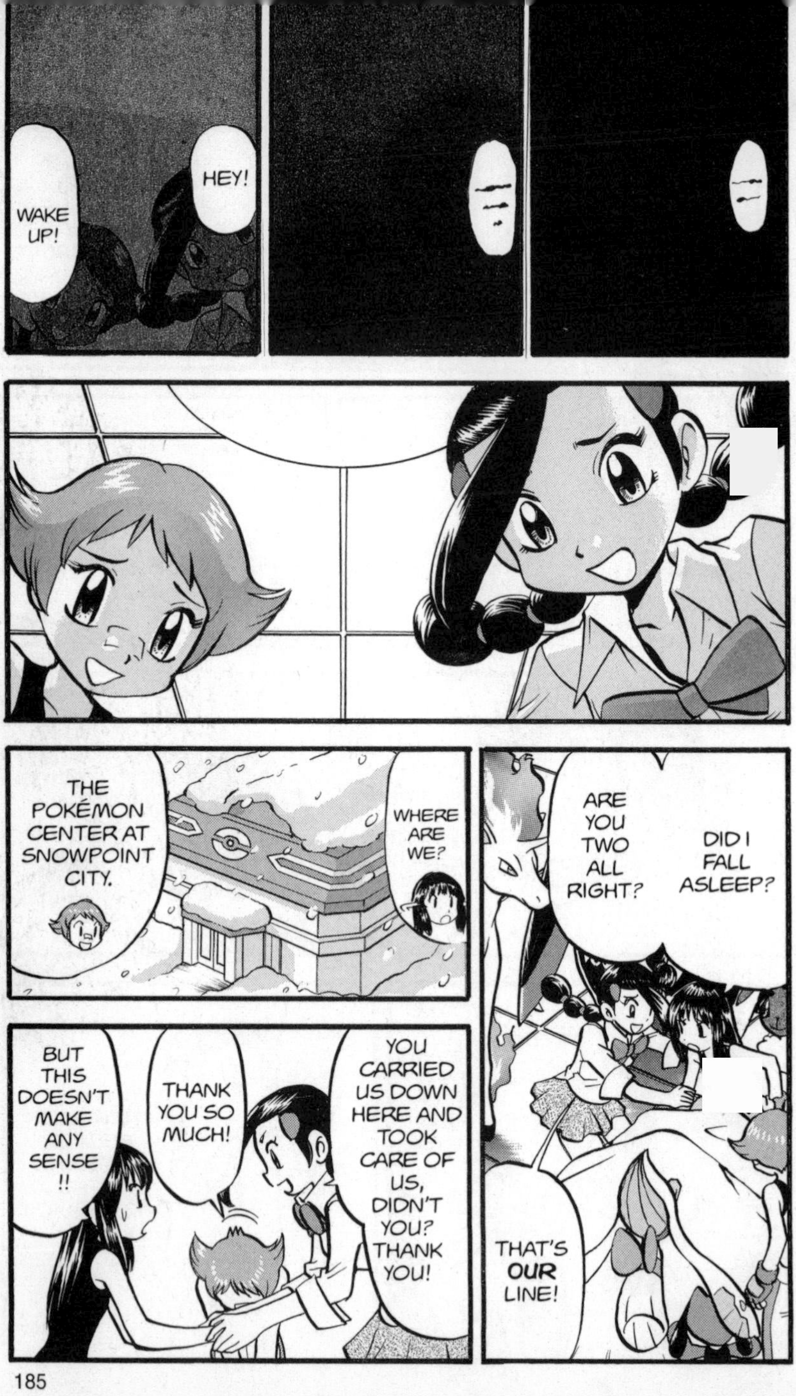
...
...
HEY!
WAKE UP!
DID I FALL ASLEEP?
ARE YOU TWO ALL RIGHT?
THAT'S **OUR** LINE!
WHERE ARE WE?
THE POKÉMON CENTER AT SNOWPOINT CITY.
YOU CARRIED US DOWN HERE AND TOOK CARE OF US, DIDN'T YOU? THANK YOU!
THANK YOU SO MUCH!
BUT THIS DOESN'T MAKE ANY SENSE!!

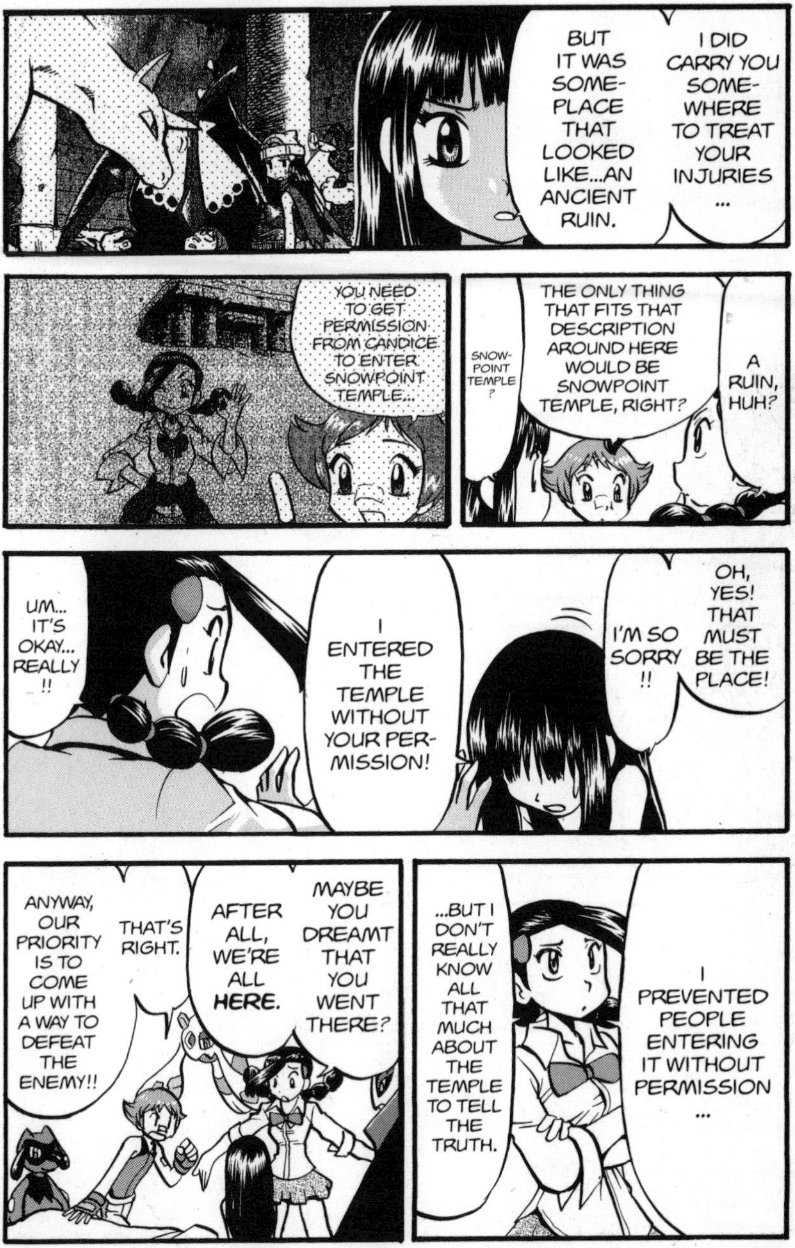
I DID CARRY YOU SOMEWHERE TO TREAT YOUR INJURIES ...
BUT IT WAS SOMEPLACE THAT LOOKED LIKE...AN ANCIENT RUIN.
A RUIN, HUH?
THE ONLY THING THAT FITS THAT DESCRIPTION AROUND HERE WOULD BE SNOWPOINT TEMPLE, RIGHT?
SNOWPOINT TEMPLE ?
YOU NEED TO GET PERMISSION FROM CANDICE TO ENTER SNOWPOINT TEMPLE...
OH, YES! THAT MUST BE THE PLACE!
I'M SO SORRY !!
I ENTERED THE TEMPLE WITHOUT YOUR PERMISSION!
UM... IT'S OKAY... REALLY !!
I PREVENTED PEOPLE ENTERING IT WITHOUT PERMISSION ...
...BUT I DON'T REALLY KNOW ALL THAT MUCH ABOUT THE TEMPLE TO TELL THE TRUTH.
MAYBE YOU DREAMT THAT YOU WENT THERE?
AFTER ALL, WE'RE ALL **HERE**.
THAT'S RIGHT.
ANYWAY, OUR PRIORITY IS TO COME UP WITH A WAY TO DEFEAT THE ENEMY!!

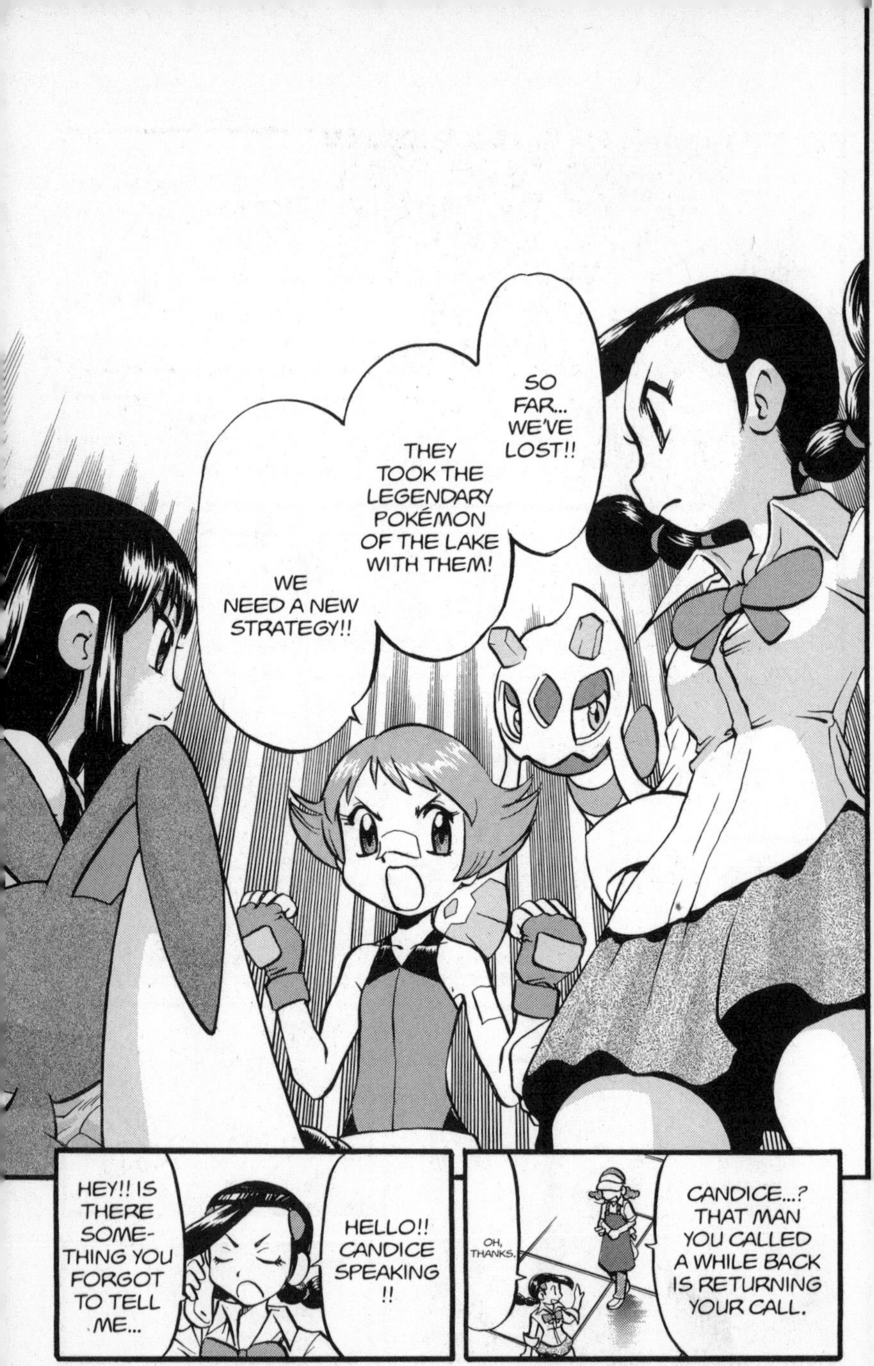
SO FAR... WE'VE LOST!!
THEY TOOK THE LEGENDARY POKÉMON OF THE LAKE WITH THEM!
WE NEED A NEW STRATEGY!!
CANDICE...? THAT MAN YOU CALLED A WHILE BACK IS RETURNING YOUR CALL.
OH, THANKS.
HELLO!! CANDICE SPEAKING !!
HEY!! IS THERE SOME-THING YOU FORGOT TO TELL ME...

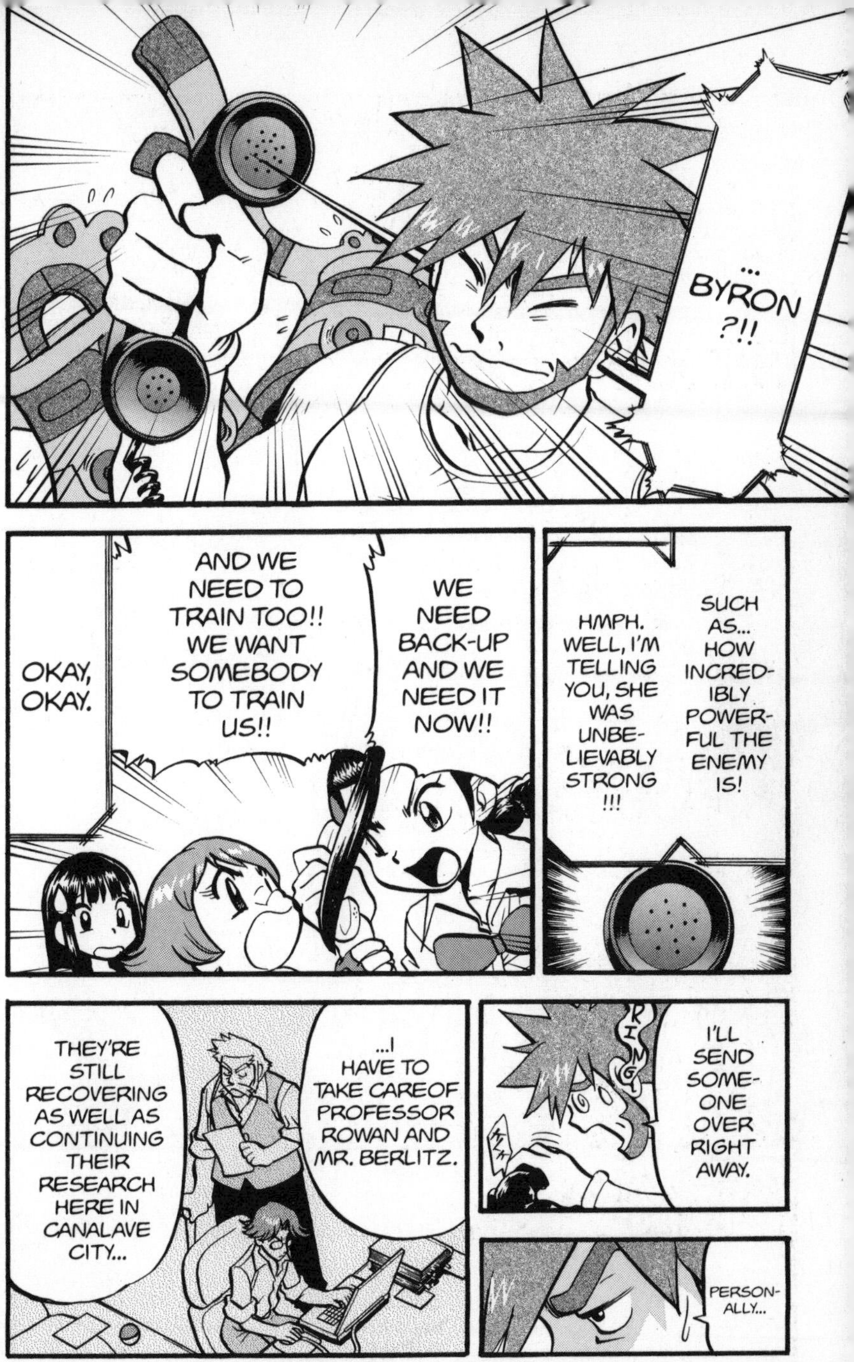
...BYRON ?!!
SUCH AS... HOW INCREDIBLY POWERFUL THE ENEMY IS!
HMPH. WELL, I'M TELLING YOU, SHE WAS UNBELIEVABLY STRONG!!!
WE NEED BACK-UP AND WE NEED IT NOW!!
AND WE NEED TO TRAIN TOO!! WE WANT SOMEBODY TO TRAIN US!!
OKAY, OKAY.
RING
I'LL SEND SOMEONE OVER RIGHT AWAY.
PERSONALLY...
...I HAVE TO TAKE CAREOF PROFESSOR ROWAN AND MR. BERLITZ.
THEY'RE STILL RECOVERING AS WELL AS CONTINUING THEIR RESEARCH HERE IN CANALAVE CITY...

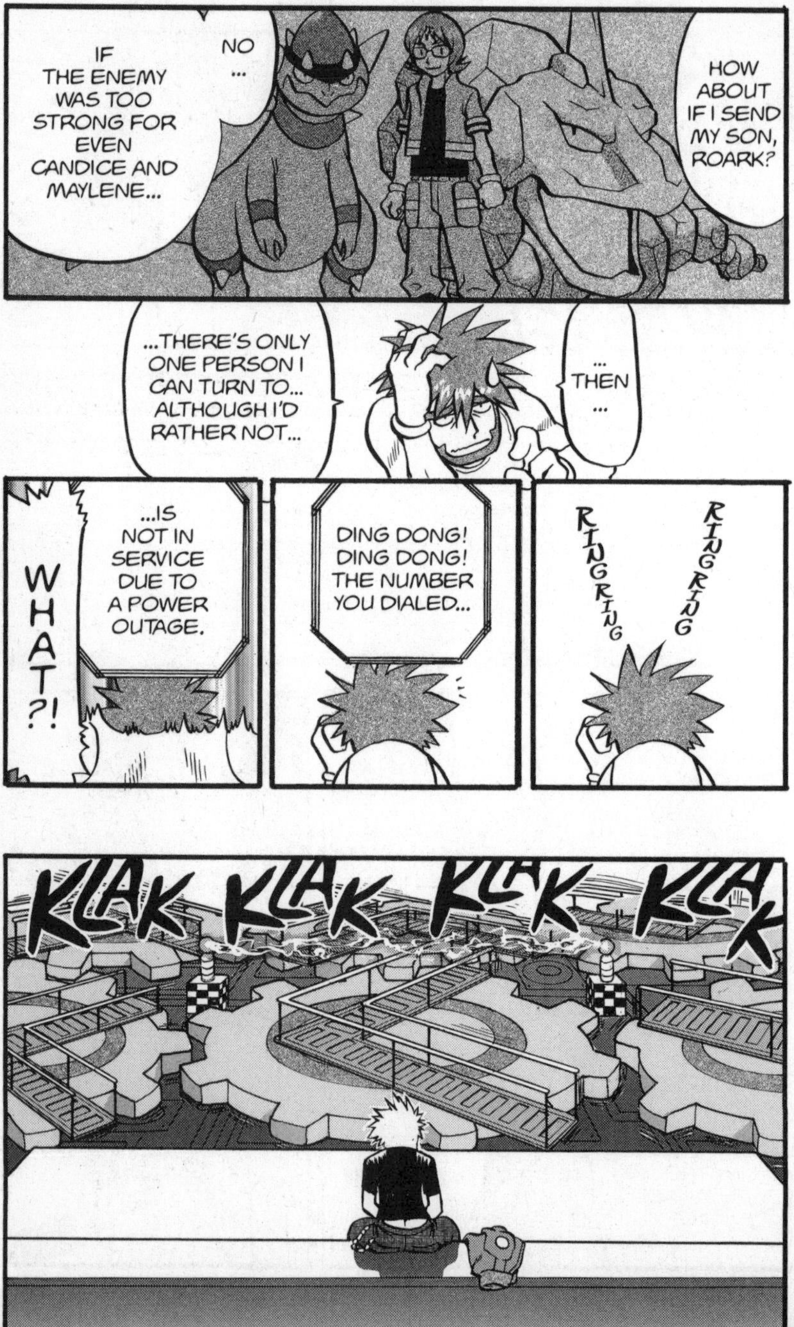
HOW ABOUT IF I SEND MY SON, ROARK?
NO ...
IF THE ENEMY WAS TOO STRONG FOR EVEN CANDICE AND MAYLENE...
... THEN ...
...THERE'S ONLY ONE PERSON I CAN TURN TO... ALTHOUGH I'D RATHER NOT...
RING RING
RING RING
DING DONG! DING DONG! THE NUMBER YOU DIALED...
...IS NOT IN SERVICE DUE TO A POWER OUTAGE.
WHAT?!
KLAK KLAK KLAK KLAK

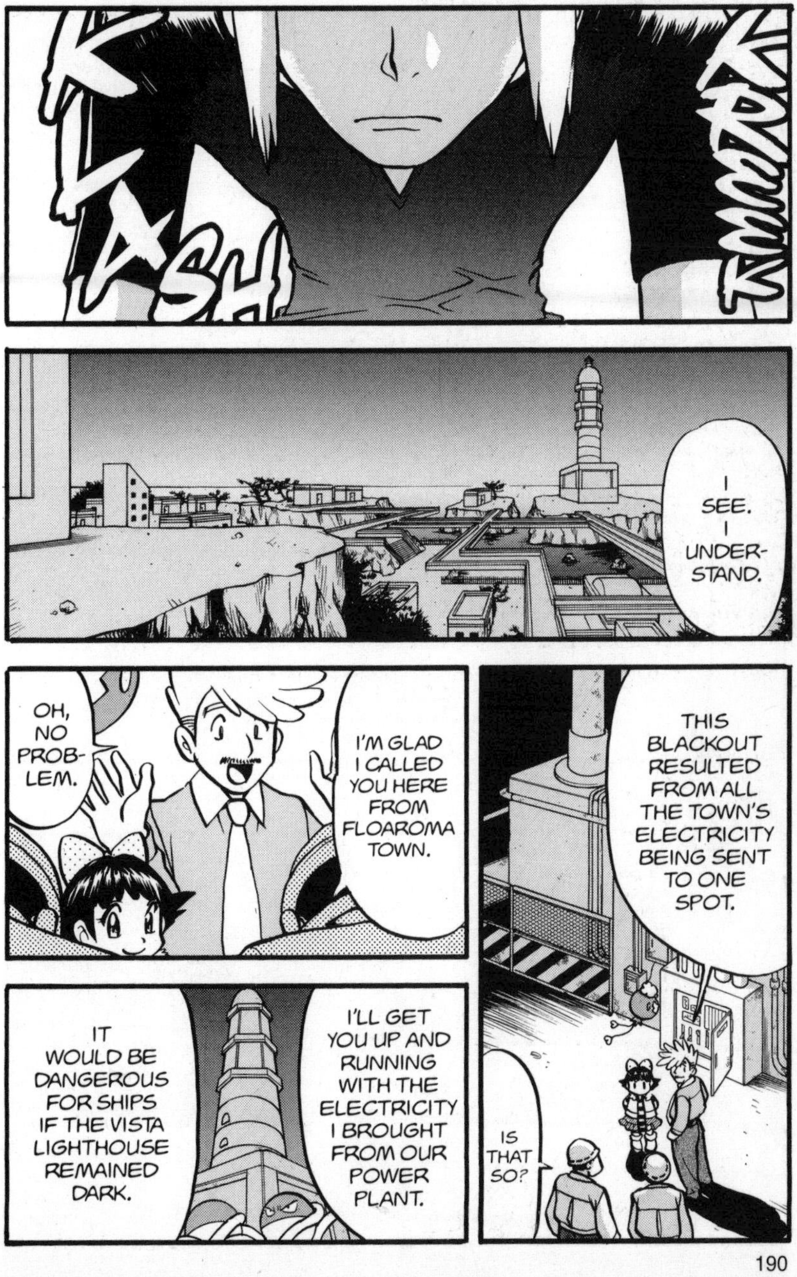
I SEE. I UNDERSTAND.
THIS BLACKOUT RESULTED FROM ALL THE TOWN'S ELECTRICITY BEING SENT TO ONE SPOT.
IS THAT SO?
I'M GLAD I CALLED YOU HERE FROM FLOAROMA TOWN.
OH, NO PROBLEM.
I'LL GET YOU UP AND RUNNING WITH THE ELECTRICITY I BROUGHT FROM OUR POWER PLANT.
IT WOULD BE DANGEROUS FOR SHIPS IF THE VISTA LIGHTHOUSE REMAINED DARK.

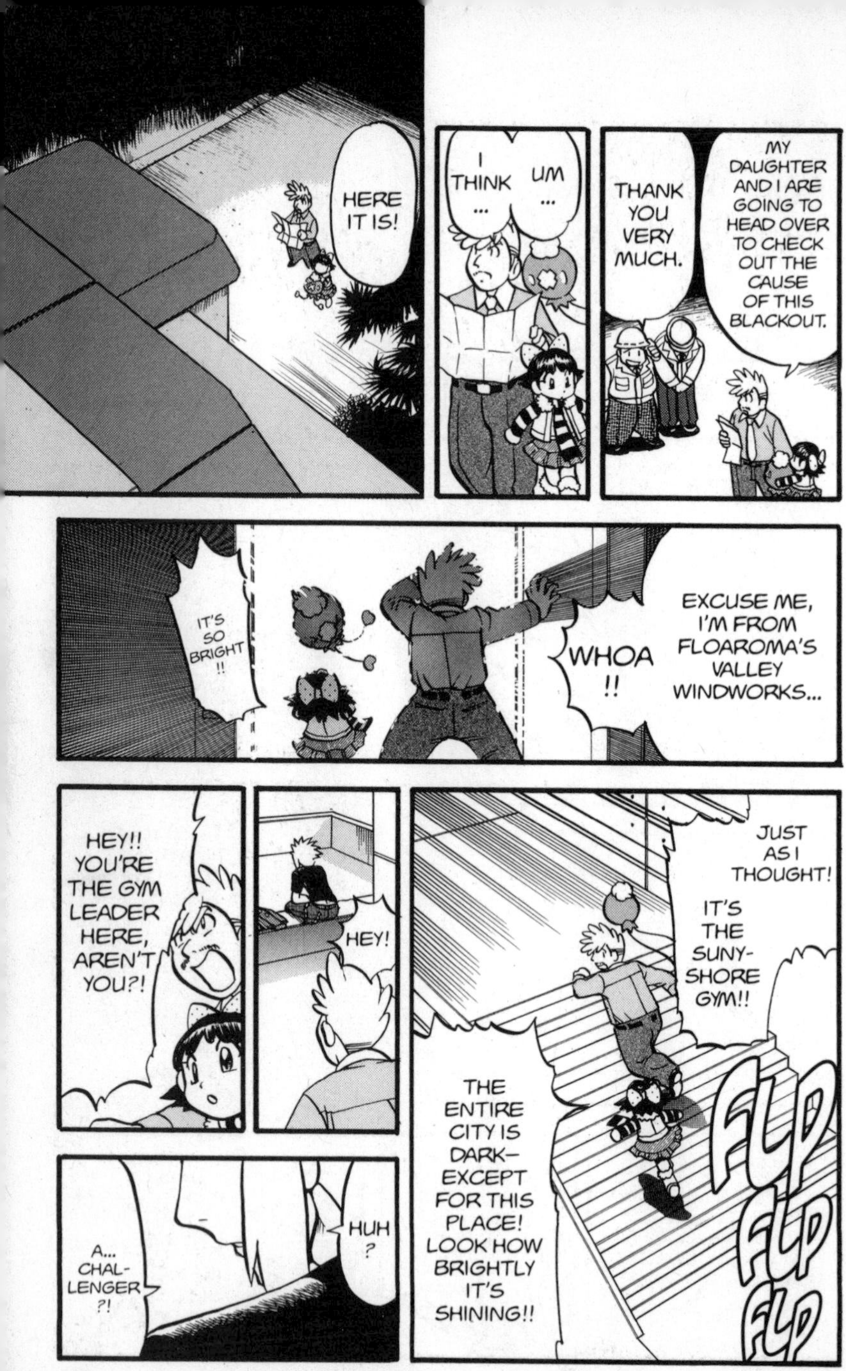
MY DAUGHTER AND I ARE GOING TO HEAD OVER TO CHECK OUT THE CAUSE OF THIS BLACKOUT.
THANK YOU VERY MUCH.
UM ...
I THINK ...
HERE IT IS!
EXCUSE ME, I'M FROM FLOAROMA'S VALLEY WINDWORKS...
WHOA !!
IT'S SO BRIGHT !!
JUST AS I THOUGHT!
IT'S THE SUNY-SHORE GYM!!
THE ENTIRE CITY IS DARK—EXCEPT FOR THIS PLACE! LOOK HOW BRIGHTLY IT'S SHINING!!
FLP FLP FLP
HEY!
HEY!! YOU'RE THE GYM LEADER HERE, AREN'T YOU?!
HUH ?
A... CHAL-LENGER ?!

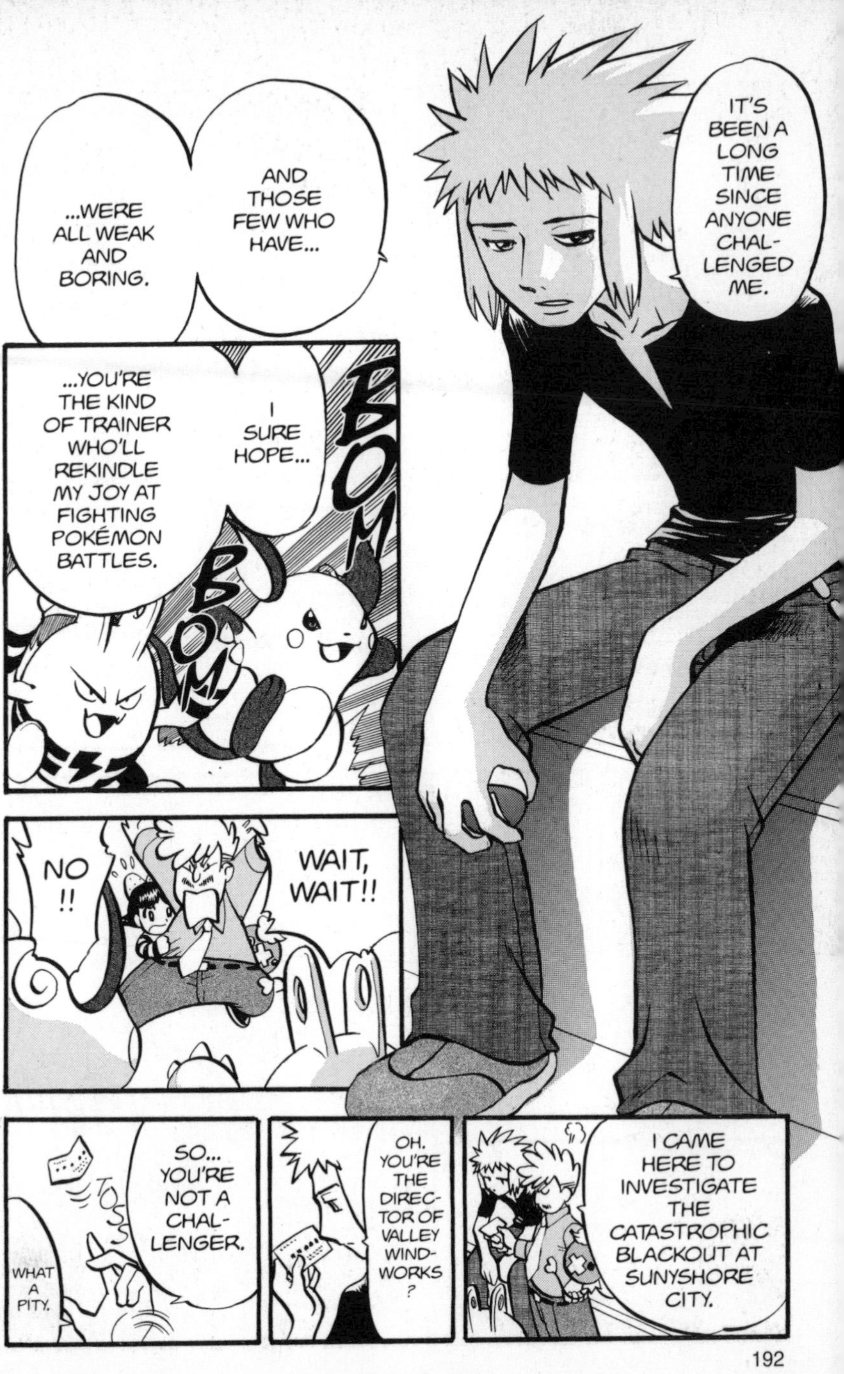
IT'S BEEN A LONG TIME SINCE ANYONE CHAL-LENGED ME.
AND THOSE FEW WHO HAVE...
...WERE ALL WEAK AND BORING.
I SURE HOPE...
...YOU'RE THE KIND OF TRAINER WHO'LL REKINDLE MY JOY AT FIGHTING POKÉMON BATTLES.
BOM
BOM
WAIT, WAIT!!
NO !!
I CAME HERE TO INVESTIGATE THE CATASTROPHIC BLACKOUT AT SUNYSHORE CITY.
OH. YOU'RE THE DIREC-TOR OF VALLEY WIND-WORKS ?
SO... YOU'RE NOT A CHAL-LENGER.
TOSS
WHAT A PITY.

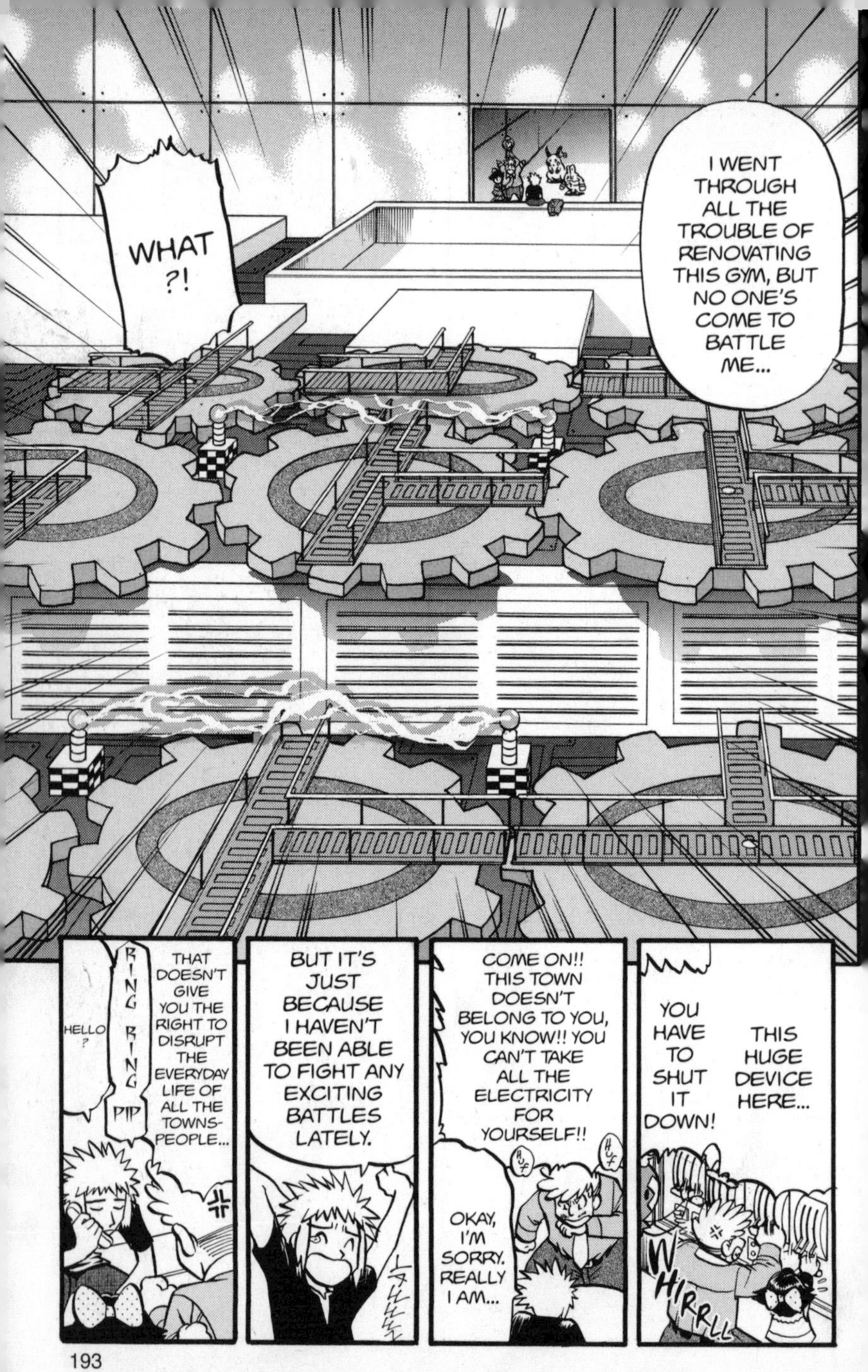
I WENT THROUGH ALL THE TROUBLE OF RENOVATING THIS GYM, BUT NO ONE'S COME TO BATTLE ME...
WHAT ?!
THIS HUGE DEVICE HERE...
YOU HAVE TO SHUT IT DOWN!
WHIRRLL
COME ON!! THIS TOWN DOESN'T BELONG TO YOU, YOU KNOW!! YOU CAN'T TAKE ALL THE ELECTRICITY FOR YOURSELF!!
HUF
HUF
OKAY, I'M SORRY. REALLY I AM...
BUT IT'S JUST BECAUSE I HAVEN'T BEEN ABLE TO FIGHT ANY EXCITING BATTLES LATELY.
THAT DOESN'T GIVE YOU THE RIGHT TO DISRUPT THE EVERYDAY LIFE OF ALL THE TOWNS-PEOPLE...
RING RING
PIP
HELLO ?

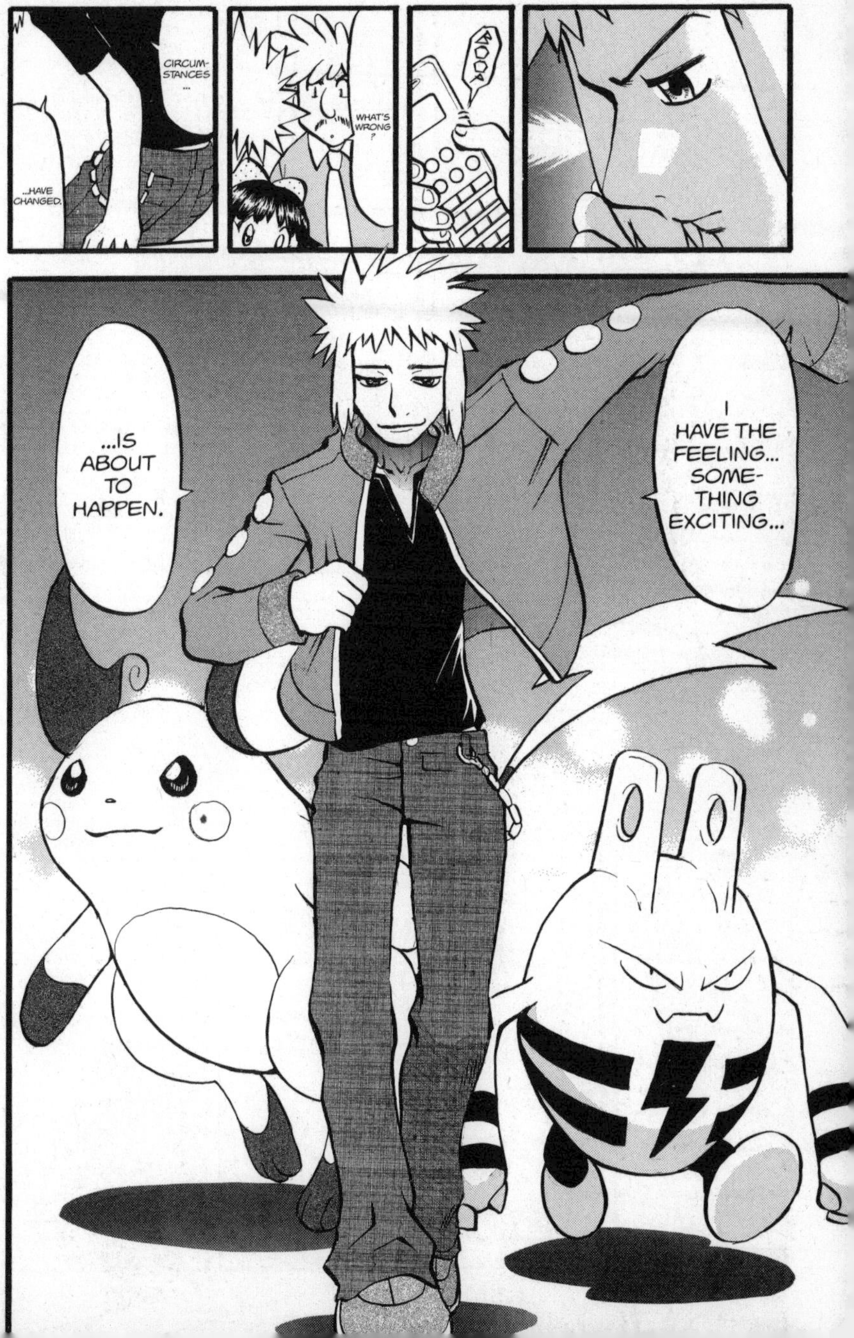
BOOP
WHAT'S WRONG?
CIRCUM-STANCES...
...HAVE CHANGED.
I HAVE THE FEELING... SOME-THING EXCITING...
...IS ABOUT TO HAPPEN.

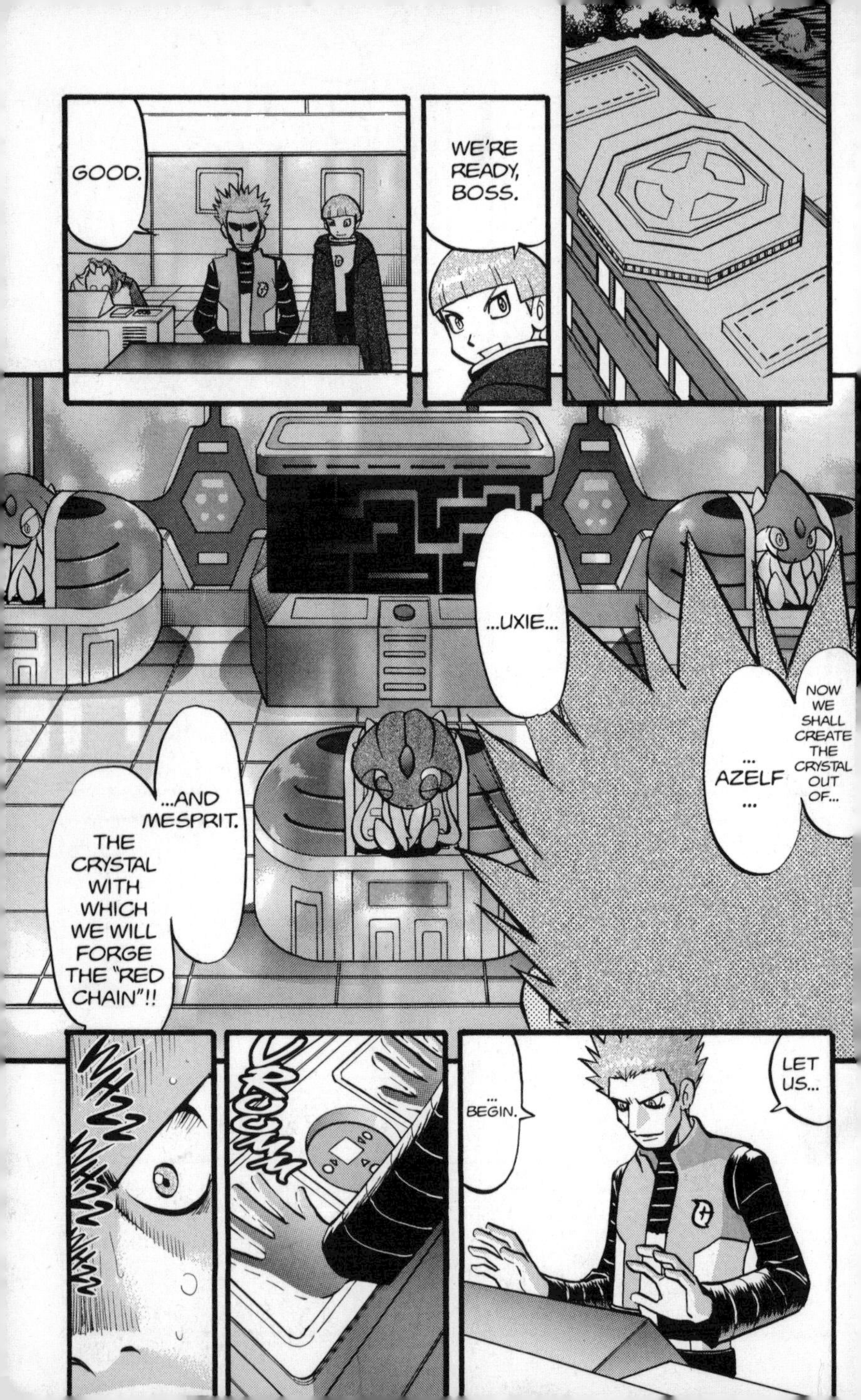
WE'RE READY, BOSS.
GOOD.
NOW WE SHALL CREATE THE CRYSTAL OUT OF...
...AZELF...
...UXIE...
...AND MESPRIT.
THE CRYSTAL WITH WHICH WE WILL FORGE THE "RED CHAIN"!!
LET US...
...BEGIN.
VROOMM
WHZZ WHZZ WHZZ

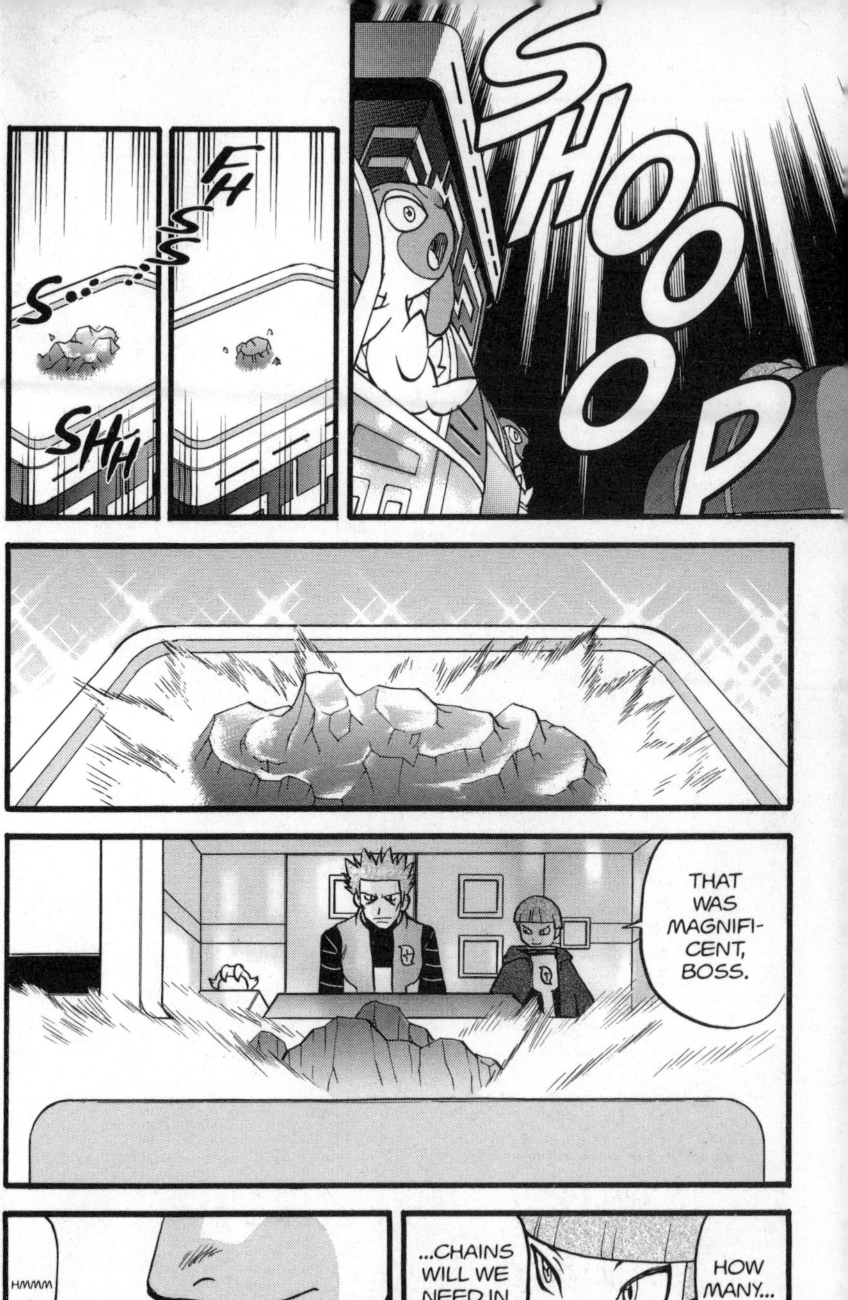
SHOOOP
FHSSS
S...
SHH
THAT WAS MAGNIFI-CENT, BOSS.
HOW MANY...
...CHAINS WILL WE NEED IN ALL?
HMMM...

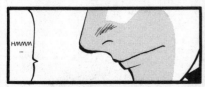

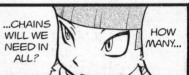

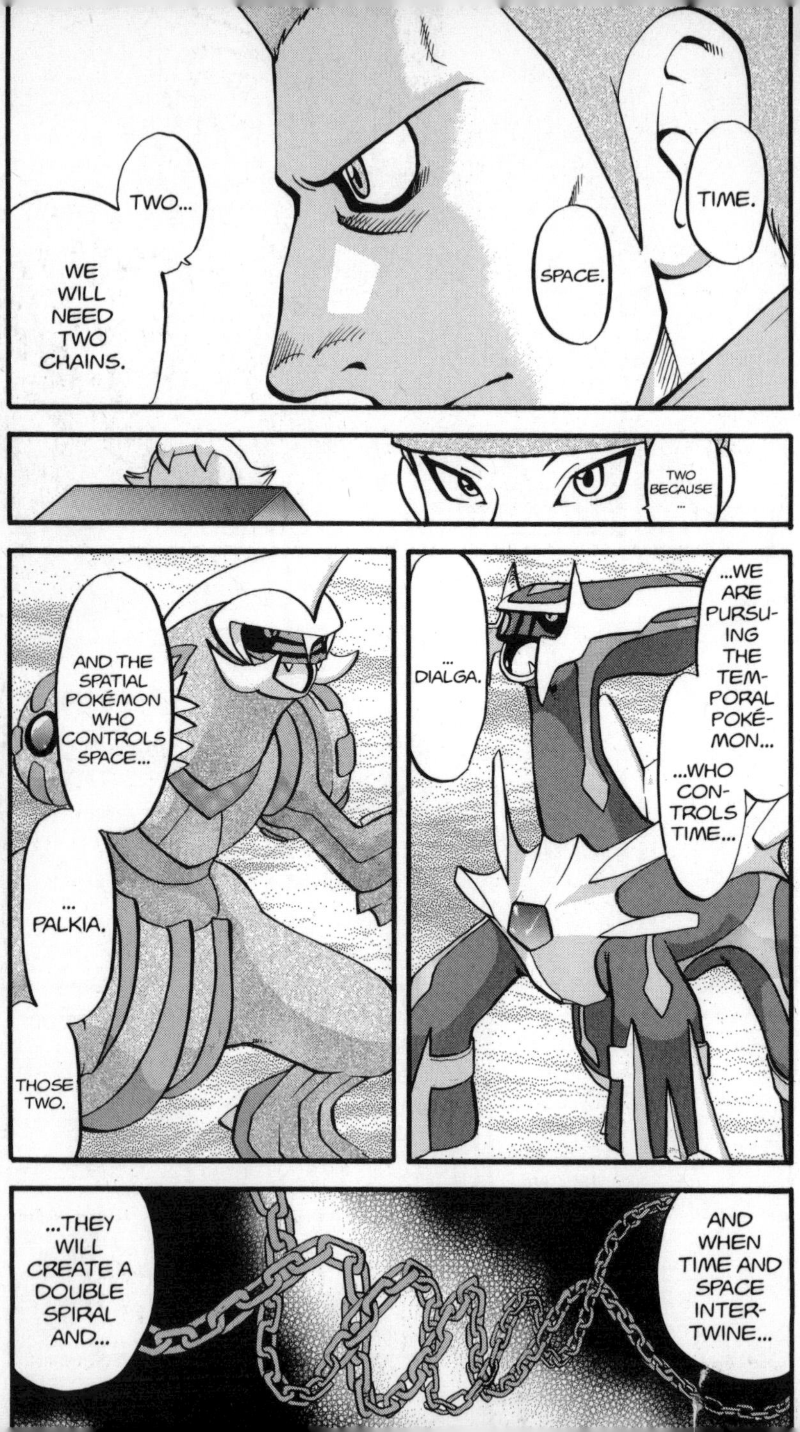
TIME.
SPACE.
TWO...
WE WILL NEED TWO CHAINS.
TWO BECAUSE ...
...WE ARE PURSUING THE TEMPORAL POKÉMON...
...WHO CONTROLS TIME...
... DIALGA.
AND THE SPATIAL POKÉMON WHO CONTROLS SPACE...
... PALKIA.
THOSE TWO.
AND WHEN TIME AND SPACE INTERTWINE...
...THEY WILL CREATE A DOUBLE SPIRAL AND...

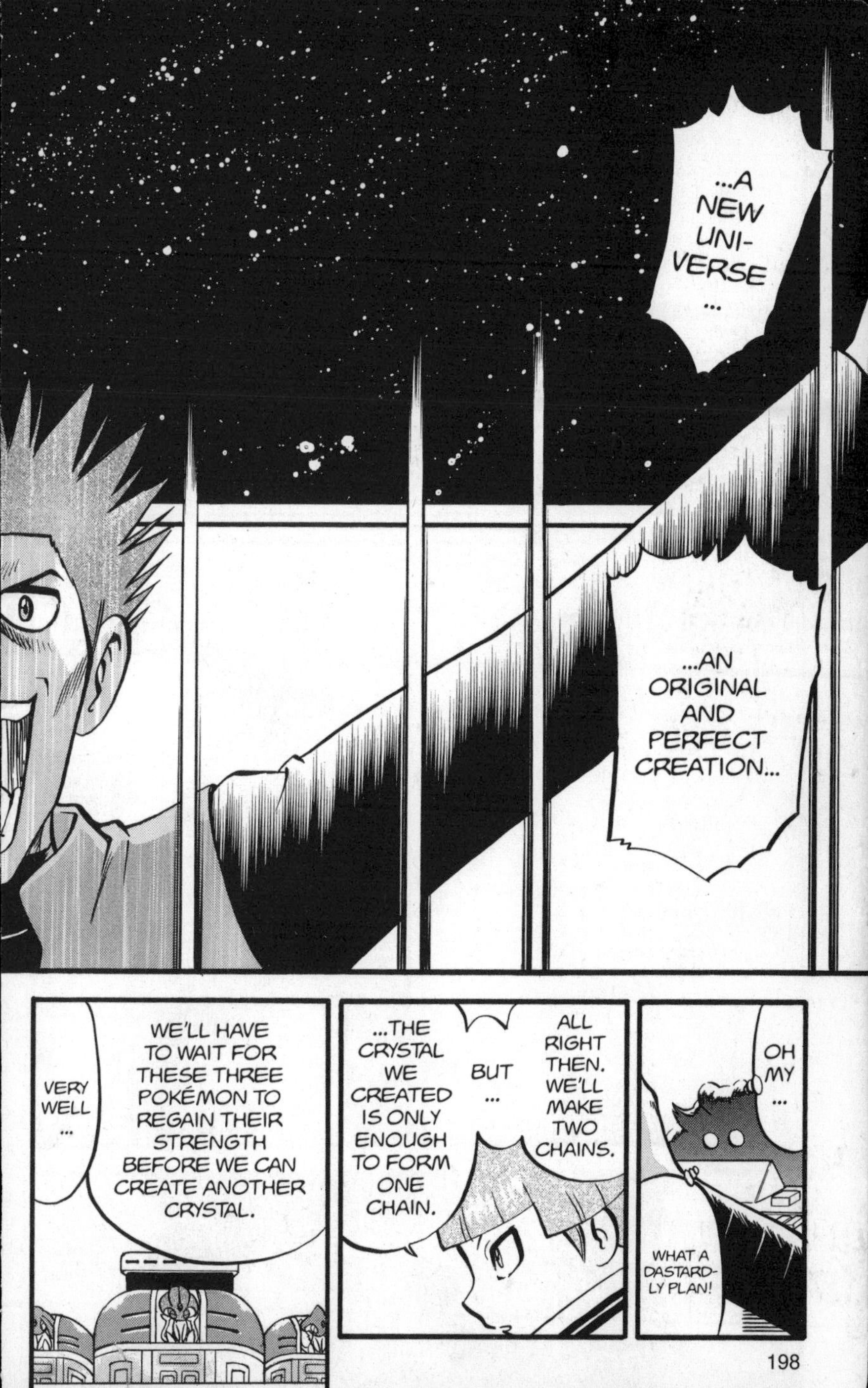
...A NEW UNI-VERSE ...
...AN ORIGINAL AND PERFECT CREATION...
OH MY ...
WHAT A DASTARD-LY PLAN!
ALL RIGHT THEN. WE'LL MAKE TWO CHAINS.
BUT ...
...THE CRYSTAL WE CREATED IS ONLY ENOUGH TO FORM ONE CHAIN.
WE'LL HAVE TO WAIT FOR THESE THREE POKÉMON TO REGAIN THEIR STRENGTH BEFORE WE CAN CREATE ANOTHER CRYSTAL.
VERY WELL ...

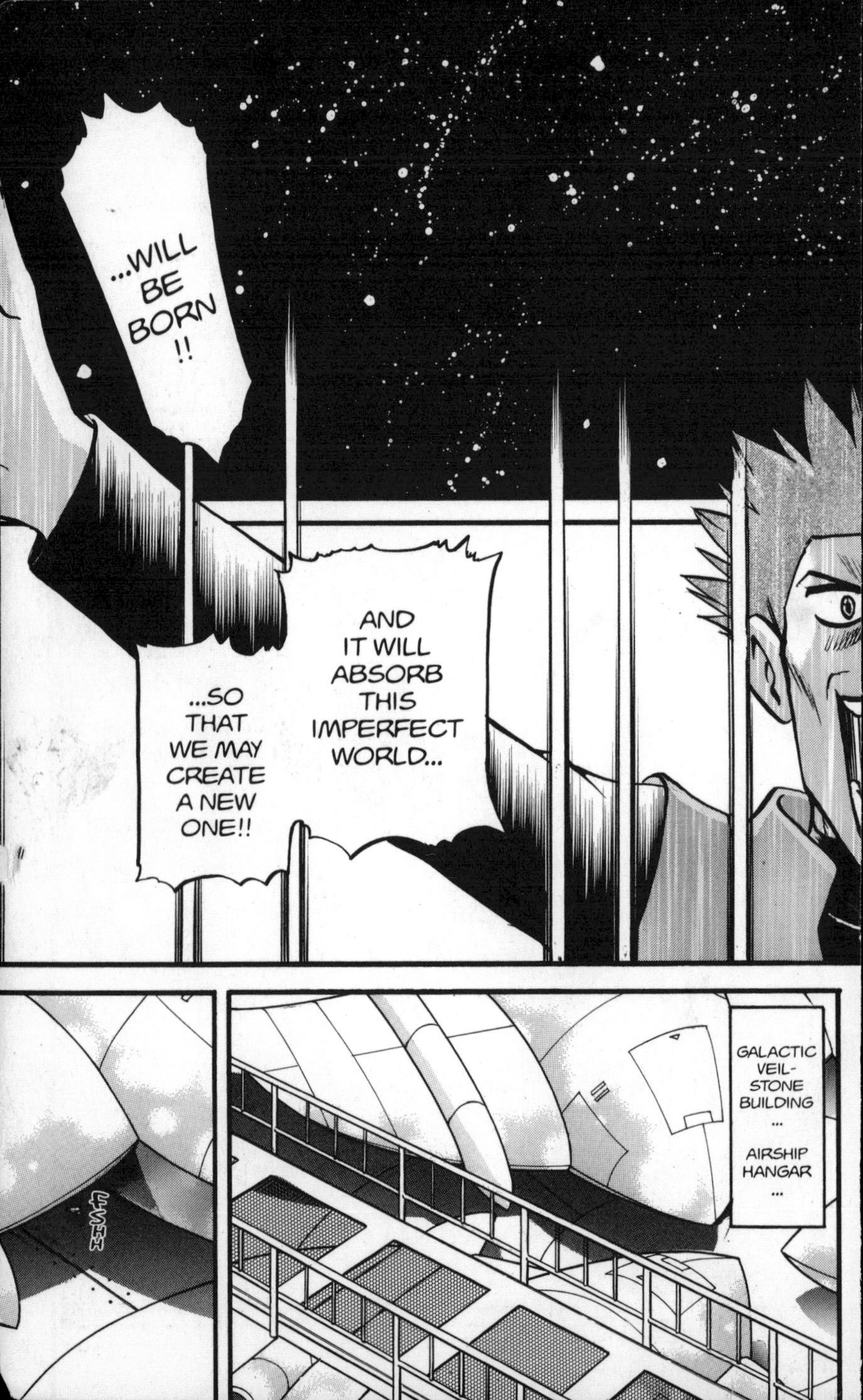
...WILL BE BORN !!
AND IT WILL ABSORB THIS IMPERFECT WORLD...
...SO THAT WE MAY CREATE A NEW ONE!!
GALACTIC VEILSTONE BUILDING ... AIRSHIP HANGAR ...

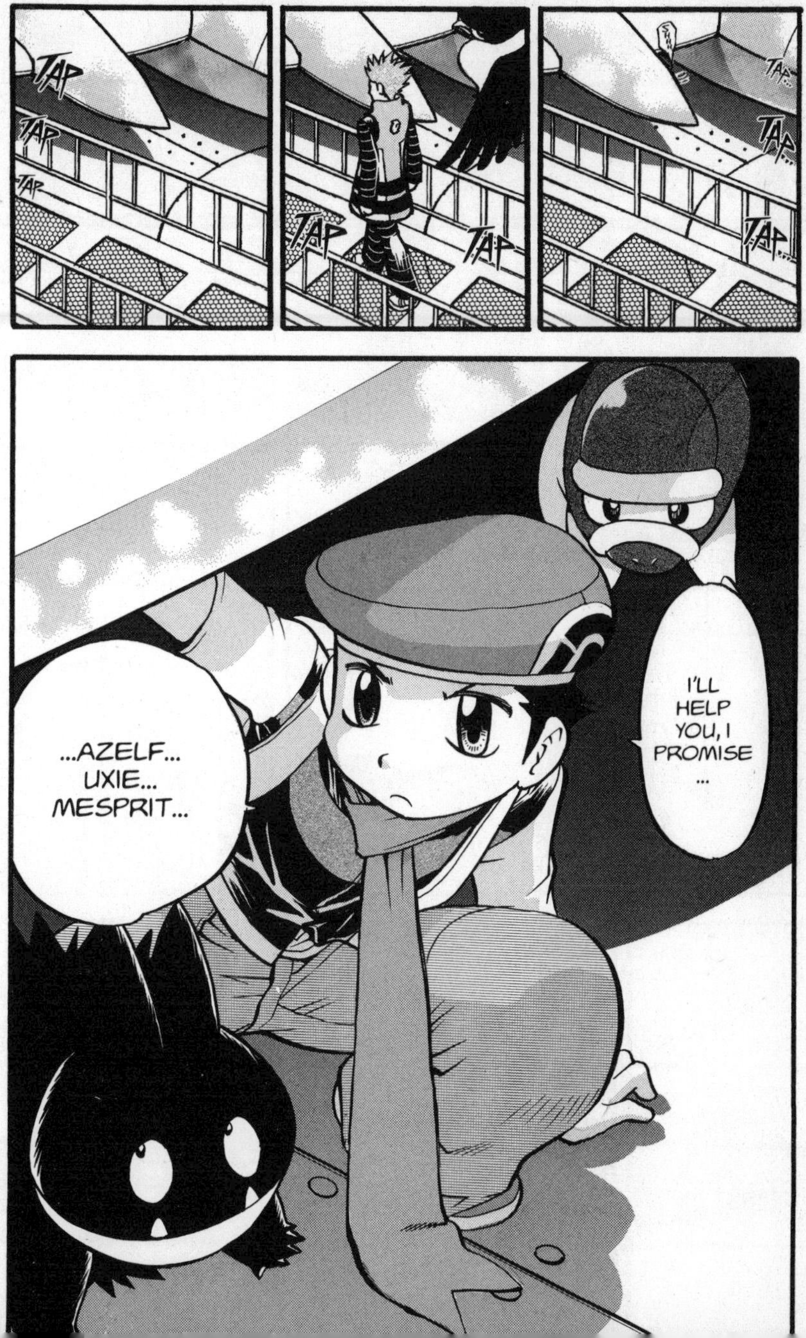
SHHH...
TAP...
TAP...
TAP...
TAP
TAP
TAP
TAP
TAP
I'LL HELP YOU, I PROMISE ...
...AZELF... UXIE... MESPRIT...

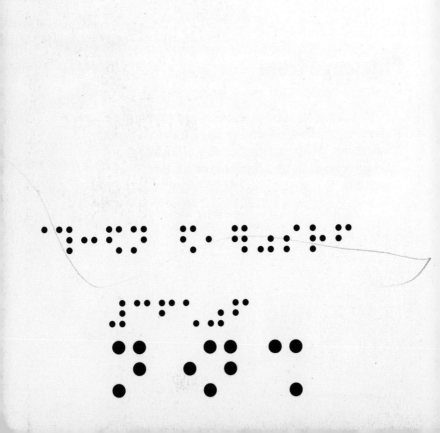

Message from
Hidenori Kusaka

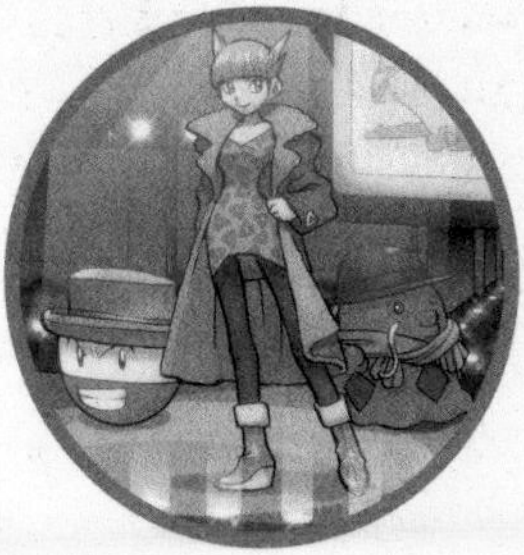

I love bicycles. That wonderful feeling of cutting through the wind... I usually use my bike to get to meetings. It's about a 25-minute ride from my house in Shinjuku to the Shogakukan building in Jinbocho. As I pedal away, what flies past my head are scenes and phrases from the manga! Come to think of it, the main characters of Pokémon all ride bicycles too.

Message from
Satoshi Yamamoto

In this volume, our trio has separated and combined with others to form three different groups. Each group has its own charm. Which configuration do you like the most...? My guess would be the original trio of Diamond, Pearl and Lady.

More Adventures Coming Soon...

To prepare for their big battle, our trio of friends each need to reach out for help—from Gym Leaders to new Pokémon. Then Lady, Pearl and Diamond are finally reunited in the very heart of Team Galactic's headquarters. Can they release the three Legendary Pokémon...before it's too late?

And who will take on Team Galactic's powerful leader *Cyrus*?!

Plus, meet Electivire, Honchkrow, Chingling, Spiritomb, Dialga and Palkia!

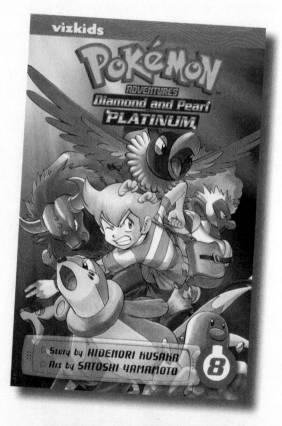

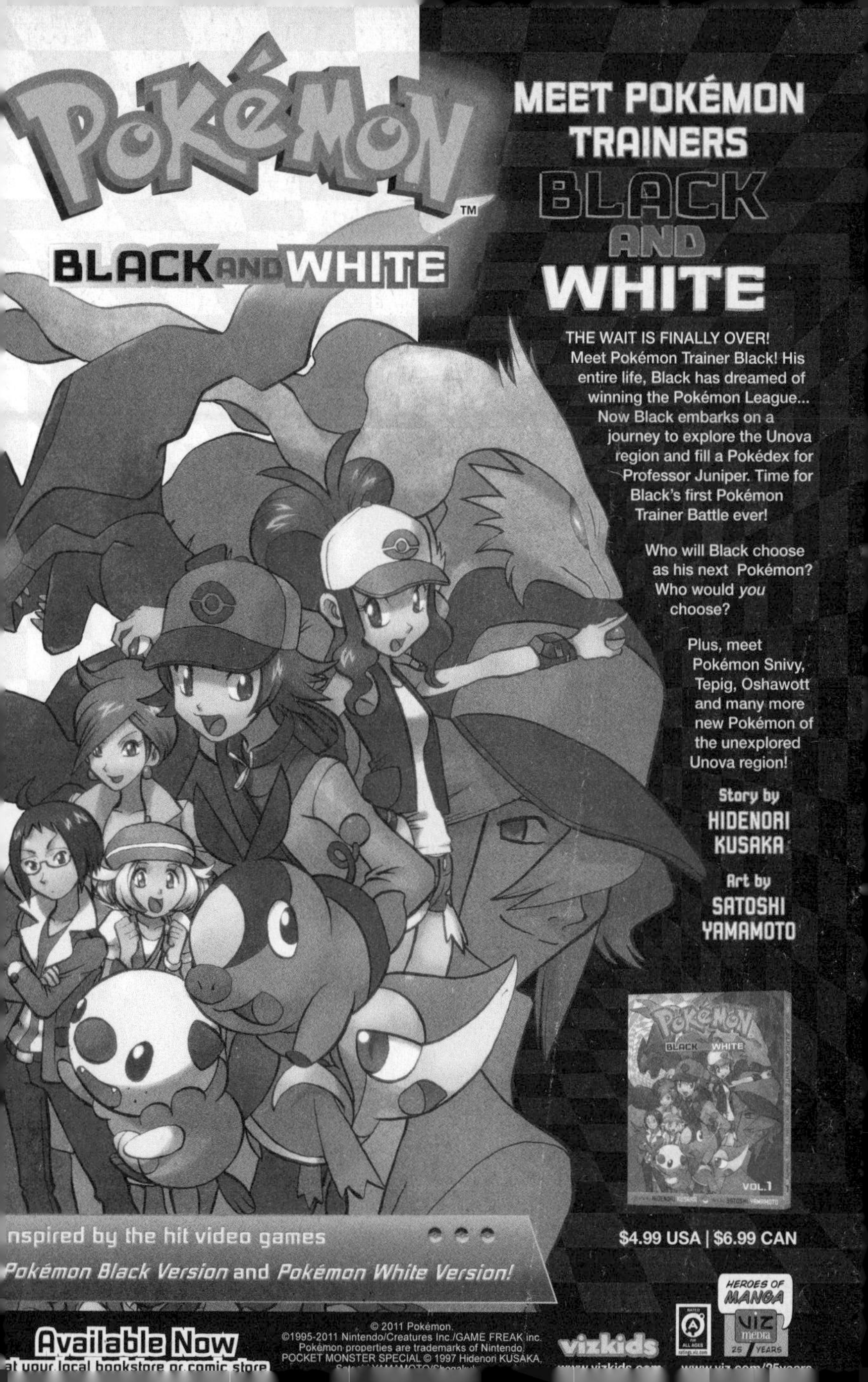

POKÉMON™
BLACK AND WHITE
MEET POKÉMON TRAINERS
BLACK AND WHITE
THE WAIT IS FINALLY OVER! Meet Pokémon Trainer Black! His entire life, Black has dreamed of winning the Pokémon League... Now Black embarks on a journey to explore the Unova region and fill a Pokédex for Professor Juniper. Time for Black's first Pokémon Trainer Battle ever!
Who will Black choose as his next Pokémon? Who would *you* choose?
Plus, meet Pokémon Snivy, Tepig, Oshawott and many more new Pokémon of the unexplored Unova region!
Story by HIDENORI KUSAKA
Art by SATOSHI YAMAMOTO
POKÉMON BLACK WHITE
VOL.1
$4.99 USA | $6.99 CAN
nspired by the hit video games
Pokémon Black Version and *Pokémon White Version!*
HEROES OF MANGA
VIZ media 25 YEARS
Available Now
at your local bookstore or comic store
© 2011 Pokémon.
©1995-2011 Nintendo/Creatures Inc./GAME FREAK inc.
Pokémon properties are trademarks of Nintendo.
POCKET MONSTER SPECIAL © 1997 Hidenori KUSAKA,
vizkids

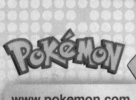

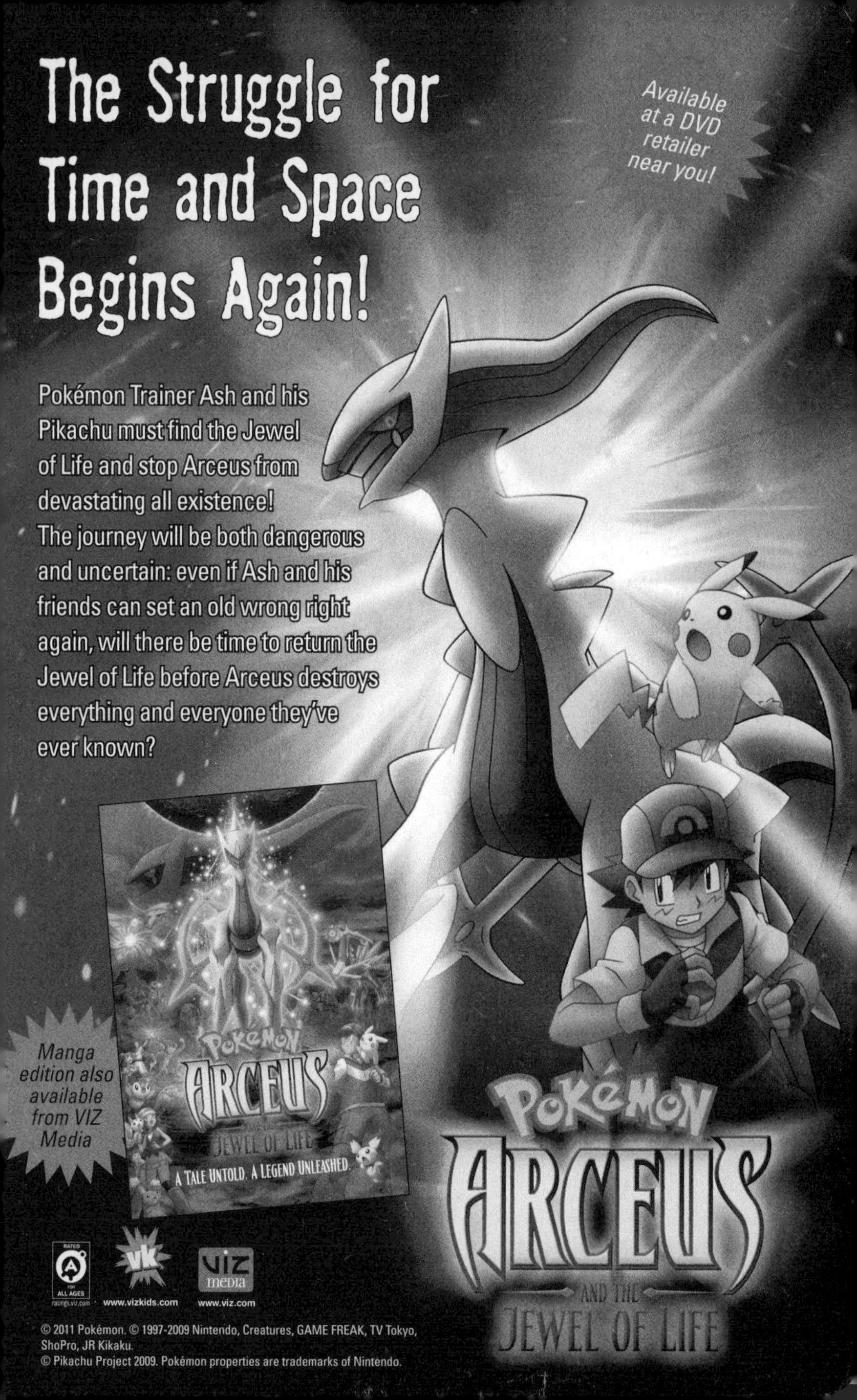
The Struggle for Time and Space Begins Again!
Available at a DVD retailer near you!
Pokémon Trainer Ash and his Pikachu must find the Jewel of Life and stop Arceus from devastating all existence! The journey will be both dangerous and uncertain: even if Ash and his friends can set an old wrong right again, will there be time to return the Jewel of Life before Arceus destroys everything and everyone they've ever known?
Pokémon
Arceus
and the
Jewel of Life
A Tale Untold. A Legend Unleashed.
Manga edition also available from VIZ Media
Rated A for All Ages
ratings.viz.com
vk
www.vizkids.com
VIZ media
www.viz.com
Pokémon
Arceus
and the
Jewel of Life
© 2011 Pokémon. © 1997-2009 Nintendo, Creatures, GAME FREAK, TV Tokyo, ShoPro, JR Kikaku.
© Pikachu Project 2009. Pokémon properties are trademarks of Nintendo.

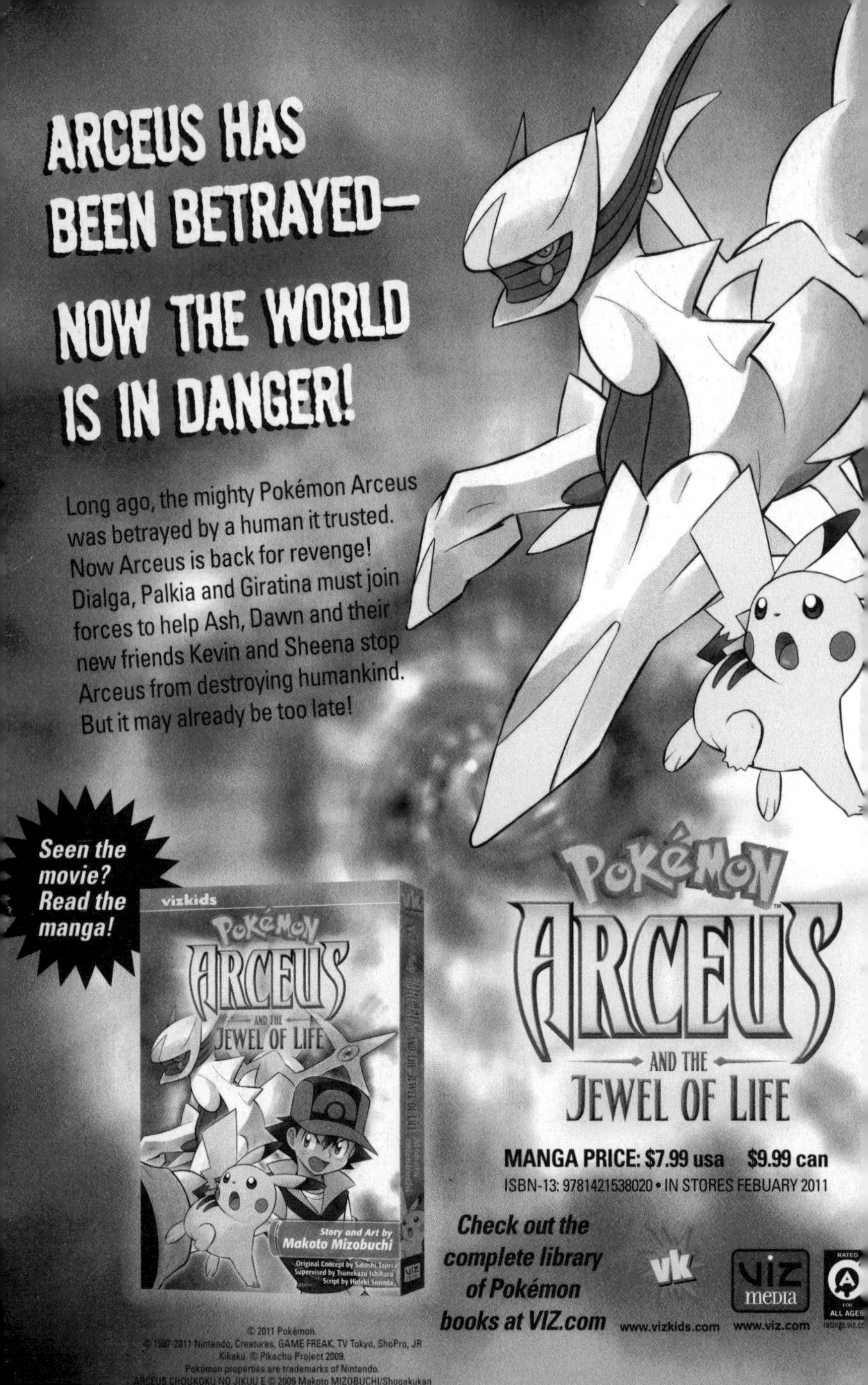
ARCEUS HAS BEEN BETRAYED—
NOW THE WORLD IS IN DANGER!
Long ago, the mighty Pokémon Arceus was betrayed by a human it trusted. Now Arceus is back for revenge! Dialga, Palkia and Giratina must join forces to help Ash, Dawn and their new friends Kevin and Sheena stop Arceus from destroying humankind. But it may already be too late!
Seen the movie? Read the manga!
vizkids
Pokémon
Arceus
and the
Jewel of Life
Story and Art by
Makoto Mizobuchi
Original Concept by Satoshi Tajiri
Supervised by Tsunekazu Ishihara
Script by Hideki Sonoda
Pokémon
Arceus
and the
Jewel of Life
MANGA PRICE: $7.99 usa $9.99 can
ISBN-13: 9781421538020 • IN STORES FEBUARY 2011
Check out the complete library of Pokémon books at VIZ.com
vk
www.vizkids.com
VIZ media
www.viz.com
RATED A FOR ALL AGES
© 2011 Pokémon.
© 1997-2011 Nintendo, Creatures, GAME FREAK, TV Tokyo, ShoPro, JR Kikaku. © Pikachu Project 2009.
Pokémon properties are trademarks of Nintendo.
ARCEUS CHOUKOKU NO JIKUU E © 2009 Makoto MIZOBUCHI/Shogakukan

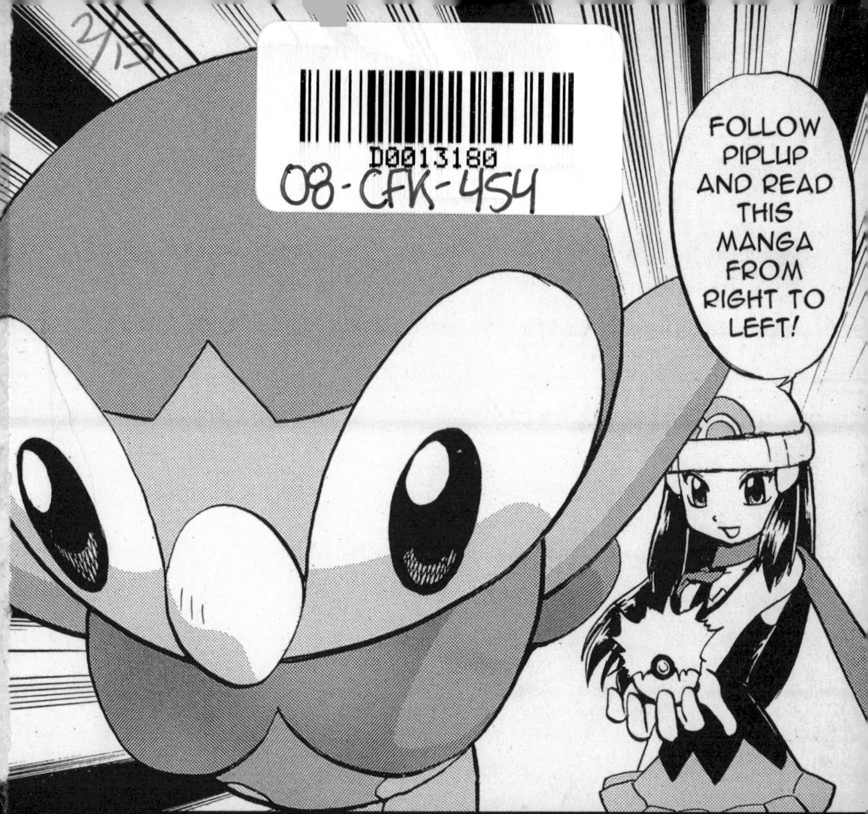
FOLLOW PIPLUP AND READ THIS MANGA FROM RIGHT TO LEFT!

THIS IS THE END OF THIS GRAPHIC NOVEL!

To properly enjoy this VIZ Media graphic novel, please turn it around and begin reading from right to left.

This book has been printed in the original Japanese format in order to preserve the orientation of the original artwork. Have fun with it!

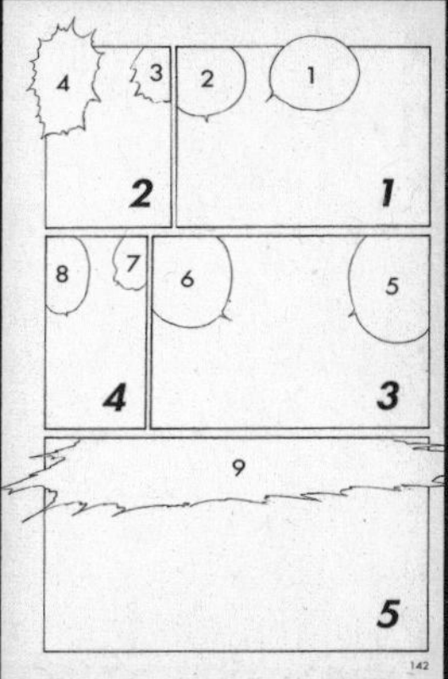
1
2
3
4
1
2
5
6
7
8
3
4
9
5

follow the action this way.